- The Phoenix Chronicles -

ALONE IN THE LIGHT

Book One

M.K Williams

The Phoenix Chronicles: Alone in the Light

Second Edition

First published by createspace in 2018

Luxon-Drake Publications

Kemp House

152-160 City Road

London EC1V 2NX

United Kingdom

www.luxon-drake.com

Illustration created by Germancreative

ISBN: 1999962814X
ISBN-13: 9781999962814

I dedicate this novel and the spirit of those to come, to
Roy Andrew Short.
My first faithful fan.
You are forever remembered.

To my close friends and family, no words could do you justice for all your support.
To Rachel, a best friend; true and dependable. I owe this much and more.

Edition Two (2019)

P: AZX32 N:015 T: E

Title: The fifteenth translation of *The Sagara Prophecy*.
Name: Winston. J. L. Eddingtons. (Chief Librarian)
Co-authors: D. Longsdale., G. A. Macksville., D. R. Rose., J. F. Griffiths.,
& A. R. Short.
Date: Started March 1st 1947, completed November 13th 1947
Code: Lower Ancient to English. 015AZX32E
Classification: Open Access. PR value: Low

Summary of findings:

The report on Prophecy AZX32 is a detailed analysis of the impact of
the events that are depicted and described. The Prophecy is divided
into three categories and is further divided into individual segments.
The translation for each segment, from the original Lower Ancient to
English, is accompanied by a detailed hypothesis on what is believed
to be the outcome prophesied. On review of the entire works several
statements can be made about the impact on civilisation.

[A]The fall of the Order of Light. [B]The death of the entities known as
the Phoenixes. [C]A war, comparable to those witnessed by the
*Ancients. [D]The return of an Ancient, the name of which is not stated.

The Prophecy: (Sagara: 015AZX32E) – *Translation to English.

Signs:

[1]Dead of night the vile attack. When the free are led by bird, and
liberty burns. A hero lost is the Defier's gain. [2]His Collection grows to
five, through vengeance blood is spilled, a Phoenix returned. The
Strong are willed, united they speak, as one they listen. [3]His faithful
returned, his army rebuilt. His pieces moved into check, marked are
those who touch the eye. [4]Blinded is he whose heart does not beat.
To the path he must return, to save his soul. No innocence is lost, due
to smoke and mirrors. Return to the earth the unstoppable walks.
[5]The Eye is destroyed; it sees only death and misery. The heart is

rubble, warriors so few. Traveller's blood frees him from his untouchable prison. Behold the betrayal, the good and the bad. [6]The followers are plenty, his kingdom great. The second war he shall start, like none have witnessed. Neither for land, nor power but for love. His plan revealed, not so divine is he, exploit his weakness and nothing shall be.

Trials:

[1]Standing alone, our hero is blinded. The path he will walk has two lanes. Through vengeance, his death is sealed, though hope returned. The lane chosen is darker, and his steps unforeseen. [2]Solid as stone your enemy shall be. His strength is his weakness. Hands are your weapons, use knowledge of Fiore. [3]The Phoenix can stand and fight, but the Phoenix will fall and perish forever. The fate of the earth is the victor's call. Witnessed are the brave, the helpless. [4]The marked are the two who think as one. Blessed is he with ancient skills. The Defier's slayer he will be.

Revelations:

[1]If Line of Passel ends before the Defier's return, he who has slain will die at the hands of the Phoenixes' greatest enemy. [2]The marked shall escape the sixth by trust and sacrifice. Enlightenment is gained through the hell. Leap into the storm, the battlefront waits. [3]Gone is the juggernaut, cursed is the Ryder with life or death. Broken is the trinity where hope lay. As the Defier walks and speaks, cursed is the earth, but free Will can survive. [4]You destroyed the queen of pain. Lost is the king, consumed by rage, his lust for power released. A desire for revenge, his heart so null. [5]Mothers teach the greatest lesson. Though borrowed, it's true. Close the box and death forfeits his claim. No light shall you see, no love or loss will you feel. Peace is yours as the dark veil falls.

- Preface -

June 12th 1919

As I write for the first time in months, I am compelled to list the evils I have witnessed in the name of good. The concept of good is one that exists on many worlds I have visited, but no version has troubled me more so, no definition of good has ever been filled with so much hypocrisy.

Murder of the innocent. Rape. Genocide – entire ways of life destroyed, removed almost entirely from record. Claiming ownership of objects and over people, and then stealing claims from others. The people of this world are corrupted by so many higher concepts. They have the will of a god but no power or wisdom to see them through.

This world knows nothing of the battle that is fought in its name, for its honour; for its own good. I have seen a war that has spread the globe, devastated a continent, yet still the people of this – Earth, seem to care not and are destined to repeat mistakes for eternity. The value of their existence means so little to people sacrificing themselves and each other as they wage war for snippets of land and wealth. Concepts so far from mine, I feel; what could only be described as rage burns within me.

I know I should not feel such emotion, that such attachment is not the way of my people. I am, for no other better word – lost.

I have spent more time here than permitted, more time than our rules govern. It has been nearly ten years and no one has looked for me, no one has ordered my return. I am truly the first to rebel; I am the first to have had these thoughts.

I know why the rules exist, I have lived through the ages of many worlds – I have witnessed the destruction of so many civilisations. There is a solution, a dangerous one to explore.

Unlike on many worlds, only a few people here seem open to the true origins of existence, only a handful are gifted with real power and actual wisdom. For an inexplicable reason the truth is held from the masses. My only conclusion is that it is due to the desire to protect them, to protect a concept of good.

Like other worlds this one has two clearly defined sides, which only help cement such simplistic thoughts of good and evil, dark and light. For reasons that escape me, a truce has held for over fifty records. Such a form of peace is unheard of. Though the humans do an excellent job of killing one another.

I had a discussion with a young man from a body that calls itself the Order of Light. I first made contact with him to gain access to their archives; I was intrigued to learn much about the truce that exists. I have known him for several weeks and tire of his naive belief in what is right and wrong. Youth in this world is often filled with unwavering absolutes

— this is all so unattractive. He would often argue that being human alone was enough to be viewed as good. He did not respond well to my arguments to the contrary. That the mere claim in itself was not proof.

A vampire, I often argued, could be deemed as equally good. Both beings clearly have the potential to carry out deeds that would fall into either of the humans' definition of a 'good act' or an 'evil' one. That just because one was at a different level of evolution, that one was possibly deemed higher on the food chain, that did not afford the inferior the right to define the other as evil. It is arbitrary. He did not like my argument of human inferiority and often argued that it was his side, the humans — the Order of Light, that had the advantage. That had the real power. This may be the case from his perspective, but numbers alone do not ensure victory, that the power of the Phoenix will not, forever, be unrivalled.

Well, I am off point. I shall write no more until I have decided to return home or if… or if I shall explore such dangerous options.

- Solasis Krull

June 14th 1919

I have decided to stay. I shall take up arms. I have chosen my side. Justice and peace will be my gift to existence. Not just to this world but to all. I am driven to break the covenant of my people.

- Solasis Krull

- Chapter One -

Not So Humble

Stephen's legs had never moved so quickly, not ever in his life, not even in his death. If his heart still beat it would have burst right out of his chest. He wasn't the youngest vampire in his order but he could still remember what it felt like to run so far and to run so hard on mortal legs. On any other day, after any other feed, at this pace he would have tired long ago; but not today. The metallic taste of the woman's blood still lingered excitingly in his mouth. Fresh human blood was everything he had imagined it to be, and the strength it gave him was tremendous. He had never felt so strong. But was he powerful enough to take on his current pursuer? As the thought entered his mind, he began to slow.

"Yes. I can," he whispered through gritted teeth; and as he did his sprint came to an end.

Stopping and placing a hand on a wall he took a long look around him for the first time since the chase began. He had been running on instinct alone and hadn't taken in his surroundings once. He had walked the old streets of London many times before and knew them well, although he had only ever seen them by moonlight.

He listened for the approach of his follower; even with enhanced hearing he heard nothing but the distant, weak cries of his recent victim.

I've done it, he thought. *I've outrun a Phoenix.*

Everything he had been told about a Phoenix would leave any vampire filled with fear and dread, but tonight he was particularly frightened after his illegal feeding. He took another quick glance around: there seemed to be nothing and no one. He allowed himself to feel smug; he had completed his task and managed to lose his deadly hunter.

"Right, now to a safe house," the words softly left his mouth.

As he began to move a bright blue light blinded him, a sharp punching pain slammed hard into his chest, lifting him off his feet and slamming him into a wall. Rubbing his eyes, his sight began to return and there standing directly over him was the thing he feared most: a Phoenix.

. . .

Zhing looked down at the vampire. To her, vampires were the worst of the underworld's dark creatures. They were always breaking the rules, they had no respect for the Treaty and their Council would often overlook their transgressions. She had hated vampires ever since she was a young girl and had witnessed three of them terrorise and destroy a village near to her hometown, Turpan in Xinjiang, China. She couldn't let her hatred get the better of her; she needed to take this vampire in for questioning. Looking at him, he seemed confident, strong and bold.

This one might cause me some trouble, she thought. But she was more than ready; dressed in her long black Phoenix attire and with her enchanted Blade, which had slain many vampires before, strapped tightly to her back.

"Get up! Resist and you'll pay with your life, understood?" She spoke with an eloquent English accent, her eyes locked with his.

Nodding his head to show he understood, Stephen slowly dragged himself to his feet. Was he going to try and escape? If she took him in he would be finished anyway. Instantly he leapt at her, he knew he had to keep any fight with a Phoenix close. They were strong and quick, much like a vampire, but they also wielded magical powers. Reacting instantly to his lunge, she rolled, flinging the vampire clean over her head. Quickly jumping to her feet, she turned to see the vampire already standing tall. Stretching out her open hand a sapphire blue energy seemed to build around her palm, until a huge bolt of sapphire light flew out from it, heading in the direction of the vampire. Diving to the ground to evade the blast, Stephen believed he could take her on this night and win. The young woman's blood had made him feel immensely powerful, made him quicker. Moving close to Zhing again, he threw a punch at her face. It was easily blocked but his second throw struck the intended target, just below her chest. Zhing flinched, but reacted with a blow to Stephen's face, knocking him to the floor. As he hit the ground, she arched her whole body and kicked him clean into the air. He rotated several times before remaking contact with the ground. One arm lifting himself up, he looked over at her; he watched her hands link together, one on top of the other with shimmering sapphire light surrounding them. With his other hand he pushed himself into the air but he hadn't been quick enough. Another, larger bolt of blue hit him hard in the stomach, throwing him with immense force at the other wall behind him, the collision so hard a crater formed. He fell to his knees in agony. As a vampire he did not often feel pain, but now every bone in his body ached.

"Resist and I shall end your existence. You're coming with me, understood?" With a slight smirk on her face, Zhing moved to stand directly over him again, her sword stretched out, its tip pointing at him.

"Yes, yes okay," Stephen said as he looked up at her; he noticed that she had not even broken into a sweat. It looked as if she could take on fifty vampires saturated with the blood of a thousand young women.

...

Across town the cold air felt bitter on Sam's face but it didn't seem to bother him; his gaze scanned the landscape around him in a panicked search. Turning his head side to side, he leaned his right ear in different directions, trying in vain to hear the young woman who was somewhere mortally wounded. He heard nothing. He wasn't alone, his good friend and colleague Rachel Winters was also out on this freezing night, both of them searching for the innocent victim, left for dead by a vile monster.

The pair ran down back-alley after back-alley in a frantic hunt, their mission to find the victim and find her fast. To them it wasn't important to catch the perpetrator of the crime; they knew someone was already on that task, someone who was more than capable of tracking the beast down.

Turning a very sharp corner at speed, Sam lost his footing and stumbled to the ground. Rachel slowed her sprint just in time to avoid tripping over him. Kneeling down, she helped him back to his feet.

"Come on, slow down, concentrate. Can you sense her presence at all?"

Rachel's words did little to comfort Sam. He had visualised the victim in his mind; he had felt her pain and now he seemed somewhat helpless to save her.

"No, I can't sense her now at all. It's strange, it almost feels like something's blocking me," Sam replied.

This seemed odd to Rachel, not because she was unaware of Sam's psychic gift, but because she had never heard of anyone being *blocked* before. She was beyond puzzled by his statement. She had a gift of her own and she didn't feel as if hers was being hindered. Rachel was gripped with a sense of urgent desire.

"What do you mean you're being blocked? Explain. Does anything look familiar at all?" she barked.

"Well, I've not been able to sense people before, either because they're too far away from me or because…" Sam paused.

"Because what?" Rachel probed.

"Because they were dead. But this is different. I know she's alive." Sam's words seemed to stem from desperation.

A feeling of failure, making her sick to her stomach, suddenly overwhelmed Rachel. She looked at him, her eyes filled with tears partially concealed by her glasses, her cheeks began to glow red.

"What now?" Rachel asked.

"We continue, we keep looking; she's not dead, Rachel. It feels different, I can't even read you. Something's not right with my head; it's all cloudy, I can't think straight." Sam strained.

Rachel listened and knew that they needed to find the victim before she 'turned', though she didn't share Sam's belief that she could be still alive. She thought he was clutching at straws.

"Come on, we still need to look for her," Sam commanded.

Rachel slowly turned away. Her face filled with disbelief, which Sam read easily. She didn't believe the girl was alive and she didn't believe him; that he was being *blocked*. Knowing this wrenched his insides, like a fist punching through his chest and twisting his heart. He and Rachel were closer than brother and sister and the thought of her not trusting him was hurtful. He had seen the woman in his dreams, and he wasn't going to let her die. Over the past four years he had seen many victims, just like this one. Four years that, if Sam was living the life of a normal twenty-two-year-old, would be filled with drink-fuelled parties and carefree days, but this wasn't Sam's life, this wasn't the life led by any of his present friends. He had been given a gift and he was determined to use it to help others. Dropping to his knees he placed his hands on his thighs and closed his eyes. With every fibre of his being he stretched out with his mind.

Walking away, Sam's shout stopped Rachel in her tracks. "Wait."

She turned and saw him kneeling and concentrating.

In his mind's eye a veil was lifting, he began to see people around him, passers-by, people on a bus, Rachel. He still couldn't see the girl and with even more of his strength, he looked further. As he poured more of his energy into the search, the more distorted his visions and the louder a thumping sounded within. His hands began to grip his trousers tightly and his nails began to dig deep into the fabric, impressing on his flesh. The more intense the thumping got, the harder he squeezed. His hands began to ache from gripping so tightly, his mind was so befogged he began to feel like passing out or bursting a blood vessel. Rachel could see sweat pouring from Sam's face, his exhaustion evident. She was overwhelmed with concern, maybe he wasn't exaggerating, and maybe he was being *blocked*. Lowering herself to his level, she spoke softly in his ear.

"Are you okay, Sam? I know you can do this."

He was dimly aware of her words but did not respond; his thoughts were entirely focused on finding the young woman. Then it happened; he could hear her heartbeat, it was fast and erratic. He now had a focal point to meditate on. Moments later he could see the white blouse she was wearing, she was becoming clearer and more vivid in his mind; he could now see her face and the wound on her neck. Suddenly a large thud vibrated in his mind and her face appeared clearer. The pain he felt was immense as his right hand released its grip from his leg and wiped his dripping nose. Slightly opening his eyes, his gaze fell upon his hand; it was covered in blood. His nose was bleeding and the more he concerned himself with that, the faster the image of the girl became clouded by fog.

6

"I can see her," he said.

Rachel had a look of complete astonishment on her face. She had never seen Sam like this before; she had never seen him bleed.

"Okay, where is she?" Rachel uttered in a tone that suggested she feared for Sam's health.

Sam focused, and with all the energy he had left, he fixed on the girl's image, and the sound of her heart beating. The fog again began to clear and the woman was back in focus. He slowly began to extend the image, not only looking at her but also at her surroundings. She lay against an iron railing that was painted black but in places had turned brown and flaky with rust. Beneath her feet was grass and, behind her, tall trees that were sparsely spread out from one another. The pain and pounding returned, but he was so close. The image expanded until he saw something else, a street sign. His concentration was instantly broken as he leapt to his feet. Recoiling in shock, Rachel stared as Sam darted off back the way they had come. Pulling herself to her feet, she quickly followed. For a man who seemed exhausted, his feet moved swiftly and Rachel found it hard to keep up. It wasn't long before they entered one of London's many parks.

Sam paused and whispered, "She's here. And we're not alone."

Rachel's concern for Sam's well-being increased to sheer panic and fear for both their lives.

"Move!" she ordered.

The pair ran off, looking around the park. It didn't take long until Rachel's eyes fell upon the girl. The wound on her neck was small but blood poured from it profusely.

"Here, over here," Rachel shouted and Sam quickly turned to see what was in her gaze. A woman who appeared to be in her early thirties lay with her back against the railings. Her blood-covered hand rested on her shoulder, having given up on its vain attempt to stop the bleeding from the neck wound. Her body appeared lifeless, spread out in full view. Moving closer to the woman, Sam and Rachel lowered their bodies. Sam quickly took off his jacket and placed it hard against her neck. Rachel moved to the woman's ear and spoke clearly and loudly.

"Hello, are you awake? We're here to help you. My name's Rachel; what's yours?"

Sam's attention drifted off, he hadn't heard or seen anything, but rather he could feel something.

"We've got to get out of here. We have to go now!" Sam's words emulated the angst he felt inside. Rachel, not wasting another second, quieted her mind and began to use her gift. Focusing on all three of them and the entrance to Headquarters, she attempted to make a switch in space. Within a few seconds of Rachel's eyes closing the three of them had vanished in a flash of bright light, resembling a small, silent explosion, each ray of light appearing as a tiny marble of energy scattering off into the night.

...

Undiscovered in the corner of the darkness, Canola stood staring at the spot where the vampire's victim had been and where the two vermin belonging to the Order of Light had been moments before. *I should have killed them and taken the girl*, he thought.

He was eager for a fight; it was his job, a low-ranking assassin in a grand sect of mercenaries. He loved the fight, he existed to kill. His early life had been spent growing up in the poorest and darkest parts of Moscow. His upbringing harsh, he often remembered the hardships his parents bore, struggling to put food on the table and to keep the fire burning. Those days were far behind him. Now his family had a large home where the fireplace was always lit and the feeling of hunger was a distant memory. His life had changed on his fifteenth birthday when he realised he was what both the Council and the Order referred to as 'gifted'; he soon found himself caught up with the Council, and the killings had begun. But this night wasn't the night for his hands to be covered in blood. He had strict orders to monitor the girl and to only take her in if she turned. The most important command he was given was not to get caught, not to get involved in a fight with agents from the Order of Light. It was time to leave; he needed to report to his client; a powerful man whose instructions were to be followed to the letter. To disobey would mean certain death.

...

One mile away another hired hand took aim with his rifle. Tom didn't have any ordinary ammunition; he knew his gun was loaded with the very thing, the only thing he currently needed to eliminate his prey. Down the sight he could see two targets, both very tempting but only one would be his victim, only one would die from his shot. The girl in his sights he had seen before, she was athletic and strong. Something about her made him tingle inside, a gentle burning sensation.

He took great pleasure in watching them fight. He already knew what the outcome would be, but to change the victor wasn't the reason he was being paid; that wasn't the reason he was there.

Several bright sapphire-blue flashes lit the entire alley below. The female yielded great power, but it wasn't the first competent Phoenix he had seen in action. He had seen many battles through his life, and during the latter part of his twenties he had seen twice as many as during the first. Tom didn't class himself as a bounty hunter or an assassin. He enjoyed being defined as a well-trained, slightly expensive but always delivering, artist of pain and slaughter. That was his pitch to his clients and that's generally what he practised. He never found himself out of work. He was good at what he did, and he enjoyed the rewards that came with his risky lifestyle. Always being in such high demand because of his deadly talents, he was well known to the Order of Light. He had always been on their radar, yet always just out of their reach. He loved antagonising the Order, flaunting his 'art' so close to them and then recoiling away before a Phoenix could pounce. He had only ever fought one Phoenix before and the battle didn't go quite as he had expected. He often duelled with other agents of the Order, the *gifted* as they were known. But ever since the day he duelled with Yi-Mao, he tried hard to always steer clear of direct confrontation with a Phoenix – that was until tonight.

...

"Yes, okay, yes."

The vampire's words were disappointing to Zhing. She enjoyed a good fight and her initial instinct told her that this vampire would put up more of a challenge. The chase and the fight, though quick, were intense for the young woman. She had fought many battles and she was trained to focus her senses during combat, listening intently to the voice from within, the voice of her Phoenix.

As her pulse began to slow, she could feel a strange, niggling burning sensation. It wasn't painful and she had felt it many times before. Responding to this intuition she knew that something wasn't right; she reverted to her training, closed her eyes, concentrated her mind and searched her soul for the voice of Athena.

Instantly reacting to gentle words within her mind, she turned her body suddenly, stretched out her arms, palms open wide and from them a sapphire light began to form a circle-like shield in front of her. In that same split second, she heard the *phut* of a silenced gun being fired and a bizarre whistling sound, which was interrupted by a thud. Then there was a moment of eerie silence.

The silence was broken by a yelp of pain from the vampire. Turning her head, Zhing could see a small black metallic projectile lodged deep in the vampire's chest. Immediately she stepped in front of him to ensure her field covered them both.

"You okay?" Zhing said as she knelt in front of him, still using the shimmering blue shield as cover. Reaching over, she pulled the dart from his chest. As it came away, broken glass fell from it.

Panting hard as if he was trying to breathe, the vampire's forehead began to glow red.

"What was that? I'm hot, it's like I'm on fire," he gasped.

On hearing this, Zhing knew that the dart had injected him with some kind of poison, but what, and how deadly was it? She had no idea.

"Don't panic. I'll take you back to Headquarters, they've got all known mystical poisons on record, and their antidotes, I'm certain Jon will…"

Before she could finish her sentence the vampire began to shake uncontrollably. Red foam started to pour from his mouth and his pale skin began to come away from the muscle. Withdrawing in sheer shock, Zhing clenched her fist, bringing her sapphire shield down. Her eyes widened; she had seen many vampires die before but this seemed, even by their standards, barbaric.

The vampire began to roll on the floor, screaming out in pain, his red fleshy muscle turned to sludge as a steam-like mist emanated from deep within his bones. His cries began to slowly quieten; what had been his liquefying body began to congeal into a pool of fleshy pulp. Even his bones began to melt as if they were on fire and the organs that lay caged within them began to turn to a foaming liquid.

Zhing stood up with a start looking with disgust at the foul remains of the vampire. Even in her aberrant memories she couldn't recall anything as gruesome as what she had just witnessed. A range of differing emotions began to whirl around her mind. Her shock, like the vampire, melted away; she was left feeling confused, weary, but most of all, angry. She had failed in her mission to bring the vampire in for questioning. Who could have been so cowardly, so meticulous, to use a poisoned dart to stop her? She knew the answer to her question before she had even thought it.

Turning her head in the direction from which the mysterious shot had been fired, she thought of the one person who was more than capable, someone who would've actually relished the task.

Zhing whispered, "It was Tom… It was Kronos!"

…

- Chapter Two -

The Chosen Life

It was the early hours of the morning and the medical team in the Andromeda-Aceso centre had not yet gone to bed; they had been up all night fighting their own battle. The centre looked like an ordinary hospital ward, apart from a few exceptions. The room was comprised of one long row of beds on either side with a wide central walkway. At one end of the ward there were three elevators, each with solid oak doors and what appeared to be gold fittings. At the other end of the room there was a narrow office and an awkwardly shaped storeroom. The medical centre was lit by bright, artificial light, glaring from a long row of fluorescent lights that stretched along the middle of the ceiling; it was the only way to illuminate such a long windowless space.

The office and storeroom were empty of people; those present were standing near a bed at the other end of the room close to the elevators. Three medical staff administered care to a young woman who lay lifeless on the bed. On the opposite side, atop a clean empty bed and facing the trio and the patient, a young woman was sitting upright; her eyes glared through her glasses and were fixed on the commotion.

"Right, are the straps secure, have you checked the IV drip again? Make sure it's the right concentration, don't overdose her." shouted Dr. Susan Gambon, whose words were orders rather than questions. Susan was fifty-two with a dark Mediterranean complexion and a strong South African accent which always gave a harshness to her words. "All right, where are those X-rays?" She barked her commands to the younger members of staff who darted around her trying to fulfil her demands.

Susan insisted on a high level of respect from her staff; she had managed the medical centre for eighteen years now and in that time she had witnessed many supernatural illnesses.

"The IV is good, X-rays are in your office and the straps are secure," said a youthful man dressed in a white overall that was unbuttoned, revealing his grey suit beneath.

"Good, thank you. Okay. We need to take another blood sample and run another 'Hormone-V2 type' test."

She looked at the two assistants who glanced at each other for an instant then quickly carried out her order. Looking over to the opposite side of the room, she noticed that Rachel was still on the end of a bed. For Susan, the last five hours had flashed by so quickly. It seemed like five minutes ago that she had gotten the emergency call, alerting her that two agents of the Order were on their way in with a vampire victim. She and her team had collected their emergency equipment and run up to meet them at the entrance to the building where they had quickly strapped the young casualty to a trolley and rushed her down to the ward.

"Where's Sam?" enquired Susan as she moved and sat beside Rachel.

"Oh, he went to bed about twenty minutes ago," Rachel replied, sheepishly.

Rachel turned her head and looked at the clock that rested above the elevator doors. "Wow, I mean – two hours ago."

"I didn't hear him leave. Time has a funny way of running away from you down here, in the darkest depths of headquarters," said Susan.

"How's she doing? Is she stable?" As Rachel spoke her eyes looked back towards the woman strapped to the bed by her arms, feet and waist.

"To be honest, I'm not really too sure. We've managed to stop the bleeding which is good, but the venom from the vampire's canines has transmitted the infection through her lymphatic system faster than expected. She is on a drip of what we call 'Dianna's cocktail', it's an intravenous solution of synthetic compounds mimicking the old mixture of garlic extracts, silver molecules and limestone that the apothecaries of old used to administer orally; of course my concoction is a bit more effective, it stops the spread of the infection." Susan spoke coldly and clinically as she often did, always providing more information than was ever sought.

"How bad is the infection?" asked Rachel. She didn't know much about the transformation process of a vampire but she asked the question in the hope of a dumbed-down answer.

"I've the X-rays now, they should show the extent of the infection; we need to check if it's spread to the organs, which I'm guessing it already has."

"You guess?" Rachel uttered. "Will the X-rays show you for sure?"

"They're not actually X-rays in the conventional sense, we just call them that round here. I think they'll confirm what I suspect though. You see, her skin is pale and green, which indicates that her liver and kidney processes have slowed. The virus attacks all organs in the body, causing them to shut down so it can complete the metamorphosis of its host. If you want, you can come with me, we can look at the images together," replied Susan.

The pair walked the seventy-metre-long ward to Susan's office. Unlocking the door and walking through, Susan took off her jacket and placed it onto her chair. Following her in, Rachel took a long look around. "It's bigger than I expected."

"Well, it's not just my office, it's for all the medical staff, but I do use it as my own personal study," Susan replied.

Susan had an element of self-importance when she spoke. Picking up a large white folder from the top of a pile of paperwork, she opened it and emptied three prints into her hand. Walking over to the light fixture on the wall, she placed them onto the screen and switched it on.

"Oh," Susan gasped after just a few seconds of analysing the images.

"What's wrong?" Rachel asked, panicked.

Susan pointed to the first image, which from the outline of the bones, showed it to be the woman's pelvis. Susan explained:

"It appears that the infection has already destroyed her uterus and constructed the vampyr minor organ from her ovaries. This is deeply worrying; I'm going to do a CT scan to confirm it," she stepped back from the screen, her hand over her mouth.

"Vampyr minor?" Rachel's inexperience with vampire anatomy was ever apparent in her tone and expression.

"There are two distinct stages of pre-vampire metamorphosis; one is the creation of the vampyr minor. This organ is made from the patient's reproductive organs, and produces the hormones for the second stage, which is the construction of the vampyr major organ from the heart. The vampyr major is responsible for producing enzymes that directly convert haemoglobin into a kind of energy source. It also regulates all the endocrine systems of the vampire," Susan explained not once showing any emotion in her voice or on her face.

"Has this vampyr major organ formed yet?" asked Rachel.

"No, not yet, but it's not long after the minor forms that the major is constructed, days, sometimes hours." Shaking her head, Susan looked like she was at a loss for a solution to the situation.

"What about Jonathon, maybe he can help her?" Rachel perked up; she thought she had the answer.

"No, unfortunately the infection has spread too fast and has consumed too much of her, there's nothing Jonathon can do at the moment. Hopefully the 'Dianna cocktail' will stop the spread, slow the progression and, fingers crossed, bring down vampyric-infection rate," Susan said as she glared at another print.

"Hopefully?" Rachel exclaimed, disheartened by Susan's pessimism.

"Don't panic. I've seen victims in a similar state recover from a vampire bite in the past; she's got a fifty–fifty chance of recovering. It's just a waiting game now." As the doctor spoke she placed a consoling hand on Rachel's shoulder.

Bowing her head, Rachel could only think about how, if she had run faster, looked harder, maybe they could have got to her in time. Rachel was never one for frontline fighting, she preferred her desk, and she preferred the less violent side to her work. Then for an instant she wondered if there was ever a non-violent side to her work anymore?

"I've got to get some sleep and so do you. If you say no, you know I can order you to." Susan looked at Rachel, whose eyes were filled with tears.

"Yeah, I'm more tired than I think," Rachel replied.

Rachel retired to one of the many accommodation rooms in the headquarters complex. As she was lying in bed, the sunlight came through the window, hitting her tear-drenched face. Her eyes had disclosed the pain she felt inside. Placing her head on the pillow she began to breathe more deeply to try to slow her sobbing so she could drift off. The image of the bleeding woman haunted her; it took nearly an hour of weeping before she finally drifted off for a few hours of uneasy sleep.

...

It wasn't the busiest day Kristian had ever worked but it was right up there with the days he knew he should have phoned in sick. He never hated making coffee; he did not see his job as hard, just boring on occasion, even when it was busy. The customers he served were often rude for no reason and their hectic lifestyle weren't appealing to him. He had moved to London to study and to get away from the close-knit community he had grown up in.

It was not that he hated home, it was just small and stagnant, and he wanted to experience the big city; the world. He enjoyed living in London; there was always something to do. It had a huge metropolitan feel but it also had history and character. He had an eye for the beauty in life, he enjoyed marvelling at the buildings London had to offer, old and new.

There was one building whose appearance he didn't appreciate; it always sent a shiver down his spine whenever he walked past it. When he had first moved to London, it seemed he couldn't avoid the place, but after nearly two years, he had perfected his ability to steer clear of it. The building and the people inside seemed far more than a distant memory; they were more like a dream. Being nearly twenty Kristian often felt he had seen many things that had made him far wiser than his years. The truth was somewhat different; in fact he knew he could be very immature at times, not just in his actions but also in his thoughts. Considering what he had been through, what he had lost, and what he had missed out on, he could understand why he felt like that. However, dwelling on the past was not something he enjoyed doing, it was the past now and he intended to let it lie there. The day seemed to go quickly considering it wasn't that busy, and before he knew it, it was ten to six. The last ten minutes seemed to drag a little, there wasn't much to do and he spent the time clearing away empty trays and pointlessly wiping clean tables.

It had gone six and the journey home took no more than twenty minutes from Leicester Square to Angel. It wasn't a direct link but it didn't take long. The two-bedroomed flat he shared with his best friend Jess was so close to Angel tube station he could lean out of his kitchen window and throw stones at the Transport for London sign. As he shut his front door behind him and began to walk up the stairs, he knew Jess was in, even before he saw her. Blasting out of the stereo were songs that clearly came from an 'Ultimate Disney' collection.

Walking into the lounge, Jess was standing there cleaning and singing along to a song from *Beauty and the Beast*. Kristian laughed out loud; he loved how Jess was so sweet, so innocent. Moreover, the fact that she didn't care what anybody thought of her inspired him.

In her own little world of 'happy ever after', Jess quickly turned to the doorway to see Kristian standing there, chuckling at her.

"Welcome home, Kris," she said as she threw the cloth she was holding at him.

"Housework, this time of the day?" Kristian wasn't surprised really; she was always doing housework. She liked a clean house, but it was nearly half six on a Sunday evening and this was slightly odd, even for her.

"As always there's an ulterior motive behind my good deeds." A little smile crossed her face to which Kristian sat down and gestured with his hands for her to continue.

"What it is… well you know it's Andy's party tonight?" Jess started.

Before she could continue, Kristian leapt to his feet.

"Oh crap! I completely forgot. What time? I've absolutely nothing to wear."

Walking around in a strange haze of self-indulgence he totally forgot that Jess was trying to tell him something. His eyes connected back with hers and he saw she was grinning at him.

"I'm sorry, Jess, carry on," he said as he fell back into his seat.

"Well…" continued Jess, "Jason's going to be there and I think tonight is the night when we're gonna," she paused, and hoped that Kristian would realise what she meant and not pursue the matter. She wasn't a virgin, she wasn't even a prude, but when it came to her own love life, she always coiled away.

"Going, to, what, sorry?" Kristian knew what she was getting at, it had been their main topic of conversation for nearly a month, but he wanted to play. Now blushing, Jess stood up, her whole body seemed to turn away from the conversation, and her hands quickly grasped for the Hoover.

"I'm kidding, I'm kidding. You know I think you're beautiful and you're the sweetest person I know, I think you worry too much. If he likes you, he won't care how clean the kitchen is or how plumped up the cushions are."

Kristian didn't like being so frank with her but she really had no idea what a catch she was. She was the same age as him, smart, kind, and pretty wasn't the word for her. She had long brown hair, with beautiful deep blue eyes'; she had a true 'English rose' look about her.

"I'm sorry. I really like him," she let go of the Hoover, she had clearly done enough cleaning for now.

"I think I'm going to leave in about an hour. Karen says they've been drinking since two." She giggled.

Andrew's monthly parties were renowned at Uni as being the event of the month; a must-go.

"Okay, I'll be ready by then. I need a shower, I stink of coffee. Which isn't a bad thing, it's just not a good one." Getting off the sofa, he made his way to the door, but before leaving the room, he turned and kissed Jess on the cheek, giving her a reassuring hug.

"We're going to have a great night and everything with you and Jason will be perfect, you deserve it."

Jess stood and stared after her friend. He was more than a best friend, he was like the older brother she never had. He was sweet and caring, and she knew everything about him, she thought. Though unbeknownst to Jess, there were some secrets he had kept even from her.

…

The air was cold with a bitter wind, the sun had just begun to rise and the rays of light still hadn't touched the heart of the Berlin streets. Michael was on his daily jog along the bank of the river Spree; he started from his home in Treptow, on one side, and he ran as far as Rummelsburg.

The run usually lasted just over an hour but today there was something different. His legs seemed to ache like never before, and the cold air was making it hard for him to breathe. He had been running for over forty minutes and he still hadn't made it back to his side of the river. He still had to jog through the woodlands.

As he finally made it to the bridge and began to cross the river the thought of just carrying on home entered his mind.

Just skip the woods; it would be the easier option. However, his second thought was, *I'm not a quitter. If it hurts it hurts. If I stop short today I will just stop short tomorrow.* He was this determined in everything he did, and it wasn't long before the greenery and tall trees began to appear in the distance.

As he entered the woodland, his pace began to quicken; the pain in his legs started to relent and soon he was almost at the end of the forest. He could hear the small waves of the river hitting the bank and the birds in the trees began to sing their early morning songs. He found these background sounds beautiful; it was part of the reason he did his early morning jog; that and the fear of getting older and looking it.

The cold air soon began to carry an awful smell with it. The bitterness that filled his lungs suddenly took over and he found it impossible to breathe at the speed he was running. Almost stumbling into a tree he halted his pace to an abrupt stop; stretching out his hands he caught his fall on the branches. Taking deep breaths in, the air entering his lungs stung and made him cough uncontrollably. Trying to bring his breathing back under control, his mind began to think what the strange smell could be. It was clearly coming from the river. *Sewage*, he thought. *Someone must have dumped something there.* As well as being a little arrogant, he was also a very curious thirty-eight-year-old. Stomping through the small bushes, breaking off a few branches from the overhanging trees, he soon found himself at the river's edge. His heart froze and the cold air that he was trying so hard not to breathe in a few moments ago, seemed to rush into his chest. His eyes widened as the reality hit him. It was obvious what it was, but he could not believe what he was seeing. The stench soon overwhelmed him completely and before he had time to turn around, he vomited straight into the river. He walked backwards, his hands trembled with the horror of it, as he slowly reached into his pocket and pulled out his mobile phone.

Sixty minutes later there was a helicopter flying overhead and a horde of forensic officers and police surrounding the riverbank. The whole park was cordoned off and sitting on a bench away from all the action was Michael and a young policewoman. Not only did he find it hard to breathe, he now also found it hard to speak; the taste of bile lingered in his mouth. The words that did leave his mouth were spoken softly with a slight hesitation behind each sentence. The policewoman seemed to just nod her head and write things down. She had not seen the crime scene yet but she had seen many horrors before and knew she wouldn't be overwhelmed.

"Then, I called you guys," Michael was glad that he had come to the end of it.

"Okay, thank you," said the policewoman. "My colleague may like to have a word with you but we understand you're in shock. If anything comes back to you later on, you have my contact details, so please get in touch, and we'll do the same for you if we feel we need to ask you any more questions. Thanks for your help." Placing a comforting hand on his leg, she slowly moved to her feet. On turning around to look in the direction of the crime scene, she saw two junior officers, crouched over, and vomiting into, a public bin. She chuckled to herself.

"Ah, what it was to be so young and innocent," she thought aloud.

Walking over, she stopped and stood next to a tall gentleman in a dodgy suit. Turning towards him she spoke.

"Sir, I have his statement, he doesn't know much."

"Did he touch the body? Did he turn him over?" asked the tall suited man.

"No he didn't come into contact with the victim; he just saw the body in the river and phoned the police straight away."

"Good," said the tall gentleman. "Because this case is going to give even me nightmares." After speaking, the man walked off.

Not even thinking of following her boss, her eyes were fixed upon the forensic team as they began to examine the body in the water. Two men in white overalls, in knee-high water, slowly began to right the overturned body of a young man, ready to extract him from his watery grave. He had blonde hair and had to be no older than twenty-five. His build was large and muscular as if he played rugby.

An attractive young man killed in his prime, thought the officer.

From where she stood, she could see marks along his arms and legs, bruises that suggested he had been restrained. Then her eyes fell to the injury that was clearly the cause of death. A hole in his chest began to empty water; a large cavity had been cut in his thorax not only through his clothing and skin, but through bone as well.

The hole was just off centre and, without even much knowledge of human anatomy, the officer knew it was where his heart would have been. From where she was standing, it looked as if someone had cut out his heart, the thought sending a chill down her spine. Her chills soon changed to pure revulsion as her eyes moved up to the young man's expression. The dreadful anguish of his death was plainly evident on his face. His eyelids stretched wide, eyes filled with terror, his mouth open and distorted. Dread clouded her mind and she had only one thought. This man must have been alive when someone had cut out his beating heart, an awful fate she couldn't imagine. The autopsy later that day confirmed her worst fears.

...

- Chapter Three -

A Fallen Hero

The outside of the building was in stark contrast to everything else about the Cardinal Office, which was the official title for the headquarters for the Order of Light. The exterior was deliberately plain and inconspicuous, but the majority of the interior was very different, it was in a grand style, extravagant and imposing. The Cardinal Office was the ultimate symbol of power and everyone who entered held it in awe. The headquarters for the Order of Light had moved several times since the organisation was created, but the Cardinal Office had always been used by the Order, in some fashion. The office itself even predated the Nariasdem's records. The site on which the mammoth building now stood was home to the world's most extensive collection of magical artifacts. It also housed the 'Great Library', the Nariasdem's largest and most comprehensive collection of both conventional and mystical texts.

The reason for the Order's consolidation on the site was due to the magical barrier found within it, which only allowed the good and true of heart to enter. This barrier was discovered over three millennia ago and ever since, the place had been used to store and protect that which was held powerful and important from the forces of darkness.

Nowadays the barrier was used to full industrial potential. The Great Library and the artifact stores now filled the entire space that the barrier protected.

The interior of the building was lavishly decorous; the walls and floors were all marble, the fixtures were all gold. The exterior, however, was somewhat different. It was 1960s grey brick with blacked-out windows. Two bulky oak doors at the centre of the building appeared to be the only entrance. The building itself wasn't distinctively ugly, it was just plain, almost as if it had been designed that way in an effort to go unnoticed. It was something that people would just walk by and give no thought to the wonders that were happening within its cold, solid walls every day.

Tucked away, deep inside the building, was the main conference room, currently being used by Jonathon Paige, Director of the Order, who was holding his weekly consolidation meeting. Today it was focusing on the upcoming half-yearly amendment summit. That amendment meeting was held twice a year between the Order of Light and representatives from the Council of Tivernal.

The Council was the largest representation of what Jonathon referred to as 'the forces that dwell in the shadows'. That underworld was made up of Vampires, Lycanthropes, Vinji, Sorcerers and several smaller factions of gifted humans who generally used their gifts to exploit others.

The business at these meetings would generally just be tit for tat, covering issues such as the amount of human blood being transferred to the Vampires or the quota of how many new Vampires and Lycanthropes were being sired. Occasionally, more pressing issues arose, like a rogue faction on either side starting an offensive to try and undermine the Treaty and cause conflict between the two sides. This usually involved a dark sorcerer of some sort, conjuring up some form of ancient magic to try to bring forth yet another apocalypse. Sometimes it was a Vinji impersonating a head of state and attempting to start a human-to-human war in some small African country; but it was usually resolved quickly by either side.

The purpose of the summit was simple: to ensure peace and stability between the two opposing factions. It seemed to have worked for as long as human records had existed, the two parties had never directly gone head to head.

Jonathon hated these meetings. When he had first started as Director, any gathering or summit with the Council had always been amicable and without stress, but over the last two years, relations had become somewhat frosty. The representatives from the Council were all very different and seemed to disagree with each other about everything. They often sat there and argued amongst themselves. It was not unlike having a meeting with a room full of schoolchildren; although children did not have the power to initiate a war and kill countless numbers of people.

The half-year amendment summit was a tricky affair and Jonathon always chose his words wisely; every time the Council met, he couldn't help but feel a little smug at the way he directed them. He did have the upper hand after all. He had more cards to play; his side was stronger and more organised.

In other conference rooms dotted around headquarters, more meetings were taking place. Jean Tanner, a young half-French, half-English man, was holding a conference on how best to assign members to different task forces set up by the Order.

Another formal discussion was being held downstairs in the smallest office in the building. Roman, a powerful wizard and a prominent member of the Order, was chairing it and the topic of conversation was the whereabouts of the Order's new office, the choices being Buenos Aires or Lima.

Tall, middle-aged and muscular Brendan Sloane was also holding an official Order meeting, which was taking place in the second-largest conference room and the subject was getting everyone a little heated. The room was beautifully decorated, oak throughout with a grand *Quercus* table in the centre. There were no windows and, right where a window would have been perfectly placed, there was a magnificent portrait of a previous Director of the Order. The stately table was large and could easily sit twenty people around it, but on this occasion there were only four, huddled at one end as if their conversation was top secret and for their ears only.

"Well, I've definitely come to the conclusion that my talks with Sauror are now beyond pointless. He knows nothing more than what he told us before and is more interested in talking about football than dark forces," Amar spoke with a deep Arabic accent, born and raised in Iraq; he never attempted to hide it.

"Come on people. I need something!" Brendan's voice was direct and stern. It was not just in this instance that he spoke in this way, it was simply the way he was.

"I'm sorry Brendan but I've entered his mind, with him awake and asleep, and I think the information you seek just isn't there. If it is, there is no way I can get at it. I hate to sound as defeatist as Amar, but there really is no point in me trying again," as Sam spoke, he looked directly at Amar who was opposite him.

Amar didn't appreciate this remark from Sam and glared right back. Their impasse was only broken when Brendan slammed his fist on the table.

"You've got to be kidding me? You're a joke, both of you. Two years we've been working on this together and now you've the temerity to come here today and tell me that we're no further along in our investigation than we were when we began?" Brendan looked at them, his face beginning to show the strain and defeat they all felt within.

Bringing a sombre tone to the conversation, Karnel leaned forward.

"We could always try the Leceth idea again?"

All three of them looked at Karnel. He wasn't the most aesthetically pleasing member of the group. His face was a moss green and serpent-like, and unlike the other three, he was in no way human. He was a Vinji, a species that had inhabited the earth for as long as man. The Vinji had a remarkable gift for shape-shifting, which nowadays was used to conceal their true selves from the world.

A long time ago, they had been a confident species, but now they were feared and hated by the world of men and after several wars with humankind, not long before the Council of Tivernal was formed, they transformed from a race of warriors to a race of impersonators and spies. Their dwindling numbers had led this once proud race to impersonate humans solely to survive the genocide of their people.

Brendan looked at Karnel knowing his offer was pointless. It hadn't worked the last time he had tried to impersonate the head of the Council and he knew it wouldn't work again.

Completely dismayed, Brendan rose to his feet.

"Guys, I'm calling this meeting to an end, and I'm cancelling all further meetings on the subject. We haven't a clue about Sauror's plans, every lead we've had has just led us back to where we are now".

The other members rose to their feet too, each with a look of disappointment on their face but also a slight look of relief. It had been two long years of following up leads and mysterious ID fits that had led to nothing. It was right for a line to be drawn. They all felt that if Sauror were up to something of any importance then there would have been more evidence. This was a comforting thought for Sam, Amar and Karnel but Brendan remained troubled. Sauror was high up in the Council and Brendan believed that something of great evil or power was often shrouded in immense secrecy.

"Well, gentlemen, if anyone does have any further suggestions then please let me know but we'll leave it at that for now," said Brendan raising his hands towards the door. The three others made their way across to the exit in silence until Brendan's voice broke the calm air again.

"Hang on a second Amar, I'd just like a word with you. I'll catch up with you two later," Brendan said to Sam and Karnel.

Not thinking anything of it, Amar made his way back towards the grand oak table and sat down whilst the other two left and closed the door firmly behind them.

· · ·

Kristian's eyes opened slowly, his head pounding and the room slightly spinning. Sunlight had crept in through the space between the closed curtains and was now starting to warm his feet. Gingerly lifting his head, he tried to work his way through the confusion he felt.

"Where am I?" he thought aloud.

It was a few more seconds before he realised that he was actually in his own lounge. Feeling slightly relieved that he had made it back to the flat, he leaned back in an attempt to go back to sleep. He felt a little cold and remained halfway between awake and asleep with the added extra of still being a little drunk. The sunlight that was warming his feet so perfectly was now rising up his legs and past his knees. The contradiction of the coldness of his torso to the warmness of his legs was slightly strange and was stopping him from dozing off again.

As the rays moved slowly up his body he suddenly had a strange sensation and realised that a part of him that didn't often get to see the sun was getting a bit more of a tanning session than he had ever hoped for. He looked down in horror to see that he was, in fact, completely naked. He sat up with a start and slowly examined his naked body. Thinking about it, his nudity didn't really bother him. After all, it was his own flat and Jess was the only other person there. She had seen him naked before and he really had nothing to be embarrassed about. Without the energy or desire to move to his bed he simply lay back and let the warmth engulf his whole body. He was just at the point of drifting back off to sleep when he heard some movement from Jess's room. He couldn't be bothered to move; *she probably wouldn't even look in the lounge, I expect she'll just go to the bathroom then back to bed*, he pondered.

With that very thought, the noise got louder and he heard a man's voice say, "So, cinema tonight, right? Just you and me."

Jumping to his feet, the memory of Jason sharing the taxi back with them from the party filled his mind; he grabbed around for something to cover himself with. Before he could do anything, Jess's door opened and the footsteps approached the lounge. As quickly as he could, Kristian picked up a cushion and just as Jason emerged, he managed to cover his modesty.

"Nice, uh, cushion mate!" smirked a tall, dark and handsome Jason.

"Uh, yeah, thanks," muttered a very embarrassed Kristian.

Jason walked towards the door to the stairway with Jess in tow, her eyes locked with Kristian's as a mixture of embarrassment and surprise covered her face. Kristian merely stood there with his cushion, his cheeks bright red. He mouthed sorry to Jess but she missed it as she followed Jason to the door.

"Well, thanks for the lovely evening, and I'm picking the film tonight," Jason's voice floated up from the stairway below and Kristian dashed into his room. It was less than ten seconds after jumping onto his bed and wrapping his duvet tightly around him that Jess came storming in.

"You moron! You just had to embarrass me didn't you?" Her voice was raised but her tone was humorous and he knew that she wasn't mad with him.

"I'm so sorry, I must've just crashed out last night and I totally forgot you had company." he smiled at her and she returned it with a cheeky grin. "So, come on," pried Kristian "what was it like? Tell all."

"It was great; he… had… big hands," as she stretched out her own hands they both began to giggle.

"Well, I'm glad it went well, and cinema tonight, I hear, I'm slightly jealous." Kristian loved the cinema. It was the greatest form of escapism for him.

"Yes, he's going to ring me later to make the arrangements. I need to go and get some beauty sleep now though. See you later, big boy!" As she left his room, she gave him a little wink. Kristian laughed and thought of how perfect it was, she was finally happy and he was delighted for her. If anyone he knew deserved to be in love, it was her. To him, she deserved the best guy out there.

…

The main conference room within the Cardinal Office had been busy for over five hours. The meeting had been going on since nine with only a half-hour break. Everyone's tempers were beginning to fray. Jonathon was starting to hate this meeting almost as much as he had hated last year's 'half-year amendment' summit. Most of the issues about the summit with the Council were done with, and now everyone was drifting into idle conversations about their own matters; things that would probably be sorted quickly but were tedious to say the least.

"So, he passed the final trials on Saturday and Roman and I both agree that he's our choice," Andrew Gilmore spoke; he was dressed in a long brown garment that was remarkably embroidered.

"Oh! So Ashleen McKenzie has been disregarded then?" asked Peter.

Andrew did not have much time for Peter. To him, Peter was a workaholic; a know-it-all who spent too much time with his books and not enough time with his staff. Andrew had met many people like Peter in his forty years with the

Order. Andrew was an older gentleman with grey hair, always clean-shaven and dressed rather strangely compared to all the suits that packed out the Order. Peter, by appearance, wasn't that much younger than Andrew. He certainly didn't carry as much respect as him, but he did carry an equally high position in the Order. As Chief Librarian of the Great Library, it made him the highest-ranking Nariasdem member in the entire Order of Light.

Peter was renowned for his knowledge of ancient texts and seemed to know all there was to know about every book in the Order's archives. If anyone had any questions about the ancients then Peter was the man to ask.

"Well, Ashleen was carefully considered by both Roman and me. She has excellent control over the magic, knowing more about the subject than almost anyone I've ever met, but she lacks the zeal, the panache for it. Magic is not a science, my friend; it's more an art. It's easy to read a book and then recite it back to someone, but magic is about instinct, emotion." Andrew was stern; he didn't feel the need to justify himself to Peter and he hated it when other parts of the Order interfered with the Coven's affairs.

"Oh! I didn't realise that such a large portion of our budget went to an art department," snapped Peter.

Seeing that this could easily get out of hand, Jonathon quickly intervened.

"Gentlemen, the matter is sorted; it is resolved. Kieran Young is to be the next member of the Trinity and his joining ceremony has been set for the twenty-third of next month. Done! Next on today's agenda please?"

Flicking through various pieces of paper, everyone at the table seemed to have lost the flow of the meeting. Jonathon's patience had all but deserted him when a young female voice suddenly said, "Oh, it's me."

Leafing through her pile of documents, Rachel Winters coughed as she attempted to clear her throat. She didn't really like the limelight and certainly never enjoyed the larger meetings. She preferred, where possible, to delegate the admin tasks to someone else.

Her timid voice just about carried throughout the room; everyone's gaze fell upon her. "It's just an update really about the lady who was bitten on Friday. She's responded well to the serums we have explored and the vampyirc-infection rate for the moment is controlled at fifty-nine point two per cent. Still not enough evidence for Jonathon to do anything I'm afraid. Dr. Gambon is hoping that with the next dose there'll be an even better response and then Jonathon can help."

Most people in the room were a little shocked. The meetings were usually concerned with petty squabblings about manpower and the distribution of resources, but this shy young woman had reminded them all about the harsh realities of why they were all there.

"Oh, and there's more," the timid voice spoke again. "She has a son. We've located him, but he's not yet been informed of his mother's condition. He's only fourteen and we don't feel it's appropriate at this time."

"I don't agree, Rachel," Jonathon spoke with a grim look on his face. "He's old enough to know and he should be allowed to see his mother while she's still the woman he knew. It may soon be too late for her and for him."

"Okay then, yes. I'll sort it," she demurred;, Rachel realised she had made the wrong decision but she still felt uncomfortable with the thought of the boy seeing his mother as she was, in that condition.

"Right, next please!" Jonathon was getting tired of hearing his own voice.

Jumping in before anyone else could speak, Zhing's voice was resolute and immediately got everyone's attention.

"While we are on the subject of this bite victim, you will all have read my report on the events of that evening and will probably all share my concern that Tom Harrowman, the host of the Dark Phoenix, is in London; and it's becoming apparent that he has a new work ethic."

This news came as a bolt from the blue; shocked gasps sounded throughout the room. Nearly everyone hurriedly and urgently looked through the mountainous bundles of papers in front of them. It was disappointingly obvious that barely any of them had bothered to even look at Zhing's report.

"Why Tom killed the vampire I was chasing is still not known; you must all agree that he has to be apprehended and as soon as possible," said Zhing with the obvious intention of wanting to take on the task herself. The room erupted with noise as everyone started shouting their suggestions on what to do about the Dark Phoenix.

Determined to end this worrying subject, Jonathon slammed his gavel on the table in front of him. There was instant silence.

"Okay, Zhing I want you to investigate Tom, try to locate him and bring him in. You can use the Alpha Team if you need."

"Good," her reply was immediate and she was clearly delighted with her new orders.

Hoping that this was the last issue of the day, Jonathon was afraid to ask the question, but once again found himself saying, "Next please?"

First to speak was Yi-Mao.

"I just wanted to remind and possibly notify everyone that I have my meeting next week with the Shing'tao and that Brendan and Amar have a conference with the Kar'sin monks, so all three of us will be out of the country. This will leave Zhing as the only Phoenix here in the UK as Adriana is at home in Spain and Oliver is still in Germany. All the other Phoenixes have now been assigned to other offices."

His accent was clearly Chinese, unlike Zhing's, who spoke with a perfect English accent. The others present all nodded as if this was irrelevant. It was in their notes, but few, if any, had taken the trouble to read them, so this was, for many, the first they heard of the arrangements.

Jonathon prayed that this was the end of the meeting. It had lasted for nearly six hours now. These meetings had long since lost their allure for him: it all seemed old hat and repetitive. In fact, with a fair amount of accuracy, he could predict every agenda item put up for discussion.

There was a stony silence, as no one gestured and no one spoke. Delight and relief filled most of their minds and then quickly turned to disappointment, when a big-haired woman with huge-rimmed glasses spoke, "Ah, I have something actually."

"Go on then, Penny," sighed Jonathon hoping it would be nothing other than money concerns, which was what she generally talked about.

"Well, what it is, is," she started, "three months ago, I was asked by the Trinity to locate an object of great importance." Penny's voice was unexciting and boring but her subject matter caught and held each person's interest. Everyone looked intently at her, no one more so than Andrew, Roman and Peter. Penny was in her early thirties and had been a member of the Order since she was eighteen. She knew the Order's workings well, but she still felt intimidated by these large meetings.

"Go on," prompted Andrew.

"Well, I have located it, but there is a problem you see, the thing, the object, that I believe to be the 'Heart of Merlin' was found in a geological dig several months ago. The stone had formed part of an exhibition, which from last night was being showcased at the Natural History Museum. So I was going to go and check it out and confirm whether it was what I thought it to be, but…"

"But what?" interrupted Andrew, who seemed quite bewildered by what Penny was saying.

"Well, somebody broke into the museum last night and stole the stone; the one I think is the 'Heart of Merlin', well, from what I can make out from the reports." Penny looked increasingly unsettled as all eyes gazed upon her.

Not wanting to continue an open discussion on the matter, Jonathon ignored Penny's statement and quickly ended the session.

"Okay, ladies and gentlemen, thank you for your time but it really is getting late now, and we must all retire and eat. Andrew, I expect you will follow things up with Penny?" Jonathon said as Andrew gestured that he would.

The room emptied within seconds and as Jonathon sat there with Peter and Yi-Mao, he pondered about the 'Heart of Merlin'. His train of thought was suddenly interrupted when in burst a distraught Brendan. His expression looked pained, but it didn't take him long to utter, "It's Oliver… Oliver's dead."

…

- Chapter Four -

Goodbye Old Friend

Jonathon had been sitting down for a while; he just watched as a young man cleared away empty tables.

I wonder if he'll recognise me? Jonathon thought. He knew to think this was pointless. The question he needed to ask himself was, *does he want to recognise me?*

It had been a hard couple of days and Jonathon knew that what he was about to do meant breaking a promise. He was going back on his word, which wasn't something he did easily.

He sat and waited for the young man to make eye contact. Jonathon was a calm man but not a patient one. Now well into his late fifties, he was proud and bold. His appearance didn't give away his age, his skin was youthful and he still had a full head of dark brown hair. His dark brown eyes followed the young man's every move. He seemed to clean every table except the one Jonathon was sitting at. It was clear to Jonathon that he had been spotted, but was being ignored. With the desire to get up and go over, he began to edge off his seat; the young man then suddenly seemed to change his mind and headed towards the table. Not making any form of contact with Jonathon, the youth merely wiped the table over limply with his cloth and looked away.

"There's no table service, sir. Not in this coffee house. You've got to go to the counter and place your order." The young man spoke with a nonchalant tone and turned to walk away; Jonathon, not wanting to be snubbed so openly, wasn't going to stand for it. He demanded respect every day from hundreds of people who put their lives on the line for the cause and he was in no mood for this boy's disdain. Not after everything that had happened recently.

"Kristian!" he barked. "I just want to talk to you."

Turning to face the man he once knew quite well, though now not familiar at all, Kristian felt almost afraid. He respected Jonathon, admired him, but he knew that there was only one thing that would've brought him here; to see him and to hear those fateful words was something Kristian certainty didn't want to face.

"I'm working," Kristian muttered, knowing that Jonathon wouldn't accept any excuse. He sighed, looked down and knew that he owed him at least five minutes of his time. "I have a half-hour break, I'll take it now. Can I get you a drink?" as Jonathon shook his head Kristian took off his apron and slowly walked towards the counter. When he came back he brought a mug of coffee for himself. He sat down and looked at Jonathon nervously. The smell of the coffee was strong, its pungency alone brought clarity and alertness to them both. Kristian was full of unease. He had spent the past two years repressing memories that still profoundly haunted him; memories that this man in front of him brought flooding back.

"Are you sure you don't want a drink?" Kristian asked again. He wasn't overly concerned with Jonathon's thirst but was endeavouring to delay any conversation about the Order and its dealings.

"No, I'm fine. So, how are you Kristian? How are you keeping? Are the studies going well?" Jonathon leaned forward, knowing subconsciously that he too was also trying to avoid the topic he had come to discuss.

"It's all going well, thank you," Kristian replied. "My lecturers are really pleased with me; they say I'm doing well and I am on course for a first. I also took up fencing and I'm actually pretty good. I'm the Uni champion. I've some great friends now, my own flat, a brilliant flatmate; I go home from time to time to see family. I party hard, and I work harder." Kristian spoke with genuine happiness and contentment, but there remained an undertone of sarcasm in his voice.

"What about you?" Kristian asked. He didn't really want to ask this of Jonathon, but the words just came out, almost like polite instinct.

"I'm okay. Keeping busy as you would expect," Jonathon sounded tired. "We have been a little stretched recently and I feel as if certain people are testing boundaries, trying to see how far they can push me before I snap. I am not just talking about the bad guys," he looked down at the table as he spoke. "So when do you finish then, for the year I mean?"

"I've finished all my lectures for the year but I've some exams coming up," Kristian replied.

"I see," Jonathon looked Kristian deep in the eyes, which sent shivers down Kristian's spine. Anticipating that the discussion would soon turn sour, the young man looked away and pretended to gaze out of the window.

"What do you plan to do when you finish, Kristian?" Jonathon was attempting to get to the point.

"Well… I've one more year left you know and then I think I may try and stay here for a few years, maybe get a manager's job, earn some extra cash so I can do my masters."

Placing his hand upon Kristian to draw the flow of conversation back to him, Jonathon spoke.

"It's good that you have plans, Kristian, but there is something that you need to know," he looked into Kristian's eyes once more and Kristian knew that something awful had happened. Jonathon's sheer presence there was a sign that something had gone massively wrong, of some terrible tragedy, and now he was about to find out. He suddenly felt cold and dead inside.

"Whatever it is, I don't care. I'm not coming back!" Kristian's words were harsh and resolute.

"Kristian, it is not as simple as you would like it to be." Kristian's expression showed that Jonathon's words had fallen on deaf ears.

"I don't care. You cannot force me to come back. I have tried so hard to have something which resembles a normal life and you can't come here and destroy it again, you just can't." Kristian's face showed the anger he felt. He had never asked for anything else, all he had ever wanted was to lead his own life and to make his own choices.

Jonathon was nothing short of stunned by Kristian's impassioned reaction. He reflected on the conversation that the pair had had just before Kristian had left the Order.

"I know I gave you my word that you were free to go for your degree, for a career, but you are what you are, and like it or not that makes you part of the Order. Regardless of the choices you make, we need you. You have a responsibility to the Order."

The more Kristian listened, the more incensed he felt. Two years ago, after his training and after his first and what he believed to be his last mission, Jonathon had promised him that he would only be called on if it became absolutely necessary. The more he thought about it, the sweatier his palms became and the angrier he got. Moving to his feet, his eyes unfocused and he vehemently said, "Whatever has happened I'm not coming back, I'm out, Jonathon. I'm out."

Acting purely on instinct, Jonathon reached out and grabbed the young man's arm, slowing his exit. "It's Oliver…"

Kristian froze and he knew what was coming, but the whole experience seemed so surreal to him, he couldn't move away, he couldn't shake off Jonathon's grip. "What's wrong with him?"

Gulping and feeling as if he couldn't say the words, Jonathon spoke with an unsteady voice.

"Oliver has died. He was killed. I am sorry you had to find out like this but we need you to come in for a briefing. It's important," Jonathon spoke fast with one quick breath, as if it made it easier to say.

Kristian's legs stiffened. *God, Was it true?* His heart pounded and every beat was like a bullet to his chest. How was it possible? Oliver was so strong and brave. He had lived for the fight. His calling had been the making of him and he had approached it with unyielding commitment. Kristian was overwhelmed with feelings of sadness, regret. Part of him felt like he should have been there with Oliver.

"When? How?" Kristian fell back into his seat.

"It happened last week and his body is being brought back to headquarters for examination. He was on a very important mission in Germany. He had been working off the record with utmost secrecy. I directed him to only make contact when he had the information we needed." Jonathon scratched his head and with guilt in his voice, he continued. "We are troubled and dismayed as it appears, though unconfirmed, that he died over a week ago and our lack of information from the seers and mystics has baffled us completely. We are at a complete loss as to who did this and what the motivations could be."

Kristian couldn't believe what he was hearing. The Order he remembered had never sounded this weak and this impotent.

"You must have some leads, Jonathon? You know what he was investigating, so you must've something?"

"He was working on something top secret and I cannot talk about it here. Moreover, the leads we do have are a lot more complicated than you can ever imagine, it's not straightforward bringing the main suspect in for questioning."

"So you've a suspect? Then it's simple, you arrest him, bring him in for interrogation, find out what he knows, then execute him for his troubles. Look, if you do that then I can still have a normal life and the bad guys still lose," Kristian paused and glanced over at the clock on the wall. "Well, time for me to get back to work". He knew how selfish he was being, but fear was holding him back and although he was filled with guilt, he knew he could never accept Jonathon's request.

"Kristian, please." Jonathon rarely begged.

"I suggest you go now, Jonathon. You knew what my answer would be before you even came here, but if you want, I will say it again; I-am-not-coming-back. That's final!" Kristian could hardly believe that these cold, cruel words were passing his lips, but he meant them and he needed to say them so badly.

"Things are so very different now. You owe this to Oliver, he was your friend as well as a colleague and it's down to you to help ensure that the person responsible for this is brought to justice," Jonathon's disheartened voice portrayed his disappointment: he had expected more of the young man. He thought that respect for his friend would have been enough to convince him.

"You bastard," Kristian was shouting now, his inhibitions gone. "How dare you come into my life and try to stir up my emotions in an attempt to get me to do your dirty work. Oliver was like a brother to me and his death hurts me inside more than you can possibly know. But he knew the risks he was taking. He knew that if you live by the sword, you would eventually die by it. He chose to live that life, and I chose not to, so let me be. I left the Order and I am not going back." His face was deep red and his eyes ablaze. As he turned to walk away, he muttered, "It's time you left, Jonathon."

Jonathon was shocked. He had expected the discussion to be hard but not impossible. *How could he be so cold?* Jonathon thought. But alas he had wasted too much time already and could do no more. He put on his jacket and left the café.

Kristian moved towards the counter and put his arm against the serving hatch whilst taking in deep breaths of air. A small chubby man with more hair on his face than his head stumbled over.

"May I remind you to keep your personal life out of my café. You're lowering the tone," he spoke with a strange accent, a mixture between Scottish and Italian.

Kristian raised his head, his eyes were bloodshot and glazed over. Wiping them before the tears formed he whispered, "I'm sorry; it was an old friend that's all; just an old friend." The impact of the conversation was now kicking in.

Forcing a smile and putting a hand through his hair he attempted to push his emotions deep down inside him; along with the rest of them.

"Sorry, Mr. Durante, he won't be back. I can assure you of that."

"Good." Mr. Durante's face lit up with a grin, which disappeared as quickly as it had come. "Now get back to work will you. Break time is over."

Kristian didn't argue, he got on with his work, a nice distraction from his nightmarish thoughts.

...

Frantically looking over a few different texts laid out over his desk, Peter endlessly looked back and forth between the police photos of Oliver's body and a book entitled *Encasement of the Divine*.

The pictures were gruesome. Any ordinary person would have been sick by now, but Peter was different. He was a cold and emotionless man and often seemed pitiless. Moreover, he was a workaholic and therefore, if a task had to be done, he didn't stop until it was completed. The large book with a yellow and brown cover took up most of his desk space. The script on the pages wasn't a language devised by man. It was a text comprised of pictograms and symbols that appeared in different colours. Straining his eyes to read it, he searched desperately for something that would give him a clue into the bizarre killing of his fellow comrade, Oliver.

A few moments later, a library clerk appeared in Peter's office with a trolley full of more books.

"Sir, I've the books you requested," said the clerk as he pushed the trolley into the only remaining space left in the room.

"If you could just leave them on the trolley," said Peter as he realised that there was nowhere else to put them.

Cursing Peter inwardly, the clerk left the trolley and exited the room. "Lazy bastard, never takes his books back, why doesn't he just go into the Great Library like everyone else."

As the clerk left, Peter looked up just in time to see a flash of brown hair pass his office; he knew that it was Kieran.

"Kieran!" he shouted and rushed to the door.

Kieran's attention had been elsewhere but on hearing his name, he turned and to his dread saw Peter Bergbeck ushering him into his office. As things stood, Peter didn't actually have any authority over him in the Order. He was a higher rank than Kieran but he was Nariasdem and Kieran was soon to undertake the blending and become the third member of the Trinity. This aside, he knew deep down that this conversation with Peter would happen eventually, so why not now?

"Kieran, do you mind? A quick chat?" Peter waved his hands in the direction of a chair.

That's all he ever does, thought Kieran, *directs people with his hands.*

"Sure, I've ten minutes spare, what can I do you for, Peter?" he walked in to the office and sat down upon a pile of books.

Peter gave him a disapproving look and then got to the point.

"I wanted to talk to you about your ascension to the third spot in the Trinity. You must be very surprised that Andrew and Roman picked you for such an honour?" He was being sly and patronising but his words did not faze Kieran. He wasn't going to bite back. He had worked hard to earn this opportunity. Blending with the Trinity power, the responsibility and everything that came with it, was all he had ever dreamt about, ever since the day he cast his first spell.

"Yes, I'm honoured," Kieran's voice was direct and true.

"Yes, a real honour," Peter continued. "I must say though that I'm surprised your name was chosen. I was sure it was going to be Ashleen, weren't you?" He was clearly trying to work Kieran up, but he was failing.

"Not at all, Peter. I agree with Andrew and Roman, I am the best all-rounder in the coven at the moment. Young, maybe; immature, not. As for Ashleen? Well, yes, she is powerful and does know her stuff, but she is a little flat with the magic and she doesn't have that natural flair," Kieran was careful with his words. Peter and Ashleen shared an almost father-and-daughter-style relationship. Everyone knew how beside himself with fury he had been when she had not been chosen to blend and become a member of the Trinity after the death of the previous member, Wendy.

"Well. Only time will tell if the coven has made the right decision; when is the ceremony again?" Peter asked.

"Next week I am told. Andrew is officiating it and Roman will be the witness. It's standard practice that the longest-standing Trinity member performs the spell," Kieran managed a quick, insincere grin at Peter and then leapt to his feet, "Well if that's all, Peter, I'd better be off, busy man, things to do, you know what it's like."

"And where are you off to exactly?" Peter enquired; he was always intrigued to know what everyone was up to at any given time.

Turning to face him, Kieran wondered what to say exactly. His plan hadn't been agreed by Jonathon, so there was no way he was telling Peter about it.

"I'm just off to see an old friend, that's all," he said as he left as quickly as he could.

Peter, not really giving much regard to Kieran's plans, sat back down at his desk and continued with his grizzly task.

…

It had been almost a week since Jonathon had visited him; Kristian's head had been in a blur ever since. His old friend and colleague was dead. As much as he wanted to know the details, he was afraid that if he did, then he might be persuaded to spiral into some harrowing mission for the Order.

He had just finished work; it was a Sunday evening and the fog outside reflected the fog in his mind. He couldn't remember what Jess was doing tonight but hoped that maybe she would be out with Jason as he wanted to be alone. He had tried to keep busy all week, working extra shifts and studying hard but now he was exhausted and needed to think things through.

Pushing his key into the front-door lock, he could hear voices coming from upstairs. A male and a female. *Must be Jess and Jason*, he thought with a pang of disappointment; he would not have a quiet night in after all. But when he reached the lounge, Kristian was surprised to see, for the second time in a week, a familiar but not-so-welcome face.

"Kieran?" he gasped.

"Kristian Wallace," Kieran rose and gave him a half smile.

Kristian placed his bag onto the couch and moved closer to him. Jess was standing uncomfortably in the corner, watching Kristian intently to see what his reaction to this stranger or old friend would be. *Why had she let him in?* Kristian wondered. *There was no way she knew him and she was usually so suspicious of strangers.*

"I, uh, I didn't think I'd be seeing you again," Kristian was still in shock at seeing his old acquaintance.

"You mean, you hoped you wouldn't?" Kieran moved slowly towards him.

The two men just stared at each other for a few seconds and then suddenly, they were shaking each other's hands.

Kristian, feeling uncomfortable, turned his attention to Jess.

"So, you just let complete strangers into our house now do you?" He sounded annoyed and Jess looked hurt.

"He was sitting on the doorstep when I got back and he said he knew you. I thought you'd be pleased to see an old friend?" Jess trailed off and stared at the floor, her cheeks flushed.

"So you just took his word for it, that he knew me?" Kristian felt bad having a go at her but he was wondering how many more times this week the Order would interfere in his life. First, his workplace, now his home.

"Well, you do know him, don't you? I thought I was doing you a favour, that's all," said Jess.

"Hey look," Kieran interrupted. "I thought you'd be a bit funny with me when I got here but don't blame her, I should have called first I know. I just wanted to catch up is all. We have a few things to talk about."

Jess and Kristian looked at one another and then at the man sitting on the sofa. He looked odd to say the least. He was a handsome man with dark brown hair but his clothes were very odd. He wore a purple corduroy jacket with bright lime-green trousers and a 'trap door' T-shirt underneath the blazer.

"So how do you two know each other?" Jess was hoping for some juicy story, but Kristian was certainly going to deny her that.

"We used to work together back home, that's all," Kristian paused for a second and then turned his attention back to Jess. "Jess, can I talk to you in the kitchen please?"

When they got into the kitchen, Jess looked up at him with concern "I'm sorry Kris, I thought…"

"Don't worry," he interrupted her. "I'm sorry I gave you a hard time back there. Listen it's just, Kieran and I, we have some stuff to talk about and it may be best if you weren't around. I just don't want you to get involved if it gets heated, okay?"

"Kristian, are you in some sort of trouble?" she asked, worry creeping ever deeper into her face.

"No, no, it's nothing like that. But please, just give us an hour, okay? For me?"

Unconvinced but not wanting to upset him further, she kissed him on the cheek then headed for her room, where a few moments later she emerged with her coat on, and swiftly left the flat. Now the two men were alone at last.

Kristian walked back into the lounge and glared down at Kieran.

"No. The answer is no, Kieran. Jonathon couldn't persuade me, so what makes you think you can?"

"Jonathon doesn't know I'm here," Kieran stood up again and walked towards the window, overlooking the tube station.

"Then why are you here?" Kristian was confused. Surely Kieran was lying.

"We need to talk, Kris. It's about Oliver. There are things you should know about his death, about the Order. Things no one would want me to tell you, but I just have to."

Kristian, although still scared of what the truth would do to him, was intrigued. Seeing Kieran again had been a shock but no matter how much he protested against the Order, he wanted so much to know what had happened to his friend. He knew that the Order was the only place he would gain that information. He slowly walked over and stood beside Kieran.

"Okay," he said softly, "tell me. How did Oliver die?"

"Well, he was on a mission in Berlin investigating Leceth. The mission was designated as a classified reconnaissance.

He left for Germany a couple of months ago and no one had heard from him since. He hadn't once reported in, not through the official channels anyway."

"Leceth? As in the head of the Council of Tivernal? And what kind of recon?" Kristian could hardly believe that the Order had taken such a bold and dangerous step.

"The Order has been concerned with Leceth's movements ever since we arrested Sauror. We believe that there is a link between them but we don't have any evidence and that is partially why Oliver was there. We couldn't prove that they had a relationship outside of the Council itself. Leceth is the chair of the Council and Sauror was a leading member but they come from different factions. Leceth is a vampire from an ancient line and Sauror was a member of Shadow," Kieran broke from talking and strode back over to the sofa, where Kristian noticed he had a small brown bag. He unzipped the bag and rummaged for a few seconds and then pulled out a large brown paper folder, bound together with blue elastic straps. "Due to the evidence that you and Oliver found on your first mission, Sauror was convicted of the murder of Anne and Preston. His motives for killing them are still, unfortunately, unclear to us, but the Order believes that his nefarious contacts are connected to Leceth himself."

"Why did the Order believe Leceth was involved?" As Kristian spoke, he leaned in closer to Kieran.

"Many reasons, but mainly due to some intelligence we obtained from within the Council. Leceth's rise to the top spot wasn't as smooth as we were led to believe. In fact, there were many who opposed his appointment. Several months ago, we learned the outcome of the vote that landed him the job. Both vampire seats had voted for him, one of the Vinji and one of the werewolf clans voted for him too. None of the dark covens voted for him. To lead the Council you need more than half the seats to support you, so at least six out of the ten available seats. To many of us at the Order, we were surprised that both Shadow seats ended up voting him in," Kieran's expression clearly showed how truly taken aback he was by this.

Kristian however, was not too shocked. He had never really understood the politics of the Council and he didn't care.

"So, he became the leader, the Shadow voted him in, that's not so strange to me."

"Oh, but it is," sighed Kieran. "Never before have both Shadow members voted for a vampire to be the Chair. The Shadow is made up from the world of man. The relationship between vampire houses and Shadow has never been one of co-operation and friendship," he spoke so fast that Kristian found it hard to keep up.

"Okay, so they hate each other. But they are both evil," Kristian still hadn't made the connection.

"It's beside the point, Kristian. We know a meeting between Sauror and Leceth took place in which Sauror swore his allegiance to Leceth and said he could get Ghost, the other Shadow member of the Council, to vote the same way. It's completely unheard of. There have been vampire leaders in the past but they generally got the six seats from the vampires, Vinji and werewolves," Kieran's voice raced on.

"Okay, okay calm down," Kristian was worried that Jess was going to come back and overhear something. "I get it, major conspiracy. So the Order asked Oliver to keep an eye on Leceth and I guess he did, but got caught and what? Leceth had him killed? That doesn't sound too smart to me, Leceth killing Oliver. If he knew he was being watched then why didn't he just make a thing of it? The Order isn't allowed to monitor the chair of the Council and killing Oliver just makes him look even more suspicious." By thinking and talking about it objectively, Kristian managed to stay emotionally detached from the situation.

"Well, you would think that," Kieran continued, "I agree, if Leceth did kill Oliver, it makes little sense, but it's the only thing we have to go on. And Oliver's death was strange. I use the word strange but what I should say is barbaric," he hesitantly placed the folder he was holding into Kristian's hands.

Kristian slowly undid the straps and cautiously opened the folder. Onto the floor slid three photographs of Oliver. Full-colour shots of his corpse floating in a river. Kristian suddenly understood why Kieran had used the word barbaric. His heart filled with rage and fear as he struggled for breath.

"What have they done to him?" Kristian gasped, not wanting a response.

"His heart was removed. We think he was alive during its removal, the autopsy suggested it, but still it's all a bit sketchy."

Slamming the photos down, Kristian screamed, "How could they do that to him? Why? Why? The bastards."

"There is more, Kristian, if you want to hear it?"

"More?" Kristian's body was unmoving but his heart was pumping faster than ever. "Go on." His hands covered his face to hide his horror.

"It has been more than two weeks since we believe Oliver lost his life and we have received no sign that his Phoenix has joined with another host. In fact, our seers have not even been able to feel its presence," for the first time, Kieran's voice was filled with fear.

Kristian released his hands from his face. *How could this be? Usually when a host dies, the Phoenix finds a new body.* Feeling utterly bewildered as well as angry, Kristian's memory took him back to a strange childhood recollection. Jerking it from his mind, he stood up fast.

"Look Kieran, thank you for coming here today and thank you for telling me what you've told me. I appreciate you've risked a lot to do so, but I need you to leave. I can't come back, Kieran. I just can't."

"What?" Kieran was gobsmacked. "You heard what I said, right? Oliver is dead and his Phoenix-Ethalon is missing? This isn't any ordinary situation. The Order needs you, you can't just stay here and hide. It's not just about you, there are others involved."

"I can do as I please. I don't owe them anything, or indeed you," as he spoke, he moved Kieran towards the stairway.

Kieran was at a loss for words. He didn't remember Kristian being so selfish, such a coward. Passing the threshold of the flat, Kieran turned around and spoke to his old friend. "It doesn't matter what you think you do and don't owe the Order. What really matters is what you owe to yourself."

With that, Kristian slammed the door and stood for a few minutes, arms crossed over his chest; his face filled with rage and his heart pumped to the pangs of guilt and pain.

. . .

- Chapter Five -

Into the Belly of the Beast

Jess sat outside a small, quaint café, one of many that lined the High Street in Angel. Staring down at her empty cup of tea, she pondered how long she had been out of the flat. Looking at her watch she was surprised to see that she had wasted nearly an hour. An hour spent drinking tea and reading newspaper after newspaper, filling the awkward time she was forced to kill while Kristian and his mysterious guest 'talked'.

Was an hour long enough? she thought. Kristian and Kieran probably had a lot to talk about from what she had gathered. Doubt was spreading through her mind about the decision to let the man into the flat. She remembered the look on Kristian's face, the one of shock and foreboding. *Was she right to let the stranger in?* After all, she hadn't a clue who he was. He seemed like a nice person but from that look of Kristian's, she was beginning to think she had done the wrong thing.

Still pondering if she had caused her best friend unnecessary heartache, she spent another ten minutes staring at the clock through the window of the café. *I think it's time to go home*, she decided.

Had Kieran left yet? She wasted no time with that thought and concluded that she didn't care. Concern for her friend now overwhelmed her; she needed to make sure he was all right. Leaving the café she paced quickly back to the flat, not really knowing what to expect when she got there. *Would they be fighting? Would she return to a bloodbath or just to two old friends catching up, laughing over old memories, with old photo albums strewn over the coffee table, or flicking through photos on Kristian's computer or phone?* She had no idea, although she was sure she had never seen any photo albums belonging to Kristian.

It was no longer than three minutes later when she was at her front door. Unlocking it and opening it gently, she inched her way into the flat. Creeping up the stairs, she listened intently and scanned the hallway for signs of a scuffle. Hearing and seeing nothing, she thought it possible that the two young men had gone out somewhere, perhaps for a drink. She reached the second door at the top of the flat that led the way into the main apartment and opened it, little by little. To her great surprise, Kristian was there, sitting on the floor in front of her.

"Kristian? What happened? Are you okay?" She sat down beside him.

He wasn't crying, he wasn't tearful at all, he wasn't bruised or scratched or, to Jess's huge relief, hurt in anyway. He was just completely lost in his own thoughts, staring into nothingness and completely unresponsive.

"I take it your friend has gone then?" Jess tried. "Are you okay? You gonna tell me what happened?"

Her unease increased, she shook him really hard "Kristian! Are you okay?" she spoke slowly and forcefully.

Kristian suddenly and abruptly came to. He sat up straight and his face infused with life once more. He turned his head toward Jess. "Sorry, Jess, totally wasn't with it, when did you get back?" He lifted himself to his feet and walked into the living room.

"Where are you going now?" shouted Jess, following him.

Sitting down on the couch, Kristian flicked the TV on and leant back, obviously not at ease.

"Kristian, are you going to speak to me?" her voice was high with emotion. "I'm worried about you."

"Hey, it was nothing," Kristian brushed her off. "He just wanted to catch up and I wasn't up for building bridges, so he left. Honestly, it's nothing. Just leave it, please," his eyes were fixed on the TV the whole time he spoke to her. Turning up the volume with the remote, he seemed to think that the conversation was over. Snatching the remote from his hand, Jess threw it across the room in disbelief and frustration, and sat down beside him on the couch.

"Okay Mr. I-have-no-problems, this 'friend' of yours has obviously done or told you something that has flustered you. You don't have to tell me, but I can sense that you're upset, that something is wrong, so don't treat me like an idiot, Kristian. Just understand that I'm concerned about you, will you? I'm your best friend for God's sake."

Kristian felt a pang of guilt. He had never seen that look on her face before; a look of mistrust and doubt. They usually talked about anything and everything together: well, almost everything.

There was something he was keeping back from her, but the thing he kept hidden was something he wanted to hide not just from Jess, but from himself. And besides, would she be able to deal with it? He couldn't even deal with it himself. Did he really want his burden to be hers as well? Then again, maybe she would understand and help him with the difficult decision he had to make. There was silence in the room for ten solid minutes as Kristian considered what to do and what to say. He was rehearsing in his mind the words that should leave his mouth. Jess was sitting sideways to him, arms folded, scrutinising him, anticipating the story he had to tell. She let out a few loud impatient sighs, which he ignored. He just wasn't sure: was he just putting off telling her or was he dumbstruck by indecision? There was so much to recount.

His story, his life and his secret. Could he really just come out with it all now? Spill his secrets right here in the lounge? What would she think? Then in an instant, he just started.

"There's something important that you need to know about me, about my past," he exclaimed.

"Whatever it is, I'm here for you," she said as she kindly placed a hand on his arm.

"You're thinking drugs. Prostitution, even a stint in jail aren't you? I only wish it was something that simple."

"Is it worse?" she looked surprised; she couldn't imagine her sweet, kind friend getting into any kind of trouble.

"No, it's not worse, it's just different; hard to explain, and I don't think you'll understand," Kristian struggled.

"Understand? Kristian, how could you say that? Of course I'll understand," Jess couldn't hide her frustrations as she spoke.

Kristian looked down, searching for the words. "Jess, I'm really sorry but this isn't any ordinary secret. Once I tell you, there will be no going back. It won't just change the way you judge me, but the way you look at the world."

"Oh, for God's sake, Kristian, tell me!" she demanded as she stood up in frustration.

"Okay!" he rose to his feet. "Put simply, I'm a Phoenix."

She glared at him, confused, "A what?" Her voice was getting higher.

He sat back down, realising that there was no going back now, she would either believe him and help him, or she wouldn't. "It's something inside me... It kind of gives me... powers."

After a few seconds of complete silence, she burst into hysterical laughter. "So it's drugs then?" she mocked sarcastically. She turned away from him in anger and in a hurt voice she spoke, "If you want to play games with me, that's fine."

He rose back to his feet. "I knew I wouldn't be able get you to understand," he muttered as he headed for the door.

She turned around quickly, "I'll bloody understand if you start off by telling me the truth. For Christ's sake, be honest with me."

He suddenly and abruptly punched the wall in front of him; she jumped back in shock. "This is me being honest with you. I'm telling you the truth but you're just not willing or able to hear me out."

"Fine. Start from the beginning, then? Come on, I'm listening," she said, uneasy at his outburst.

He walked back into the centre of the room and took a deep breath. "Okay, I'll tell you everything, just promise me that you'll hear me out, let me finish, then I will answer any questions. You just need to be open-minded, really open-minded."

"I promise," she said as she raised her hand.

"No sly comments, no filthy looks, no laughing. Just listen! And when I'm done you can either believe me or not; that's your call."

She eyed him suspiciously but knew that she had to give him his chance to explain; she walked back and perched herself back on to the couch, facing him and watching him intently.

"I'm the host to a Phoenix," he repeated, moving to sit beside her again.

She scanned his face for a sign of deception, but there was none. This left her with one of three conclusions. Either her friend was crazy, telling the truth or an even better liar than she could've ever imagined.

"You're serious?" she whispered.

"Deadly," he replied.

"So what does it mean? What is it? What's a Phoenix?" she asked.

"Well," he started, he hesitated slightly, shocked by her willing tone, "a Phoenix, and wait for this, is an incorporeal being of great power that can only live in this world in a symbiotic relationship with a human host. At least, that's how it was first explained to me," he paused for another second. "It's as complicated as it sounds; it started for me about—"

Jess interrupted. "Whoa, whoa, whoa, wait a second. Leave out all the long words. You said something about powers just then."

He sat up straight and coughed slightly. "I know that you've always thought of me as a bit of a wimp, but I'm actually a lot stronger than I look. I heal really fast as well and there's more."

"How strong?" she asked suspiciously. Before the words had finished leaving her mouth, Kristian had made his way across the room and effortlessly lifted up the bookcase and held it up with one hand so it touched the ceiling.

Jess stood up and gasped. As he put the bookcase down he continued, "There's a lot more too."

She walked over to the bookcase; thinking that it was all some sort of stunt, she attempted to lift it as well, but for her, it was impossible. Only by using both hands did she manage to move it slightly. He had really lifted it; it was no trick.

"More?" she probed, to which he grinned slightly.

"Oh yes," he said. "Do you want me to show you or tell you?"

She hesitated. "You're not going to cut yourself, are you?"

"No," he laughed. "There's more than the super strength and the fast healing. The Phoenix has this power. It's like an energy, one that I can mould into stuff. A well-trained Phoenix host can make all manner of things, from blasts to shields. I used to be able to do it, I'm not sure if I could now, it's been a while."

She looked at him with astonishment. Teetering on the edge of understanding and disbelief she willed him to show her more. "So what do you mean, you could blow something up?"

"Maybe if I tried, I haven't done it for so long. It's a skill that needs constant practice. But I'll try. Stand to one side. It could be dangerous." Using his arm, he manoeuvred her out of the way of his acquired target: an ugly old vase that was given to Jess by an unattractive ex.

"You don't like that tat?" he asked pointing at the homemade creation resting on the floor next to the fireplace.

"As much as I liked Rick," she replied.

The answer gave him the green light to go ahead. Trying desperately to remember his training, he stretched out his hand as jade light flickered from the tips of his fingers. Hissing through the air it struck the vase smashing it into several pieces.

She gasped again, as her hand rose to her mouth; she looked over to Kristian in bewilderment to see him looking equally shocked by his own destructive achievement.

Wiping his brow he spoke in disbelief, "I didn't think I still had it in me. Though to be honest I've a bit of a migraine now." He said "migraine" but what he meant was discomfort. The task did cause him actual pain, but what disturbed him the most was hearing the voice of his Phoenix; he had suppressed that voice for nearly two years, and now it echoed through his thoughts.

"Wow. Okay, super strength I can deal with, healing fast I get, but I didn't actually believe that you could or would blow something up. That was amazing. So when did you last do it? How long is a long time?"

"About two years now. Just before I left the Order."

"The what?" she asked.

"The Order of Light; it's an old secretive organisation; I used to work for them. I left, but now they want me to go back," he said as the burden of returning once again filled his heart.

"I've never heard of the Order of Light." she blurted out.

"That's because it's a secret, it's not like the Freemasons or anything."

"Who are they? What's their game? Are they bad or something?" Jess asked, sounding genuinely intrigued by it all.

"No, no, they are actually the good guys," he said.

"Good guys… then who are the bad guys?"

"God, so many questions. Do you really want me to start from the beginning?" Jess responded to Kristian's question nodding enthusiastically, she wanted to hear it all, now she was more than simply a believer; she was captivated.

"Well three years ago, I started to have these nightmares. There was this woman, I found out later her name was Anne. In my dreams she was murdered, I had the same macabre dream repeatedly. Every night for weeks on end I watched her die; I felt her die. It was tangible, as real as you are to me now. That's how it started."

Jess looked fondly at her friend; she could almost see the horror of these memories in his eyes. If there was a single moment in this bizarre conversation, when she truly believed him, it was now.

"The dreams were just the start of something called the 'blending'. That's what the Order calls it when a Phoenix joins with a new host. It doesn't hurt, well, not physically. The legend of the Phoenix is rooted in some truth. When a host dies the Phoenix is reborn into a new body; it never dies, it just lives through us, the hosts. And a consequence of that, is that there are many lifetimes worth of memories. I don't see them all, I can't recall them as if they were my own, but sometimes they play out in my sleep. The memories themselves aren't too horrific, what's bad is feeling Saranthea's emotions, the pain and the joy."

"Saranthea?" asked Jess.

"That's her name," Kristian said in almost a whisper, he hadn't uttered her name since his departure from the Order. Saying it aloud brought mixed emotions. "She isn't the only one. There are twelve out there, well thirteen if you include the Dark Phoenix. The story goes that the twelve were born into light and one in the darkness. Usually the twelve pick hosts similar to them, good and pure," he chuckled to himself. "The Dark Phoenix on the other hand chooses a host who is similar to him, someone who he can cause the most pain and misery with," he paused for breath and examined Jess's face.

"There are people out there that can do what you can do? There are real superheroes?" she asked, already knowing what the answer would be.

"Yes, I've met the occasional hero but they wouldn't class themselves as that, most people who blend with a Phoenix see it as an honour, a privilege; a calling that gives their lives meaning."

"And you don't?" she said, hearing in his voice that he had some reservations.

"I'm not the hero type, don't think I'll ever be."

She chuckled on hearing his words; to her he was the best friend she ever had, he was caring, honest and had a moral compass that never wavered.

"So what exactly is the hero type then?" she asked.

"Well, someone brave, loyal, strong, someone who is willing to always do the right thing regardless of their own needs, that's the hero I would want to be," said Kristian.

"To me, you are all of those things," Jess said without hesitation.

"You really have no idea, I'm none of those things. I'm a coward," he said genuinely believing his words.

"What do you mean you're a coward?" she exclaimed.

"You don't understand the world that I used to live in," he replied.

"Then tell me more, I want to know." Jess said grabbing Kristian's hand and squeezing it reassuringly.

"Well, after the blending, after the Order found me, I started my training, that's when I learned the truth. You asked me who the bad guys are; the Order doesn't protect people from muggers, murderers, and drug-dealers. There are things much worse out there."

"Like what?" She didn't really want to know, but she was falling down the rabbit hole, she had been told about the fantastic, the good; now she knew it was time for the bad.

"The easiest way for me to explain it is…" he thought for a moment, "well, imagine everything you have seen in horror movies, monsters, vampires, werewolves, that sort of thing. It makes sense if you think about it, folklore was influenced by reality, they actually exist and I am not talking about the clichéd cheesy versions you get in the movies. I'm talking about real evil, real monsters!" he looked at her for a reaction but she wasn't actually finding this part hard to believe; for some strange reason it was human nature to believe in the bad rather than the good.

It was easy for her to picture the vampires, the werewolves, she could see the images of them from something she had seen on TV or had read. The Phoenixes, on the other hand, were unknown to her, they were unimaginable to her, she didn't know who they were or what they wanted. And her friend's obvious reluctance to embrace them made them seem chilling.

Her face showed the angst she was feeling, and Kristian could read it plainly.

"You okay? Sorry, I know it's a lot to take in. It's not easy finding out what really lurks in the dark and there is so much more to tell you."

She considered his words; it wasn't just the thought of monsters that made her feel uneasy, it was different now; he was; she was.

"Do you mind if we take a break? There's a lot to sink in," she asked.

He nodded in agreement; he too found the conversation hard, digging around in his memories and discussing the past was not something he enjoyed.

An hour soon passed, and the pair had not ventured once to re-enter the minefield that was the Phoenix conversation. Kristian spent the time sitting in the front room staring into nothing; he only moved to make a cup of tea, and he was on his sixth brew. Jess was now laid in lukewarm bath water, she tried hard to think of anything else, but her mind was racing, her imagination was working overtime. As the bubbles around her flickered out of existence so did her belief that everything would remain the same. She didn't know what emotion to focus on first, the confusion, the fear, the hurt. There were so many questions she wanted answers to and with every answer a new emotion would enter her heart, a new thought would cross her mind.

She was surprised at how she felt, the worry for her friend, the confusion in her mind was obvious, but the niggling feeling of betrayal that had started off seeping into her thoughts was now flowing like a river through her head. Mixed in with the feeling of betrayal was a feeling of stupidity. How could she have been so naïve as to not realise the hidden depths that Kristian had guarded so closely; not seen the signs that hid the dark world she was now so very aware of? As she reflected on her feelings, she soon began to feel guilty at seeing her friend in such a light. *He is still Kristian, isn't he?*

She wasn't entirely sure anymore, and that hurt.

Suddenly there was a knock on the door. "Are you okay in there Jess?" Kristian said, barely audible through the door.

She sat up abruptly, splashing water onto the floor around the bathtub. "Um, yes, I'm fine, just give me a minute, okay?"

"Sure, okay, I just wanted to check on you. You've been in there forever."

As she heard his footsteps walk away from the bathroom, a sadness crept over her. She immersed her whole body and head under the water and let the ripples wash over her, attempting to let them take her away to a place of safety and calm. That momentary tranquillity did not last long, as she knew that the conversation was not finished.

It wasn't long before she was back in the lounge, perched once again on the sofa in her cosy dressing gown and slippers, with a cup of tea in her hands, freshly made by Kristian.

"I guess the main question I have to ask you is why did you leave?" she asked tentatively.

"You have to understand how the Order works, Jess, it's not just about the Phoenix. I left about two years ago, just after completing my training, after my first mission. From the months I spent there I knew it wasn't for me. You're constantly reminded of the worst aspects of this world. I wanted my own life and I wanted to choose my own destiny," he paused for a second. "So I made a deal. They let me leave and go to university and I said that I would get my degree, get a real career but would return to help if they ever needed me. It may sound selfish, but they have eleven other Phoenixes out there to take my place. They have witches and wizards and other people with extraordinary powers. They can easily get by without me," he looked at Jess hoping for her acceptance, her understanding.

"I get it," she put her arm on his. "So what's happened and what does Kieran have to do with it?"

Kristian took a few seconds before starting; he took in a deep breath and began, "There was a guy called Oliver. We became Phoenix hosts at the same time, we trained together, took our first mission together," he paused again; he couldn't bear to say it aloud. "He was killed. They want me to find out what happened, find whoever did it."

Jess hugged him tightly. "What are you going to do?" she asked

"I don't know. I really don't want to go back. But I feel like I owe it to him, he was my friend. He was older than me and looked out for me, like a brother. He was brave and I feel like I disappointed him so much when I left. I want to make it up to him, but I don't think I can."

"Well, you don't have to go back for good do you?" Jess wasn't sure she wanted her best friend to be out there fighting monsters, but she could tell that Oliver had meant a lot to him.

"I know Jess, but I'm scared. I'm not brave or courageous like the others. I don't want to die," his voice trembled.

"Now you listen to me," said Jess firmly. "You are brave. You may not think so, but you're very courageous and a lot stronger than most people. Let me tell you what my crazy Sergeant Major father used to say: courage isn't about being fearless. It's about being filled with fear, knowing that fear, embracing it and doing the right thing in the face of that fear."

He studied her. She was strong; she had a remarkable ability to make everything make sense to him. He knew it would take more than a quick chat with her before he entered the belly of the beast again, but she was helping him more than he had thought she could. She was making his decision easier, giving his decision-making clarity.

"Look," she said "I know, as you do, that you will go back Kris, and here's why: you're a good person and good people don't run away. They stand and fight for what they believe in and you've always done that in the past. I didn't know Oliver and I won't pretend to, but I think you would honour me and fight for my justice, just as much as you are going to fight for Oliver's," she kissed him on the head and stood up.

As he listened to her words, he knew that she was right; he knew that he was going to go back, even though the thought scared him shitless. He knew that it was the right thing to do. He stood up and embraced her tightly.

"Thank you, Jess, you're right. I am going to go back, that's exactly what I have to do."

She smiled at him and sighed heavily.

"So, am I going to wake up now?" she chuckled.

He laughed. "If only," he replied. "Now, are you hungry? It's late and we haven't eaten. I will cook if you like."

"Are you putting off the phone call?" Jess asked.

"What phone call?" he answered.

"I think you know what I mean."

"Give me a chance. I've only just made the decision myself." he replied, smiling for the first time in the conversation.

"Well, I don't want you to ponder on it for too long, you might change both our minds."

"I don't think I'll change my mind. There's not really any going back now is there? It's time for me to be your hero."

She gazed up into his deep blue eyes and smiled affectionately at him. She placed a hand on his arm softly, and uttered the words he needed to hear.

"You've always been my hero, Kris."

. . .

Jonathon stood in his office contemplating his next move. Kristian was a no-show. *'If he were going to come back to the fold, he would have done it days ago,'* he thought.

Six days had passed since his meeting with him in the café and not a word. Moving people around to fill the tasks he needed them to do now plagued his mind. It was now going to have to be Zhing. The investigation needed to be carried out with or without Kristian and Zhing was the only one he could spare. Maybe he could get Adriana to come back from Spain, but she was already on another mission and she had not even been told about Oliver's death yet. Perhaps Kara could take up the mission, but she had just taken command of the New York office. His head was throbbing; the stress was getting to him. He knew that neither Adriana nor Kara would be able to lead the investigation; he just did not want to have to tell Zhing that she was being reassigned away from the Dark Phoenix mission. She was likely to go berserk: it was her most important mission yet and she was determined to complete it.

The Order had always taken a half-cocked approach towards the Dark Phoenix problem and for the last ten years practically ignored it, but the time for action was now and it needed to be resolved quickly. Frustration completely overwhelmed him; he placed his whole arm on his desk and with one long swipe, he tossed all of his paperwork on to the floor. Pens, pencils and paper went everywhere, the phone too, and the lamp smashed hard against the stone floor. Placing his head on the desk, the old man began to sing quietly to himself. His song and thoughts were cut short by a hard rapping on his door. "Go away," Jonathon shouted.

Entering the office, Andrew Gilmore walked in; dressed in his usual worn overall, he spoke softly and gently. "Well, old friend," he smiled "I sensed you didn't really mean it."

"Oh, I'm sorry Andrew, do sit down." Jonathon raised his head and smiled back at him. Closing the door behind him, Andrew slowly walked towards the chair opposite Jonathon and then realised the chair and every other chair in the room was covered in paperwork. "It's as bad as Peter's office," Andrew spoke his thought aloud.

"Oh dear, I'm sorry, let me move some of this," said Jonathon rising and pointing toward the chair.

"Not to worry," Andrew had already stretched out his hand and the cluttered chair was suddenly clear again.

"Nice trick," Jonathon never failed to be impressed by magic, even though he had seen it used many times.

"Well, you now know why we members of the Trinity have such tidy offices, Jon. And some people are just easily pleased," he smiled widely at his friend.

"Oh, I wish I was still easily pleased," sighed Jonathon as he lowered himself back into his chair. "I really do, it would be nice if things went the way I planned them."

"Still troubled by how to investigate young Oliver's death? Expecting old friends to be more receptive, are you?" Andrew said, appreciating Jonathon's situation. The entire Order knew how overstretched the resources were at the moment and Oliver's sad and strange death, along with Kristian's resistance to return, were additional strains.

"He died on my watch, Andrew. I sent him on that mission; I got him killed. We have no leads except you-know-what and we cannot even bring that person in for questioning. The last two years have been so difficult and for the first time since I got this chair, I really don't know what to do," Andrew had never heard Jonathon sound so disheartened.

"Yes, he did die in unfortunate circumstances Jonathon, but he wasn't the first and he certainly won't be the last. It is the nature of the devil with whom we dance. Oliver's death was far from ordinary and to suggest that you are in some way responsible is utter nonsense. He died doing what he was born to do: to fight. I know this sounds heartless, Jonathon, but everybody dies, it's simply a matter of when and how. Oliver died a hero, doing a hero's job. What is tragic is that he died so young. Your only job now is to try and find out who did it and why. And as far as Leceth goes, if he is responsible, we will get to the bottom of it. I feel in time we will bring him in, he will answer for it, if he's involved," Andrew's words reawakened Jonathon's determined spirit.

"Yes I know you're right, Andrew. However, feeling responsible is part of being human. It is the part of me that drives me to find the culprit and bring him to justice. I only wish Kristian was on board, we do need him. I really believe that. But I know I can't force him and the boy is as stubborn as a…"

Andrew interrupted: "I could use a spell on him, make him think he wants to return?" he winked at Jonathon.

"You can do that?"

"Well, it is a little tricky. His Phoenix protects him from a lot of magic but I'm not just any old magician, you know?" As Andrew spoke it was clear he was thinking of all the spells he would like to cast if he could, for a man of such prestige and wisdom, he had a mischievous streak.

"Well, as much as I would like that, we mustn't," Jonathon sighed deeply.

"Well, if you're sure," Andrew looked disappointed. "You could always try talking to him again," Andrew's smile returned to his old face. Jonathon laughed at his friend's sarcasm. Talking to Kristian again was the last thing on his mind.

"Well, I have things to do, must get on with it. I assume you are going to hand the Oliver investigation over to Zhing?" Andrew asked.

"Yes, that's the plan. One hopes it all works out for the best," Jonathon replied.

"I'm sure everything will work out just fine," Andrew turned and walked towards the door when he heard the sound of a phone ringing and turned to see Jonathon staring aimlessly at the floor.

"Damn, where is it?" Jonathon said, regretting that he had let his frustration get the better of him.

With one flick of the hand, Andrew made the telephone appear out from the pile of papers on the floor and come to rest next to Jonathon's ear. As the receiver magically picked up and was held by an invisible force, Jonathon mouthed a "thanks" to Andrew.

"Hello, Jonathon Paige speaking," Jonathon's face drained of all colour as he heard the voice on the other end and as he took in the words that followed, he was filled with astonishment, wonder and hope.

"Hello, Jonathon, it's Kristian. Can we talk?"

. . .

The bulky, solid oak doors opened slowly, and the sight of the interior of the Cardinal Office hit Kristian hard. He tentatively stepped forward and as soon as he walked over the threshold of the building a tingle of unease travelled through his body. He had almost forgotten what it felt like to cross through one of the many magical barriers in the Order's headquarters.

Kristian was an expert at keeping control of his emotions; he had many things bottled up inside him. His secret life at the Order, the years of hiding his feelings from the people he held dear, but now he could not stop the stirrings of fear edging deep within his chest. What was it about this place that caused so much terror in him? This was a temple of good and the people who resided here were equally as good, they were worthy of being here. It was the prospect of seeing those people, his old friends, that rattled his nerves, made his palms sweat. Was it too late to back out? He scanned the lobby of the building. It was small, lit by artificial light; it contained only one long desk opposite the grand entrance. Behind the desk were two more solid oak doors. One was a lift and the other was the entrance to the public hall. And there at the desk in front of him, casually chatting amongst themselves, were some of the faces he had once known very well. It was the old team, minus Kieran and Oliver. Sam was sitting on the floor looking up at the others. It was the same old Sam, looking carefree, slightly overweight with chubby red cheeks. Standing above him was the friendly face of Rachel; she looked different. Her hair was shoulder-length now, her clothes not as casual as he remembered. The most familiar thing about her still were the thick-rimmed glasses that she got a lot of stick for, but she refused to get more fashionable ones. The team had always poked fun at Rachel for her stubbornness on the subject but they all knew deep down that Rachel would not be Rachel without those awful glasses! Next to her was the unchanging face of Jean Tanner. To look at Jean you would think he was stand-offish and a snob, but the reality was that he was one of the most kind, compassionate and approachable people that Kristian had ever met. Although, Jean did like to play the odd practical joke utilising his telekinetic abilities.

Kristian was so nervous about them spotting him, he felt sick. He was contemplating turning on the spot and running back out the way he had come in. *Are they here waiting for me?* he wondered. He had not thought about the Alpha Team for a long time. He had buried the memories of them along with his memories of the Order. But to see the team standing in front of him made him feel nostalgic and he then realised how much he had missed the faithful companions he once had. He coughed, as if to clear his throat, and the three of them turned to look at him. The first to respond was Rachel;

71

she squealed with delight and rushed towards him, then hugged him tightly. As she backed away Jean moved in, hugged him as well, and kissed him on both cheeks. As Jean cleared out of Kristian's line of sight he saw Sam smiling at him and he leapt to his feet. The two men stared at each other smiling for what seemed like forever and then, suddenly, the pair embraced each other with such force Rachel and Jean thought for a second that they were fighting.

"You don't know how good it is to see you," Sam said, as he could not stop smiling.

"Thanks guys," Kristian was overwhelmed with their welcome. He had thought they would be angry and be disappointed with him for leaving the Order in the first place, that they may even blame him for Oliver's death, but this greeting was surprisingly wonderful.

"You haven't changed at all," said Rachel excitedly, "except your hair is longer and you're more attractive than ever."

Before Kristian could respond, Jean jumped in. "Yes, it's great to see you, are you well? Things have not been the same since you left."

A pang of guilt and regret filled Kristian and he quickly changed the subject of 'leaving'.

"So, uh, what's new?" he asked awkwardly. "I take it Peter is still here, huh? Nosey as ever, I bet? I know that Jonathon is still running the place, uh, yeah so, what's new?" Kristian felt stupid and awkward for saying that but was lost for words. Sam placed his hand on Kristian's shoulder.

"Yes, Peter is still here and no he hasn't changed; he's still the same old Peter you remember. In fact, I would say he has got worse!"

"Worse?" exclaimed Kristian. "I didn't think that was possible. Are Wendy, Susan and Penny still here?" There was a pause and Kristian sensed a despondency between the three of them. "What?" he said, "Are they okay?"

"Well," said Rachel, "Penny still has her job and Susan is running Andromeda, but Wendy, well…"

"What?" Kristian was waiting to hear the dreaded words, that she had been killed by some dark force just like Oliver.

"I'm afraid she passed away," Sam spoke softly.

Kristian waited to hear the words 'killed' or 'murdered', but Sam spoke again

"Don't worry, it wasn't anything sinister, she died in her sleep a couple months ago. She was eighty-six, you know."

Kristian felt relieved that Wendy had not been killed but still felt sad for the loss. He knew Wendy was a frail old woman, even though she was a member of the Trinity and could make herself look as young as she wished. She was an incredibly kind and thoughtful woman and had fully supported Kristian when he had chosen to leave the Order. He had often thought that Jonathon wouldn't have let him leave if Wendy hadn't backed him up. He felt a deep sadness now and the joy of seeing his old comrades was being overtaken by the weight of sorrow that he felt was around his neck. Hiding his emotions well, as always, Kristian smiled at the gang and said, "Hey, she had a good life didn't she? She was a great woman and let's hope she taught us all something valuable. Now, I've got to go and see Jonathon and get my briefing so I better get a move on."

"You certainly picked your moment to return, fella." Sam said whilst shaking his head.

"Yes, it's all go here at the moment. My suggestion is to keep us close Kristian. We were and still are a good tactical team and sticking together, we're the best in the Order," said Jean.

Kristian let out a little laugh. "Us? A tactical team! You three in action I would love to see, and as for me? Well I must be the most unreliable Phoenix host in the history of the Order. And what about Kieran? I've seen better magic from a magician at a kids' party."

The four of them laughed. They all knew it was true. Individually they were all talented and unique, but as a team, none of them really thought they were the best the Order had to offer. They had only completed one mission as a whole team, they had trained together, and that first mission was still a topic of conversation and ridicule for the office staff two years on.

"Hey, come on. We're not that bad," chuckled Rachel.

"Yeah I know, I was just kidding. I'm sure all evil creatures tremble at the sound of our names and once they discover that we are on the trail of Oliver's killer, they will be quaking in their boots, or whatever it is they wear." Kristian realised what he had said almost as soon as he said it; he noticed the group tense up at the sound of Oliver's name. Luckily, the doors to the elevator opened and out walked Kieran to break the silence that had overcome them. He walked straight over to Kristian and like the others had done, hugged him.

"It's marvellous to see you, Kris."

"You too," Kristian replied. "You guys have really made me feel welcome and have made coming back a hell of a lot easier for me. Thank you so much. I thought this was going to be so hard. You all know I don't really want to be here, but I want to find those responsible. It's just this life I don't want, it's nothing personal, you know?"

"Listen," said Kieran, "as long as you do what you came here to do, that's all we want from you. Now Kristian, are you ready to enter, are you ready to get swallowed up by the beast?"

"I can hold your hand if you want?" smirked Rachel, and before he could respond, she grabbed a hold of his hand.

"Thanks," replied a bemused and still somewhat nervous Kristian.

They all walked towards the elevator and once the five of them were inside, Kristian was overcome with the feelings of claustrophobia and being completely trapped. His hands stiffened and his grip on Rachel's hand tightened. She turned to him and whispered in his ear, "You'll be fine, and if you really want to leave, I'll whizz us out of here in a flash."

Her words comforted him. He had forgotten about her special gift. And to think of her power as a gift made him, for an instant, think about his in a similar way.

...

- Chapter Six -

For the Love of Gaia

The elevator doors opened on to the central level to the complex. It was called the central level or the hub. Kristian thought it had to be a good thirty metres below ground. A long corridor now stretched away from the group, with a row of more elevators on one side and a row of doors on the other. Each elevator and door had a large plaque above it indicating its purpose.

This part of the building had remained untouched for near on a century and the only change made was to replace the large staircases that had once stood on one side of the corridor with modern elevators.

Moving swiftly down the corridor, the five of them passed the elevator signposted 'Andromeda-Aceso Medical Centre'. Kristian hoped he would not find himself having to enter that elevator any time soon. On the right-hand side of the corridor, the first door they passed was very much like all the other doors in headquarters, solid oak, but this one had the name 'Holy Order Of The Trinity' written on its plaque. Kristian remembered this room well. It was one of the most comfortable in the entire building, spacious and full of lots of very interesting people. The decor inside was also different, it was nothing like the macho, imperialistic decor that made up the rest of the premises, it was gentle and soft, and had an almost feminine touch to it.

The next door they passed read 'Office of the Chief Librarian of the Nariasdems' Great Library'. Underneath that sign, another smaller one read 'Chief Librarian Peter Bergbeck'.

The group continued their walk down the long, wide corridor, passing door after door, each one marked accordingly, 'Artifact Stores', 'Offices of the Nariasdem', 'Offices of the Phoenix Legacy', 'Sleeping Quarters'. The doors they passed were exactly the same in appearance. They were the general offices of the hierarchy of the Order. They passed Andrew Gilmore's, which, as head of the Coven of the Trinity, he rarely used.

Towards the end of the corridor there was the last elevator labelled 'To conference rooms 2–39'; to the right of this was Jonathon Paige's office, designated as 'Head of The Order Of Light' and next to that was a set of double doors marked 'Conference Room 1'.

The whole corridor was twenty foot high and each door at least eight foot tall. The double doors at the very end of the corridor, however, stretched the entire width and length of the wall and seemed huge in comparison with the rest. These doors, like every door, were solid oak but unlike any other door in the entire Order, they were furnished with no handles, no distinctive locks or keyholes. An elaborate pattern was etched out on the surface in gold.

It sent shivers down people's spines when they first laid eyes upon it and for Kristian it had been such a long time since he had first laid eyes upon it that this gaze felt like the first time all over again. The door had no plaque, no sign. It did not need one, because everybody in the Order knew what lay behind them; it was the Great Library.

The locks and mechanisms of the door lay on the other side. It was more like a safe than a library. The room contained the most extensive collection of books ever collated, and not just magical ones, but every book ever written by man or beast alike.

Very few people actually entered the library and it was widely believed that the clerks who maintained it lived permanently inside.

To gain access to the library would require a password, a magical word that when spoken would release the locks on the inside of the enormous doors. Many people in the Order knew the password, but only a few would ever use it. The word was not the only protection given to the library; it was also protected by the greatest of all magic. A powerful mystical barrier that began at the threshold and encompassed the entire library; one that would only allow those who were good and pure of heart to enter.

Many members of staff were too afraid to enter; the ever-present fear that one wasn't completely pure of heart and knowing that of oneself frightened many to the core. After all, most of the staff at the Order were human, and like most humans, no one was perfect.

Kristian himself had only ever entered the library once and believed he would never enter again. Not for the usual fear of being rejected by the barrier. For him, there was only ever the one justifiable reason to enter.

"Are you just going to stand there all day or are you coming to the meeting with the rest of us?" Rachel's voice echoed slightly as it bounced off the walls. She pulled Kristian's arm in the direction of the main conference room – 'Conference Room 1'.

"Sorry, I'm coming," he muttered, shaking off the haze and the chills that the Great Library's doors gave rise to.

Kieran slowly opened the doors to the conference room and he, Sam, Jean and Rachel walked in. Kristian followed tentatively keeping his head down avoiding looking at those awaiting him. He was nervous. As he glanced up, he could feel his cheeks burning and saw at the very end of the table, five faces examining him. Four of them he had not seen for over two years and the fifth was Jonathon.

"Take your seats please," bellowed Jonathon. All five obeyed the command, with Rachel and Kristian sitting down at one side of the huge table and the other three sitting opposite them. Kristian felt like the faces at the far end were taunting him, he didn't want to look at them, to see the looks in their eyes as they scrutinised him. Jonathon sat at the head of the table and next to him on his left, sitting alone, was Peter. As their eyes met, Kristian felt a surge of anger as he became aware of the way Peter glared at him. On the other side of Jonathon was Andrew Gilmore, the leader of the Trinity. Next to him, Yi-Mao, head of The Phoenix Legacy and sat next to him was Brendan, who was generally regarded as Yi-Mao's number two, but this position had never been officially recognised.

"Before you start asking questions, Kristian, you should know that Brendan and I are leaving this afternoon for China and Japan, on important Order business that is completely unavoidable. Bringing you back was necessary and I, like everyone here, am very pleased to see you've chosen to return," said Yi-Mao, smiling.

Kristian took on board every word his former mentor said. He had the utmost respect for Yi-Mao and felt relieved that he had welcomed him in the way he had. He was just beginning to relax again when he caught a glimpse of the look on Brendan's face.

"Okay, thank you, of course I completely understand that you have important work to conduct, it's just that I would like to get started on my mission, ASAP," Kristian said, his eyes locked with Brendan's.

Brendan did not like him, and Kristian knew it.

Brendan was to Kristian a typical 'warrior'. He was built to fight, very tall and muscular, balding, roguish and very brash. He spoke with a deep bass East End London accent, and was altogether very intimidating.

Brendan's disdain for Kristian stemmed from his own devotion to his calling. Like most of the hosts he regarded his blending with his Phoenix to be a great honour and the fact that Kristian had been so keen to give his up was an affront to Brendan's entire belief system.

"Let's get straight to business then," Jonathon's voice was loud and clear, that of a man in control. No one would have guessed that this was the same man who, not long ago, was throwing the entire contents of his desk onto the floor of his office in frustration. "You all know why you are here, it's simple! The task has been laid out clearly for you in the briefing notes I'm about to circulate. The long and short of it is, I want to know what happened to our good friend and comrade, Oliver. I want answers and I expect those responsible to be brought to justice," as Jonathon spoke he passed out brown folders strapped together with blue elastic.

All five began to skim through the notes about the mission that Oliver had been on before he died.

Three of them gasped.

Two of them, Kieran and Kristian, did not. Jonathon looked at them, watching their reactions, and wondered how much Kieran knew and how much he had told Kristian.

It did not matter now though, not at this precise moment, Jonathon thought.

"So, I take it I have to go to Berlin then?" asked Kristian.

Brendan, who was also glaring over notes, snapped his head around to face Kristian and sneered, "Yes, well, it does look like that doesn't it? Think you can handle it?" he leaned back in his chair and placed his arms behind his head, not taking his eyes off Kristian once. Everyone but Kristian ignored Brendan's blatant sarcasm.

"So all of us are now fully assigned to this case?" Sam was thinking aloud more than asking a question.

"Yes, that's right Sam," said Jonathon. "Well, Kieran will not be fully assigned; he will merely be a point of support and help for you, what with the blending ceremony next week, it's not standard procedure to have a Trinity member acting as a member of a tactical unit."

Kristian's ears perked up. *What was that? Kieran was going to be taking Wendy's place as part of the Trinity. That can't be possible!* he exclaimed to himself.

"But he's so young to be a Trinity member, and he's…" Kristian stopped himself from talking any further in case he had offended Kieran.

Peter was quick to latch on to Kristian's surprise. "Yes, it is a little shocking," he said. "It was quite a surprise for all of us when we were informed."

Andrew gave Peter a glare which clearly conveyed, 'Keep your nose out of Trinity business once and for all'.

Kristian noticed the hurt look on Kieran's face; he felt immensely remorseful. It was not that he thought Kieran wasn't good enough to be one of the three members of the Trinity; it was just so unusual for someone so young. It hadn't been his intention to offend his friend, he was merely thinking aloud; a knee-jerk reaction to the surprising news. "Well, if Andrew thinks you're ready then I won't say anymore. Besides you were always good at that paper clip trick!" Kristian said in an attempt to restore the friendship he suspected he had just ruined.

Kieran couldn't believe his ears; he just wished that Kristian would quickly shut up.

"Tell me about it, that paper clip trick troubled me for years," laughed Andrew and soon everyone except Peter was chuckling. As Andrew was speaking, he looked at Kieran and winked.

"Okay, moving on please," Jonathon sounded more than a little agitated, "no more talk of the Trinity, back to the task at hand. You four will leave for Berlin in three days," he pointed at Kristian, Sam, Jean and Rachel.

"Three days?" Kristian's voice was more raised than he had intended. "Why three days when we could leave tomorrow? We are all good to go, aren't we?" he glanced at the others, the three of them nodded their heads.

"Yes, *they* are, but your skills still need to be tested. We need to see how much you remember and how much of the sacred skills you have simply abandoned." Brendan enjoyed saying this; it was evidenced by the smirk on his face.

"What Brendan means," interrupted Yi-Mao, "is that you have been away for over two years and we just need to see how strong and fast you are and how finely tuned your Kar'sin is."

"Have you continued with any of the meditation techniques you were taught? Can you still even hear Saranthea's voice?" Brendan said again, clearly trying to provoke him to retaliate.

Kristian was about ready to hit back and tell Brendan where to go when Jonathon interrupted, "The discussion is over, Kristian. You will work with Andrew and Sam on the meditation, your fighting skills and Kar'sin will be tested by Yi-Mao this afternoon, and you will leave for Berlin in three days. Furthermore I would like a day-by-day plan of your investigation drawn up before you go."

"That's fine," said Kristian. He was exasperated with Brendan for bringing to everyone's attention that he had deserted the Order and was consequently not as connected to his own Phoenix as Brendan was to his. He knew Brendan was right, but he was still annoyed with his attitude and he felt humiliated.

"Right, everyone. Back here at six please so we can review tactics. I would like you all to complete sections one to three of the briefing notes by then as well," as Jonathon spoke, he rose out of his chair.

As Jonathon, Peter, Andrew, Yi-Mao and Brendan left the room, the others quickly opened their notes again and began scanning sections one to three.

After a few moments of frantically reading, Yi-Mao suddenly re-entered the room and asked Kristian to step outside with him.

Silently and obediently, Kristian stood up and followed his old Master's lead as he walked out of the room.

Standing outside the door, Yi-Mao looked around to check that nobody was listening, "So how are you feeling, young man?"

"I'm good, sir. I thought that coming back here would be more difficult than it has been. I guess I forgot about all the things I liked about the Order," Kristian said, attempting not to sound daunted.

"Umm, yes," replied Yi-Mao, "we do have a habit of doing that when we don't like something; repressing all the good things about it. It's your subconscious trying to help you move on and justifying the reasons why you left."

Kristian stared at the floor, almost afraid to look the old man full in the face. "Yes, I guess you're right."

"So, are you planning to stay this time? Or is it just the one mission?" said Yi-Mao.

"Just the one I hope," Kristian replied; he had decided it was pointless beating about the bush, especially with Yi-Mao. "This whole world-within-a-world thing was never really me. I like partying, I like studying, and I like being me too much."

"You like not having responsibility?" Yi-Mao's words were kindly said, not an attack, just a question. "You know you can still have all those things that make you who you are, Kristian. At least to a degree. Those people in there have had a tough time of it and we are all counting on you to stick with us through what is likely to be a harrowing investigation. You can always go back to your life once the task is done but, for now, you need to be the focused, determined young man we all hope you are."

Those words stung Kristian; he sombrely replied, "I hope I am as well, for all our sakes."

"You must focus all your energies, my son, and help bring in Oliver's killer. Report all your progress to me, won't you?"

"Yes, sir." Kristian had nothing but respect for this great man; he was the fastest and most formidable Phoenix in the

Order, as wise as he was strong. "I will not fail you, Master. I'm going to get him," Kristian boldly spoke.

"Him?" Yi-Mao's eyes widened with mock surprise. "Already you know who the culprit is, do you? Do not be foolhardy, Kristian, no rushing in. Only patience will bring you the answers you seek. You are smart, level-headed; let those traits be your weapons. You are much more of a warrior than you know. It doesn't just take strength and courage to be a hero, you know?" Yi-Mao turned to leave as if the conversation was over.

"Courage?" Kristian muttered to himself, "I could certainly do with some of that."

Somehow Yi-Mao became aware of Kristian's doubts, "You have more courage than many people I know. Not everyone is strong enough to be who they really want to be, and to stand up to Jonathon as well. You have proved you have all the courage you will ever need. Now you must channel that courage," Yi-Mao spoke quietly and with conviction, but did not turn around.

"I guess I just wish I was a little bit more like everyone else around here," said Kristian despondently.

"Maybe in time, Kristian, you will obtain that which you most desire. Have you ever asked yourself why Saranthea chose you as her host?" Yi-Mao still did not turn to face him.

"I've asked myself that many times, Master, and the answer still escapes me. I guess there wasn't anyone better around that day, huh?" Kristian mocked.

This time, Kristian's former Mentor did turn around as he spoke and he looked at him intently as if trying to imprint his words on Kristian's memory.

"A Phoenix selects its host because that is the person whom it believes it will be able to do the most with. A Phoenix does not see, nor hear, nor think as we do. They are beings from a world we know little about, their wisdom and power is far greater than our own. Your Phoenix chose you and there is a reason for that, whether you want to believe it or not. Stop doubting her, she is far smarter than you, smarter than me. You need to have faith in her, and in yourself!" As he finished he walked determinedly away, leaving an astounded Kristian to reflect on what he had just heard.

My Phoenix chose *me; she picked me!* Kristian declared within himself. His train of thought continued: *And she is not going to leave me no matter how much I want her to. Yi-Mao is right, I must focus all my energies on getting the most from Saranthea and completing the tasks that are expected of me.* With that, he stood up straight and with a look of utter determination on his face, he turned and walked back into the conference room. In a clear and commanding voice, he said to his four companions, "Come on guys, we've a lot of work to do. Let's do this!"

...

Kristian had now been training for over two hours, repeating duel after duel with Amar. Amar was a competent Phoenix host, and a keen believer in Brendan's philosophy on the role of the Phoenix. Like Brendan, Amar had a strong contempt for Kristian and sparring with him now gave him the perfect opportunity to vent his aggression, and Kristian was feeling it.

Yi-Mao had always described Kristian's hand-to-hand combat as inventive at best, and the last two years had not done much to change his style at all. Amar had won every single hand-to-hand combat that had taken place since Kristian had reluctantly agreed to revisit fight training. Kristian, however, protested that the sparring arena was a 'controlled' environment and nothing like the reality of the world outside the building. He liked to believe that in an attack, adrenaline would just take over and his sparring skills would be a great match for any opponent that came along.

The sword duels that followed on the other hand were a different matter altogether. Amar was barely able to stand his ground against Kristian who had always had a talent for the blades. Even during his time absent from the Order, Kristian was a keen fencer, even good enough to captain the university fencing team to the semi-finals last year, and his technique was impressive.

Calling an end to combat, Yi-Mao dismissed Amar and sent him to find Brendan and to prepare for the long journey to the Kar'sin monastery in Japan. Yi-Mao and Kristian watched Amar leave the sparring arena, a large open space with markings on the floor and an impressive array of weapons adorning the walls with the duelling ring in the centre. As soon as Amar had exited, Yi-Mao turned to face Kristian and looked relieved that it was just the two of them.

"I must say, your swordsmanship skills are very impressive. In fact, your use of the blade seems perfect. Your moves were almost seamless and effortless. The sword glided through the air with ease. Well done!" Yi-Mao paused for a second. "I know you haven't summoned your sword since you have been away, but do you still think you can?"

Feeling a little smug with Yi-Mao's initial comments, Kristian gave a modest shrug, "You sound too surprised! And I haven't tried, I didn't want to. I still think I could, do you want me to try now?"

"No, not now," continued Yi-Mao, "we need to talk about your fighting techniques. Your hand-to-hand combat leaves a lot to be desired. You are undisciplined and unorthodox. You are far too defensive and when you do attack you leave much of your body exposed."

This second comment did not provoke the same reaction in Kristian as the first. He wasn't overly concerned. He knew his combat skills were not the best in the Order, but as he had thought before, if the time came to actually put them to use, he was sure he could wing it. His response again was to shrug his shoulders. This time though it was as if to say 'so what?'

"Now that I have assessed your fighting skills, it's time to evaluate your Kar'sin," said Yi-Mao, sounding somewhat disappointed with Kristian's response to the critique just given. This filled Kristian with dread. There would be no shrugging of the shoulders. He had not practised these skills at all since he had left. assuming that he would never need them again, and it wasn't practical to practise them when you lived in the middle of a bustling city.

"Ah, yes, my Kar'sin" Kristian hesitated, "well, to be truthful I haven't really had much opportunity to practise them, what with, you know, school and stuff."

"School and stuff?" questioned Yi-Mao with a curious smirk.

"Yeah, my Uni life leaves very little time for me and what with living in London, in a shared flat, it's kinda hard." Kristian knew that these were lame excuses; the truth was, he really hadn't been that bothered about his Kar'sin.

When he had left the Order he had not intended to ever return and he had not given a second thought to practising any of the skills he had learnt. In fact, he had buried them along with all the memories he had made whilst active in the Order.

Yi-Mao was scrutinising Kristian wondering just how bad this was going to be.

"Well, we shall just have to see, won't we?" Yi-Mao said, "We shall begin with the basics, maybe the palm projection technique. I assume you won't find that too hard?"

Kristian didn't know what to say; he felt ashamed of himself for his lack of enthusiasm. He knew he was going to be in big trouble if he could not even achieve palm projection.

"With luck, concentration and commitment on your part," Yi-Mao began to pace around Kristian before he continued, "once you have shown me this technique, we can take a look at your object projection and your non-palm projection, okay? However, I understand this may take some time. These techniques are always hard to master and too easy to forget, without constant practice. It's almost like Peter doing ballet." Yi-Mao had a twinkle in his eyes but was obviously quite worried.

Kristian smiled. Although Yi-Mao's words were an underlying warning, his old master had a kind way about him, which made Kristian believe he was capable of anything with his guidance. He was right, though, he hadn't practised at all, and even when he was in the Order, his techniques were lousy and uncoordinated.

"Well, Master, I shall endeavour to try and impress," said Kristian in a rather mocking tone.

"Let us hope so. Now shall we begin? Basic palm projection, do you remember the technique? You need to concentrate all of your mind and focus inwards to your Phoenix, let her come through and imagine your body being engulfed with her light and energy. Focus this energy into your palm and project the light out of it. I want you to put up a basic shield around yourself," Yi-Mao said as he came to a halt behind Kristian.

Kristian stretched out his right arm. He was right-handed and it was more comfortable to project with this arm. Closing his eyes, he thought back to all his Kar'sin training. Reaching deep into his mind, he tried to pass beyond the barriers of thought and tap into his innermost energy: his Phoenix.

"Don't try too hard, Kristian, let her come through naturally," said Yi-Mao noticing the strain on the young man's face.

Kristian took a deep, slow breath and let his thoughts fade away; he continued to breathe gently and deeply, and slowly but surely he closed his conscious mind. He could hear a low ringing in his ears and a buzz in his head, then a sort of calm engulfed his whole body and he felt his insides glowing with energy. He had done it! Saranthea had come through and was moulding her energy with his imagination. Automatically and without even thinking about it, he held open the palm of his right hand and imagined a barrier of light bursting from it. His hand tingled, the sensation was strange but comforting. Slowly opening his eyes, he was amazed and relieved to see a shield of shimmering jade green light in front of him, emanating from his right palm.

Yi-Mao could not help but be impressed. Kristian had put up an imposing shield and had shown more promise than he had originally thought Kristian capable of.

"Well done. Now, lower it slowly," Yi-Mao commanded.

Without even moving an inch of his body, Kristian allowed Saranthea's energy to lower the shield she had helped him create. The bright green light flowed backwards, into his palm. He opened his eyes again and let out a huge sigh and a smile. "Wow," he said, "impressive, even if I do say so myself."

"Don't be too hasty," Yi-Mao answered. He *was* impressed but it was only the beginning. Kristian's arrogance was his downfall; Yi-Mao became aware of this two years ago and was not inclined to let Kristian indulge this weakness again.

However, it wasn't long before Kristian was sending bolts of energy from his right hand. Within an hour of beginning the training he was throwing bolts, varying in size from that of a tennis ball to that of a large beach ball, across the room. Yi-Mao was quick to point out the reliance on his right hand and explained that this could cause problems in the future. Kristian's response was to attempt to send some energy bolts from his left hand. They were not as strong, but even Yi-Mao could not argue that they were feeble.

"Good, but you still have a lot to work on, you must continue developing your concentration technique, you can't keep shutting your eyes like that. They are one of your greatest assets when fighting an enemy."

Kristian nodded. He knew Yi-Mao would notice all these faults, but he knew how necessary it was for Yi-Mao to be critical; it was just so hard to concentrate with his eyes open.

"With more practice and lots of focus I'm sure that you will improve your technique, I have every faith in you," Yi-Mao smiled at Kristian then went on to say, "shall we move on to the tricky stuff now?" Yi-Mao again began to walk in a circle around Kristian. "How well do you remember object projection training?"

"Umm," replied a dubious Kristian. He did remember the techniques but still he doubted his abilities. "There's the rope, the dagger, the hand and the, um, general forces. Is that right, Master?"

"Very good. That's the basics. Now show me them all," said Yi-Mao who walked over to the far wall, picked up a chair from the darkened corner and returned to the centre of the duelling ring with it. Kristian looked at the chair and wondered which object he could use on it. The rope or the hand would probably be easiest; maybe he should start with the hand. He closed his eyes and stretched out his hand once more. Suddenly remembering his Master's critiques, he opened his eyes and tried to concentrate. Using the same technique as before, he reached inside himself and called Saranthea forward. He began to imagine a hand gripping the bottom of the chair. Realising he had his eyes shut, yet again, he opened them to see that nothing had happened. Staring intently at the chair, he tried again. Suddenly he saw a blur of dull jade light, lit at the very spot he was focused on. It was not as he imagined; it wasn't hand-shaped, but more like a ball of light fixed around the chair's leg. In his mind, using his imagination, he could see the chair lift off the ground and hover in the air. The real chair did not levitate as he had hoped, in fact, it barely moved. Trying even harder than before, he saw it lift up again in his mind. Again, the chair did not respond as he had hoped. It slowly began to float but its rise was not as smooth and weightless as it had been in his thoughts. It jerked about, up and down, side to side until eventually the green ball of light disappeared and the chair fell back down the couple of inches it had risen. He looked at Yi-Mao, expecting a look of disappointment and frustration.

"For a first attempt, that was not so bad," was Yi-Mao's response. He patted the young man on the back, "Why not try it again with a different object, perhaps the rope?"

Kristian was feeling out of breath as if he had just returned from a jog; he really wanted to pack it in for the day. "Can we take a break?"

Yi-Mao's response was cold and instant, "No. Now. Your enemies in combat will not let you have a break every time you need to catch your breath. Through pain and hard work come results. Now come on. Try again."

Kristian was shocked by his tone, but he was unwilling to argue with this great man. Kristian agreed that the rope was the best option against the chair. The rope was a good skill and one he had managed to pull off a few times before when he had first learnt the technique. It enabled the Phoenix to project a rope-like energy, which would wrap itself around one's opponent or object and completely imprison them.

Stretching his arm out, he closed his hand so his fingers met his thumb, forming an 'O' shape if looked at from above. Not closing his eyes this time, he began to reach inside himself once more. He was so tired and he felt completely drained. Imagining the rope lasso resting in the gap in his hand, he could begin to see the green disk form on the top of his index finger and thumb. That was the easy part. Staying completely focused, he flicked his wrist and arm as if throwing a lasso through the air. With his hand in mid-swing, he opened his palm and released a ring of radiant green energy. As the ring flew seamlessly through the air, it expanded to a size that would easily fit around the chair. Using his outstretched fingers to control the rope's direction, he attempted to lasso the chair. It wrapped itself around the chair, but around the legs, not the back as he had hoped. With a mighty crunch, the rope squeezed the chair's legs together. It instantly exploded and shards of wood flew in every direction.

Yi-Mao reacted instantly with non-palm projection, as a formidable yellow shield encased him to deflect shards of wood. Kristian dived to the floor placing his hands over his head. After a few seconds, he looked up at Yi-Mao's perfectly projected shield and was inspired to produce an equally good one through non-palm projection.

"Well, if your intention was not to catch your opponent but to split them in two, you certainly succeeded," said a smiling Yi-Mao as his yellow shield lowered.

"Yeah, that's exactly what I was going for," replied an embarrassed Kristian, giggling.

"Perhaps we should move on and try the non-palm projection," Yi-Mao said as he watched Kristian get back to his feet.

Kristian felt worse, he remembered that his non-palm projection was terrible and was feeling even more drained from the day's efforts. "What do you want me to project?" he asked hesitantly.

"The basics again. A shield to start with, then maybe a bolt or two," Yi-Mao replied.

The technique for non-palm projection was the same as before but this time he had to produce the Kar'sin energy without using his hands as a base. It required a vast deal more concentration and a much better grasp of the surroundings and one's place in it. Closing his mind he began to pull his Phoenix through. He imagined his hand stretched out, but kept his hands firmly beside him. He began to imagine his palm opening with a bright green light emanating from it. In his mind's eye he could see the energy build up around his hand, much the same as in the palm projection. He continued to build the shield up in his mind. Again, he had his eyes closed and when he quickly peeked through half-closed eyelids, he could see no shield in front of him, no green energy.

He tried again, but it felt like he was fighting a losing battle. Trying harder than he thought possible he focused on the image in his head, on the thought of the light radiating from his hand. His breathing quickened, as did his heartbeat. He kept delving deep within himself, pouring more and more energy into the imaginary shield.

Yi-Mao was just off centre to him, his gaze locked on to Kristian. Bright jade-coloured sparks were lighting up in front of them but disappeared as quickly as they appeared. The sparks were about a metre in front of Kristian and seemed to appear as from nowhere. The eighth spark he conjured materialised and moulded itself into a ball and then started to spread out like a starfish.

Its size quickly doubled and soon it was covering the young man's chest. Suddenly, Kristian lost his concentration, and the jade green light vanished. Relaxing his body, he took a deep breath.

"You did well. You almost had it back there. But you gave up too quickly," Yi-Mao remarked.

Kristian, angry with himself, out of breath and panting, snapped back at his master, "My chest was hurting and I couldn't breathe, my head's pounding."

"That pain would have left you once the shield was fully formed. You must learn to push yourself more," said Yi-Mao completely unfazed by Kristian's tone of voice.

"What?" Kristian snapped. "My chest really hurts, it's not easy," Kristian was incredulous. He knew that not many in the Order would dare speak to Yi-Mao like this, but he didn't care, he was exhausted and he had tried his best.

"No, it is not easy, and I know it hurts, but as long as it hurts, you know you are still alive and that will not be for long if you do not practise your technique. Or indeed, if you speak to me in that tone again," Yi-Mao's first comment was seriously meant, the second, less so. However, Kristian's frustration made him feel more than peeved. He was angry with Yi-Mao. Kristian believed Yi-Mao was being selfish and unfairly pushing him this hard after his two years' absence from the Order.

Who did he think he was, telling him not to talk to him like that? He was an adult and he was doing Yi-Mao a favour, and he all was getting in return was criticism and he was being patronised too.

"These basic skills should be second nature to you, your life will depend on it," Yi-Mao spoke, noticing the irritation on Kristian's face.

"Second nature?" shouted Kristian. "You're aware, are you not, that I've been out of the loop for two years? You know I'm not suited for this crap, so cut me some slack will you? God, it doesn't help having this sensation in my chest. I'm exhausted and I need a break. What am I doing back here? I knew this was a mistake. I'm going to get us all killed."

Yi-Mao was silent as he walked towards Kristian when the two were almost nose to nose, he said in a calm voice, "You are here because we need you; that burning in your chest is your Phoenix acknowledging that she is in the presence of another. She has a lot respect for her peers, as you apparently do not. You cannot have a break, you must push yourself. Only then will you achieve your optimum best, and I expect nothing less from you. Two years away from the Order or not, it makes no difference to Saranthea, and nor should it to you. You are a Phoenix host, and that is all there is to it."

As his master spoke, anger once again spread across Kristian's face.

"Good," whispered Yi-Mao, "anger and aggression will only make you stronger, as long as you can focus that aggression. Use it to produce some truly remarkable bolts through non-palm projection." As he finished he retreated back several metres.

Kristian eventually responded well to these words. *Fine, if he wants me to send a bolt of energy at him, so be it*, he thought.

He turned his body towards Yi-Mao. With his eyes open, he again focused on his anger and frustration and began to mould the energy within him into a bolt of light, and in his mind, he saw it head straight in Yi-Mao's direction. Without warning, dazzling jade light emanated from his chest where it formed a huge bolt, which sped quickly and powerfully towards the old man. Kristian fell back due to the force of the bolt he had just produced.

Yi-Mao stretched out his palms and a small intense yellow field of energy twisted out from them, forming a whirling palm-sized bowl. The green bolt hit Yi-Mao's yellow swirling saucer with immense force but Yi-Mao did not move. Within seconds, the yellow light spiralled further and then completely engulfed the dwindling green energy. Closing his palms, Yi-Mao seemed to absorb the energy into his being.

Kristian regained his balance; he was totally amazed. He had never seen anything like that before.

Rolling his eyes, Yi-Mao smiled at him and said, "Well, I bet you couldn't do that again on demand."

Kristian's amazement turned again to anger and he proceeded to launch another powerful bolt of energy from his chest. Yi-Mao was startled by the speed of this bolt and he arched his body backwards to avoid the high-speed bolt from hitting him. It raced past him and ploughed into the wall.

A huge thud rocked the room. As Yi-Mao squinted through the dust and smoke, he twisted his head sideways and was able to perceive a huge breach in the stonewall.

As the smoke and dust cleared, two faces could clearly be seen peering through the hole. They looked in complete shock. It was Jean and Sam, they were on a field training tactical course in the next room. Turning his head back to face a very embarrassed Kristian, Yi-Mao spoke quietly, "Actually, it's probably best if you don't do that again, at least not in here!" he let out a small chuckle and moved towards Kristian.

"I'm so sorry, Master," said a red-faced Kristian. He suddenly felt very small and was ashamed of his earlier outburst at Yi-Mao.

"Walls can be rebuilt; young men sadly cannot, not even by the remarkable Dr. Gambon. Remember that, you will be much harder to replace than that wall. Now I think I will take this as my cue to leave you. Please keep practising until the six o'clock meeting. I will not be there, as I have to leave in a few hours. Andrew will be continuing your training tomorrow, please resist trying to blow him up!" As he finished speaking, Yi-Mao bowed to Kristian and placed his hand on his shoulder. Squeezing it gently he said, "Be careful, be safe. And remember, your Phoenix chose you, listen to her when she speaks to you, that's all she asks." Kristian returned the bow as Yi-Mao slowly turned and made his way towards the door.

"Master," Yi-Mao slowly turned back around on hearing Kristian's words. "Thank you for today. You may not think it but I've remembered a lot and have learnt much from you. I know I'm a pain in the arse and I don't mean to be, it's just…" He stopped mid-flow as he realised this conversation was not entirely exclusive. His gaze fell upon the hole in the wall, and on to Jean and Sam who were listening intently from the other side.

"Just do me one thing," Yi-Mao said.

"What's that, Master?"

"For the love of Gaia, PRACTISE!" Yi-Mao grinned widely and made his way out of the door. Kristian smiled back and watched his mentor leave. Something inside him made him wonder if he would see him again and the thought worried him. It would not take too long to complete this mission and then he would be back to his normal life, the life he wanted. Or was it? Did he still want it? Kristian felt uneasy as he questioned himself. What else would he do once the mission was completed? He couldn't stay in the Order; or maybe he could? The thought did not provoke the same fear in him it once had. The idea of staying here, amongst these people he called friends, was not so scary anymore, in fact it comforted him to think of himself here with Sam, Jean and Rachel. Maybe this was the life he was supposed to have; and if so, then maybe he was born to fight.

"Hey. Aren't you two supposed to be training?" he said as he turned his attention to Sam and Jean, who replied in harmony, "Yeah we are, but you're the one who blew a hole in our training room!" Kristian laughed, turned away and spoke under his breath proudly, "Yeah, yeah I did."

...

Jonathon and Brendan had been sitting in the main conference room for over an hour and as time ticked on and approached six o'clock, the two men were lost in discussion at the far end of the huge table. The reason for their pre-meeting was cloaked in secrecy. No minutes were taken and no one knew that the meeting was taking place, except the two of them. The room was dimly lit, shadows were cast on their faces. They both seemed tense and worried.

"Of course, I'll continue looking into it, but to assign Amar, Karnel and Sam to it seems pointless. Over the past two years only one lead has ever been generated from Sauror," Brendan's voice was dry and croaky.

"The more I think about it, the more concerned I become. The whole Sauror thing, the strange death of Oliver, the diminishing relations with Tivernal. It all points to troubled times ahead," Jonathon's whisper was softer, and more audible than Brendan's.

"Jonathon, we've faced many things in the past. Some stranger and more terrifying than I had ever imagined possible and we have always come through. If there is trouble ahead, we shall face it and overcome it."

"I wish I shared your optimism, but something doesn't feel right this time. I fear there are far deadlier forces at work here," Jonathon said as Brendan raised himself off the chair.

"Hmm, it does feel strange I agree, but that's only because we have been one step behind. As soon as we get on top of it, find out what's really been going on, it won't look so bad," Brendan's tone deceived his words. He was clearly agitated and as he paced the length of the room, looking up at the magnificent paintings that adorned the walls, his face fell into a deep, thoughtful frown.

"Yes, you are probably correct. But when are we going to get on top of it? I'm running out of patience and our resources are stretched to the max as it is," as Jonathon spoke he too joined Brendan's pace around the room. The two men came to a halt and looked at one another. Brendan had always admired Jonathon's leadership, even though he secretly believed that a Phoenix should lead the Order.

"I will find you a lead, my friend. It will all become clear soon enough," Brendan said, sounding determined.

"Thank you Brendan and we shall get that lead together," replied Jonathon.

"Together it is," said Brendan, walking back over to the table, "have you thought about bringing someone like Peter in on this? I admit I'm not his biggest fan, but he may have some knowledge of what the sign could be."

"Ah, I doubt he will be able to help. I have already checked the records and there is only one source that remotely knows what the symbol is," said Jonathon, looking up at the portrait above him.

"The diaries of Alexander Surich?" said Brendan.

"Yes and a lot of good that was," Jonathon released his gaze from the portrait and returned slowly to his seat.

"Well, you and I are the only two who have seen it on Sauror's chest. No one else here knows anything about it and Sam didn't even pick it up when he entered Sauror's mind," said Brendan as he too returned to his seat and continued, "which means that Sauror has found a way to block Sam, which is an altogether unsavoury thought. Or someone else is blocking Sam's powers. He did mention to me that he felt a strange sensation when he was searching the other day for that vampire's victim."

Jonathon frowned and looked down at the papers in front of him.

"Perhaps the symbol was burnt into Sauror's chest without him knowing; or after being marked, he might have had his memory wiped. Either way it does not bode well for the investigation. So what exactly do the diaries of Alexander

Surich say about the symbol?" Brendan let out a long sigh and looked at Jonathon intently.

Jonathon laughed half-heartedly. He had gone over the passages of the diaries many times in the vain hope that the text would leap out at him and reveal all he wanted to know.

"It merely points out that Alexander Surich once killed a vampire who bore the symbol, and as the vampire was dying he uttered the words 'Long live the Defier of Death, long live the Quartet. Long live Sola…' He also had the symbol on his chest, the exact same symbol," Jonathon recited, remembering he had spoken the words to Brendan many times before.

"Well his own investigation into the symbol was just as fruitless as ours. Maybe we should bring in others; someone might know what Sola means?" said Brendan, as Jonathon's voice initiated memories within Brendan to play out.

Jonathon cut Brendan off suddenly and stood up, "Yes, his investigation was not only into the symbol but also into the vampire's dying words. There is no record of Sola; personally I believe he died before he could finish his last, defiant sentence, but I have run searches on the Quartet, Sola, the defier of death, but nothing definitive has come…"

No more than a second later, the chime on the grand clock chimed six times and the doors to the conference room opened and in walked a mass of people. Kieran was first, followed by Jean and Sam, and behind them, Rachel and Kristian.

"Well according to Penny, the hole is huge and it's going to cost a bomb to fix," said Rachel.

"Cost a bomb," laughed Jean, "you'd think it would be expected really, it is a training room."

"Yes, I suppose. So are you planning to destroy any other walls in the building, Kristian?" Kieran shouted back.

Before he could respond, Brendan was already in front of them speaking, "Interesting conversation. I do hope you spent more time going over your mission notes and meeting deadlines than partaking in idle chit-chat, no matter how engrossing it is."

All five of them stopped dead in their tracks and stared at Brendan; none of them said a word. As they started for their seats, they exchanged looks, which clearly said, 'What a git'.

As Kristian made his way to move past Brendan, Brendan grabbed Kristian's arm and whispered into his ear, "Good luck with the mission, please try not to screw up." Kristian tried to ignore the malice in his voice but was tempted to do a replay of his earlier run-in with Yi-Mao.

"Well," continued Brendan, this time to the whole group, "I have to catch a plane. I don't see why Rachel could not just teleport Amar and myself there to be honest, Jonathon, surely it would be so much easier, and more cost-effective?" Laughing at his own sarcastic wit, Brendan turned on his heels and left the room. Kristian glared after him until the doors closed.

"Please take your seats," Jonathon sounded impatient and exasperated. "We have a lot to get through."

Kristian was lost in thought, chilled by Brendan's words; 'Try not to screw up'.

"Kristian, please take your seat," shouted Jonathon, annoyed at his distraction, whatever it was.

Kristian walked around the table and took his place next to Kieran.

"Right," continued Jonathon, "Yi-Mao was singing your praises Kristian, and Brendan tells me that Sam, Jean and Rachel are all prepared to leave?"

"Yes sir," they all spoke at once in the same monotone voice that echoed around the room. None of them were in the mood for this meeting, they wanted to get out there and get started. It carried on like this for half an hour, with every response to every question being answered in the same dry, emotionless, collective way.

...

- Chapter Seven -

Echoes

Rachel strained her eyes as she looked to see if anyone else was around. The ward was extremely dim; the only light source came from two bedside lamps, one near Rachel and the other halfway down the room. The familiar face of Dr. Gambon was somewhat far away; she was lying on her back on one of the many beds, directly in the middle of the ward. She was clearly fast asleep.

An open book rested on the doctor's chest, it moved ever so slightly up and down with every breath that she took in her sleep. Rachel turned her attention away and looked towards the other lamp. Turning her head Rachel saw a face glaring over at her from the closer bed. Staring at her, awake and wide-eyed, was the very pale face of Tanya Morgan.

Rachel knew many things about this woman, due to her efforts of trying to locate her family. She took a deep breath, gulped and then walked slowly towards the bed. Tanya did not move, she did not flinch or even blink, her eyes were drawn back into her skull, her complexion pasty and her lips were a blue-grey colour.

In less than ten average-sized steps, Rachel found herself standing directly by Tanya's bedside. Her mind clouded over as she felt the urge to say something, but no words left her lips. She soon found herself whispering, "Hi, I'm Rachel. What's your name?"

Tanya's eyes opened as wide as they could and in a skeptical tone replied, "My name? Surely you must know my name?"

Rachel was a little taken aback. Of course, she knew her name, but in that moment there wasn't anything else she felt she could have said. She cursed herself for asking such an idiotic question, and then racked her brain for a suitable response. However, before she could continue, Tanya spoke again.

"Rachel? The Rachel who found me?"

"Yes, that's me. I'm sorry I asked you for your name, that was really dumb of me; I just didn't know what else to say to you. I'm so terribly sorry about what has happened to you," replied Rachel, again in a whisper making an effort not to wake Dr. Gambon.

"There's no need to apologise, I'm glad to have the opportunity to thank you," Tanya's voice was croaky and rather grating.

"Well, I cannot take all the credit, my friend Sam was also with me that night and it was he who found you, I simply brought you back here. I happened just to be there."

"I'm sure that's not true," said Tanya as she reached out and clutched Rachel's hand. Rachel was surprised at the firmness of her grip.

"Thank you again and please thank Sam for me, that is unless I see him first." Tanya managed a small smile as she spoke.

Rachel returned the smile; her eyes showed the empathy she felt for the woman, "I'll have a word with him, he's very busy at the moment but I'm sure he would wish to see you and to make sure you are okay."

Tanya nodded her head in recognition watching Rachel closely. *How kind and caring she appeared*, Tanya thought to herself.

"Be honest, how are you feeling now?" Rachel asked.

Tanya spluttered a small laugh, which quickly turned into a cough.

"Well, mainly I feel tired. Very, very tired. Also confused, I guess. Shocked. Surprised. I just can't get my head around this whole thing."

"That's totally understandable and expected, I guess. What have you been told about the attack?" Rachel asked tentatively

Again, Tanya let a snicker escape, "They've told me a lot. How much of it I actually believe I'm not sure. But some of it does fit I suppose," as she spoke, she moved her hand away from Rachel's and placed it upon the bandage around her neck.

"Dr. Gambon is the best, Tanya, I'm sure she is doing everything she can to help you. Whatever she has told you will be spot on and she will have you out of here and back to your life in no time," Rachel attempted a smile but could not quite manage it; a strange, contorted smirk emerged on her face instead.

Tanya must have noticed because she suddenly looked uncomfortable and Rachel tried, with great effort, to force her face back to its normal contours.

"Well, I hope so, but you can understand why I'm skeptical, right?" Tanya's voice suddenly seemed less croaky but more determined and strong.

"Yes, of course I can." It was Rachel's turn to feel uncomfortable. "I understand what you mean, obviously I cannot completely relate to it. However, I believe that the younger you are when you first hear it, the easier it is to take in. I was brought into this organisation when I was very young. I had just turned ten when I came here. I remember feeling excited and special. But I was also fearful of never seeing my family again. There are things I've seen, some of them are unbelievable, but they're second nature to me now. It's gonna take time but you will come to terms with what happened to you."

Rachel's words, although meant to be comforting, seemed to stir Tanya's fears. Her eyes filled with tears, and tiny droplets began to fall, forming rivulets, running down on her cheeks. As they fell down her face, they seemed to thin out and evaporate before they reached her neck.

"I wonder if I'll ever see George again?" Tanya managed to utter.

Rachel, realising her error, moved closer to Tanya, took the seat next to the bed and reached into her pocket, pulled out a handkerchief and offered it to her. Tanya took it and began to dab at her eyes.

"I'm sorry," Rachel said, feeling tearful herself, "I really didn't mean to upset you, I was just…"

"Oh, it's not your fault," said Tanya through her obvious misery, "I just, I just want to see, to see my boy. That's all. He's so young you see and I—" as she attempted to finish her sentence she was suddenly overcome by emotion and began to sob more loudly, her shoulders shuddering with every breath she drew in. Crying without tears seemed to upset and frustrate her more as her eyes began to dry out. Rachel, not knowing whether to hug her or not, watched the poor woman weep into her hands and then no longer able to control her own emotions, she too began to sob.

The tears fell thick and fast. The two women sat there in the dark, dingy ward and let emotion overwhelm them. It was a sorry sight, and would have evoked tender sentiments in the coldest of hearts.

Rachel eventually managed to compose herself and sat up straight. As she stifled the last of her tears, she placed a hand on Tanya and said reassuringly, "Come on now, don't cry. We've located your son and he's fine. He is with your father at the moment. They're both obviously concerned about you, but they're both okay. They just want to know where you are, which at the moment is a rather tricky question to answer."

Tanya sat upright suddenly and gripped Rachel tightly, "My George? You've seen my boy?" her voice was more powerful this time and filled with hope, "Well, would I—" unable to form a structured sentence, Tanya's mind raced with thoughts of seeing her son. "Well, I need to see him. Could he come here? Can I go to him?" Tanya pleaded aloud, not purposefully directed towards Rachel.

"He would have to come here, I am afraid," said Rachel. "It would not be possible for you to leave here at the moment, not with your current state of health."

"My current state?" Tanya's words were laced with bitterness and sarcasm. "Yes, I suppose you're right, I haven't left this bed for what feels like weeks, so I know I can't go home. He'll have to come here," as Tanya spoke these words aloud, her heart froze as the reality hit her. She held back more tears. Tears that were triggered not from the physical and emotional pain she felt, or by the thought of seeing George again, but by the thought of having him come to the hospital and for him to see her like this.

"I can't let him come here; he mustn't be allowed to see me in this state. And this place is so strange; he would ask too many questions. And he can't know, he mustn't know what has happened to me. You haven't told him have you?" Tanya asked sharply.

"No, I haven't personally made any contact with him or your father," Rachel reassured her, "I merely checked up on him to ensure he was safe."

"Good. Thank you." Tanya breathed out a long sigh as she contemplated the situation.

"No, no, I do not want him to come here, how could I explain this to him, a fourteen-year-old boy? How do you tell your child that you have been bitten by a vampire and may be turning into one? I don't want him to experience this alien world. No, it's for the best," her words were resolute but her tone was not. She sounded as though she was trying to convince herself that it was the best thing to do, although deep down, she knew that she wanted to see George, to hold him and kiss him and tell him that his mummy was going to be okay.

Rachel looked down upon her with immense pity, trying hard to imagine the pain Tanya was most likely feeling.

"I understand what you are thinking, and I do not know what I'd do if I was in your position. But everyone here is doing their best for you and to be brutally honest, I'm afraid you may never get the chance again to see your son," as Rachel said this, her eyes, yet again, filled up with tears.

"I've started to realise that might be the case of course," Tanya snapped back immediately. She looked down at her hands; the colour of her skin was fading away, and the grey-blue colour was getting darker. "I'm sorry; I didn't mean to freak out, Rachel. But if I had him brought here to me, it would be for me. For the selfish reason that I want to see him one more time, not because it's in George's best interests. If he saw me now, I'm not sure how it would affect him."

"I know," said Rachel almost in a whisper, "but if my mother was dying, I think I would like the chance to say goodbye."

Tanya looked at Rachel and shook her head slowly, "I *did* say goodbye to my mother when she was dying. I was eighteen. She was in bed for months before she passed away. I avoided going to see her; I was scared of what I would see. Then, two days before she died, I mustered up the courage to go and see her. When I walked into her room, she was rambling about chickens. Her pale skin was clinging to her bones as though gripping on for its life. Her eyes fell upon me, but they looked right through me. I knew that it was too late to say a proper goodbye. My own mother could not even see me," Tanya paused and stared into space as though remembering the moment. "I did say goodbye, I even kissed her on the cheek, but the only words that left her lips were, 'don't let the chickens out'. I ran out of that room as fast as I could. I didn't return. I didn't even go to the funeral."

Tears again flowed down Rachel's cheeks. *I'm so rubbish at this*, she thought, *why do I keep crying, I'm the healthy one here, I should be offering support, not crying every two seconds.*

"I'm so sorry," Rachel said to Tanya as she wiped her tears away, "but surely it's better that you did say goodbye? Your son deserves the same, doesn't he? You're not crazy, you're awake and you are sane, he would not leave here thinking that you had looked right through him, or didn't understand him. It wouldn't just be him saying goodbye to you, it would be you getting that chance to say goodbye to him," Rachel spoke slowly and her tone was soft and non-confrontational.

"No, it's not. The memory haunts me and I don't want the memories of me to haunt him like that forever. I would prefer to leave him with the memories he already has," Tanya finished, feeling confortable with her decision.

Rachel could see what Tanya was saying, but to her the two situations were very different.

"Besides," Tanya continued, "I might even get better. I know the diagnosis is gloomy and the doctors haven't exactly been positive, but I have hope. I have my faith."

Rising to her feet, Rachel couldn't look Tanya in the eyes. She thought that when a victim was as far gone as Tanya, they never came back. Though, if a full recovery were given to those who truly deserved it, then this woman would have every chance of getting better. And Tanya had the strongest motivation to: a mother wanting to return to her son.

"I should be leaving now," said Rachel.

"Will you come and visit me again?" Tanya asked tentatively.

Rachel contemplated it for a second, she didn't really want to witness this poor woman's continuing deterioration, but she knew that Tanya had no one else. She reluctantly agreed, "Of course I will," she said with a smile. "Would you like me to bring you anything?"

"Perhaps a magazine, something to distract me, with some juicy gossip in it. It might help me to take my mind off things," Tanya attempted a smile.

Rachel moved in and kissed Tanya on the cheek, "I will see what I can do," Rachel began to move towards the middle of the ward.

"Thank you again," murmured Tanya.

Rachel turned and mouthed 'You're welcome'; she continued walking towards the centre of the ward to the bed where Dr. Gambon lay. Standing above her, Rachel envied how peaceful she looked, and decided not to wake her, but as she turned to leave, Dr. Gambon suddenly sat bolt upright, throwing the book which had been on her chest onto the floor.

"Morning, Doctor," Rachel said with a grin.

Susan's face was filled with confusion, her mind still embroiled in the dreams she had been having. Squinting her eyes to determine who was next to her, she recognised Rachel by her glasses.

"Good morning, Rachel. Sorry, I was just having a power nap. Been on my feet for hours." Rachel smiled as she watched the doctor attempt to shake off the sleep and make coherent sentences.

"How is she doing? Honestly?" Rachel wasted no more time with pleasantries, she jumped straight in with the reason she had come down there.

"Well," said Susan, still rubbing her eyes and gathering her composure, "for vampire bite victims, there's something called the vampyric-infection rate, it's a calculation we do. It takes into account chemical and biological changes and gives a score, usually a percentage. We've worked out Tanya's level, and so far we've got it down to fifty-three point seven per cent."

"That's good isn't it?" Rachel said, radiating hope. "The level is dropping, that's a good thing surely?"

"Well, usually it is a good sign," Susan replied, "but I'm afraid that the rate at which the infection is dropping has plateaued, and that, unfortunately, is not good at all! We are going to try mixing up the cocktail, but she is already on the strongest dose of a number of the drugs we have. Obviously it's a good sign that the rate of infection hasn't begun to rise again, although I would say that it's only a matter of time," she glanced over Rachel's shoulder in the direction of Tanya.

"Will mixing up the cocktail work? Can Jonathon help now?" Although she spoke in a whisper, Rachel's voice was filled with dread and panic.

"Trying to find the right cocktail is a trial and error process, Rachel. Different serums work at different stages," Susan spoke in the cold, blunt tone that was usual for a doctor. Life and death were daily events for them, and although Susan herself was a compassionate and warm person, she knew that the bad outweighed the good in this situation and didn't want to give anyone, including Rachel, false hope.

"And each transformation is different, don't forget that. I'm sad to say that Jonathon will not be able to help here. His gift of healing people works in a way I can only guess at, but one thing I do know is that it heals everything, the good and the bad. If he tried to heal her now, his powers would recognise the dominant aspect of the genome and physiology. In other words, it would recognise the vampire part of Tanya as the true form. He would end up attacking her human aspect and speed up the rate of infection, resulting in only speeding up her metamorphism," Susan looked at Rachel and saw her dejection.
She could tell that Rachel harboured hope for this woman. Rachel was a very emotional person often allowing herself to get too involved in situations like this.

"Look, I'm trying my hardest here, I can promise you that," Tanya said, the only thing she thought she could say to sound reassuring.

Susan's words had sent a shiver down Rachel's spine. She had always imagined the gifted as people of the light, she had never once thought of a gift as neutral.

"What is going to happen to her?" No longer whispering, Rachel seemed determined to find some solution, some loophole to help save Tanya.

"Well, there are two outcomes. The first is that the rate of infection speeds up, and she will be a fully formed vampire in a matter of days, possibly weeks. The other depends on whether I can get that vampyric-infection score below fifty per cent, then Jonathon can help her. I must warn you though that if this is the case, his gift will not restore the damage done to her by the vampire virus, it will simply remove the infection."

"Damage? What damage? Surely, the infection is the damage?" Rachel was confused. For all the years she had worked for the Order, the metamorphic change of humans to vampires was something she was not too familiar with and she was still naïve with regards to the potential and limitations of the medicines and many talents of those in the Order.

"Even if the infection is removed successfully, Tanya will still have to spend the rest of her life on very powerful drugs. Many of her organs will perform below optimum levels. Her reproductive organs will have been completely destroyed; she will never be able have children again."

Rachel was dismayed by Dr. Gambon's somewhat emotionless tone and she gasped at the thought of what Tanya would still have to suffer, and for the rest of her life. And in spite of any intervention by Jonathon, Tanya would still lose the war, even if she somehow won this battle.

"She won't have children ever again?" Rachel was incredulous, but deep down she believed Dr. Gambon's prognosis, she knew what she had heard was correct.

Susan nodded at Rachel, who seemed lost in her thoughts and was crying silent tears. Rachel wondered if she had ever cried so much in her life.

"Bastard! I'm glad the vampire is dead and I hope Zhing kills Tom as well," Susan was taken aback by Rachel's blunt words. The Rachel she knew was usually so quiet and timid, but then she had let herself get too emotionally involved once again.

"Okay, Doctor, I have to go," Rachel sighed as she wiped away her tears.

Walking fast, she passed Tanya's bed and saw that she had fallen fast asleep. Rachel approached the elevators and stepped in, not able to take her mind off the fate that poor Tanya lying across the room from her had to endure. She had believed that she had saved her, but had she really? Would she ever be saved? As the doors to the elevator began to close, an arm suddenly popped through the gap and forced the doors back open. It was Susan. "I will do my best, I promise. She will get through this somehow."

The words, although meant kindly, sounded empty to Rachel and she was suddenly overcome with rage with the doctor. "It doesn't matter now does it? The damage has been done," she spat, she pushed one of the many buttons on the elevator's panel and Susan hurriedly stepped back as the doors closed. Rachel turned to her reflection in the gold panelling and saw her face looking darker than she had ever seen it before. She looked so angry, so ruthless.

...

Kristian was standing on a packed underground train. As he looked around, he realised that it was not a London underground tube train, but in fact a New York subway train. Confusion invaded his mind. How? Why? His head filled with questions. He had not been to New York for ten years. Had Rachel brought him here? With that thought, he turned and gazed out of the doors. He saw Rachel standing on the platform with Sam and Jean in tow.

"It wasn't me. I'm not doing this," said Rachel. As she spoke, the doors of the train closed and the train prepared to leave the platform. Kristian frantically reached for the 'open door' button but before he could push it, it vanished from the panel on which it sat. Jumping back, he let out a gasp, what was happening? Turning and looking down the carriage, none of the faces seemed familiar. The people on the train all looked at him, moving their heads and gazed in sync, their mouths opened and they all spoke at once.

In unison the passenger chorus spoke, "Alone you must go," Kristian flinched and took a step backwards; he grasped hold of one of the support bars to stop him losing his footing.

"Got to go where alone? What's happening?" his voice was trembling with fear and bewilderment. The people on the train repeated their bizarre chant, "Alone you must go." Then suddenly and oddly, they all went back to their previous mundane tasks, of travelling to work, reading their papers and pushing each other out of the way, marking their own territory attempting to gain some personal space in the packed carriage. Freaked out and scared, Kristian clutched hold of the nearest passenger to him, pulling the man to his feet.

"What's happening to me? What's going on? Who are you people?" he demanded. The passenger was completely flaccid, drooping in Kristian's grasp. His face was emotionless and he stared right through him, as if he wasn't there. Completely unresponsive, his deadpan, completely vacant eyes were glassed over and he could have been dead if it were not for the colour in his cheeks.

Kristian repeated his questions, pleading for answers, but the passenger remained unresponsive, he did not move nor utter a single word. Kristian slowly released him and the man flopped back into his seat.

Collapsing against the support of the train's fabric, Kristian was mystified; he sought answers to a number of troublesome questions. He was completely baffled. How had he got here? Where was he? Moreover, why was he here? Who were all these people and why did they seem to know him one minute and then completely ignore him the next?

Kristian had never been in a situation like this before, and yet, somewhere in the back of his mind was a sense of familiarity, a feeling of déjà vu. It was inexplicable, but it was there. As he pondered on this thought, the train drew to a halt.

Kristian assumed the train had arrived at a station, but there was no place name, no passengers waiting on the platform. As the doors slowly opened, he had the sudden urge to jump off. Heading for the door he was just about to leap onto the platform when a tall, curly-haired man appeared from nowhere and stepped onto the train. Pushing past him, Kristian attempted to flee from the carriage but before he could get his foot over the threshold, the doors closed.

"This is not your stop," said the curly-haired man who had just entered the carriage. Kristian immediately lunged at the man and wrapped his hands around his throat, lifting him into the air.

"Are you doing this to me?" Kristian shouted, his face turning blood-red with anger.

The man, who was taller than anyone else on the train, and dressed in remarkably odd clothes, tried to smile at Kristian. "Perhaps, if you release me, maybe I can explain." On hearing the whispered half-words, Kristian lowered the man to the floor and released his grip.

"What is happening?" Kristian demanded, but the man merely stared at him, grinning. He was wearing a strange robe and a waistcoat with symbols dotted all over it, symbols that Kristian could not quite make out but he was sure he had never seen anything quite like it before.

Suddenly, the man pointed towards Kristian's forehead; Kristian returned the point with a look of exasperation, "I'm not up for playing mind games okay?" Kristian said sounding even more agitated.

Then, in an instant, the penny dropped for him. Kristian's thoughts became concise and ordered; the answer came to him as he scratched his head, "Oh. You're in my mind?"

"Well, in a manner of speaking," the man replied, placing down a large blue suitcase on the floor; opening it he took out a white container and removed two chocolate cookies from it. "I'm not in your head, you're dreaming my friend." As he spoke he offered a cookie to Kristian.

Kristian shook his head in frustration, "No thanks," he barked, "I'm good. So you're in my dreams, which means you are in my head?" the man looked at him and then down at the cookie. He seemed to take the refusal of the biscuit as a personal insult. He then bit into his cookie and spoke, "Suit yourself, but these are very good cookies, and believe me I have eaten lots of cookies in my time. Oh, and to answer your question, no I am not in your head, I'm not really me."

Kristian's expression showed the baffled state of his mind, what did this stranger mean?

"Well, consider me as part of your dream; I'm merely an echo of someone you once met. The name is Zelupzs, but my friends call me Zel! My close friends call me something else."

His words hit Kristian like a ton of bricks. The man's face had seemed familiar to him and he suddenly remembered where he had seen him before. It had been a long time ago yet Kristian could still remember that day clearly now.

"Zelupzs," Kristian uttered, "yes, you are familiar to me, you're the man I met—" before he could finish his sentence, he turned and looked down the train, the memory came flooding back to him. "Here, I met you here, this is the day I met you." Zelupzs nodded his head and pointed down the carriage to the very back of the carriage. Standing there were a man and a woman; Kristian was sure they had not been there before. They looked to be in their mid to late twenties, the man was reading a map of the city and the woman was holding several shopping bags. In front of the couple stood a young boy with blonde hair. His youthful face was filled with innocence, his smile would have melted the coldest of hearts.

Kristian stared at the boy, his appearance all too familiar to him, but it had been a long time since he had seen that smile. "It's me. And that's my mum and dad."

114

"It is indeed," said Zelupzs as he checked his watch, "and right about now is when it happened."

Kristian just stood there motionless, his legs were frozen. The carriage rocked and a blinding white flash filled the whole train with bright light. As the light dissipated, Kristian rubbed his eyes, regaining his focus. The carriage went silent; every single person on the train seemed frozen in time. Everyone except Kristian, his younger self and Zelupzs. The young Kristian turned, his face changed. His smile no longer present, his happy joyful look was replaced with a look of fear. He began to tug on his mother's jacket and tried to speak but no sound came out.

"Mum, Mum," the older Kristian spoke in time with the boy, remembering the events of this day all too well. The younger Kristian then began to tug at his dad's jacket, again mouthing more words, which the older version spoke loudly and clearly.

"Look Zel, I was so scared. I had no idea what was going on." As he spoke, he turned and looked at Zelupzs.

"I am sorry," replied the man. "My intentions were not to frighten you. I needed to speak with you. Do you remember what I said to you that day?"

Kristian nodded to imply he did and turned back to look at his younger self. There out of nowhere, another Zelupzs appeared at the end of the carriage and slowly began to make his way towards the younger Kristian. The boy was clearly startled; he could see no one else but this strange figure coming towards him. He tried to scream but yet again no sound came out. Backed into a corner, the young boy fell to the floor and wrapped his arms around his legs, closed his eyes and began to silently sob. After a few seconds, the Zelupzs of the memory knelt down and began to pry the boy's arms away from his legs. He too began to speak but no sound came out of his mouth.

"Do you remember what I said to you that day?" repeated Zelupzs over Kristian's shoulder.

"Every word," Kristian replied, still fixed on the younger version of himself. The conversation between his younger self and the memory Zelupzs did not last long, no longer than a couple of minutes, although Kristian remembered it feeling like hours. After about a minute, the Zelupzs that spoke to the young boy vanished and as he went a bright white light flashed again down the train and the people in the carriage suddenly returned to life. Kristian's parents looked down at the young boy as he sat near the door. They appeared to be shouting at him as he sat there wiping his tears. His father seemed to be very cross with his son's outward expression of emotion, but the mother, realising that her son had been crying, soon softened and embraced him, stroking his hair and making shushing noises. The father rolled his eyes and continued to read his map.

"He was so mad at me, I don't think he spoke to me for the rest of the day," said the older Kristian. As he finished talking the train stopped at another station where his parents and his younger self left the carriage. The doors closed behind them, every other person on the carriage had seemed to vanish, leaving just Kristian with Zelupzs as they turned to look at one another.

"So you remember everything I said to you. Do you believe me now?" said Zel.

"Yes, I remember. Do you want me to repeat it to you or something? And as to whether I believe you, I think I always did. Even before the Order found me and before the joining," Kristian spoke as he slowly made his way towards one of the empty seats and sat down.

"Yes, I would like you to repeat it to me; I want to know that you remember it all. I hate to rush you kid but this dream is nearly over and I need to be sure of what you heard."

Kristian sniggered, it was defensive, and he always seemed to want to laugh when he was challenged. "Well, okay. You told me to read the Sagara prophecy. You told me that in seven years' time I would be joining with a cosmological incorporeal being," he sniggered, "you then told me that it was very important that I read some prophecy. I remember asking you why, and you said that I was in them. That the future that the prophecy describes would happen in my lifetime. Is that right?"

"Yeah, spot on kiddo." replied Zelupzs winking.

"So is that the only reason to come to me tonight, to make sure I remembered?" Kristian asked, still perplexed, wondering what the significance of meeting Zelupzs really was.

"In a way, yes, but also to tell you that we do need to meet again. We have to meet again. You will need to find me," Zelupzs commanded.

"Pardon me?"

"My friend, the dire parts of that prophecy are far beyond their planning stages; there are dark forces working overtime at this very moment. These forces are even more powerful than you could ever imagine. As he was speaking, he moved toward the doors.

"Well, what am I supposed to do about it?" snapped Kristian, "I've read that prophecy and to describe it as cryptic is an understatement. No one around me has the inclination or the time to be deciphering old dusty prophecies. If you really want me to do something, then perhaps furnish me with some names or dates that would be useful. Have you got anything, anything at all?" Kristian rose to his feet.

"Look, I wish I could give you more, I really do. It's not that I don't know; I hate to have to remind you, but this is only a dream, I am merely an echo! I have only two more things left to leave with you. Firstly, there is more you need to read. George Caparin was a former Order member. He was very meticulous about recording absolutely everything in his life. The stuff around March 1919 is a most interesting read.

The train began to slow again as if coming to yet another station. "This is my stop, kid, not yours though; you've a long way to go yet," Zel said as he looked fondly after Kristian.

"Wait!" shouted Kristian. "And the second thing?"

"Ah, yes, there is one more thing – Trafalgar," Zel exclaimed as the train came to a halt; the doors opened for a second and he quickly exited.

Kristian appeared confused and before he could move the train doors closed. Not sure what Zel's final word meant, he moved to the door and looked through the glass at Zel. Kristian could see Zel standing a few feet away and was struck by the fact that the strange man's eyes were focused on a large poster to his right. Kristian followed Zel's gaze and focused on the poster, he could see large white writing on a red background, and whispered the words as he read.

'You can no longer Hyde, your battle of Trafalgar awaits'

Zel moved off as Kristian pondered over the message on the wall. As Zel neared the exit to the platform, he stopped once more, looked back over his shoulder and he shouted to Kristian over the noise of the train, "I like you kiddo, you've got a big heart underneath all that anger and pain," as he finished speaking, the 'open door' button on the train materialised next to the door; Kristian immediately stretched out his hand and slammed the button quickly, fearing it might disappear.

Before the doors opened, Kristian yelled at the glass towards Zel in desperation, "I don't understand! I'm not a hero. I can't stop what's coming."

The doors suddenly slid back open and Kristian jumped onto the platform and started to run in Zel's direction. He suddenly slid to a halt in panic, as he saw three bodies lying on the platform floor in front of him. He paused and tried to take in the horror of what was there in front of him: three bodies soaked in blood. Moving quickly towards the carnage, he knelt down and turned one of the corpses towards him.

The face, though stained with blood and dreadfully scared, was more than familiar.

"Rachel. Rachel!" screamed Kristian. He looked over towards the other two bodies and realised that they too were known to him. Jean and Sam both lay face up, the injuries on their bodies as severe as Rachel's. Kristian scrambled to see any sign of life through the wet, red veils that covered their faces.

"Sam. Jean!" Kristian was now weeping and quivering with fear.

In the dread and frustration he looked around him to see what might have committed such a vicious act. He then quickly became aware of the fact that he was dreaming. He began to stroke Rachel's hair, he gazed upon her face, her trademark glasses askew and smashed, his heart pounded as her eyes opened.

"You can't take us with you. Don't take us with you!" she spattered her words, her mouth and throat choked with blood. The shock rushed through Kristian as he flinched backwards.

Opening his eyes, he scanned the space around him. The surroundings were different, no blood-soaked bodies, no train, he was now back in his sleeping quarters at the Order; back in his bed. He was sitting upright, sweat dripping from his face.

"It was just a dream, it was just a dream," he affirmed. As the words left his mouth, he slowly laid back into his sweat-drenched sheets and pondered on the revelations. *Was it all just a dream, what did it mean?* he thought. In his confusion he was unsure of what Zel's or Rachel's words meant, nor did he have any insight into what the cryptic poster meant. Kristian remained in his soaked sheets and spent the next couple of hours contemplating his nightmare.

...

- Chapter Eight -

The Trinity

Following several hours of fractured sleep, Kristian awoke to the sound of a mobile phone ringing. Sitting bolt upright, he wiped his eyes to try and clear them of sleep, and began to look around the room for his mobile. Listening to the ringtone and trying to determine where the noise was coming from, he scrambled for his trousers, which rested on the back of the chair at a desk. Rummaging through, he quickly found his phone in the back pocket.

"Hello," he answered. The male voice on the other end was loud and played heavily on his ear.

"Are you up? Where are you? Do you know what time it is?"

"Yeah," Kristian replied as he moved the phone from his ear and looked at the time. It was half past eleven. Slamming himself in the head with his free hand, it suddenly dawned on him that he had overslept; badly. "Sorry, I had a bad night's sleep."

"Well, this is your wake-up call! You have a busy day ahead," the disembodied voice replied.

"Sorry, Jonathon. Thanks for the wake-up call; I will go and find the others now." Kristian hung up the phone and threw it onto the bed. Looking into the mirror he was shocked to see how awful he looked. His eyes were dark, his skin red and blotchy and his hair was all over the place. It didn't take him long to get ready; within ten minutes, he was in the elevator heading down to the main corridor, often referred to as the hub. He walked from office to office, investigating all the training rooms; he was looking for the rest of the gang. He spent near on half an hour searching and was beginning to get fed up with looking.

He had bumped into nearly half a dozen people, all of them patting him on the back and telling him how nice it was to see him again. He couldn't be so sure that he felt the same about many of them; he hardly recognised most of them. They were the office clerks and research assistants with whom he had never really spent much time whilst in the Order. The only friendly face he happened upon was that of Karnel, the Vinji. His appearance alone was not particularly welcoming and to say he had a friendly face would be misleading. But he had been a good friend to Kristian, and what he·lacked in looks, he made up for in personality.

Kristian was glad to see the large, overpowering and yet very kind Vinji. Of all the people he liked and admired in that building, Karnel was one of the dearest. Kristian had often wondered about his past, how he had come to betray his people and how he ended up working for the Order, but as friendly as Karnel was, they were questions that Kristian had been warned never to ask.

They stood and chatted for going on fifteen minutes, about everything from university to coffee, then Kristian thought to ask him if he had seen his companions. Asking Karnel on the off chance he had seen Sam, Jean or Rachel, the Vinji replied with a smirk, "Ah, yes, they are in the Crown."

Kristian could have hit himself for not thinking of looking there; of course, that is where they would be. For the few months that he had spent in the Order, a lot of that time had been spent in the Crown. Leaving Karnel with a grunt and a wave for a goodbye, he leapt into a fast-paced jog and left the complex, running around the corner towards the pub, which sat directly behind headquarters.

It was a nice little place, with envious views over the Thames, and the South Bank. Pushing through the doors, Kristian instantly spotted the team. They were sitting in the same old booth, which he remembered well.

Of all his time in the Order, he remembered the moments spent in this place most fondly.

They all noticed him enter and each of them raised their hands and waved him over. Sam, Jean, Rachel and Kieran all returned to their conversation as Kristian walked over and sat next to Rachel and Jean.

"Morning guys, eaten, have we?" Kristian said as he pointed down at the empty plates on the table.

"Yeah, breakfast as usual. Oversleep did we?" replied Kieran who sat directly opposite him.

"A little. So, what have you all been chatting about?"

"Well, loads actually. But it's all about the mission," said Rachel.

"Would you like a drink, Kristian, it's sadly my round," said Kieran, rising to his feet.

"Yes please, I'll have a cranberry juice."

"Okay, so is everybody else having the same?" asked Kieran, pointing at the empty glasses. Everyone said yes and Kieran made his way towards the bar. Kristian looked down at the array of glasses on the table in front of him. Two pint glasses, one wine glass and a tumbler, which he picked up and smelt.

"Ooh, gin in the morning?" said Kristian, cringing.

"Yeah, that's mine!" replied Rachel, laughing.

"I thought yours was the wine."

"No, that's Kieran's. I think he thinks it's sophisticated." chuckled Sam.

"It's never sophisticated drinking alcohol before midday!" said a smirking Kristian.

It wasn't long before Kieran had returned to the table with the tray of drinks. Everyone began to launch back into their conversation. They all seemed worked up, the discussion heated, each one suggesting what place to search first, how the group should split up, even how they were going to write it all up.

Clutching his cranberry juice, Kristian downed it in one, feeling unbelievably nervous; his dream was still haunting him. The point of the dream was clear to him now; he knew he had to go to Berlin alone, but how could he break that to them? His mind began to race as he thought of how to word it, methods he could use to persuade them. He was aware that he didn't have much time to do it; it had to be done now.

"I'm going to Berlin alone, guys," Kristian's words cut through the conversation, stunning them into silence as they all turned as one towards him.

"I beg your pardon?" asked Jean, looking surprised.

"I'm going alone. I can't take you. It's hard to explain, but it's just something that I need to do on my own." Everyone looked shocked at Kristian's revelation and they all shook their heads in sync.

"You cannot just not take us, Kristian. We're not children. Sorry, but Jonathon wants us all to go, so we are all going," said Sam, his voice unusually high.

"Sam, you can't come. I can't tell you why but I have to do this. I have to do this alone," Kristian said, his tone attempting to convey a deeper meaning to his request.

They all looked at each other; all of them except Kieran who was trying to think of what to say that would change Kristian's mind. Sam went to reply to Kristian but Rachel interrupted him. "Fine, we don't need to know. I for one trust you Kristian, but a word of warning, if you go alone you will be open to even more danger than you would be with us. Oliver was alone, remember."

"Don't bring him into this please. Trust me, it'll be a lot safer if you don't come; that's my word of warning," said Kristian defensively.

"How can you say don't bring Oliver into this? It's about Oliver; he's the reason we're going in the first place. And what does Jonathon think of your plan? Huh?" Sam was shouting, angry and frustrated. "And how are you going to get there without Rachel?"

"I was going to take a train, later on today," Kristian replied.

"Today?" said Rachel, Sam and Jean incredulously.

"Kristian, just think about what you are saying," pleaded Rachel, "at least let me take you there. I would need a few hours to prepare before I teleport you and Saranthea, but if you just give me some time, I can do it, I've teleported other Phoenixes before."

"I just don't have the time," replied Kristian adamantly. "I need to leave today!"

"Look, there is no way you can leave today and by train. Come on Kristian, Jonathon will not let you go alone," Sam's voice was still raised.

"I'm doing this, guys, and Jonathon will come round to the idea, especially if you are all on board," Kristian paused as he examined all their expressions. "Please, I need you to do this for me," Kristian was now pleading with them.

"Okay, Kristian, but even if we all agree to come on board with your ridiculous plan, Jonathon will not," said Jean.

"Well, I hate to put you in this position, but I was just going to leave. I wasn't going to tell him," he said, avoiding eye contact with all of them.

"What?" said a bemused Sam. "And you want us to tell him what exactly?"

"Just leave it as late as possible, and then tell him I chose to go alone and that I knew he would stop me if I told him."

The three of them were looking at Kristian as if they hoped he was joking, but it was obvious that he wasn't. There was a steady determination in his voice.

"Look, I'm not up for this. Listen to reason, will you? You just cannot do this alone," said Jean.

Rachel was lost for words; Kristian thought about his next move. What else could he say? How could he win them over? Rachel had sounded like she may be able to come to terms with the idea, maybe she could say something to support him, but she just looked empty and abandoned.

"Guys. If he wants to go it alone, we will have to let him. He may have only just returned to the Order but he's a Phoenix, which means he outranks us all. Just relax about Jonathon, I will talk to him. I'm sure he'll be okay in the end." As Kieran spoke, they all turned to look at him. They had almost forgotten that he was there. This was the first time in the conversation that he had got involved; he had just been sitting there, sipping his wine.

Sam and Jean looked at each other, then at Kristian and then shrugged their shoulders. Kieran finished his wine with one long sip, and then moved towards the bar without a word to anyone. Kristian leaned in towards the table and on his move, the other three followed.

"Look," Kristian spoke, "please try and understand, I'm doing this because I must. I know that you think I'm being foolish but my intentions are good. Besides, I want you three to do something really important for me. I want you to help Zhing find the Dark Phoenix."

These words were exactly what Rachel had wanted to hear. She had been dying to get in on that case ever since she had been to the hospital wing to visit Tanya.

"Okay," Rachel said without hesitation.

"Even if we are on board, Zhing was already offered our help and she refused. She wants to do this without any outside interference," said Jean.

"Fine, then help her somehow from headquarters," said Kristian, hoping that this new mission may help the team come to terms with his plan.

Kristian continued after he momentarily glanced over his shoulder at Kieran. "Sam, you can use your gift to try and find him; Rachel and Jean you can stay in touch with Zhing and me and be ready at all times for any other operations that may arise."

The three of them stared at Kristian, all with bemused expressions, wondering if this was really a good course of action. Without saying a word they watched as Kristian stood. "Guys, if we're going to pull this off, we're going to have to get going. I know that you think this is a bad idea, but trust me, I know what I am doing. Why don't we go our separate ways now, think about what I'm saying then meet back here at three?" As he finished his sentence, Rachel's mobile phone started ringing.

Reaching into her pocket she pulled it out and looked at the screen. "It's Jonathon," she said with a look of panic in her eyes.

Before she could answer it, Kristian signalled 'three' with his fingers followed by tapping the back of his wrist where a watch would be. He then made for the bar.

Taking up the place next to Kieran, Kristian leaned against the bar and spoke, "Thank you for that back there; you helped me a lot."

Kieran slowly moved his head; his eyes gazed over at him. "You can keep your thanks, Kristian. I didn't do it for you."

Kristian was completely thrown by Kieran's tone and attitude. *Why was he being aggressive?*

"What's your problem, Kieran?"

"My problem? You can push us all away if you want, you can rush the mission through as fast as you feel you need, you can even go back to your pathetic little life when all this is over. But for you to risk your life like this is beyond reckless. When will you realise that the world doesn't revolve around you? You make me so—" Kieran's voice was raised, strain was showing on his face. Trying hard not to shout, Kieran turned towards the barman, "Oh, just forget it," he then moved past Kristian, pushing into him as he went and walked out the door. The barman stood there with a glass of wine in one hand and a cranberry juice in the other, looking completely bewildered.

"Sorry," Kristian said to the barman as he raced after Kieran. Pushing through the doors, he saw Kieran not far ahead of him.

"Hey!" he shouted. Kieran stopped and looked back.

"I'm not going alone because I'm afraid of becoming too attached to everyone. I'm not pushing anyone away. I just have to go alone," Kristian shouted down the street to the bemusement of many passers-by.

"Why? Why do you have to go alone? Just tell me that. Why is it only your fight?" Kieran again struggled to keep his voice from shouting.

"I can't tell you, Kieran, I just don't think you will understand," his voice was lowering, he was trying to stay calm, and he hated fighting with one of the team.

"Fine! Whatever. Just don't expect a welcome back again," Kieran said sounding defeated. "You're so mysterious. In two years, you haven't changed at all," Kieran's voice was now as measured as Kristian's, but as he finished speaking, he just turned away and started walking off again. Kristian stood there, stunned by Kieran's comments. Of all the outcomes he had expected, this wasn't one of them. *Did Kieran really feel so much anger towards him?* Looking down the street, he pondered on what to do next; he thought that he should go and buy a train ticket, sort out some accommodation.

The doors to the pub suddenly swung open and to Kristian's surprise, there was Rachel, her face looking defeated, crumpled by emotion. She was being supported by Sam who looked equally upset, her face filled with tears. They both looked at Kristian. *What had happened whilst he had been away*, he wondered. But before he could ask the question, Rachel spoke, "It's Tanya, the girl who got attacked, she's… it's… she died," her voice cracked and the tears started afresh; she whipped her nose on the back of her hand.

"Her heart stopped," Sam said, as he wiped away the beginnings of a tear from his eyes.

Kristian looked stunned. He knew that there was a girl in the ward and he knew why she was there, but he had not come into contact with her himself. However, he knew that Rachel and Sam had played a big part in the girl's rescue and completely understood their turmoil. He moved closer to Rachel, hugging her tight.

"I'm sorry; I know you felt responsible for her," he held his head over Rachel's and the image of her bloody hair from the dream crept back into his mind. He pulled away sharply; to cover his reaction he quietly asked, "What is going to happen?"

"Her heart's stopped; Susan says she will wake up within the next twenty-four hours as a Vampire," Sam said as a tear ran down his cheek; he then looked back and saw Jean behind him and without warning, gripped hold of the Frenchman and began to gently sob on his shoulder. Kristian shook the image of the dream out of his mind and his eyes locked with Jean's. Both of them stared at one another and smiled half-heartedly. Both of them wondered what the other was thinking, but neither of them had a clue!

...

Standing in front of the Great Library, Kristian peered down at his train ticket and hotel confirmation. Placing the pieces of paper deep into his pocket he felt the urge to hide them away from any prying eyes. Filled with a sense of anticipation mixed with fear and dread, Kristian was anxious to enter the Library again. The large magnificent doors that lay right in front of him were intimidating and did nothing to relieve his tensions. He had entered the Library before; he had passed the magical barrier that protected it. It had granted him access; it had decided he was pure of heart. But had things changed? Was he now less worthy? Pushing his emotions to one side he placed his hand onto a square gold fitting that rested on the door at chest height. The panel, which was roughly the size of a sheet of A4 paper, began to heat; pulling his hand away he watched as a shape began to appear from the fitting. A large golden ear now protruded out from the fitting. Lowering his head Kristian whispered into the ear. Instantly it vanished back into the door as the locks and cogs of the door sprang into life. Unable to see them as they lay on the inside of the door, Kristian knew the door was opening; the noise of the unlocking was louder then he remembered. Within seconds the large oak doors swung outwards as Kristian took a few steps back.

Mesmerised, Kristian's eyes widened. The memory of the Great Library was as nothing compared to revisiting it. The length of the room extended far beyond what he could see at the door, as he pondered how such a large room could exist within the headquarters complex.

It was noisy as libraries go, and hundreds of people all dressed in grey suits darted around, some carrying books, some just talking to themselves. As Kristian crossed the threshold he felt a tingling sensation somewhat like the feeling he felt when he first entered the complex. As the feeling passed he turned on his heels to see that the doors had already silently closed behind him. Twisting back to face the library Kristian was surprised to see that nearly everybody had stopped what they had been doing and were now glaring at him. A split second later they had all returned to their previous tasks. All but one.

An extremely tall, gaunt-looking man made his way towards Kristian.

"Sorry about that. Not many Black Suits venture into the Great Library. I guess they worry too much about their own purity. Not you, though? This is not your first time. You've entered before, June 16th 2007? Am I right? Of course I am!"

Kristian, startled by the speed and the words of the strange man's speech, could do nothing but nod in agreement.

"How can we help you today young sir?" his voice so very deep it almost broke into whisper.

"I'm not sure. I'm looking for a book," Kristian said being discreet as ever.

"Well you have come to the right place," he laughed as he swept his arm round the vast space.

"Sorry, stupid answer. My name's Kristian by the way."

"Yes I know. And I am Saresh." The tall man paused and smiled at Kristian, "So this book, you have a title?"

"Not exactly," Kristian replied as he turned and tried to take in the library in all its glory. Aisle after aisle filled with row after row of books stretching up so high he could hardly believe the building extended so far. Spiral staircases were dotted all around. The task, suddenly, of him finding the book he sought seemed to be a mammoth one, to say the least.

"Not exactly?" Saresh replied as he stared at the young man's wide-eyed and open-mouthed expression of awe. "Well you know how to search?"

"Search… there's an order to this chaos!?"

"Of course. A magical one. Just head for the desk, fill out a card and I am sure even a Black Suit can find the book he is looking for."

"Desk?" Kristian said as he pivoted on his heels. To his amazement, a small desk which he had overlooked previously stood out of place; the desk had a huge stack of white cards teetering on top of it, behind the desk, practically hidden by the stack of cards, was a short plump woman almost engulfing the chair on which she perched.

"Simply fill out the card and the rest will be done for you," as Saresh spoke he gestured softly with his hand and tilted his head to signal goodbye.

Kristian, pressed for time, paced purposefully towards the desk, not even returning the physical gesture of goodbye.

Grabbing a card he glanced at the tiny writing, only three columns lay on the credit card-sized paper: Title, Author and Details. Scribbling in the details section Kristian wrote everything he remembered Zel telling him:

- *George Caparin / March 1919.*

Kristian stood back and glared at the card on the table he had just written on. The card without warning lifted into the air hovering in front of him at eye level. Floating there, the card began twisting as if it had a mind of its own, or contained a computer that had begun processing the minimal information. The card's revolutions stopped abruptly and shortly afterwards the card darted off. Kristian gave chase as the card flew erratically through the air, weaving in and around busy librarians as they went about their business. It wasn't that the card was travelling too fast that made it hard to keep up with, it was the route it was taking; Kristian had no idea how busy a workplace the library was.

Turning a sharp corner, a large empty aisle stocked with thousands of books on both sides lay in front of him. The card had stopped a short distance ahead; it began to float upwards until it stopped a few metres high next to a small brown leather-strapped book. The book now began to move itself out from the shelf until it was hovering in the air. It opened as pages flipped over and the card slotted in and the book closed. Slowly it floated down until it rested in Kristian's hands.

Finding an empty desk Kristian sat down and opened the book at the page where the card had rested itself. Clipping the page and the front cover with his finger and thumb he glanced at the front cover – *Diary: G. Caparin. 76.*

Returning to the marked-out section he began to read. The diary contained six references for the month of March 1919. It didn't take him long to finish reading all of the passages for that month. Nothing from the texts leaped out, no words plagued his mind. He reread the passages several times but he could not help but think that it contained nothing important. It was just like most diaries, he thought; a description of mundane daily tasks written as if by any ordinary person.

As Kristian read the text again he scribbled down words and lines that he hoped were important and contained deeper meaning.

Serucio's translation of Dwarf Word Magic / Brancrock / Wilson's collection / Solasis Krull / his sister I believe is a member of the council / tempest / I lost corban's key / Drancrock

Looking at his list and then at his watch he was left feeling that he had wasted enough time on his very cryptic search. His list seemed so vague; nothing really jumped out at him, though he did feel a slight tingle to one reference, to a name he had found. There was no logic to his feeling; it was instinctual, from the gut. With that he underlined *Solasis Krull* on his notes.

"Interesting," a voice interrupted from over Kristian's shoulder.

Kristian was so engrossed in his work, the sudden interruption by Saresh startled him and Kristian merely responded by echoing the word. "Interesting?" he spoke in such a tone that gave away his annoyance and surprise. What's more, was Saresh spying on him?

"Oh, I am sorry. I don't mean to snoop," Saresh responded to Kristian's strained tone.

"It's okay. What's interesting?"

"That name. 'Solasis Krull'. It's an odd name. What are you reading?"

"Just some diary," Kristian said as he showed the front cover, "what's so interesting about a name?"

"Its structure is interesting. Looking at it, I would say it wasn't man-made. It looks 'Ancient', 'Elvish' perhaps. Maybe even 'Traveller'," Saresh said as he pondered out loud.

"It looks what? What do you mean? It just looks like a name to me," Kristian replied.

"Ha! Such a young mind. A name is more than just a scribe, more than just a series of symbols or letters you know. It can hold a wonder of secrets." Tilting his head and repeating the name in a whisper, Saresh's eyes focused intently, "No, no, no. Not an Ancient's name. Though I would imagine it's written in lower Ancient."

Kristian stood glaring at the strange, intrusive librarian. He didn't understand what he was being told, but listened. It sounded odd, it sounded important.

"Lower Ancient? Ancient?" Kristian asked.

"You know about the Ancients? You can at least name one? Surely!"

Kristian had heard about them previously, about beings of great power. But the way it was explained to him, even in the world in which he lived, it all sounded too mythical. "Well, there's Gaia."

"Well, I'm glad you know that. Mother of the Phoenixes, protector of Earth. There are many more than just her, and the language they spoke is referred to as Ancient. Our interpretation, our literal translation of it is called Lower Ancient."

"There's a difference?" Kristian asked, his tone slightly sarcastic.

"Well, to read Ancient you need to be Ancient or very gifted. It's written like Lower Ancient, but the words, the structure of the sentences, contain more meaning. Meaning that can only be understood by seeing the underprint," Saresh said with a smile on his face; he always enjoyed passing on his knowledge.

"Okay – I'm so confused. Underprint?" Kristian asked.

"You really don't know? Well, I've said it before and I shall say it again. Those who work in the field need more than just combat training. You should be forced to pick up a book!" Saresh said as he now stepped back and glared at the young man. "The underprint is hard to describe. Never experiencing it we only have written testimonies to go by. It is like a psychic or magical imprint that is left on a word. Take the word 'Crankel'; in Lower Ancient, the translation is mountain. But written and read in original Ancient it could mean something more specific. Like the name of a mountain, a view from it, it could even leave the reader seeing the mountain in his or her mind's eye. It could be as wondrous as a feeling or an emotion. See, it could change the meaning of a text. It's easily said that we have had more than difficulty translating anything written in Ancient."

Kristian stood there thinking about what he had heard. He understood it, or at least he thought he did.

"So there could be more meaning to this name? This Solasis Krull?" Kristian asked.

"Yes if written and read in its original form. Names in Ancient are most interesting. Like word-magic itself a name can project power over its owner. Hence some names are well-guarded secrets by their owners."

"Cool," Kristian said; he was impressed with what Saresh was saying. He knew then he would have to look further into this 'Solasis Krull', he could feel in his bones that it was important.

Glancing down at his watch it instantly dawned on him that he had let time escape from him. He had a train to catch; his investigation into this mysterious name would have to wait. There was a more important mission at hand – justice for Oliver.

"I'm sorry. I have to go. Thanks for your help. It's truly been helpful," Kristian moved away and began to pace back towards the entrance.

"No worries, young man," Saresh called after him. As the boy disappeared from view, Saresh turned back to the table and to the diary that was left there.

"Interesting, very interesting," he muttered to himself, "Solasis Krull – I wonder," he picked up the book and turned on the spot with a very inquisitive and thoughtful expression on his face.

…

It had been nearly twenty-four hours since he had had the discussion with his companions, since Kristian had found out about the death of Tanya.

Many things had happened in those hours: his visit to the Great Library, his discussion with Saresh, the long non-direct train journey to Berlin, the awakening of Tanya as a vampire and the early morning phone call from an enraged Jonathon, threatening to send Rachel to bring him back.

It was after midday when Kristian finally got out of bed; the room he had slept in was cold and damp, not unlike the rest of the rooms in the youth hostel he was staying in. He wasn't overly concerned by the conditions of the hostel but was more surprised about the fact that it was owned by the Order.

The Order owned a lot of property in over a hundred countries and the few he had visited were in no way as bad as this.

Putting his clothes and watch on, he glanced at the time and was annoyed at how late it was. He had arrived in Berlin in the early hours of the morning and had spent his first two hours searching for the hostel which had been walking distance from the station, but he had got lost on the dark streets of the capital.

Grabbing his rucksack from the floor, he pulled open his mission file and began to look through it. Examining the photos and maps of marked locations on the Berlin landscape he wondered which he should visit first. There were so many locations to investigate, lots of people to question. Due to the lack of factual information that Oliver had failed to gather prior to his death, little if nothing was known about the events leading up to it.

Throwing the pictures on the floor, he began to feel side-tracked as his belly roared with hunger. Leaving the hostel, Kristian began to walk down a long street on his quest for food. The buildings around him were so different from the ones back home. They were smaller than those in London and yet they didn't feel foreign to him. Couples kept passing him on the street, their conversations clear and audible. Kristian stared at them, it was strange. He had never been to Germany before but he could understand everything the people were saying; he knew why he could comprehend a language he had never spent time learning, but the experience for him was very strange. He continued to think about how amazing and bizarre it was until his belly let out another great rumble of hunger. Remembering that he was on the hunt for food he turned and noticed a bakery a few shops down. Walking in he began to greet everyone in the shop, the customers and staff, all in word-perfect German. After a long ten-minute conversation with the counter assistant, Kristian left the store with a large handful of pastries. Standing outside the shop, he began to gorge himself on the delicious treats he had just purchased. People continued to pass by and he was still able to understand them perfectly; he thanked Sam aloud for implanting the language in his subconscious. Sam's physic ability that allowed him to enter people's minds also allowed him to implant information into one's subconscious as well. The technique of transferring knowledge and skills into people's psyche had been used by the Order for many years, but never had anyone been better at it than Sam.

Walking back to the hostel, Kristian had eaten four of the pastries he had been carrying and on entering reception he placed the remainder of them on a large table. Heading back up to his room, it wasn't long before he was once again flicking through his mission file. Placing the locations in order, one behind the other, he carefully planned out the week ahead. Lingering over some of the photographs, he could almost picture Oliver in them. His imaginings quickly disappeared by the ringing of his phone. Stretching over to answer it he saw that it was Jonathon calling yet again. He knew what the conversation would entail. It would be Jonathon agreeing to disagree about Kristian disobeying orders and that he was going to accept the idea that he was going it alone as long as Kristian agreed to use support from the Munich office if he needed. He would also give some kind of empty threat to Kristian about what would happen to him if he ever tried to pull off a stunt like this again.

The phone call proceeded exactly as he predicted it would, even the empty threat was present, which Kristian had quietly sniggered at. When it was over, he stood looking down on his bed at the mass of photos and notes he had spread out on it. He began to question if he had been right to go it alone after all. He looked around his room and the dark and dank decor was a real indication of exactly how he felt.

...

One week after Kristian's departure, in the most prestigious casting room of the Order, Andrew was standing in the centre; kneeling a metre in front of him was Kieran, his head bowed towards the floor. Behind him, about five metres away stood Roman, his eyes closed and his palms together. All three of them were wearing long white overalls, just like those Andrew always wore.

Kieran was concentrating hard, trying only to think of the ritual ahead. He had been so young when he had first heard of the Trinity. It wasn't long before that he had been told that the things that were happening to him were caused by magic. Ever since that day, he had fantasised about being in the Trinity, and now that honour was being bestowed upon him, he was filled with joy, pride and trepidation.

Andrew began to chant softly the ancient scriptures, "*El es undo moni*," over and over again. His chanting lasted three minutes and then silence fell on the room. Kieran opened his eyes to be greeted by Andrew who was emitting a blinding light. Rising to his feet, Kieran kept eye contact. He had imagined this experience to be overwhelming and the image in front of him was truly awe-inspiring.

"The ritual is bound by words, the noblest of magic's. You must be open and willing to receive your third. Do you promise to wield this magic to aid those who are fearful, to protect those who are innocent and to stand by those who are brave? Will you honour the lore of the Trinity?" Andrew's voice quietly echoed through the room, his face the only part of his body that was visible through the light.

"I will always aid, protect and stand by. The name of the Trinity shall be my own, I will honour it with my life, and may my death be a tribute to all those who bore the gift before." Kieran spoke slowly to avoid making any mistakes; he had spent hours practising those words but was still worried about messing up. As he finished his reply, he closed his eyes and began to empty his mind of words and imbued his heart with the will to accept.

"*El sueot, fal ma, geu,*" Andrew intoned. Light began to leave Andrew and floated through the air like a weightless fog. Wrapping itself around Kieran, it resembled a snake wrapping itself around its prey. Andrew began to look faint, he began to sway on his feet, and his face looked pale and drained.

"I accept this gift. *El sueot,*" Kieran said, his voice high and jubilant.

Roman took three steps towards Kieran, his palms still locked together. He spoke "*El es undo moni,*" as a veil of light spewed from within him and surrounded him like thick mist.

"*Fal ma, contu,*" Roman spoke again and as he did, the light shot quickly from around him and latched onto the light engulfing Kieran. The two lights coalesced into a powerful vortex swirling around Kieran. Roman now looked as white and drained as Andrew.

Kieran was consumed with bright light.

"*El sueot,*" Kieran spoke as the light continued to float around him. Taking a deep breath Kieran continued, "*Sueot, eux mans trinity.*" A few seconds later, the light that was coiled around Kieran tore into three separate sections. Two shot off in opposite directions, one hit Andrew, the other hit Roman. Kieran stood amongst the light that remained as it slowly began to filter into his body. Andrew and Roman's faces regained their colour as the light that hit them entered their bodies.

All three of them took long deep breaths, the ritual itself was over and all three of them were showing signs of the stress.

Andrew looked at Roman and smiled, both of them seemed pleased to no longer carry the extra part of the Trinity that they had to bear after the death of Wendy. Their smiles fell upon Kieran who looked strained. His eyes were wide open and his jubilant smile was etched from ear to ear. He had read many accounts of what the ritual would entail and what it was going to feel like to bear a third of the Trinity. The words he had read offered him little comfort now. He could feel the energy burning up inside him; he struggled to keep it buried and not unleash any unwanted spells. All of his senses seemed to be heightened and every nerve in his body was tingling. He had never felt so alive!

"How are you feeling?" Andrew said as he moved towards Kieran.

"If I said high, like ecstasy high, would you think badly of me?" The two men sniggered and patted him on the back.

"You will need to do some spells, it will relieve some of the pain," Roman said as he noticed Kieran rubbing his chest.

"It's just a matter of time, it will get a lot easier," said Andrew.

Kieran knew that what they were saying was true, he had read the accounts of all the past members of the Trinity and each had described the discomfort he felt' it didn't help him now though.

Through gritted teeth, he looked at the pair, "I'm sure I'll be fine."

…

- Chapter Nine -

Soon to be Slain

Navigating the streets of London during the day wasn't an easy task for any courier, but for those employed by the Order the job entailed added risks. Dodging past cars and whizzing through the odd red light, it didn't take David long before he was making his way across the river. His destination was a prestigious gallery on the south side owned by Isobel O'Hara.

After a twenty-minute ride, David soon found himself parking his bicycle and walking up the long and beautiful stone steps to the entrance to Isobel's home. Not only did she work there, it was her place of comfort, her refuge. The gallery was unlike the Order's headquarters or, indeed, any of the Order's buildings. It was far from the drab and basic concept that most designers of the Order's buildings were tasked with when planning the exteriors of those properties.

The gallery was large and grandiose both within and without. The exterior was made from an astonishingly white marble with several lighter colours, red, blue and yellow, running through it. The front entrance consisted of four large pillars with a huge door in the centre. The pillars were made of the same remarkable marble as the rest of the building and the door was made out of a combination of Bocote wood and rhodium and platinum metals. The metal covered most of the door and it beautifully reflected the light away from it, as if it was a sign that light wasn't welcome inside. The large window above the pillars appeared to let through lots of light as did the two windows either side of the door. David thought to himself that they must be tinted. It was a well-known fact to the members of the Order that there were several forms of tinted windows that allowed vampires to see the sunlight, to see the sun rise and set.

The thought of not seeing the sun set or rise again directly quickly played out in David's head. It saddened him. For him it was one of the many reasons why being a vampire was so undesirable. Edging closer to the door, David's eyes fell upon two large golden knockers. As he reached to knock, his eyes flicked towards a small sign with a buzzer underneath.

'Do not use knockers. Please ring the bell.'

He immediately stopped his hand as it gripped the left knocker; slowly and quietly he removed it. He then hit the buzzer. He could not hear the loud ringing that played out behind the doors, but he sensed that the buzzer worked.

The left door opened creakily and to David's surprise, there was no one there.

"Hello?" he said as he peered through the opening.

"Enter," said a soft male voice from within.

David did as he was told, although his intuition told him not to; fear attempted to freeze his walk, but his limbs still moved. The room into which he entered was large and open. There were several people working at the far end, lit by the sunlight coming through the windows. Walking in a few steps, the door slammed hard behind him and his heart jumped into his throat.

"Can I help you?" said a man, dressed in a dark blue suit and walking toward David.

David moved slowly, the man's voice was disarming. With one flick, he unstrapped his bag and swung it around into his hands. In one swift move, he pulled out the envelope.

"I have a letter for Miss O'Hara," he said, stretching out his hand, keen to maintain his distance.

"Oh!" replied the man, intrigued. He took the envelope from David and examined it intensely.

"Is she here? I just need her to sign for it," as David said this he pulled an electronic pad from the holster on his side.

"Maybe. Who is it from?" questioned the man.

"It's from the Order of Light. I have been told to make sure she gets it," David said importantly, puffing out his chest slightly.

"Okay, she will read it, don't worry. I will make sure of that," the man sounded untrustworthy to him and as intimidated as he was, David stood his ground.

"I'm sorry sir, but I need her to sign this herself and I cannot leave until I have her signature on record."

The man eyed David up and down. He knew he was just like every other Order employee: obnoxious, self-important and defiantly persistent.

"Fine. Don't move," growled the man as he turned and walked off.

Standing there on his own, David began to look around the building. For a gallery it appeared to be very bare. Only two portraits adorned the walls. They were of a man and a woman, both old in appearance. It was clear to him that they were vampires. The woman's eyes seemed to have a lock on him and something about them sent a shiver down his spine and made the hairs on the back of his neck stand up. Frozen to the spot, he found it hard to move his eyes from the woman's. His gaze only broke free when a stern female voice echoed in his ears.

"Hello? Thank you for the letter. I'm told I have to sign something?"

David stood there for a second, blank. Isobel O' Hara had a presence about her that would make any room stand to attention. David found her attractive, which was strange, he thought, not because she was a vampire, but because of her age. He knew that she was one of the oldest vampires around today.

"Hello?" she repeated, waving the letter in front of his eyes.

David shook himself, "Ah, yes. Sorry. Sign here please."

She signed it quickly and then gave him a little nod as if to ask if there was anything else. As he slid the pad back into the holster and made his way back towards the door, he glanced up at the paintings again and said, "It's a bit bare in here isn't it? For an art gallery I mean." He then pointed to the portrait of the woman and asked, "And who is she?"

"Oh," Isobel said as she glanced over her shoulder to the painting. "This is just the lobby. There are one hundred other rooms in this building and I can assure you that our collection fills them all quite substantially. That woman, my inquisitive young friend, is Passel, one of the original vampires of this world."

David glared at the painting for another ten seconds as if the connection was remade. He had heard of the famous vampire of course, but had never seen a painting of her.

"I'm sorry, but if you would like a tour you'll have to book; there is a long waiting list," as Isobel spoke she pointed towards the door.

David took the hint and began moving in the same direction as Isobel had indicated. As he turned back to say goodbye, he saw Isobel talking to the suited man he had spoken to earlier. As he stepped through the door, he quickly glanced back again and had one last look at the painting.

Isobel ran her hand along the envelope as though reading a hidden message trapped within the paper.

"It's from him isn't it?" questioned the man.

"I believe so," she replied. She ran a long, pretty black fingernail along the seam of the envelope and slit it open. She quickly but gracefully pulled out the parchment from within and read.

Isobel,

I am sorry to have to put my request in writing; I know how you frown upon it. There are several things I urgently need to discuss with you. If you are able, I would like to meet you at our place tonight (10:30 pm).

Yours
Jon

Isobel clutched the letter in her hand and brought it to her side.

"Are you going to go?" asked the man who had read the letter over her shoulder.

"To not would be a mistake," she replied. With that, she left her companion and made haste to her office. She read the letter another ten times before disposing of it in her fireplace.

...

The sun had set only a few minutes ago but already Isobel was in her car, making her way to meet Jonathon Paige – Head of the Order of Light. They had met several times in the past, secretively. Both of their affiliations would disapprove of such meetings, but for Isobel and Jonathon, it was important to ensure that a line of communication was always open between the two sides.

The long summer days had quickly come around, Isobel thought. Summertime, to most vampires, was the worst time of the year. The sun was not only stronger in its intensity but it stretched longer and higher in the sky. As the centuries had passed, vampires had made many advances in avoiding the sun and getting around the rules that governed their deaths.

As the car pulled up, it parked on double yellow lines. Isobel stepped out and signalled to her driver to do the ride around the block. She could see the faces of the clock tower of the houses of Westminster. From across the water, the lights of the houses reflected beautifully on the river. As Isobel gazed upon it she stood in admiration; democracy was one of the human concepts she greatly admired.

Looking across the road, she could see Lambeth Palace, the home of the Archbishop of Canterbury. It sent shudders down her spine as the images of Christ looked down at her from afar. Vampires were not affected by the church but the concepts of God repulsed many. Walking over the grass, her heels did not dig deeply into the mud, as it was dry from the constant rays of sun.

Jonathon's silhouette was clearly visible from where she walked and as she got closer she could see his dark, greasy hair. Within seconds, she elegantly slid next to him on the bench where he sat.

"Nice view, isn't it?" she said.

"There are better ones," replied Jonathon.

Isobel crossed her legs and wrapped her coat tightly around her body.

"Well, it is one of my favourites," she said, pausing for a second, "so why have you broken our routine? What could be so urgent that you couldn't wait another fortnight?"

Jonathon pulled out a file and without making eye contact, slid it into her soft, pale hands. "I love how cliché this is," he smiled.

"Well, you do like to keep to your beliefs of hiding things in plain sight!" she grinned back.

As she opened the file Jonathon spoke, more sombre than before, "Her name is Tanya. And she turned a week ago."

"Is this the attack of the fifteenth?" Isobel asked.

"Yes. You were aware of it then?"

"Of course!" she exclaimed. "The whole Council were made aware. We were naturally concerned. I was charged with the investigation. But I must congratulate you on your excellent cleaning-up skills," Isobel closed the folder and returned it to him.

"Thank you. So will you take her off our hands?" Jonathon said, still not making eye contact.

"Of course. We would never turn away one of our own. I suppose you are asking me to keep this from the Council?"

"Could you?" Jonathon requested, with a tone that conveyed he was sure she would.

"Yes," she replied, "I do not see it as a major problem. I will send a car for her tomorrow. It will have to be a secret location. The Council monitors your headquarters."

"Yes. The Hampstead house will be sufficient, I think?" he looked at her and nodded.

"Agreed. So what else?" she asked, looking at her watch.

Jonathon considered asking her about Oliver, to see if she knew anything, to examine her response. Questions popped into his head about Leceth. He considered asking them, but the conditions of their meetings ruled out espionage. She did not like to be asked direct questions about Council members. She was a true lady, never asking questions about the Order. She always followed the rules that they had set up seven years ago when they had had their first meeting together.

"Have you learnt about the death of Oliver McKenzie?" he asked, turning to watch her expression.

"The Council has been informed. I'm not sure why. Môn'ark was asked to start an investigation. I too was asked to look into it. The Council is worried about your response, but I tell you this: they had nothing to do with his death," she said darkly.

"What about Leceth?" as the words left his lips he regretted them.

"If he is behind it, then we are in trouble. If you want the truth, I do not know if he is. Following Leceth's activities is dangerous, especially for me. We do not see eye to eye on a lot of issues within the Council. He is more than suspicious about my activities and, given the chance, he would gladly see me replaced," as she said this, she looked at Jonathon with gloom. Jonathon mulled over her expression and wondered if it was more from sadness than fear.

"Really?" Jonathon considered just how dangerous this meeting was for her.

"Well, I am an asset to the Council," she said with more confidence, "I am clearly the most knowledgeable person in the Council with regards to the Order and the Treaty. Leceth might wish to remove me, but he does need me. So, as you can imagine, we have an interesting working relationship," she took a long look around.

"Well, perhaps we should meet somewhere else in the future? Cliché or not, this is not very secretive," Jonathon replied as he too looked around.

"No, this is fine. If we keep to the usual dates it should be okay," she rose to her feet, sensing that the meeting was nearing an end. "The car will arrive tomorrow at 2am. How is the woman anyway? How is she coping?"

"She is okay," Jonathon, replied less than enthusiastically, "she is disorientated and scared, but I have told her about you and the work that you do."

"Good. Well I have lots to do, Jon. I have several sisters to show around the amazing works of Gastro Sinclair. One of the more appealing vampire artists of the seventeenth century," she began to walk back to her car as it pulled up just at the right time.

"Goodnight," he said, but Isobel was clearly too far away to hear. He said it more to himself really. He looked at her and smiled. Perhaps it was a vampire thing but she looked so graceful as she moved towards her car and slowly stepped in.

As the car drove away, he turned his attention back to the Houses of Parliament.

He took the view in again. *Well if it is one of Isobel's favourite views, who was I to argue?* he thought.

...

Days soon turned into weeks and before Kristian could really gather his bearings, five whole weeks had passed and he was still no closer to completing his investigation than when he started. He had visited all thirty-nine locations laid out in the mission file, from bars and dark magic bookshops to warehouses and factories. Not one of the sites produced any leads, not one scrap of evidence was found.

Each day he reported to headquarters, generally phoning in at around five in the evening. More often than not he reported to Rachel. A couple of times Jonathon had logged his reports, he often sounded very weary. Kristian's investigation was not the only one that was not going as well as had been expected. Sam had told him that Zhing was also having trouble. Tom was always one step ahead of her, skipping from country to country by any means possible. She had managed to track him down in Edinburgh and had a brief scuffle with him, but due to the risk to members of the public, Zhing had backed off and he had once again escaped her grasp and vanished without a trace.

Everything seemed to be an obstacle in the Order's day-to-day running at the moment. Jonathon found it difficult just chairing the simplest of meetings of late. Both Zhing and Kristian's investigations played heavily on his mind. His train of thought often drifted and as the days went on he became more and more concerned for their well-being. To top it all off the worst date in his calendar seemed to be approaching more quickly than it had ever done in the past. The days and weeks flashed by and the meeting between the Order and the Council of Tivernal had crept up on him filling him with a bilious feeling as he readied himself for the event. The half-year Amendment summit was a half-day affair when the Order and the Council would meet to discuss the events of the past six months and the future six months.

The second meeting for this year was as bad as Jonathon had imagined it would be. It was the first meeting he had attended without anyone from the Phoenix Legacy with him. Their presence at these meetings always symbolised the strength of the Order and was viewed by the Council as the Order's greatest weapon. Representing the Order of Light was Jonathon, Peter, Dr. Gambon, and Andrew. The Council had sent four delegates as well which was the standard protocol. Leceth headed his delegation, which included Isobel O'Hara from one of the Noble Vampire houses. She was named the Keeper of Knowledge and was a prominent member of the Council.

The two other companions were Ghost from the Warriors Guild of the Shadow, who represented the many gifted organisations affiliated to the Council, and Volvir Santiago, a dark warlock whom the Order knew very little about; other than that he was an avid practitioner in dark magic and had used expertise in this to preserve his age.

The Treaty Scriptures demanded that the meeting be held in a truly neutral place but this had always been difficult as both sides had different opinions as to what was to be considered neutral. The venue for the meeting was always confirmed by the Arbitrators, who made it quite clear that they were watching the proceedings. This year it was being held in an unmarked mansion, just outside of Oxford, unknown by either side.

The house was grand, clean and empty, the present owners having put it up for sale several months previously. Both delegations arrived in the dead of night, under cloaks of secrecy and security. As well as the eight actual delegates each side was allowed two members of their security forces. It was mid-July and the meeting started at 11.30pm.

Jonathon found the meetings tiresome, as nothing ever really got resolved. The Council was always concerned that the Order was being far too oppressive to their people and that they desired more freedom. The Order would argue that the numbers of vampires, werewolves and other demonic forms were always high and this would stretch the Order's resources too far. Each side always listened to the other, nodding in agreement but never agreeing a way forward in words. The only thing that was ever secured by the half-year Amendment meeting was the relative peace it allowed to continue.

The meeting lasted into the early hours of the following morning and many issues were adjourned or postponed until the next conference as the vampires had requested to leave before sunrise. Jonathon agreed eagerly. He was more than happy to bring the meeting to an end for another six months. His eyes drooped down as the bags underneath them weighed heavily. Andrew and Peter were both exhausted, whilst Susan was still full of energy. It had been her first time attending one of these meetings and she was always keen to learn more about the intricate duplicity between the Order and the Council.

Returning to Headquarters Jonathon considered what he would define as the successes and failures of the meeting. He managed to count the successes on one hand but when thinking of the failures he quickly ran out of digits. He reflected on what the outcome of an all-out war would be. He knew deep down that the Order could muster far more resources than the Council; both of the magical kind and manpower, including the gifted and non-gifted. They also had the Phoenix Legacy at their command, a never-ending legion of warriors who would continue the fight until victory was achieved. He knew that any war between the Order and the Council would have only one outcome – victory for the Order.

He then began to think about the cost of such a victory. Millions dead, even more maimed, countless displaced.

The devastation would be unimaginable; that was the reason the Order had never struck first. Not because it was ever worried about losing, but the fact that winning such a war would come at such an unacceptably high price meant it would not taste like victory at all.

...

Kristian sat on the river's edge looking into the water wondering about Oliver's last hours on earth. The soothing sound of the water lapping the verge of the bank and the birds flying overhead were the only noises he could hear. In the distance and beyond he could see boats, and on the other side of the bank there were several tower blocks of flats. The noise from the boats and the flats drifted over towards Kristian who somehow managed to block them out.

This was the spot, he realised. This is where Oliver's lonely body had drifted, where it had been discovered.

Kristian noticed his backside was wet from sitting on the damp grass, and the jeans he was wearing were turning a dirty shade of green.

The last hours of Oliver's life haunted Kristian; he wondered what would go through his mind if he were in a similar situation. Oliver was probably the bravest man that he had ever met and considering who his friends were, that was no easy feat.

The sun had set many hours ago and Kristian had wanted to be out patrolling the streets but his legs were tired and his mind drained. He had spent the long weeks searching in vain for some small clue. Nothing ever came his way; he never seemed to have that lucky break he so desperately needed.

As the evening drifted on he felt the urge to go home, get some sleep and to re-evaluate his plan tomorrow. The thought of giving up and going back to London crossed his mind, but he had little to go home for. Term was over and exams were finished. Jess was having a wonderful time with Jason, as she had told him on the phone.

If there was one thing he wanted to go home for it was Jess, but she was happy enough without him. Sure, she worried about him, but she was in love and that took up most of her time. The memory of her face disarmed him in a way he never thought it would, and her voice had brought a clarity to his chaotic mind. Even the thought of investigating Solasis Krull could not motivate him to go back; he was staying put for as long as he needed.

Moving back into the main grounds, trees blocked out most of the light from the city and the parks lamps. Slowly making his way through the gloom he reached the path; nerves jangled, the feeling that he was being watched crept over him, prickling. He turned suddenly, jumping on the spot ready to face whatever was behind him but to his surprise there was nothing and nobody there. Heaving a sigh of relief, he turned back to the path but was taken aback to find it blocked by an ominous silhouette right in front him. Preparing his defence, he raised his fists and awaited a blow. When one did not come, he cautiously looked through his arms and made out a tall, thin woman. Her full appearance was hard to discern in the dark but it was clear that she was a vampire, her complexion pale and figure slim. He hesitated for an instant over whether to launch into an attack but something told him he wasn't in direct danger and that he should ask some questions of his would-be attacker.

"Who are you?" he shouted threateningly.

The vampire responded instantly, fearing that if she did not calm this man's nerves, she would soon be dead, "My name is Leandra. I honestly mean you no harm."

Kristian scanned the area around him, looking for others. He was sure she would not be alone, and he was certain she was a vampire, and no vampire could be trusted.

"Mean me no harm, huh?" he scoffed with his arms still raised, defensively, but ready to attack. "So I suppose creeping up on people in the dead of night is normal for friendly vampires in Germany is it?"

She was taken aback the instant he said vampire; she was astonished. She had been told that the Phoenix held impressive intuitive powers, but she could not help feeling impressed.

"I'm sorry for creeping up on you, but it's not safe for me to talk to you openly. You see, my friend, not all vampires are your enemies," her voice was soft and gentle.

Listening to the tone of her voice as well as what Leandra had said, Kristian relaxed a little. Feeling slightly more at ease, he lowered his fists.

"Well, I have never met one who isn't. I assume Leceth sent you to warn me off?"

"No!" she said emphatically and somewhat abruptly, "I do not serve Leceth. My master is far braver and more honourable than he will ever be. As I've said, I'm your friend. Not all vampires are bad, believe it or not. There are still some who hold up the foundations of the Treaty. There are loads like me that believe that peace is beneficial for all races, not just humanity."

Kristian could hardly believe his ears; never before had he heard anything like this. If there were factions out there who supported the Treaty and the Order, he was sure he would have been told. *Wouldn't he?* he thought.

"Okay," he said warily, "just say that I believe you, why are you telling me this? And why are you here now?"

"The truth is, I've been following you for weeks now, and this has been the first chance I have had to speak to you away from prying eyes. Just as I have followed you, I followed your friend – the other Phoenix."

His heart stood still. Suddenly a breakthrough. He fought back the urge to attack this woman, to hurt her. Where had she and her 'we can all be friends' sentiments been when Oliver was having his heart ripped out of his chest? Casting these thoughts aside, he realised that she had information; she may be able to help him.

"Oliver," he whispered, "do you know what happened to him?" His voice was trembling with emotion.

The vampire looked down at the ground, a look of sorrow on her face.

"Well, I had managed to keep track of him most of the time. His death, I did not witness. I lost him several days before that occurred." Her explanation going some way to placate Kristian's initial anger, she stretched out her hand and held out a piece of paper. Taking it from her immediately, Kristian smoothed it out into his palm. It was a receipt of some kind.

"What is this?" Kristian barked, bemused.

Leandra looked over her shoulder, "We must move quickly. It is a shipping order receipt for an ancient artifact – for what? I know not. All I do know is that the Phoenix obtained it from a barman at *Das Ferkel*. The next day he went to the address on the receipt," as she spoke she pointed to an address at the top of the piece of paper.

"It's a warehouse on the outskirts of the city. A Herr Bauch, who shows up on none of our records, owns it. The Phoenix broke into the premises and that is the last time I saw him."

Kristian had finally got the clue he was after. He moved closer to the vampire and in a moment, which in retrospect he deemed foolish, he embraced her tightly. Pulling himself back, he whispered, "Thank you."

"Please, there is no need to thank me. Just be careful, okay? I cannot help you if you go there alone. You will need help if you plan to break in. Help I cannot offer." Again, as she spoke, she looked over her shoulder scanning the outline of the trees. "I must leave." Wasting no time at all, she darted backwards and was soon lost to the shadows.

Kristian remained on his spot for what seemed like an eternity. He thought about what he had just been told and knew he must head to *Das Ferkel* and speak to the barman Leandra had told him about. He suddenly remembered that he had already visited this bar and that the barman had told him that he had never seen Oliver. *Lying swine*, he thought. Crunching the receipt in his left hand, he began to make a plan of action in his head. He would go to the tavern and this time be more forceful with the barman. Then he would return to the hostel and report straight back to Jonathon. A smile crossed his face; finally, he was getting somewhere. He started into a jog, which soon became a sprint and in no time at all he was leaping over the fence at the edge of the park.

...

It was not long before Kristian found himself walking down the stone stairs and pushing through the glass doors of *Das Ferkel*. As soon as he entered, all the heads turned to look at him warily, and then quickly returned to their drinks. He instantly clocked the barman who on seeing Kristian looked panicked. Walking over to the bar, Kristian calmly drifted through the sea of people and with one hand signal, gently leaned over the counter at the bar and loudly spoke in the barman's ear. Shaking and almost dropping the bottle in his hands, the barman heard every word Kristian said. "We need a little chat. I don't think that you have been entirely honest with me."

Gulping, the barman nodded and pointed in the direction of an empty booth in the corner. Walking around the bar, he whistled at one of the three barmaids who were all busy flirting with the many leery male customers and with one arm, pointed towards the bar.

Kristian allowed the barman to walk in front of him; there was a part of him that felt more than uncomfortable turning his back on this lowlife. Sitting down in the booth, Kristian smiled and then quickly jumped into questions about the warehouse, Oliver and the receipt.

The conversation lasted for twenty minutes and the barman was more than compliant, divulging everything that Kristian wanted to know. He told him that the building was once owned by a Herr Bauch who passed away last year and that there were vampires living there now.

Kristian felt like the exchange was going well; the barman had found out about the delivery of an ancient artifact to the warehouse and told Oliver about it. Oliver had been far more intimidating the first time they had met and the barman was not so witless as to try to keep information from him. This sounded feasible to Kristian. He now had two accounts of Oliver knowing about this special delivery and going to the warehouse. It seemed to him that Oliver would have visited the place searching for answers. Suppressing the urge to go to the warehouse immediately and break in himself, he realised that he had to be smarter than that if he wanted to last longer than Oliver. Besides, Leandra, the vampire, and the barman could just be telling him exactly what he wanted to hear! However, his Phoenix intuition was telling him that he was not being lied to this time. He knew he should return to the hostel and call Jonathon. He thought about waiting for backup, then with reinforcements, pounce on the warehouse, and make the bastards pay.

Once Kristian believed that he had extracted all relevant information he left the bar feeling much more hopeful. He sensed that nothing could now go wrong, he had his lead; Oliver's killers would soon be brought to justice and he could return home to London, to Jess.

However, unbeknown to Kristian, his hopes might have be misplaced; he had been so engrossed in his conversation with the barman that he had not maintained a watch of his surroundings, as he had been trained to do. Kristian was completely unaware that his conversation and movements in *Das Ferkel* had been closely watched by a hooded figure in the corner. His eyes had not once left Kristian and as Kristian left, the man in the hood had followed him out. Looking across the street, ducking in and out of the shadows, he followed Kristian, staying a few steps behind him. His feet moved gracefully; he was swift and cunning. He had been well coached, his job required this special tactical gift. Staying far enough back not be noticed, he was close enough to hear the boy's mobile phone conversation. Jess had phoned Kristian to see how he was getting on. After his breakthrough with the investigation, Kristian was so happy that he began to tell Jess every detail of what he was doing. His joy was making him more open and honest than he was normally.

Still following closely behind, the hooded figure slowly steadied his pace, so as to keep a safe distance from Kristian. Kristian slowed to concentrate more on his chat with Jess.

After tracking Kristian for thirty minutes, the hooded man was getting weary; luckily for him though, they had eventually reached the hostel. Kristian fumbled for his keys and unlocked the outer door and let himself in.

Stepping even further back, the man watched Kristian enter his hostel. *This is it*, he thought to himself. This boy was a Phoenix and he had just explained his entire mission to his friend on the phone. Reaching for his own phone, the man found a number and placed it to his ear.

A few seconds later he spoke, "Hey, this is Canola. You will not believe this. They have sent another Phoenix. Come here quick. He is going to pay us a lot for this one!"

...

- Chapter Ten -

The Face of the Enemy

Walking through the door Kristian managed to take off his jacket whilst still on the phone to Jess and threw it onto the sofa. The room still had a mouldy smell to it, even though he had left the windows open for the last three weeks. Discarded takeaway trays were everywhere. Although he had paid not to share his room at the hostel with anyone it was still smelly and mould-ridden; fortunately it was large in size and split into two separate rooms. One half had a single bed and cupboards, it was separated from the other room by two short walls that stretched a metre out from either side. This other room contained a sofa bed, angled towards a bookshelf with three German and one Polish book on it.

"Okay. Okay. I've got to go now. I need to check in," Kristian said in a tone that suggested that he really didn't want to go.

"All right but I want you to ring me tomorrow when you have checked the place out, okay? Take care," Jess replied.

"I Will," said Kristian, as he ended the call and tossed the phone onto the sofa. Walking into the bedroom he sat on the bed he was using and began to take his shoes off, then his watch. Placing his watch on the bedside cabinet he glanced at the time as he put it down. It was ten to one German time, which made it ten to twelve back home; he wondered for an instant who would be up if he called now. It was a thought that wasn't designed to put him off making the call, he was just curious and his mind was wondering. Probably Rachel, she always seemed to be up these days, always doing the extra shift. *She is soon going to work herself ill*, he thought.

Walking back towards the sofa he looked around the floor, his eyes scanning for any food that looked edible. There was clearly nothing on the floor that he could eat without running the risk of spending the next day with his face down the toilet. He then spotted a half-full bottle of now flat and warm Coke on the floor. Picking it up and quickly taking off the top with barely a fizz, Kristian drained the remainder of the two-litre bottle without taking a breath. Wiping his face he chucked the empty plastic bottle on the floor with the rest of the rubbish. Looking around at the mess, he felt a little disgusted in himself, he had never been such a slob before, it was just the mission, he told himself.

Report in, he thought as he picked up his phone and walked back to the bed. Sitting on the edge of the bed he began to flip through his contact list until he came across the phone number he needed. His thumb hovered over the number for a second and just before he could press it the lights in the room went out. Standing up instantly his eyes strained to adapt to the sudden darkness and before he could think of anything else a large explosion sounded in his room. Blue light lit the room as the front door flew off its hinges and smashed against the opposing wall. Diving for cover without thought, Kristian found himself sprawled out behind the sofa. Lying there, filled with a sense of shock, he heard two quietly spoken voices.

"Where is he?" enquired the first.

"He has to be in here. Shit," the second replied.

Both spoke in English with distinctive accents that were clearly not British. *Two of them*, Kristian thought to himself. The room was pitch-black and he was hard-pressed to see anything, the blue flash having ruined his night vision completely. Raising himself up slightly, his hand gripped tightly to the top of the sofa as he gingerly peered over the top. The silhouettes of two large men were visible in the doorway; squinting his eyes to try and pinpoint their position exactly, Kristian realised he was going to be forced to act on his instincts, rather than skill.

Lifting himself upright to his knees, he threw out his hand in the direction of the doorway. The room was suddenly lit by a flash of dazzling jade light as a bolt of energy left Kristian's hand and flew towards the intruders. As he began to drop back down to the safety of his sofa hiding place, he glimpsed the bolt of light he had just launched hit its intended target square and cleanly in the face. Down on the floor Kristian was unable to see the outcome of the impact but merely heard a loud thud as his victim's body landed heavily on the floor.

A jubilant smile crossed his face, *I will definitely be trying that again!* he thought to himself, but before he could move, blue light jetted across the room accompanied by a deafening crackle. Originating from where Kristian presumed the second man must be a further bolt of lightning-like energy arced towards him. As these forks of blue electricity-like energy hit the sofa, sparks and flames flew off in every direction, instantly transforming into a blazing inferno; chunks of material and wood rained down about the room. Kristian, covered in tiny flames that began to burn his body, rolled on the floor in an attempt to extinguish them; he knew he had to escape quickly before he succumbed to fire or his tormentor. Briskly leaping to his feet, he dived forward and rolled alongside his bed; clambering backwards he found refuge against the separating wall. As he moved swiftly and elegantly through the room his attacker tried in vain to blast him with the blue jets of energy. The electrical charge bounced off everything it hit, discharging sparks up into the air and setting fire to the carpet and bed covers. The air soon began to thicken quickly with smoke and fumes. Kristian was finding it increasingly difficult to breathe, he knew he had to move against the last attacker; now or never.

Closing his eyes, he thought back to the training he had been taught over two years ago; listening hard for his Phoenix, he was asking for advice. The noise in the room was deafening, the several small fires burning throughout were crackling and spitting, the constant blasting of the wall Kristian was pinned against by his attacker made it nigh on impossible to concentrate. With so much going on around him he knew he would never be able to reach the level of meditation and focus he would need to talk to his Phoenix. What he needed to do was to act expeditiously.

Moving back towards the sofa and his unseen foe, Kristian nimbly stretched out his hand from which emanated a large gleaming jade-coloured shield protecting his entire body. His attacker's energy impacted it with immense force, but no flames came off it, no sparks were produced. Kristian began to navigate past the sofa, through the flames, ensuring his arm was out and his shield was up. He angled it towards his attacker and with each step he got closer and closer to him. Using both hands his attacker's face was showing signs of fatigue as his blue jets of electricity started to become weaker and sporadic. It wasn't long before Kristian stood directly in front of the shadowy figure, with his green force field still emerging from his palms, large and strong. His attacker, weakened, could no longer stretch out his hands; he was pressed against the wall, arms forced against his sides. Sensing his opponent was now compromised Kristian quickly dropped his shield; as he lowered the projecting hand his other fist speedily swung through the air until it connected with the man's face with a rather squelching thud.

Falling to the floor, the figure was rendered unconscious from one clean and perfect punch. Turning around and looking at his room he couldn't believe his eyes: in no more than ten minutes, the place that had been his home from home was now unrecognisable and fiercely ablaze, his possessions, the file; all was lost.

Wanting to waste no more time dwelling on what was lost he quickly exited the door. The alarm in the hostel suddenly began to clang, the hallway instantly flooded with people, all trying to escape. Quickly glancing behind him he could see the figures of his attackers sprawled out, unmoving on the floor, almost one on top of the other. He contemplated going back and dragging them from the burning room but he shrugged off the thought. *I'm not that kind of hero*, he told himself.

Brushing past person after person he exited the hallway and entered a stairway; he wanted to leave the area before any official arrived. The fire door at the bottom of the stairs was wide open and jostling through the crowds Kristian was finally outside staring up at his window above, now fiery red with smoke billowing out of it. Around him hordes of people were all staring and pointing up towards his room.

"Are you okay?" a voice asked.

"Yes, I'm good thanks," replied Kristian, pausing in mid-sentence to realise that he was speaking English, responding to a question that had been asked in English.

Turning to look more closely at the man who had spoken, he jerked his arm out and grabbed the man's outstretched hand, which had been reaching for his chest. Kristian's grip locked tightly onto his questioner's wrist, which now pressed against Kristian's chest. Though his reflexes were fast they weren't quick enough! He had been determined to throw the hand off his chest but was finding himself becoming immobile. A weird sensation drifted throughout his entire body, a freezing bleakness steadily permeated his being; his mind drifted, he could think of nothing else other than the death of his brother so many years ago. Kristian's eyes became increasingly heavy; the numbness spread, along with the cold, all over his body and into his limbs. His hands dropped to his sides, releasing the lock he had on his opponent's wrist.

Staring into the man's eyes, they seemed somewhat familiar to him. Looking down, his eyes drifted to his hands, his veins appeared thick and dark green. Unable to concentrate on anything at all, his eyes finally closed and as he slumped forward his vanquisher caught him before he hit the ground. Kristian's head flopped, now pale and looking lifeless, veins protruding, ropey thick and seaweed green.

...

Not sure whether he had opened his eyes or not Kristian turned his head in both directions unable to make anything out. The room was darker than anything he had experienced before, a sudden dread pervaded his mind: *I'm dead!* The feeling in his chest felt like a blade, penetrating deep, the sensation though painful was strangely reassuring, at least he could feel something and logically this meant he was still alive! His heartbeat was loud and fast, the sound reverberated across the room; apart from his breathing, it was the only thing he could hear.

He began to think about the last thing he could remember; the events of the attack were being played out in his mind. Analysing it step by step, he could not help but be critical of his performance; he was much too slow and made the wrong decisions. As he tried to rise to his feet pain shot up through his legs and into his arms. Though unable to see them he could feel restraints holding his limbs tightly to the chair he was sitting on. Feeling for what he could touch, Kristian could tell that the chair was wooden and he was bound to it with a thin plastic-fibre rope.

He began to wriggle, furiously attempting to loosen the straps and break free. But as he struggled the ropes seem to tighten and the pain increased as they began to dig deep into his flesh. His skin began to crack under his frantic movements; blood began to trickle down his hands and drip onto the floor. His heart raced faster and with it the blood trickled more rapidly from the deep wounds; he knew he had to think of a way to escape as his efforts, so far, were less than fruitless.

Trying to calm himself down he took a breath and identified his first priority – 'survey and evaluate one's surroundings', in the wise words of Yi-Mao. For this it was obvious he desperately needed a source of light to illuminate the room and to achieve this he was going to have to rely on his non-palm projection technique, which, he would freely admit, he had never mastered to an adequate level. But he had to try; closing his mind and searching deep within, he revisited his training, the skills he had been taught. Using the energy from his Phoenix, he began to imagine a small sphere of light hovering a metre in front of him. Within seconds a soft jade light started to fill the room, as there, floating above him, a shining, swirling globe of green light had materialised.

Kristian attempted to twist himself as best he could, quickly glancing at his surroundings. The room was bare, grey brick walls with no paint or wallpaper. Covered in damp and dirt the only objects in the room other than the chair appeared to be some old shelf fittings, the shelving itself missing, fastened to the walls. Though rusty, and at least two metres from the ground, the iron brackets appeared sturdy and appeared to have somewhat sharp edges. Shadows darkened, the globe overhead that had started the size of a tennis ball had shrunk over the preceding seconds and was now no bigger than a spinning penny. The green light continued to diminish until it finally vanished from sight and the room returned to darkness.

Closing his eyes and doing his best to concentrate, Kristian was just in the midst of producing another ball of energy when a loud screeching noise broke the quiet and an intensive white light pervaded the room. Looking up, Kristian could see a door directly opposite him; light flooded into the room like water through a dam. Appearing to curve, the light bent around a figure standing in the doorway. Striding rapidly straight towards him, the figure lifted his left arm above his head and immediately swung it swiftly down to strike Kristian's face violently.

Dazed by the sudden blow and spitting a mouthful of blood to the floor, Kristian raised his head to find the face of his abuser. There, standing in front of him, was the man who had so easily apprehended him earlier, or however long ago it was now. There had been a spark of recognition at their prior meeting at the hostel but now a sudden realisation hit Kristian and a name projected itself across his mind: Canola.

Canola, a renowned hired hand for those who required a cold, callous brute to do their dirty work, a man to fear.

Kristian had seen his face many times during his early training; though he had perused many mugshots and files of those the Order had regular encounters with, Canola was one of a few that had stuck in his mind both for his ugliness and the fearsome attacks and murders he was responsible for.

"Well, well. I'm more than a little surprised that the Order has sent you on your own or did you come with someone else? Have you got to check back with the Order?" Canola rubbed his hands together as he spoke, his voice cold and with a hint of glee.

Kristian considered not speaking; would silence work, he wondered? Though he could have answered the man with the repetition of name, rank and number, toeing the line to try and placate Canola, he felt he would give a little sass.

"Check in, should've done it hours ago. And alone, well maybe, maybe not. The Order is fully aware of my whereabouts and I'm sure by now that they're already on their way." Kristian spoke with confidence; even though he knew his words were false, his lips stretched in an effort to form a smile.

Canola laughed, the sound deep and echoing in the dank, neglected room.

"You can wish, kid, you can wish! Let me tell you this. You, my friend, need to check in at three later today. You came alone. And no one is coming for you. Not in time anyway," Canola mocked.

Kristian's lips twitched for an instant but his smile remained, "Well, if that's what you think. But if I don't check in, they'll know something's not right."

Canola's eyes looked deep into Kristian's, greatly unnerving Kristian who could do nothing but stare back. Lowering his body Canola moved closer and began to put his weight onto Kristian's firmly tied legs.

Leaning further forward Canola said without any emphasis, "Maybe after about a day or two, your guys might begin to get suspicious." Kristian nodded in agreement.

"But that will not do you any good. Because you'll be dead by then," Canola said with a dark sinister grin.

The words hit Kristian like another blow to his face. His smile faded as Canola's grew.

Rising to his feet Canola walked out of the room.

Sitting there imprisoned by the rope Kristian could not help but be overwhelmed with fear; he knew that he needed to be level-headed and emotionless, be collected and resolute, but his mind flooded with thoughts about the prospect of his own death.

Re-entering the room some minutes later, Canola walked in with another figure; again the face seemed familiar to Kristian. The astonished look on Kristian's face made Cable laugh, "Thought I burned alive back in your room? Left me there to die, that wasn't very good of you! Your friends at the Order wouldn't be too impressed."

With his head angled towards the floor only Kristian's eyes looked up to watch Cable as he spoke. Shifting his eyes between the pair he began to work on his escape plan once again. To his delight Canola flicked a switch on the wall and the room lit up. Though only a dull white light, less like that which had flooded the room from outside, it was still illuminating enough.

Cable and Canola began to move towards him, Canola resumed his place resting on Kristian's knees whilst Cable circled him and then stopped behind him placing his hands on to his shoulders.

"I can't believe they sent you on your own. I was so hoping to kill more of your scum myself," Cable's voice sounded much like Canola's but younger almost childlike.

"I'm sorry about that. You're just going to have to put up with just my blood on your hands," Kristian replied, feeling glad for once that he had come alone.

A roar of laughter burst from both men.

"We wish, *I* wish," said Canola raising a knife towards Kristian's throat, "you see, we're not allowed to kill you. Unfortunately for you."

"Unfortunately?" said Kristian.

"Yeah, unfortunately. Well, you see, I would like to, just want to place my hands on your head and fry your brain, while Canola would more than likely wish to drain your body of every drop of energy it has. But, alas, we are forbidden to; we have our orders," Cable leant down almost whispering into his ear.

"Orders? To be honest, I wouldn't like to die in either of those ways, thank you," said Kristian.

Both men guffawed in unison, their eyes meeting over Kristian's head.

"Oh you will be wishing for us to kill you. Trust me. As you probably know, we're just the hired help, paid to bring scum like you in. Our boss wants to, I mean he needs to, finish you off himself," Cable said, his back straight and speaking forward as if proudly to the world.

"Why?" Kristian said his voice inquisitive.

"Well," pausing for an instant Canola began to think about what he was about to say. He enjoyed antagonising the Phoenix. Such a stuck-up bunch, so pompous, so bold, so very over-confident were they. It was an amazing feeling to be the one with the power! With that in mind, he wondered what he would be allowed to say? If his boss knew what he had already divulged he would be in trouble. But then again he isn't ever going to find out and Canola was having so much fun!

"Well our boss is into collecting," both men sniggered again, "he has this ritual he performs, awful painful it is, but so fun to watch. He chants several haunting incantations and then takes out some old blade, something called the 'Sword of Conccoti' or something like that, and he uses it to cut out your beating heart," Canola's words instantly permeated through Kristian's muddled thoughts into his consciousness. He had finally got the answers to his questions but they offered him no comfort, as all he could think about now was, *That's how I'm going to die.*

"Well, when Leceth cuts out your heart, you'll still be awake and aware. Well, for a bit, the previous guy didn't last long, a couple of seconds before he conked out," said Cable with a sadistic smile on his face that was wiped off when he looked at Canola and realised what he had just said.

Kristian heard Cable's words but it took him a few seconds to process them; his mind was deliberating about death, the ritual and Oliver.

"Leceth," Kristian mouthed, almost soundlessly. Canola rose to his feet and struck Kristian across the face in a vain belief that he may forget Cable's words. Cable wondered if what he had said would get him into serious trouble, but on second thoughts he knew it didn't matter. Soon Leceth would be here, soon the Phoenix would be dead and the Order of Light would be none the wiser.

Canola left the room again with Cable quickly following. Kristian's body uncontrollably burst into frantic wriggling, again his skin bled but he didn't feel pain, it was drowned out by the panic swimming through his mind.

"That's not going to cut it. You won't get out of those restraints," said Canola walking back into the room brandishing a grey-coloured piece of pottery. "You see this," he said raising the distinctive vase-shaped pottery in front of Kristian's eyes, "well, Leceth is on his way here now, three hours he will be back in Berlin and performing the ritual. And not long after that, kiddo, your heart will be in this jar!" Canola jigged the urn in front of Kristian's eyes, taunting him with it.

The urn was the size of large jug, it had strange engravings all around it and was dark grey in colour; it was like nothing Kristian had ever seen before. A large distinctive mark, a symbol, stretched across both the face of the urn and its lid.

"What is it?" asked Kristian.

Canola withdrew it towards his chest, covering it with his hand, as though protecting it from Kristian's question.

"It's an urn, an incredibly old urn made by someone very powerful, a long time ago. There are only a few around apparently. Hard to come by, rare I'm told. But I've seen two, once you've seen one though, you've seen them all," Canola's words did little to relieve Kristian's curiosity, Canola merely exaggerating his own importance.

Staring at it, his mind raced trying to commit to memory every detail of the urn. Canola held the vessel close to his chest; he began to worry about what he had revealed. He knew it had been a mistake. To inform your enemy of your plans was a sign of being the weaker. A stupid blunder, so rarely made out in the real world. It didn't matter to him, he thought, it wasn't even his plan, he didn't even understand the purpose or why Leceth was going to so much trouble, all Canola cared about was getting well paid.

"Well, sweet dreams. See you at three!" Canola sniggered as he backed out of the room, his hip pushing the door open, one hand clasping the urn, the other reaching for the light.

As the darkness returned to the room Kristian tried to bring his thoughts back round to escaping, but his brooding over Oliver's fate kept intruding. There was to be one thought and one thought only, Oliver's death! Those that had murdered Oliver were going to do away with him in the same dreadful way. Kristian's whole being was overtaken by a strong and fearful emotion. Revenge. His paramount wish was to kill Cable, Canola and this Leceth! Rage fuelled him, his only friend at this time. He was going to make them pay, all of them, anyone who had had a hand in Oliver's death. Informing the Order of Light of what had happened to Oliver, what had happened here today, all seemed so irrelevant. Revenge was his *raison d'être* now, and to fulfill his desire he had to escape.

His mind raced, *Okay. I am tied firmly to a wooden chair by rope. Okay, I have tried jiggling and I didn't move at all. The room is empty, maybe use the iron hooks on the walls. No, not possible.* That train of thought repeated in his mind, as though the answer was there and he was just too blind to see it. *Right, tied to a chair, jiggled a lot, haven't moved at all, the room is… I've jiggled and not moved.*

Desperately focusing hard, Kristian again produced another swirling ball of jade energy; the strength of his feelings seemed to enhance his power, the ball was bigger than the previous and shone even more brightly.

Looking down to his feet he could see the bottom of the chair. The wooden chair was fastened to the floor by metal screws that were fixed to the legs of the chair by metal brackets. Focusing his eyes, Kristian could barely believe what he was seeing. The screws appeared to be loose; they had been screwed into the floor but had somehow been slightly unwound back out.

How? Kristian wondered if it was his frantic moving that had lessened the screws' hold. The morbid answer came to him suddenly: *It was Oliver,* he thought. He had been sitting in this chair before his own murder; he had painstakingly used his power to free the screws and then himself. Kristian instantly realised that Oliver must have shared similar thoughts to his; that it would be too dangerous to try and cut through the rope or the chair; you could accidently slice a limb off!

Limited time was not only a factor for Kristian, it must have been one for Oliver too; and for him time had obviously run out. Blankness and nothingness engulfed his mind, the green light vanished as he gazed at the floor.

Don't die here today. Don't let Oliver have died in vain. With that thought he snapped out of the emptiness. "Time to focus, time to concentrate," he said.

Using non-palm projection, he began to focus on the screws, he began to visualise them in his mind. Holding onto that image, he started to use his powers to form a ring of energy around them. Sure enough, just as in his mind, rings of jade energy began to loop around the four screws holding the front two legs. The rings of thick green light began to tighten around the screw. This was the trickiest thing Kristian had ever tried with projection but also the most crucial. He needed to form energy tight around the screws but not so tight to cause the screws to break in half.

The rings formed, wrapping around the screws as closely as he was able to make them. He now needed to force them upwards towards his body. Straining to lift them, a slight stabbing pain pierced his mind. The screws weren't budging. It was clear to him that pure force wasn't going to remove them, he had to twist them out! Concentrating like he had never concentrated before, he began to turn the screws; the light twisted as did the screws, clockwise for nearly half a rotation, but in his mind's eye he could see the screws sinking deeper into the ground. Instantly realising he was rotating the energy force in the wrong direction he began to spin it anti-clockwise. The screws slowly began to move upwards. Sweat began to pour from his face, he could feel it trickle down his forehead, into his eyes, making them sting, and then downwards over his cheeks, dripping off his nose and chin.

It seemed as if his own body was trying to distract him, to break his single-mindedness. His face started to crease up and become increasingly flushed as he renewed his efforts to remain focused, the increased strain started to turn the slight stabbing pain in his temples into a full-blown throbbing headache.

Not allowing the pain to intrude on his state of mind, his breathing became laboured; he was not sure how much longer he could keep up this level of concentration. A small but significant sound suddenly rippled through the air: three clinking sounds followed by another. The four screws rolled along the floor, ringing as they spun. Letting out one big sigh of relief, Kristian wondered how long it had taken him to remove the screws; it must have been over fifteen minutes, he thought to himself.

His chest still pained him as his lungs sucked much-needed oxygen into his body; his heart was thumping, pounding away with the tremendous effort that had been necessary to fulfill his task. Yet, at this poignant moment, he was almost brought to tears as the reassurance of success engulfed him.

Not only did he have two enemies to consider, he also had time to contest with. Without thinking, he pushed out, forcefully; a combination of pent-up energy and muscular release propelled him backwards. The chair arms that his wrists were tied to instantly snapped. The left arm broke into thousands of tiny splinters whilst the right broke in two, one fragment forced through his shirt, digging deep into his arm causing Kristian to let out a short cry of pain. The rest of the chair collided with the ground moments later creating a resounding noise, one that must have been heard outside.

The rope loosened around his arms and he quickly untangled himself. His left arm was peppered with several small splinters cutting his arm in places. The deep rope-inflicted wounds around his wrists were also bleeding. His right arm was another story: the large shard of wood dug into his arm, its sharp point penetrating muscle and pushing against bone. With his left hand he quickly yanked the wooden stake clean out of his arm.

Blood began to flow profusely from the open wound. Removing his blackened jumper he tore the arms off and wrapped them around his right arm stemming the bleeding. Although he gritted his teeth in an attempt to stop himself yelling, he was unable to control a small moan and then a howl of pain which he stifled with a bloodied hand.

With his now untethered hands he quickly released his feet realising that someone was bound to burst through the door in response to the loud noise. Freeing himself eventually from every restraint, Kristian darted for where he believed the door to be. Feeling his way in the darkness, he quickly found the door and, moving to the left, he backed onto the wall. The light switch was prodding him in the back; he knew he couldn't turn it on, he had to wait and pounce on anyone that walked in.

Standing against the wall, not moving a muscle, time passed quickly; before he knew it, twenty minutes had gone by and no one had entered the room. What was to be his next move? He was alert, his heart beating fast, responding to the excess adrenaline coursing through his body. Reaching for the door handle, Kristian decided to exit his prison and to his delight the handle twisted and the door opened freely, thankfully with little noise.

Slowly opening the door, Kristian was on tenterhooks wondering if Cable or Canola, or worse both, were waiting to ambush him on the other side of the doorway. Surely one of them must have heard the chair smash and his involuntarily cries of pain? They must have been otherwise occupied or they would have investigated by now.

Peering through the door, another sign of good fortune was waiting for him. A long corridor now lay in front of him devoid of anyone. Slowly and noiselessly he exited the room, pulling the door shut behind him. The corridor, lit only with dull light, was at least thirty metres long with only one other door at the far side. He rapidly scanned the hallway for windows, vents, anything he could escape through, but there was absolutely nothing. The door at the end was the only route; it was his door to freedom, a door through which he was going to have to pass no matter what was on the other side.

...

- Chapter Eleven -

The Party Crasher

Standing resting his head against the door, Kristian strained to hear the voices beyond. Three distinct male voices could be heard through the door; two were familiar, that of Canola and Cable, the third was unknown to him.

"So Leceth will arrive in two hours," said Canola.

"It's risky having him here. We should have Kronos here too. We did last time. When the other Phoenix was here." said the third unknown man.

Kristian's mind was in turmoil as he endeavoured to fathom what was going on. The Dark Phoenix, Tom was in on this whole thing too. Leceth's plans were far grander than he or anyone else in the Order could possibly imagine. He felt relieved that Kronos the Dark Phoenix wasn't there; he needed to escape, to send word. A fleeting thought of worry interrupted his mind: *If Kronos is a part of this, then I hope Zhing is safe*. He instinctively knew that she; there something about hosting Phoenixes that connected them all together.

His mind drifted back to his plan of escape; he knew that the door was his only exit and he was going to have to confront all those that lay behind it. The pain in his right arm suddenly intensified and shot though his entire body. He grabbed the wound with his left hand and squeezed tightly; the pain increased. All his muscles ached dreadfully and were tightening up. He could smell the blood from the wound and could think of only one thought. *I'm going to kill them, I'm going to kill them all.*

"Well he can't be here, he's being tracked by one of them. And for that reason Leceth doesn't want him anywhere near here. I don't trust him anyway. Tom might be contracted to the Council, but he's still one of them. Carrying one of those things inside him. I'm glad he's in La Cumbrecita, out of the way. Away from me," the voice was clearly Canola's, but not so cold, it was more somewhat resentful.

"You wouldn't say that to his face, Canola. Leceth trusts him and that's enough for me. Anyway, hasn't one of us got to pick Leceth up from the airport?" the third voice said.

"Yes I'll go, I have plenty of time. And I agree with Canola. All Phoenixes are scum, and when Leceth is finished with the ones born in the Light he will deal with the Dark Phoenix," said Cable.

Kristian realised that he'd heard enough and though still fixed on revenge, his sense of duty asserted itself; he could now complete his original mission. He could return and report to Zhing on Tom's whereabouts; he wanted to tell the Order that it was Leceth.

He pushed the thoughts of what he had heard to the back of his mind and began to focus on his plan of attack. *Surprise is key*, he told himself. Summoning his Phoenix Blade crossed his mind, but the loud noise that would accompany such a calling would surely ruin any surprise. Deciding against it, Kristian was content to rely on his Kar'sin and hand-to-hand combat skills; and in the midst of battle, if needed, he could call upon his sword.

...

On the other side of the door to Kristian the three Council's agents were completely unaware of Kristian's escape. Closest to the door was Volesh, the owner of the voice that Kristian hadn't recognised. A vampire from a house in Leceth's dynasty, Volesh was sitting on a sofa watching flickering television. Further from the door sitting at a table playing cards, gambling mountain-loads of money, were Cable and Canola glancing every five minutes at their watches.

The discussion about Leceth and the Dark Phoenix had ended some time ago and they were now debating who would win in a fight between various different breeds of demons and monsters.

"Okay, so a vampire versus a werewolf?" shouted Canola.

"Come on, you really think I'm going to say werewolf? So what, a wolf just three nights a month, I could take one as a man and I could take one as a wolf," Volesh shouted back.

Canola and Cable both laughed; they both had graphic images of Volesh being ripped to shreds by a werewolf in their heads.

"Come on mate, even I wouldn't be stupid enough to take on a werewolf when he's all fur and fangs," said Canola, his voice still raised.

"Well you're not me. You two, at the end of the day, are just guys with powers. So what, Canola, if you're a bit strong because you can 'feed on energy', big whoop! I am a creature of the night, of legends."

Canola and Cable stopped playing cards, they began to contemplate whether they were offended by his remarks and before they could decide on an appropriate retort, they both just burst out into hysterical laughter.

"Creature of the night, hey! Well, with you on our side, why are we bothering with this ritual crap. We should just send you out against the Phoenixes," Cable sniggered.

"Well I reckon I could take one. So what if they're fast and strong, so am I. So what if they do that energy thing, I'm so quick they wouldn't have a chance to hit me," Volesh said tensing his muscles and enhancing his posture.

"You've changed your tune, sonny. It wasn't that long ago you were all worried about the energy-drained Phoenix we have tied up in there, it wasn't so long ago you were begging for that Dark Phoenix to be here holding your hand. It seems to me you are full of shit," Canola said as Cable burst into fits of laughter again.

Rising to his feet, Volesh was outraged, not so much by their words, but by their constant laughing. "Stop laughing or I shall show you what vampires can really do."

Both Canola and Cable took a breath and, not bothering to get up, merely glanced in Volesh's direction. A few seconds of silence passed, suddenly broken by the pair laughing again.

"Right, that's it!" Volesh said looking around for a weapon, but as he spoke a massive explosion reverberated through the room, deafening the three occupants. The room instantly filled with blinding jade light as the door near Volesh flew out of its frame and shattered against the opposite wall.

Leaping to their feet Cable and Canola strained to see what was happening, each of them rubbing their eyes. Moving quickly into the room Kristian could see a tall figure directly in front of him; having listened in to the trio's banal conversation Kristian knew this figure to be the vampire and in no time at all Kristian was upon him. With a blow to the face and several high kicks to the chest Kristian had quickly grabbed Volesh's arm, swung him back and arched his spine exposing the vampire's chest. With his spare hand Kristian reached into his pocket and pulled out the large splinter of wood that not so long ago been impaled in his right arm. With one swift movement he plunged the wooden stake deep into Volesh's heart; thick black mucus-like liquid began to spew out from the wound.

The other two men were still sitting at the card table as the speed of Kristian's entrance was quicker than their reflexes. Having managed to shift their attention from the game to the doorway, Cable and Canola were taken by complete surprise to see Kristian stake Volesh so deftly. As Volesh's limp body fell to the floor like a discarded coat the table clattered, overturned, as the pair leapt at Kristian.

Not even taking the trouble to look over, Kristian knew that the two men were now swiftly barrelling through the air towards him. His hand moving to face them faster than he could turn his head, a flash of fierce jade energy left his palm and smacked Canola cleanly in the chest, throwing him back against the wall.

Landing on his feet, Cable quickly realised he was far too close to Kristian; his advantage lay in fighting from a distance but he would have to make do and immediately raised his hand to send out blasts of his electrical energy. A bolt of blue energy forked through the air but Kristian reacted without thought and twisted himself out of the way, dodging the blast. Cable's eyes now locked onto Kristian's arched body; as his last blast dissipated, Cable slightly repositioned his hands, and with a flick of his fingers he sent more bolts roaring towards Kristian.

Kristian instantly dropped to the floor, again dodging the blast. His movements seemed to be taking only milliseconds not even seconds and before he could think about it he had already swung his leg out catching Cable behind the knee and bringing him to the floor. Cable hit the floor hard, completely taken by surprise; his lightning stopped abruptly. Quickly trying to scramble back to his feet and away he soon found himself with Kristian's hands wrapped around his face.

Kristian now had one arm locked round Cable's neck, the other hand clung tightly onto his head. He held himself back from his initial thought of killing him; one quick jolt and this man's life would be extinguished. Cable's humanity, no matter how tenuous that was, made Kristian start to question the morality of his options, but without any more thought, Kristian's grip tightened and jerked suddenly and violently to the left.

There was a crunch as Cable's neck was broken; his eyes rolled back and his body stopped writhing within seconds.

Standing up, Kristian released his grip on Cable's lifeless body, it slumped to the floor. Staring at it, a weird sensation ran through Kristian's body. What was it he wondered to himself? Without time to think about it further he sensed Canola was rising to his feet.

Looking over towards Canola, Kristian could see the dent in the wall made when he had flung him across the room and Canola had smashed into it. Suddenly the two men launched themselves towards one another, Canola diving at Kristian head first, his arms outstretched before him. Kristian soared through the air, his body appearing weightless. The two men collided and tumbled to the floor. Canola tried frantically to get a firm grip on Kristian's chest. Pinning Canola's arms to his chest with his own, Kristian was on top of him and with one deft cartwheel-like motion flipped himself off and back onto his feet.

Quickly jumping to his feet Canola launched into a fast-paced attack, punching and kicking with an athletic style of martial arts. He attempted to break through Kristian's defence so he could get a hold of him to be able to siphon the energy out of him. Kristian effortlessly seemed to block every attack, every kick and every punch. He was faster and much stronger than Canola and as long as he didn't drop his guard he would survive.

Canola threw a wild punch that was way off target; he lost his balance and frenziedly scrambled to maintain his footing, but fell and landed awkwardly. Seizing the moment without hesitation Kristian launched an aggressive attack. Kicking his leg up, his foot impacted on Canola's chest; a second kick smashed into his face. Canola's arms swung apart from the collision. Kristian took a step forward and threw his fist towards Canola's head and landed a screeching blow to his face. With a graceful quick spin-kick, he launched Canola backwards to collide with the wall yet again. He landed with such force, bits of grey brickwork were broken off. He bounced off the wall, his body slumped to the floor in one big heap. He looked up at Kristian, his eyes fearful and slightly envious.

Kristian walked towards and then knelt down in front of Canola. "So, when exactly am I going to 'beg' *you* to kill me?"

Canola quickly stretched out his hand, but a large swirling green shield had instantly appeared in front of Kristian's chest protecting him and forcing Canola's hand away. As he lowered the shield, Kristian felt impressed with himself, how well he had controlled his thoughts; all the training and all the practice sessions had come together at last and made it all seem worthwhile. Canola looked drained; sweat dripped from his face, his arms flaccid at his sides.

"You going to kill me now?," asked Canola. Kristian blinked and dropped his eyes.

"Ah, I knew you wouldn't have it in you," Canola teased.

Kristian glared at Canola's face and could feel nothing but contempt for him. Looking over his shoulder quickly Kristian was pleased to see that the room was much like the one in which he had been imprisoned. Rusty metal shelf fittings adorned the walls; with one quick movement he gripped tightly onto Canola's clothes, cleanly lifted him into the air and launched him against the opposing wall.

Canola's back struck the wall with a slap. He could see Kristian in front of him, his gaze locked onto him. A few seconds passed before Canola weakly began to wonder why he had not fallen to the floor. A strange sensation became evident: his legs felt warm as if a viscous water was trickling down them. Tilting his head downward he could see a large jagged iron rod protruding from his chest. His clothes were completely soaked in blood. Pain suddenly engulfed him. He began to cough blood, he was unable to speak; he was choking on his own blood! His eyes still followed Kristian's movements.

Walking towards the table Kristian found the urn that Canola had taunted him with earlier. With his thoughts returning to the original mission he realised that this was something significant, he knew he had to get it back to the Order. Maybe the urn that he now held in his hands may not explain *how* his friend had died but the secret for which he had died. Kristian could feel an energy from it.

Grabbing a wedge of cash from the pile on the table, Kristian placed it in his pocket.

"Do you mind?" Kristian asked turning towards Canola whose pale face remained impassive. "I guess not," he answered himself.

He looked around: three dead bodies. No sense of remorse or regret invaded his mind, instead he felt relieved and an odd sensation of pleasure. It was strange, he had never thought of death as something a person could get pleasure from; he'd thought only of the pain of it. But a part of him had enjoyed the battle, a part of him enjoyed the killing. He began to bury the emotions with the rest he did not understand or was frightened of. He could think of only one thing now: home.

...

- Chapter Twelve -

Homeward Bound

The summer in London had been a beautifully pleasant one, it was far hotter than the previous three years. The sun was often high and uninhibited in the sky, shining brightly, and when it eventually set, the stars in the night sky were more vivid and clear than anyone could remember. As Kristian arrived back to the big city he wondered if the rumours of all the nice weather had been just that. The day of his return was wet and grey, just as he remembered them always being. The rain came down like stair-rods and the streets were covered in long stretches of puddles. The air was hot and humid and the sky was often lit by bright blue flashes of lightening, which were soon followed by the earth-trembling rumble of thunder.

Walking through the streets, Kristian's feet began to tire from the hours of constant movement. Despite the ache and stiffness of his muscles and the loss of blood from his encounter with Cable, Canola and Volesh, he wanted to avoid as much public transport as possible. His newly purchased clothes were soaked through not only from the rain but also from sweat. As he walked past people, they stared at his blood-stained sleeve and his drenched-through shirt. The night had quickly fallen upon him; he knocked softly on the door and pressed the bell once.

Opening the door to the smile she had longed to see, Jess stood in the doorway with an expression of complete surprise upon her face. Her eyes widened with dismay as she began to take in Kristian's appearance. His tousled hair drooped over his eyes and wet locks clung to his face. Not saying a word, merely communicating through looks, Jess stood aside to allow Kristian to enter their flat.

Walking straight to the kitchen table, Kristian flopped his body onto a chair, his expression inscrutable as he placed the urn on the table. Entering the kitchen closely behind him, Jess threw a towel over him, "Dry yourself. Drink?" Her tone was flat.

In response to his nodding acceptance, Jess filled the kettle up and flicked it on. Placing teabags and sugar into two cups, she opened the fridge and took out the milk, placing it next to them. Turning around to face him, she spoke.

"So are you going to talk or just sit there and drip?"

He looked up. Hearing her questions, his expression softened and he began to look more 'with it'; he focused himself.

Smiling, he recognised Jess's infamous 'attitude'. Kristian tried to muster his thoughts; the last two days had been overwhelming, leaving a residue of jumbled thoughts and memories. He found himself unable to form clear and concise sentences.

"Yeah good. Yes, I'm good. You okay? Where to start? Where do I start?" he garbled.

Jess finished pouring the water and the milk into the cups and placed one in front of him whilst she took the seat next to him and sat down.

"Well, you can start by telling me what happened to your arm," as she spoke her hands moved to gently touch Kristian's wounded right arm.

"Oh this? It's nothing, looks worse and all that," he replied moving his throbbing arm away. Taking a sip of his drink, he placed the cup back on the table. Although the boiling hot drink scalded his tongue and lip, he was completely unaware of the pain; the pulsating, aching pain that pervaded the whole of his body swamped any pain a hot drink could cause. Standing up he looked down at her as his thoughts became clear.

"I need you to leave," he proclaimed.

Jess was baffled by the outburst and offended by his tone. "Come again," she barked at him still remaining in her seat.

"Oh. I'm sorry. Didn't mean for it to sound quite like an order. But I need you to go home, back to your folks." When he spoke he just stared at her, devoid of all emotion.

"When? Why?" she demanded.

"Tonight," his eyes didn't move, his expression didn't change. "I'm sorry to ask this of you. But things aren't going to be safe for me round here. Not for a while anyway. If I'm to do the job I must, I can't do it with you around. I can't risk you getting hurt."

Jess was outraged, not at the thought that she was defenceless and needed protecting, but because Kristian was asking this of her and not giving her a truthful reason. "WHY?" she challenged.

Kristian's face finally showed emotion. "I've done something. I've killed people." His eyes reddened with fatigue and his pupils seemed to grow bold and dark. Jess could do nothing; sitting there open-mouthed, her thoughts raced. She had often wondered, ever since he had told her about the Order and his involvement with it, if he had ever killed. Now she knew.

"I'm sure you were doing only what you had to do. I'm sure it was self-defence. This doesn't make you a bad person, Kris." She softened, moved towards him and hugged him tightly.

Speaking over her shoulder, Kristian seemed to freeze within himself contemplating the swirling mess of thoughts in his mind.

"I killed them. They were in my way; I had no choice. It wasn't self-defence though, I killed because I wanted them dead; they killed Oliver. It was justice." His words were not directed at Jess but at himself. He was troubled by the way he was feeling; death was a subject he avoided, afraid not so much of the questions, but of talking about the answers.

"I'm sure it wasn't like that. You say they were in your way. You knew they had killed before, you were just protecting yourself." Jess pulled Kristian's face back and looked deep into his eyes. Her words rang true; they were in his way and they were indubitably going to kill him.

"You're right," he said as he nodded agreement, his eyes still red. He thought about Jess's words, it may seem like self-defence to her, but it didn't feel like it, not to him.

"What are you going to do? What's that?" as Jess spoke tears began to well up; wiping them away with one hand she used the other to point to the urn on the table.

"I've to go into the Order, I'll leave in a minute. That. I have no idea what that is."

As he spoke he regained the tight embrace placing her tearful and slightly wet face against his shoulder. "Don't cry for me. I'm fine really. It's part of the job; I've been trained for this. I'm just sorry that I have to ask you to leave."

"It doesn't matter. I have nothing to do here for a month. The parentals have been harassing me to go home for a bit anyway. It seems they're going to get their wish." As soon as she had finished speaking she broke away from the hug and walked to the window.

"So what's going to happen now? You're going to be all right, you say?" Jess said, her tone sounding overly concerned.

"I'm going to be fine. Trust me," he walked over to the window, stood beside her and took her hands. "Listen, I'm asking you to go, because I can't risk anything happening to

186

you because of me. I can't risk someone using you to get to me, using you as leverage. I know I can cope with the fighting and the rest, but if something was to happen to you, well, that would just be the final straw. I love you too much to lose you as well," his words were spoken softly and truly his eyes showed his feelings towards her.

"You better not be lying to me. You pray that nothing happens to you because if something does I will find you, wherever you are, Kris, and I'll kick your tight, cute ass," her eyes now dry, her face lit up and her laugh filled the air briefly for a split second.

"I promise, everything will be fine. Give it a month, and I'll be right as rain. Now please, I want you to leave tonight, so we don't have a lot of time to get you on the train." He looked at her, letting go of her hands, and gently nudging her to move towards her room.

Walking slowly to the door Jess couldn't help but feel the complexity of her emotions overwhelm her; life had a funny way of changing around her so fast, tonight was just another example of that. Turning to face Kristian she knew what she was going to say but something about the way she said it made it seem so final.

"It is so strange, just over a month ago I didn't know anything about the Phoenix, I didn't know about your past, I didn't know about the life you lead. But now it is the only thing that seems to matter. I still haven't got my head around it completely, I still feel like it's all some kind of dream. I do trust you, what you've told me, what you have shown me. You recall what I said about courage? It's true! You are the most courageous person I've ever met. Trust me," she said exiting the room. She deliberately planned it like that so Kristian couldn't reply. Standing there he turned and looked out of the window. Jess thought he was courageous, the most courageous person she had ever met; he tried to trust her judgment but he knew her to be mistaken.

...

It had been over an hour since he had seen Jess off at the train station. Now he was standing in front of the Order's Cardinal Office, staring at the entrance, almost afraid to enter through the big oak doors. The rain had relented somewhat so Kristian's clothes were not as wet as they had been a few hours ago. He had made Jess rush to pack her stuff, pestered her to leave quickly, he convinced her and possibly himself that he urgently needed to return to the headquarters complex. The only thing he had left time to do was find an old bag to carry the grey urn in. As he stared at the bland, intimidating building he found that he wasn't filled with the same sense of urgency that he had felt when he was with Jess.

Slowly he walked up the grey stone steps and pushed the oak doors open – he was now inside. Standing in the entrance hallway he could see the reception desk and the familiar face of Stanley, who was the only staff member assigned to this position. Stanley stood up as Kristian walked past the reception desk. Ignoring him, Kristian continued on and headed straight into an elevator that indicated that it was going to descend.

"Hey. You okay, son?" Stanley's body seemed awkward as he leant over his desk trying to look into the lift.

Kristian smiled at him and politely replied, "Yes," as the lift doors closed; as he began to descend he wondered who was he going to see first; perhaps he should have just called?

Standing upright once more Stanley picked up a phone, surprised and shocked at what he had just seen, the state of the boy. Stanley had a long desk with several phones, television screens and several other gizmos on it.

"Hello sir, Kristian just got into a lift. He looks all beat up." Stanley fell silent as the voice on the other end spoke and within a few seconds the call was over. Replacing the phone into its cradle, Stanley resumed his seat and then carried on with the variety of tasks his job entailed.

As the lift doors opened onto the hub, all was quiet, he could see a few people at the other end of the corridor but apart from them, it was empty. Leaving the lift, Kristian moved slowly and clumsily as though he was only putting the minimal amount of effort into it. Gazing around he wondered where to go, who to talk to. The whole place seemed dim and lifeless, it was late at night, but he had never seen it like this, he had always imagined headquarters as a twenty-four-hour workplace, busy and lively all the time.

"Kristian," a voice echoed through the air. It emanated from the far end and was clearly the voice of Jonathon. As his eyes connected the body to the voice he could see Jonathon pacing towards him. Two members of staff in the distance just looked on as Jonathon ran the length of the corridor.

Jonathon, within seconds, was now right in front of Kristian; his eyes widened as Kristian's appearance impacted on him. Kristian seemed completely worn out; his clothes were drenched, with bloodstains on the arms. He was still wearing the clothes he purchased in Germany, the blood on the sleeve was no longer dark red but more of a light brown as the rain had dispersed it.

Not caring about Kristian's appearance, Jonathon lunged forward and hugged him tightly; he whispered in his ear, "I'm sorry."

Kristian backed off, loosening Jonathon's grip.

"Don't worry. I'm still alive," Kristian sniggered, "barely; but I'm still here."

Jonathon examined the state that Kristian was in, trying to take in his full appearance; Jonathon could tell Kristian had been through hell.

"I… I mean we, have been so worried. Since you didn't check in, we had started to fear the very worst. I was planning to set up a full investigation team. We were leaving for Berlin tonight."

"You were planning to go to Berlin?" Kristian spoke with a sense of shock.

"Yes. It's not a large group, just a few of us in the boardroom. We are a little stretched, remember, I couldn't risk losing another Phoenix," Jonathon knew what he was saying was true but that wasn't the real reason he had wanted to go.

"Well, I appreciate the thought. But just to let you know, if I hadn't manage to escape by myself, you would have been too late!" Kristian let out a small laugh as he began to walk up the corridor with Jonathon in close pursuit.

"Really? Let's go into my office," Jonathon had quickly overtaken him and was now leading Kristian in the direction of his office.

Moments later they had arrived at Jonathon's office and closing the door quickly Jonathon was glad that they had made it there without anyone else seeing. Moving across the room he cleared a chair for Kristian and sat him down and then sat upon his desk. "So, from the beginning?"

Where was the beginning? Where did it start and what was the beginning? These questions passed through Kristian's still befuddled mind. Then he remembered, quite suddenly, Leandra in the park. He had completely forgotten about her until now. His thoughts were so fixated on his capture and his imprisonment that she had slipped his mind altogether.

Within seconds, Kristian began to recount; he gave Jonathon a step-by-step report of how the last month had been largely uneventful. It wasn't long before he was talking about the park, Leandra and the chilling and fateful events that followed. Jonathon's face screwed up as he listened carefully to Kristian's account, becoming consumed in deep thought.

Kristian carried on, "Well, Leandra said she was a friend, I felt like I could trust her. She couldn't really help and before I knew it she was gone. Even though I trusted her, I didn't know why. Though I did know I needed to find out if what she was saying was true, so the only thing I could think of doing was going to *Das Ferkel*, a tavern Leandra had told me about, and questioning the barman," Kristian carried on with his recollection of that evening, his thoughts flowing more easily now. He told how he had interrogated the barman and that nothing seemed out of place.

A few minutes had passed and Kristian only stopped talking to take breath. He had explained about the attack in the apartment, his capture and moved on to describe the exchange he had with Cable and Canola.

"You see, it's Leceth. They told me it was Leceth who killed Oliver. And he was going to do the same to me! He was going to put my heart in a jar; into this," as Kristian spoke he unveiled what he had stored in his bag. Pulling out the urn from his bag he placed it into Jonathon's hands. Jonathon's jaw dropped, he was completely flabbergasted! Not so much at Kristian's assertions but by what now lay in his hands.

"You've any idea what this thing is?" Kristian asked.

Shaking his head, Jonathon looked up into the young man's eyes.

"No! I don't know what it is, though it's clearly an urn. Not sure what its purpose is though, I haven't seen any urn like this before. The markings look odd." He wasn't exactly lying; it was true he had never seen the urn before, nor had he any idea of its purpose. But something about it was familiar to him, something about it was exactly what Jonathon was hoping to find.

Kristian could tell by Jonathon's expression that he was being economical with the truth, but to pursue that line of questioning would be pointless. The fact that he was sure Jonathon was hiding something was knowledge he knew he would have to keep close to his chest, for now.

"So do you want me to go on?"

"Of course, of course," Jonathon said his eyes moving off the urn and back to Kristian. Kristian recounted the intricate events of his escape from his prison, he now found himself talking about what he had heard Canola, Cable and Volesh saying on the other side of the door which had led to his freedom.

"Well I overheard them talking, they were saying that Tom, the Dark Phoenix was also working for Leceth. He's in La something, La Cumbrecita! Yeah, that's right, La Cumbrecita, wherever that is."

Jonathon rose to his feet, gazing into the middle distance.

"Come again? When did you hear that?" Jonathon sounded a little tense; moving to the desk, he placed the urn on it.

"Well, this morning," Kristian replied.

"Excellent. There's only one La Cumbrecita that I can think of. It's in Argentina Nice place to hide. We must tell the others," Jonathon immediately headed for the door.

"The others?" Kristian enquired.

"Yes there are a few people in the main conference room, some of the ones I was going to take with me, to find you!" Jonathon explained opening the door. Kristian walked towards him and Jonathon took a good look at the urn.

He began to think about what lay ahead of him, Brendan must be told about the urn, he thought, before anyone else.

Before leaving he closed the door and held Kristian back. "I'm going to ask you to do something for me, I can't tell you why, not at the moment but I need you to trust me. Do you think you can do that?"

Kristian remembered the promises Jonathon had made to him in the past: *You're free to go to university, free to get a career.* He even thought about Jonathon's face when he looked at the urn. Trusting Jonathon was becoming increasingly difficult for Kristian, harder than he had thought possible, so he kept silent.

"Kristian, I'm not ordering you to do this, and I know I have not always been true to my word. But this is more important than you or me, or even them out there. I can't tell you why, maybe in time I can find the words. But I do need you to do this for me, more than anything."

Kristian carefully mulled over Jonathon's words. He understood why trusting Jonathon was so difficult at the moment, but he realised, deep down in his heart, that Jonathon was a good man, true to his beliefs and when he asked you do something like this, there was no real choice; there was only compliance. It had to be done.

"Okay, what is it?"

"The urn, I need you to drop it from your account. When you tell the others I need you to tell them about the ritual, tell them everything, just do not tell them you took or saw the urn."

Kristian squinted, scanning Jonathon's face looking for some truth. Fighting the urge to ask why, as he knew Jonathon would not answer, he could do nothing but agree to his request. Not understanding why, he said, "Okay, you have my word. But one day you owe me the truth, you owe me an explanation. And to be frank you ask too much of me."

"I know I do. But it's because I trust you. You are a good boy and one day you will be a great man. Far from here, far from all this, I promise."

Jonathon stretched out his hand and Kristian gripped it tightly and began to shake it. The pair then quickly exited the room making their way to the main conference room. On entering everyone in the room looked towards the doors, each one had a slightly different expression of complete surprise. The gang, Kieran, Sam, Rachel and Jean, all came rushing over, each letting out little sighs of his name. As they hugged him deeply, Kristian peered over the top of the group to see who else was there. At the far end were Peter, Andrew, Roman and Susan all standing looking in his direction all smiling all mouthing 'Okays.'

As the group hug broke up they descended into frivolous chit-chat about the past day. Kristian, overwhelmed by the questioning, didn't know whose to respond to first. Jonathon quickly ushered them all towards seats and it wasn't long before he ordered Kristian to divulge his experience.

Much like the explanation he had given to Jonathon alone, Kristian described the incident in detail, step by step, but leaving out one crucial piece of information: the urn. He elaborated on the specifics of what Canola had told him about Leceth, the ritual and Oliver. Rachel gasped as he explained and shocked faces were worn by most of them. It wasn't long before he mentioned the location of the Dark Phoenix to which a few gasped, one cheered and Sam looked a little annoyed. Finishing with his explanation of how he had escaped, with the detail of how he callously disposed of his enemies, Kristian finally came to the end. Explaining it twice wasn't exactly what he had imagined himself doing but the second time was a lot easier than the first.

"Well, if we know where Tom is we should tell Zhing," Rachel said.

"She is right. But we have more pressing concerns on our hands." As Peter spoke, his voice calm, all eyes looked at him; only a few understood what he was implying.

"Yeah, I thought the same. They most probably will send someone over here within days, maybe hours," said Jonathon.

"Sounds fun," Andrew said rising to his feet. "One shall prepare for them."

"Good, first I want you to contact Yi-Mao. Update him he might be able to cut his trip short, though I very much doubt it. Rachel, I want you to contact Zhing, find her and take her to La Cumbrecita, Argentina. Peter help Andrew prepare for our guests. Susan take Kristian downstairs and give him a check-up. The rest of you, get some sleep," Jonathon stood up as he delegated, his voice stern.

The room quickly dispersed with Roman the first to leave, his face showing his inner disappointment of being completely sidetracked in the delegation of tasks. Within seconds Kristian found himself standing looking around with Sam, Jean Kieran and Susan for company.

"Hey, if you go on ahead I'll be down in bit," Kristian said looking at Susan.

Agreeing to his request Susan quickly left the room; as soon as she was gone Kristian turned to the others. "What was that? Prepare for whom?"

Sam and Jean were as confused about the conversation as Kristian. Kieran, though, was quick to answer. "They have gone to prepare for the Council."

The three men gazed at Kieran; his words did little to elevate their bewilderment. Recognising their dumbfounded expressions Kieran continued explaining. "Well, Jonathon and the others believe that the Council will send an envoy here. Because of what you did," as he spoke he looked at Kristian.

"What I did. You mean my escape?" asked Kristian, his face a little panic-stricken.

"Sorry to say this. Yes. I wouldn't worry, to me it sounded like you acted in self-defence. But you need to realise that we live in a world that exists because of the Treaty and that Treaty has certain rules. Ones that clearly state that killing members of either side is permitted only when there is no other choice, only when it is clear that it is the last action possible. Even the deaths of these low level thugs will stir up some kind of investigation on the Council's side. One that will no doubt bring someone to our door," as Kieran spoke, each word seemed to change Kristian's face, making it more afraid, more panic-ridden.

"They were going to kill me. I had no other choice," Kristian defended.

"I believe you, so does everyone here. I wouldn't worry, it's more formality than anything. The council will need to look like they are doing something. You acted in self-defence, they have no grounds for anything," said Kieran as his arm collided with Kristian's shoulder sending a friendly jolt his way. "Come on, I'll take you down to the doc."

"Sure. Hey you two, you going to bed? I'm not tired, fancy a chat when I'm done?" Kristian said in the direction of Sam and Jean. Each of them replied with a simple "Yes, see you later." Leaving the room Kieran and Kristian walked towards the Andromeda-Aceso-marked lift.

"Again, don't panic. We have all got your back. Especially Jonathon," said Kieran. Though his words were meant to alleviate his anxiety it did more to hinder than to help. Did Jonathon really have his back? What was with all the secrets? Could he really trust him? His mind began to wander uncontrollably; he thought for an instant of telling Kieran the whole truth but he quickly persuaded himself otherwise.

"So how are you? I hear you can't stop doing spells?" Kristian said just a few steps from the lift.

"Where did you hear that?" Kieran replied. "Well, it's been hard. Being part of the Trinity is like, well, it's hard to explain. I have this energy, and spells that I used to find hard to do, that needed complex incantations to complete last year, now just thinking of them makes it happen. Control is something I have a whole new understanding of now," he chuckled to himself as they reached the lift. "Well, I shall see you later, we will be in the television room in the dormitory."

Kristian entered the lift and as the doors closed he gazed through the space looking at Kieran, feeling relieved that he had seen him again, that he had seen them all again.

. . .

- Chapter Thirteen -

The Ultimatum

It was a few hours after the sun had set that three identical black cars – Jaguars, with bulletproof tinted windows – pulled up in front of the main entrance of the Order. The rear passenger door of the lead car opened and gracefully from it stepped the long, pale, beautiful legs of Isobel O'Hara. She elegantly glided up the steps to the entrance, closely followed by three tall gentlemen who were clearly her bodyguards. The doors on the second car opened, almost swinging clean off their hinges. Getting out was not easy for the seven foot seven mountain of a monster that was Môn'ark Toral, the warrior general of the Vinji clans. He cleared the steps with just two long strides of his enormous legs.

It was early evening and people were still walking by on the street below; this fact did not seem to persuade Môn'ark to changing his appearance, he had never been one for disguising his looks from the world. He was large and reptilian, much like Karnel in appearance but taller and he had a long scar on his face from left to right, crossing his eye and finishing at the top of his neck. He followed Isobel through the oak doors but unlike her, he did not carry the company of bodyguards. He had only one accomplice, a small Vinji who slithered behind him, his head facing the ground, his small feet moving quickly to keep up with the beast ahead of him.

The door to the third Jag opened and from it a tall man dressed in a black jacket that flowed out behind him emerged. The jacket looked as though it was not made from any known kind of material but was simply made from darkness itself. The man under the jacket seemed to be made of the same shadowy colour; only his eyes were distinguishable, a deep yellow with red spiky pupils. Followed by no one this figure answered to the name of 'Ghost' and he walked elegantly and effortlessly up the stone steps into the Order's headquarters.

…

Peter and Andrew stood at the main reception desk in the entrance surrounded by several security guards and Stanley. They waited in anticipation for the unannounced but expected visitors to walk through the doors and demand an audience. The sun had set just under an hour ago and the rain had relented. Peter knew that it would not be long before the Council's envoys arrived.

"Right, give it another ten minutes and I bet you a week's holiday that they will come through that door," pointing towards the entrance doors, Peter said to Andrew.

"Okay, I shall agree to your bet, but only if you can tell me exactly who you think it will be," replied Andrew.

"Well, it shall be Isobel for sure. Now, an angry Isobel, umm. That would be interesting to see. They will also send some of their more unattractive members so I'm guessing Môn'ark Toral."

"All right, so just the two of them then?" said Andrew as though he knew who was about to enter.

"Well, they will have bodyguards of course. They usually come in threes, but I doubt Leceth will show his face. Well, if you get it right, I shall give you two weeks of my holiday." said Peter smugly.

"Okay," replied Andrew, "it will be Isobel and Môn'ark."

Peter interrupted Andrew and pointed out that he was not allowed to copy him.

"Well, if you let me finish Peter, I was going to say Isobel, Môn'ark and Ghost. And their bodyguards of course although Ghost won't have any."

Peter gave an inquisitive glance at Andrew wondering if he had cheated somehow. However, before he could protest, the doors swung open and in walked Isobel. Andrew immediately walked around the desk and moved to greet her.

"Isobel, welcome," said Andrew and Peter simultaneously copied.

"So, we were expected then?" Isobel spoke, her words as cold as her skin. Peter glanced over her shoulder to see who would be next to enter. To his glee, in walked Môn'ark just after Isobel's bodyguards cleared the threshold.

"Greetings, High General Toral, I am Andrew Gilmore. Welcome to the Order," as Andrew spoke his eyes took in the daunting size of the being in front of him.

"Save your pleasantries, human. You know why we are here," Môn'ark's voice was so deep it filled the air like a heavy fog.

"Indeed, and Jonathon is waiting for you to discuss the matter," said Andrew as politely as he could. Peter kept his eyes fixed on the door, hoping that no one else would enter. A small Vinji entered quickly, scuttling across the lobby and to Peter's disappointment he was followed by the shadowy figure of Ghost.

"Greetings, Ghost, it is a pleasure to meet you," said Andrew, the tone of his voice slightly high to indicate his delight. It was partly aimed at Peter whose face had dropped. "Is this all of you?" he said, in the same tone.

"YES," barked Môn'ark, his temper evident.

"Well, if you would just like to make your way through to the gallery, there," pointing towards the door next to the elevator. "Jonathon is inside and he awaits your company to begin this meeting," as he spoke, Andrew allowed each of the guests to walk past him as they made their way towards the gallery.

The Order's security guards followed closely behind the Council's envoys. Andrew slowly paced towards the door as Peter took up the place by his side. "You swine!" Peter exclaimed. "You knew, somehow you knew. It doesn't count, the deal is off – you used magic," Peter's voice was filled with cynicism and annoyance.

…

Jean, Sam and Kieran had been sitting in the television room for over an hour, waiting for Kristian to return from the medical wing. The TV was switched on and was showing a twenty-four-hour news programme. None of them were really watching it; it was for background noise only. All three jumped as the creaky wooden door arced open. Entering the room to three sighs, Rachel instantly realised that they were expecting Kristian.

"Sorry to disappoint you, guys," she said as she slumped down onto one of the dark leather sofas.

"Nah, it's all right. We are just waiting to have a proper chat with Kristian, that's all. So, what happened with you?" said Kieran.

"Long story," Rachel replied. "Well, I say long, what I mean is not that interesting."

Her tone was coy and they all knew that what she was about to tell them was going to be far from boring. "Well, before I left the office, Peter and I cross-referenced all the Council-owned buildings in La Cumbrecita and by luck or providence we found a property owned by none other than Leceth. Coincidence? I think not. So I immediately contacted Zhing and updated her on the whole Kristian–Berlin situation, she told me where she was; I went to her then took her to La Cumbrecita. She told me to come back to London and that she would check in with the Order once she had finished recon. So, I came back, everyone is in a meeting so you are the first people I have seen. And that's it, not interesting really," after finishing this long speech, she rose to her feet, walked towards the corner table, and flicked the switch on the kettle, which rested there.

"So Zhing's okay then? God it's all go here tonight isn't it?" Jean said, his voice drenched with concern.

"Zhing will be fine, she's the last person you should be worried about, Jean. She can kick some serious demonic rear when she gets going! In my opinion, she is the third strongest out of all the Phoenixes in the Order," said Sam.

"Third?" exclaimed Rachel as she poured milk into a mug with coffee. "What, so you think it goes Yi-Mao, Brendan then Zhing? What about Kara?"

"Yeah, Kara is tough," Jean nodded.

"True, but Zhing would definitely kick her ass in a fight," replied Sam.

Kieran guffawed loudly and shook his head, "No way would Zhing kick Kara's ass. It goes Yi-Mao, Brendan, Kara then Zhing."

"You're crazy!" Sam shouted. "Kara is so rarely here, when have you even seen her fight, huh? Zhing could take her easily."

Kieran was about to react when Rachel interrupted, "Guys, guys, calm down. Does it really matter who can take who? It's never going to happen is it? Why are you even arguing about it?"

On hearing Rachel speak, the two men turned away from each other with folded arms like children being separated in the playground. Rachel smiled to herself at their reaction, as did Jean who was now holding the remote control and flicking through the channels on the television. Silence filled the room as the volume on the TV increased.

"And now we cross over to our US correspondent who is in New York."

"Hello. Thanks Julia, I'm standing in front of what is one of the biggest tourist attractions in the world, which last night became the scene of a horrific blaze. Less than eight hours ago, the statue of Liberty was on fire. As you can see, there has been extensive damage to the exterior of the statue, which officials are estimating will cost millions of dollars to repair. I'm having to stand this far away as there are concerns that the copper is still too hot and the structure itself may be unstable. President John Finch is set to visit the scene later today. We are being told that there are no fatalities but so far fifteen people have been injured with five of those sustaining critical injuries."

Switching the TV off, Jean threw the remote on to the table. "Always the same, bad news. Fire here, war there. I hate British television."

"Hey, that's not just British TV, you know? It's the news and they have that in all countries, Jean, even your beloved France. And if you didn't watch the news all the time, perhaps you wouldn't feel so crappy about it," Rachel replied as Sam and Kieran started to get back into their heated discussion about who was the strongest Phoenix.

"Well, what else am I supposed to watch? Your country is obsessed with nothing else except reality shows. Always reality shows with you English."

Rachel was a little infuriated by his comments although what he was saying wasn't really bothering her personally. She realised that she was just ridiculously tired and feeling slightly strained. She felt the urge to start an argument with Jean but as she glanced over to Sam and Kieran, who were still going strong in their discussion, she decided to let it go.

The door to the room opened and in walked Kristian who looked to be deep in thought. Rising to their feet, the four of them moved to greet him as he walked towards them.

"Are you okay?" Rachel asked as she moved out of his way.

His eyes didn't meet anyone's, he simply slumped heavily into the chair before him and placed his head in his hands.

Moving over and perching on the armrest, Rachel began to stroke his back. "What did the doc say?"

"She said I'm fine," Kristian still did not look up but just continued to sit there with his head down. "She said I have hardly any signs of a fight and most of my wounds have already healed," as he spoke, he lifted up the sleeve of his shirt to reveal his arm that less than twenty-four hours ago was deeply wounded and bleeding; now all that remained were a few scabs.

As Rachel and the rest of the gang glanced at Kristian's healed wounds, they all wondered what must be going on in his head. As a Phoenix, he knew that he healed faster than a normal human. Before anyone could speak, he looked up at them. They were all hovering above him, looking down inquisitively.

"Guys. Seriously, I'm good, okay?" The agitation was clear in his voice. The trio moved slowly to the sofa as Kristian followed them with his eyes. Kieran was the last to sit and as he did, he caught Kristian's eye and said, "We are just concerned about you, Kris."

The others all nodded their heads in agreement with him and then quickly turned back to Kristian. "So the doc gave you the all-clear, you're not worried about that. Are you worried about the Council's envoy?" said Rachel.

He did not respond with words to her question but his lips curved and his eyes twitched, his face showed the inner turmoil he now faced. The signs were missed by Sam and Jean but with female intuition and Kieran's close friendship, the pair picked up the discreet signal.

"I told you, it's just a formality, tit for tat. No need to worry," Kieran responded. "And you know that Jonathon has got your back, he won't let anything happen to you."

Again, these words did very little to comfort Kristian whose opinion of Jonathon had changed somewhat in the last few hours. Rachel's hand continued to stroke his back in a gesture of support.

"You're not surprised that the Council have reacted are you? I mean you must've had some sort of inkling that what you did would have some repercussions?" said Sam.

"I wouldn't say I'm surprised, not really. It's just the way that they are going about it. I imagined that the Council would have me killed or something, not all this diplomatic shit, envoys and that crap. It's so bureaucratic, tit for tat as they say."

Kristian felt angry and confused but his voice portrayed a being that was calm and coherent, as if he had known that it would all turn out like this. He really hated the world he was in. "Like, I could deal with them sending some assassin or something. Vampires and monsters I can cope with, but them all sitting around a nice little table, discussing my punishment is something I have no control over. I feel like some naughty kid at school. Look guys as much as I tried to distance myself from this life, I can't escape the training I've had. That training was to teach me one thing – to kill, to survive," as he spoke Kieran looked as though he wanted to interrupt and explain to Kristian that killing was a last resort, but he decided to let him continue. "And now all I can think of is my training, it's all I have."

"That is not all you have, Kristian," Rachel stopped stroking his back and looked hurt.

Cutting her off and throwing her arm away from him, he raised his voice. "If you come out with some American crap like we'll have each other, you can keep it because I don't want your psychological bullshit right now."

"She's right though, Kris, you don't have to face this alone. This is the Order of Light. We all stick together. We're all in this as well and we will all support each other."

Kristian's response to Sam's words was to simply to look him up and down.

"Look, don't get me wrong, guys, I appreciate what you are trying to do but I feel helpless at the moment. There are people deciding my life for me, and there is nothing I or any of you can do about it."

"Kristian, you have made your own decisions so far. You decided to go to Berlin alone, and I'm sorry to say it but you decided to kill those men." Kieran's words were harsh but true. "And don't think for one second that Jonathon, Peter or Andrew will sell you out; because I promise you, they won't."

"I dunno. I just feel alone and helpless. I don't wanna talk about it anymore, I think I'm gonna go to bed," he pulled himself to his feet and all of them followed him with their eyes. As he walked through the door he heard a few of them say goodnight but did not respond. He closed the door and listened for them to speak. There was silence for about a minute after he had left the room. He suspected that they were waiting until he was a safe distance away before they started talking about him. Kristian rarely trusted anyone. He felt at ease keeping his emotions in check and although he knew that he could trust the gang with his life, that wasn't what he had to question. He felt so alone, in a building that contained hundreds of workers, in a city that contained millions of people. The one person in his life whom he felt he could trust was now safely on her way out of the city, but even from Jess, he had concealed too much.

His right ear began to hurt as he pressed it hard against the door, then after the silence, all of a sudden, the gang began to speak from within. He wasn't sure if they were attempting to speak in hushed tones or not but he could hear every word. He listened intently for about fifteen minutes. A part of him wanted them to slate him in some way but the group only uttered words of concern, each of them trying to figure out ways in which to help him and why he was so withdrawn. Not one of them had a clue. He began to tire of his eavesdropping and was about to leave when he heard Kieran's voice: his ears perked up. "To be honest, I think I would feel the same in his position. I suppose, in a sense he really doesn't have a choice, unlike us four. Each of us made the choice to be in this world, he didn't. This world only offers him pain and misery whereas we all enjoy our jobs, we relish our gifts. It's a life he doesn't understand. I doubt any of us will ever know the burden he carries. None of us will carry it, not even me."

Kristian froze. Something about the tone of Kieran's voice sent a shiver down his spine, "He knows," the words sneaked out of his mouth. Clutching both hands over his mouth, he stepped away from the door. His thoughts dwelled on Kieran; did he know? How could he?

Later that night, lying in his bed, the two questions kept going round in his head; he was unable to reach an answer to them. Before he drifted off to sleep, he was left with the thought that perhaps Kieran's knowledge had been gained through magic.

…

Slamming his fists firm on the table so that the sound hit everyone's ears hard, Môn'ark Toral spoke, his voice deep and angry. "How long must we continue to play these games? You have heard our request, now what is your response?"

The three men all appeared relaxed and unintimidated by Môn'ark's aggressive stance. Peter was the first to respond, leaning forwards, his voice soft and probing. "We have gone over this many times. Our response is: your claims are absurd, as is your request."

As Peter spoke each word, a new level of rage crossed Môn'ark's face; his eyes were squinting as his forehead caved. "Absurd!" he yelled.

"Calm yourself, Môn'ark," Isobel's soft, gentle voice was met by a deadly stare. "Môn'ark, please?" glancing over towards Jonathon she gave him a look as if to initiate a reaction.

"Thank you, Isobel," he said. "You understand that we cannot simply hand over one of our members on your say-so. We need evidence," he spoke directly to Isobel as if reaching out to her, sending her a hidden message.

"Yes, I agree," Isobel replied and as she did, delight crossed Jonathon, Andrew and Peter's faces. Môn'ark and Ghost both looked towards Isobel. Their look was not angry, but inquisitive.

"Well, I'm glad you agree, now if we could draw a line under this event. I will order a full investigation into the happenings in Berlin and you will receive a copy when it is complete," Jonathon's voice though drenched with tiredness was also arrogant and insincere.

"Oh, you misunderstand me, Jonathon. I agree that the request is absurd without evidence, but evidence is what we bring," as she spoke, she pulled out a compact disc and slid it towards him. Gripping it softly, he flicked his wrist and passed it to Peter who was already gesturing to one of the security guards who instantly nodded and left the room. An eerie silence filled the room, and there were tense faces on all those who sat around the table. The minute was long and not one word was uttered. The sound of heavy breathing and the humming from the air conditioning system were the only noises that filled the room. This was interrupted by the opening of the door and the re-entering of the guard, who had in his arms a small white notepad computer. The guard placed the screen in front of Peter who was already opening the disk drive and placing the CD in. After a few seconds of loading and several clicks, a window appeared on the screen. There in front of the three men, a CCTV film of the events in Berlin. What could be made out from the fuzzy image was three men in a room, sitting around; two of them appeared to be playing cards. The video was coloured but the quality low and there was no sound.

"What you can see there is the closed circuit footage from a property in Berlin, a warehouse. These three men were considered employees of Leceth, and therefore entitled to the protection of the Council and, therefore, the Treaty. The door behind them is the entrance, I am told," Isobel's words drifted, quietly threatening, through the ears of the three leaders of the Order, but their eyes remained transfixed on the monitor in front of them.

The events quickly unfolded just as Kristian had described them. The view from the camera was distorted. Jonathon, Andrew and Peter's eyes glazed over in horror as they witnessed Kristian bursting through the door and ruthlessly disposing of one of the men swiftly, looking like he had taken him unawares, before a short and brutal fight resulting in the deaths of the remaining two.

Smiles of delight crossed the faces of Môn'ark Toral and Ghost on witnessing the looks of worry from the men across from them. Jonathon quickly shook the look from his face, closed the notepad and with a stern look, he stared at Isobel and crossed his arms.

"As you can see, your man clearly violated the code; his actions were brutal and calculated with murderous intent," said Isobel, undeterred by Jonathon's glare.

"Our claims are not so absurd now are they?" said Môn'ark with sinister glee.

Peter and Andrew both drew deep breaths and looked at Jonathon who was deep in thought. Both of them were about to respond when Jonathon released his arms and told them both to be calm.

"You can't expect us to take this footage as unequivocal evidence, can you? Not at first glance anyway. Thank you for bringing it to our attention though. I shall certainly include it in my investigation," Jonathon rose to his feet to signal that the meeting was at an end.

Slamming his fist again on the table, Môn'ark, too, rose to his feet. "Do not patronise us, human. We are not here for show. Give us the boy, or else."

"Or else? That sounds like a threat," said Peter as he and Andrew stood up.

"It is not a threat," interrupted Isobel. "He is merely frustrated. Please all sit down, I am sure we can resolve this."

No one returned to their seats and instead Môn'ark, in anger, kicked his chair backwards. As it collided with the wall the back broke. Peter jumped at the jarring crack.

"No Isobel, it is a threat. You have one option. That is to hand over the boy or there shall be consequences. The Council has no time for your human games now," Môn'ark signalled to his companions with a menacing glare.

"You can't seriously expect us to turn him over to you just because you demand it based on a few minutes of unverified, unclear footage?" Peter's voice was still shaky due to the start that the chair had given him.

"Yes we can. We turned Sauror over to you on your say-so. He was a member of our Council and we placed him in your custody as a sign of our commitment. It is clear that this Treaty is one-sided. We want Kristian in our hands. You have twelve hours," Ghost said, his eerie voice echoing through the room.

Jonathon was more than exasperated with the direction of the conversation; he had expected things to be more amicable. He knew that he was walking on thin ice, but he was in no doubt that he was not going to meet their demands.

"Twelve hours, twelve weeks or twelve years, I wouldn't wait if I were you. The Sauror situation was completely different; there was more than ample evidence from an investigation that lasted months. I'm not going to spend this entire evening playing games with you. Now I am telling you, this meeting is over. Get out of my house," Jonathon's voice was unwavering and his eyes penetrated deep into those of his guests. Isobel showed signs of conceding as she slowly made her way towards the door. Ghost and Môn'ark however were resolute and just stood where they were, staring Jonathon down. Their glares were only released when Môn'ark turned and headed to the door, followed by a reluctant Ghost. Turning to face Jonathon just before his exit, Môn'ark's eyes locked with Jonathon's as he spoke. "I am sad to say that you have forced our hand. The demand stands. You will deliver this Kristian to me by two o'clock tomorrow or else we shall release the Jakyll onto the streets of this city."

Jonathon, Andrew and Peter all felt the same dread wash over them. They couldn't quite believe what they were hearing. The shock almost stopped them from formulating any kind of sentence, until Jonathon wrangled his mind together. "Môn'ark! What is the purpose, what would that achieve? You cannot release the Jakyll. If you do, we shall take it as an act of war and respond accordingly."

Môn'ark merely shrugged off Jonathon's comments. "Take it any way you will, human. If a war is started on this day then the responsibility shall rest with you," finishing his words, he flicked his cape over his shoulder and left the room and then the building. On his exit, Môn'ark was swiftly followed by his entourage and then Ghost. Walking slowly through the corridor, Isobel was making for the exit until she was halted by the sound of a panicked Jonathon.

In a matter of seconds he was at her side, his face was red and his eyes were puffy.

"Môn'ark can't be serious. He can't do this," Jonathon uttered.

"He can and he will. The Council and Leceth have already voted on it. You have twelve hours, Jonathon, and I suggest you hand over the Phoenix," as she spoke, he manoeuvred himself directly in front of her so her exit was blocked. She tried to walk around him but he stopped her again.

"What is this? The Council cannot be serious? This could lead to war. I will take this to the Arbitrators if anyone dies."

"Jonathon, you must understand that for years the Council has believed that you do not take them seriously. They have reached the point where they have to, as you would say, put their money where their mouth is. This is not my decision. It would be simpler for you if you met our demands," she again attempted to pass Jonathon but he intercepted. Her guards moved towards her, suspecting that she might be under attack but on seeing them advance, she waved her arms and ushered them away.

"Isobel, you must go to the Council and convince them to stop this madness."

"It is too late for that. They will not change their mind unless you hand over the boy. And in fact even if they were inclined to change their mind, I'm not sure that I am inclined to do anything." Once again, after finishing her sentence, she stepped towards the door.

Enraged by a combination of lack of sleep, the recent meeting and her comments, Jonathon grabbed her arm and pulled her around so they were face to face. "What are you playing at, Isobel? You know that this is wrong. The Jakyll is no joke. The Council knows that if somebody, a member of the public, is hurt or killed, as I fear will be the case and is obviously intended, we will be forced to retaliate. This will simply escalate out of control. I know you don't want that, you know that I don't want that. Please, you have to try and stop this," Jonathon's voice was filled with despair, he was begging now.

"Release me, Jonathon. For your information, I did try to stop this before it went to a vote, but I failed and the motion was passed. And by opposing this I have lost a lot of influence on the Council. I am not sure I can do much more. And we have a tape that shows the boy killing our men, we have evidence. If you really want my opinion, play tough. Leceth is a coward. Underneath his words and actions he is afraid of the Order. He will buckle before there is a war. The Council does not really want a confrontation; all they want is your respect, which I think you should give them. And about the Jakyll, I suggest that you get to him before he gets to the public," Isobel's voice was soft and seemed to comfort Jonathon for now.

"Thank you. I know that you risk a lot by telling me this. I trust you, Isobel, and I hope you trust me."

"I do, my friend. But it is down to you to avert this war. You have to stop the Jakyll."

"Do you know where they plan to release it?"

"I do not; all I know is that it will be somewhere very open; a tourist attraction," Isobel this time walked uninhibited towards the door as she spoke. Turning to watch her leave, Jonathon gave her a smile of thanks and admiration.

...

- Chapter Fourteen -

Public Places

The doors opened and the four of them, Kristian, Jean, Sam and Rachel, walked out. The long corridor had changed so much in just a few short hours. Eight hours ago it had been empty and silent and now it was packed, filled with people busily rushing about. The hustle and bustle of the workplace was in full swing, people hurrying from office to office, noise filled the air. None of them had seen the Order as hectic before, it was clear that something significant had happened during the night-time meeting with the Council's envoy but what that was, for the moment, was unclear to them.

Heading down the corridor towards Jonathon's office the group passed small clumps of workers; overhearing their conversations saturated with anxious tones they noticed a few repeated words: 'Môn'ark', 'Jakyll', '… which public places?' and 'deaths'. Their interests were piqued, and with concern rising, they turned to one another, "What do you think's happened? What's a Jakyll?" queried Sam, a confused look crossing his face.

"It has to be something to do with the meeting last night, the one about Kristian, I wonder what trouble you've caused?" said Jean, attempting to be light-hearted but coming across as blunt as ever. Jean's words spun around Kristian's head, he knew what Jean had said to be true but he did not want to hear it.

"Hey! Not fair Jean." snapped Rachel to which he merely shrugged. As the four continued down the corridor closing in on Jonathon's office, it just seemed to get busier and busier with frantic staff everywhere. Soon the walkway was too packed for the four of them to walk side by side so instead they opted for a single-file march, lead by a boisterous Sam, with Jean, Rachel and Kristian following.

With a few dodges and sneaky elbows, the group finally stumbled up to the doors to the office which were slightly ajar. Halting outside and peeking through they could spy a throng of people rushing around to Jonathon's muffled orders. They had to jump out of the way a couple of times as people darted in and out of the room.

Jonathon's strained voice just carried over the general drone of people's voices, it was hard to distinguish any one conversation. Kristian tried to concentrate on Jonathon, his barks being slightly easier to make out. "Good. Michael, good. Keep an eye out. Oh Joe, I need you to go to the Tate Modern. I have Michael at the British Museum and the other museums are now covered too. Go now… Sally, do you have the papers from Andrew yet?" It was not clear if anyone was responding to him, not to Kristian anyway.

Jonathon kept blasting out his orders, he was keen to seize the moment, he had less than six hours to locate the Jakyll and deploy adequate measures to contain him. He had positioned his staff in all the major landmarks in London, every hotspot he had covered. He knew that he was spreading his resources at central office thinly, but he had no other option; locating the beast was his top priority now. He had sent out messages to Yi-Mao and Brendan and was hoping that they would receive them in time and maybe head back early. He knew that the chances of that were slim; they were both on important missions and in remote monasteries in the Far East.

As he was about to tell a group of his staff to head to Parliament Square his eyes fell upon the four young faces in the doorway. He instantly fell silent, as did everyone in the room when they realised that Jonathon's gaze had fallen heavily upon Kristian. Jonathon knew that he couldn't put this off, and he didn't have the time he felt he owed the young man.

"Clear the room," Jonathon shouted, breaking the silence like a hammer shattering ice. Within ten seconds, the room had emptied and he was ushering Kristian inside. The other three looked as though they were about to back away but Kristian turned to them and made it clear that he wanted them to follow him.

"Well, I suppose you are wondering what is going on here?" Jonathon said as he closed the door.

"Yes, we heard some talk in the corridor and we're slightly confused," said Jean as he sat on Jonathon's desk.

"Not to mention worried," chipped in Sam. "What's the Jakyll?"

They all waited in anticipation for what he was about to say.

"I apologise but this will have to be quick, okay? I don't have much time to explain. Now, where to start? We have a problem." He grimaced slightly and took his seat at his desk. "The Council have reacted badly to the 'situation' regarding Kristian's actions in Berlin, and are unwilling to compromise on their demands, therefore they have threatened to set this creature of which you speak, the Jakyll, loose onto the general population of London, a tyrannical move and a completely disproportionate response," he coughed as he finished his sentence.

"Who?… What?… Where?" a barrage of unfinished questions left Rachel's mouth.

"It's a creature which we have not directly come across before. The Jakyll has never been used as a weapon before, never released to kill civilians like this. We only have a matter of hours before the proposed attack begins and we don't know where."

"But what is it, this Jakyll?" Rachel demanded, her voice quivering, evidently afraid.

Jonathon sighed as he conjured up the image of the beast in his head; he had never come across it himself but had read of the evil and had seen countless pictures and drawings.

"The Jakyll is a primordial evil, it is closely related to the Phoenix," as he spoke he looked at Kristian. "It is an incorporeal life form which acts like a parasite; taking control of its host, it transforms the shell into a ruthless killing machine."

The room was filled with gasps and Rachel squeaked as she brought her hand to her mouth.

"The Jakyll is a human-hosted monster, taking control of its host and rapidly changing its physical form using a catalyst which is always water. There is only ever one Jakyll and it is one of the most dangerous incorporeal life forms on record. The sheer ease of locating a source for catalysing the change obviously makes this all the more problematic for us, it's so easy. A host will either die of dehydration or let the evil take over. If and when a host dies, the Jakyll merely finds another one," Jonathon looked around him to see four blank faces.

"I take it they are going to release the monster form, not just a host?" Sam said to no one directly.

"How can the Council do this? Surely it breaks the Treaty?" Jean shouted, standing up and holding up his arms in disbelief.

"They are responding to our refusal to, err, hand Kristian over to them and I'm afraid we can do nothing more than try to stop it. I will, as a minimum, lodge a formal complaint with the Arbitrators if they carry out their plan," said Jonathon, sounding slightly bureaucratic.

Kristian felt himself flush bright red and couldn't face looking at anyone. The Council wanted him; and Jonathon had refused.

"What is the creature like?" Sam asked.

"Well, it could be described as being very similar to a werewolf although it is different in that it forms an exoskeleton around the host; it modifies the body to have elongated scythe-like claws and teeth which release a deadly venom, for which, I'm afraid, we know of no antidote. From our understanding it is also impervious to almost all types of magic and conventional weapons."

As Jonathon finished his description a new sense of urgency rushed through him with the realisation of how little time remained in which to prevent the attack.

"Look, I don't have much time and I need to focus all my energy on this at the moment. I don't want any of you being involved in this, especially you, Kristian. That's exactly what the Council will want. I want you to continue with your work on Oliver's death and try to find some way of clearing Kristian's name. Do this in-house, stay in the building. If I do need you, I will let you know," he opened the door and patted each of them on the back as they exited. They all wanted to stay, they had more questions and they wanted to help but they knew that Jonathon was doing his best, and that he had everyone else in the building fully committed to the problem.

When Kristian reached the door he paused and, making sure that the others were well ahead of him, he grabbed the doorknob slamming it shut, much to Jonathon's shock.

"Kristian, do not argue with my decision," his hand reached for the knob but it was beaten by Kristian's.

"This is because of me, sir. The Council is punishing the Order because of what I did. Let me help."

Jonathon knew that Kristian was probably the only other person in the building besides the members of the Trinity who could take on the Jakyll but he did not want to play into the Council's hands. He could not send him out to face the wrath, the power and evil of the Jakyll.

"The Council demanded that we hand you over and we refused. Not because we wanted to get one over on them but because we know that you are innocent in this. This is exactly what Leceth wants. I will not have you fighting that thing."

"But if I don't fight it, who will? Somebody will have to take it down and I know I'm not the best in the Order but my Phoenix is strong. Jonathon, I don't regret what I did in Berlin. Perhaps you should hand me over. Surely the safety of the public is more important than me."

"The offer is noble, but you are just as innocent as is everyone out there. We will not bow to pressure. I will let you help me locate the monster but you must stay out of the fight." As Jonathon said these words, Kristian removed his hand from the door handle and Jonathon pulled open the door. Kristian began to walk away and after a few steps, Jonathon spoke, "What you did in Berlin was you acting on instinct, and that is what we taught you. You did nothing wrong."

Kristian smiled, it was nice to hear some reassuring words, especially from the head of the Order. Turning his back, he knew that he still wanted to be the one to fight the Jakyll, he just didn't know how to convince Jonathon to let him.

Rachel was waiting just down the corridor so Kristian headed straight towards her.

"Are you okay?" Rachel asked.

"Of course, I just want to help. I want to make things right!" Kristian replied.

"Like Jonathon said, you getting involved in the fight is exactly what the Council wants. You can't go up against this Jakyll. You just can't," Rachel pleaded, her tone empathetic.

Kristian ignored Rachel's words of concern. "Damn, I need to do something. I just can't sit around in this building and hide."

"For the moment that's probably all you can do, that and some research. I've never heard of the Jakyll, but we should at least check out the Great Library. Maybe the origins of this creature inspired other folklore, like Dr Jekyll and Mr Hyde." As Rachel finished talking a strange expression crossed Kristian's face.

"What did you just say?" Kristian asked.

"What, that we should do some research?" Rachel replied.

"No. Mr Hyde…" Before Kristian could continue talking a sudden and unbidden distant memory drifted into his mind, the image of a man dressed in strange clothes was there gesturing to him. Then it hit him, eyes glazing over as the answer revealed itself.

Darting back and bursting into the Director's office, Kristian shouted, "Jonathon, I know! I know where the Jakyll will be!"

...

The lift doors opened and Kristian stepped out; as he did the lights in the room clicked on. The room was a long corridor with twelve glass cabinets spanning the length of it. He had not been here for more than two years and at the prospect of what lay within he was filled with anticipation. Following him as he made a slow pace down the corridor was Jonathon who had a strange, proud look about him.

No more than ten metres down the corridor, Kristian stopped and stared into one of the cabinets. It suddenly burst into green light, which reflected in his eyes.

It wasn't long before Jonathon was standing behind him, staring into the light.

"How long are you going to stare at it?"

Jonathon placed a hand on his shoulder. Kristian tilted his head to look at the suit, which lay beyond the glass.

"You know, the last time I wore that and used that blade I was with Oliver on our first mission. So much has changed since then," Kristian's voice was not sad, just reminiscent.

He gazed down at the arms of the suit. The beautiful dark blue, of distinctly Chinese design, had a strange emblem embroidered on each cuff. On the right arm was the Phoenix emblem, a sharp silver outline of an impressive majestic bird, the Phoenix rising from the ashes. On the left cuff, the symbol of Saranthea, his Phoenix. Its shape was similar to a hash symbol on a keyboard but the left vertical stripe was longer and the two horizontal lines came to a point on the right-hand side with a semicircle intersecting the lower half of the vertical line.

Both emblems were also engraved onto the handle of the blade and the sheath. "I know I was never really a fan of all this but seeing my old uniform and sword, it fills me with awe. In my head I had hoped that I wouldn't have to ever put it on again, not because of bad memories but because I like how it fits. I'm afraid I wouldn't be able to turn my back on you again once I put that suit on a further time. Well, that is, if it still fits!" he sniggered.

"Well, Kristian, time is nearly up. Put it on. I shall meet you downstairs."

Jonathon walked off towards the elevator as Kristian glared after him. When Jonathon entered the lift, Kristian paused and waited for the doors to close before he returned his attention back to the glass cabinet. Staring at the uniform Kristian felt a sense of eagerness to put it on; his eyes darted to the Phoenix Blade and his emotions turned to dread. The sword was beautiful in design and as his eyes took in all its glory he recounted in his mind the mythology of the Phoenix Blades. The story of how the swords were forged by a group of Water-Women played out, he struggled for a few seconds before uttering the group's name.

"The Sisters of the Sea," he whispered.

This, the Phoenixes' most revered tale of their origins, was first told to Kristian by Yi-Mao early in his training. The story of how twelve blades had been forged and gifted to the twelve Phoenixes, and of the powerful magic used in the deepest depths of the ocean. Kristian instantly remembered how he had been told that the blades were indestructible and each irrevocably bonded to their respective Phoenix and therefore the hosts.

At that moment, in Kristian's mind, Yi-Mao's voice from old rang out.

They shall not bend,
They shall not break,
They shall never yield.
Ready to be summoned,
By the Phoenix in the field.

In the two years that Kristian had been away from the Order he had never once felt the need or the desire to call for the blade; he didn't want anything to enter his hideaway and shatter the illusion of his normal life. Feeling the pressure of time Kristian dared to see if he could use the summoning skills he had once mastered. He stretched out his right arm towards the cabinet; palm open, he closed his eyes and spoke the same words Yi-Mao had once spoken to him; he knew he didn't need to, but it helped him focus.

"They shall not bend, they shall not break, they shall never yield, ready to be summoned by the Phoenix in the field."

In that moment the sword behind the glass faded into nothingness and instantly reappeared in Kristian's right hand, which coincided with a loud whistling sound that ended in a deafening pop. The sword didn't feel as heavy as Kristian remembered; he recalled its weight, it had been substantial, a burden to carry around with him. That wasn't his impression now, it felt light, it felt true. He lifted the sword high as he enjoyed the way it made him feel; this was soon broken as the thought of the Jakyll entered his mind and brought him back to the room. He quickly opened the glass cabinet and took out his Phoenix uniform.

The suit was a little tight around the shoulders and waist but he managed to get it on. After strapping the sword to his back he stood and admired how he looked in the mirror. He soon stepped back into the elevator and made his way back up to the main complex. As the doors opened, he was surprised to see how many people were in the lobby. Walking stiffly out, he was soon accompanied by Kieran.

"Still fits then?" Kieran said behind a cheeky grin.

Kristian's reply was to grunt as he lifted his arms up, just over his head to stretch the material. "Good material, luckily it's stretchy." he said as he turned his attention to the crowd of people near the door.

There standing in front of him were Andrew, Peter and Jonathon along with Roman and an entourage of security guards and assistants. They all had a look of concern and deep thought on their faces, although when they noticed Kristian's approach, they let out smiles filled with hope. Andrew moved over and patted him on the shoulder. "It looks snug!" he said. "To see you in your Phoenix attire makes me very proud of you, very proud indeed."

Jonathon did not speak to the assembled group, he merely turned his head and whispered into Peter's ear. On receiving Jonathon's instructions Peter nodded and headed past Kristian back to the elevators.

The door next to the elevator opened and a red-faced, very flustered Rachel came storming out. She quickly moved past Peter and acknowledged him with a soft "Peter". Peter nodded and proceeded to the elevator but let his finger linger on the 'open' button for a few seconds.

"Jonathon?" Rachel said, out of breath as she passed Kristian. As Jonathon turned, Rachel looked over to Kristian. "Wow," she exclaimed. "You look good in that. You do know what you're doing though, right?"

"Don't worry about me. I know what this means," Kristian replied.

"Rachel," Jonathon said as he swung his arm around her, moving her to one side and concealing the conversation from the rest of them. "Is it good news?" he asked.

"The package has been delivered. Kara said she will look into it," Rachel replied between breaths.

"Good. Now what about Zhing?"

"No word as yet, I'm afraid. Her phone is not connecting, I went back to where I dropped her off but I couldn't locate her. Do you think something may have happened to her?" her breathing was slowly returning to normal.

"No," Jonathon said, not too convincingly. "She can handle the Dark Phoenix, I'm certain of it. Please keep all of this to yourself. You've done a great job." As he spoke, the elevator doors behind them closed. The pair separated, Jonathon returned to Andrew and Roman's side while Rachel moved next to Kristian and Kieran.

"Hey, good luck, okay? And please, be careful!" As she spoke she held his gaze a moment too long. She turned to Kieran who was looking a little bemused.

"You too, Kieran. Look after each other, okay? And Kristian? Kick ass like a real Phoenix". She ended by kissing them both on the cheek, Kristian first then Kieran. Looking like she was about to break into floods of tears, she turned hastily to leave, but her exit was blocked by Jonathon who, accompanied by Andrew and Roman, had walked over to the younger group.

"You still here, Miss Winters?" Jonathon asked.

"I'm sorry," Rachel replied as she manoeuvred herself past the men and left the lobby.

The five men then all turned and looked to the main doors as a group of guards opened them, revealing two cars that were parked up outside.

"Right, is everyone ready? We all know the plan, right?" Jonathon's voice was firm and determined and he sounded strong. Kristian knew that many people questioned Jonathon's leadership of the Order and there were many who considered him too weak, but there were moments when, like this, danger loomed and Jonathon showed his true, strong character and it was then that you realised why this man was their leader.

"Yes," they all nodded, the adrenaline prickling through their bodies. Kristian ran through the plan in his head. He was the bait, he was to lure the Jakyll into a magical circle, which Kieran and Roman were to create. The magical circle would trap the Jakyll and teleport it into one of the magically reinforced prison cells that the Order maintained. Kristian thought it was a good plan and he was pleased to be part of it. A part of him wondered why Rachel had not been included in the plan, but he was glad she wasn't.

This is going to be dangerous, Kristian inwardly thought. He stood up straight and put his hand on his blade; pushing his hair away from his eyes with the other hand, he looked at Jonathon and with an unwavering voice said, "I'm ready!"

...

The sound of nails scraping against metal had etched itself deep into Bryan's head. The sound had been going on for over an hour now and was really starting to get to him. Banging his fist against the partition grill he yelled, "Shut up." Leaning forward and resting his arms on the steering wheel he glanced at his watch.

Ten minutes left, he thought. The butterflies in his stomach took full flight as nerves kicked in. He and his companion, James, had been entrusted with a dangerous mission, one that could create mayhem and destruction.

Sitting in a large white transit van that had a sliding door on one side, Bryan and James looked out onto the unsuspecting crowd, each passing person oblivious to the horror that lay within. It was past midday and the square was packed with hundreds of tourists and lunching office workers. The pair shared a look with each other as they contemplated what was about to happen to those here, blissfully enjoying the sunshine and the beautiful sights of the city.

His watch beeped; flicking the switch on the side, Bryan turned and smirked; it was time. Exiting the van the pair walked around to the sliding door. They opened it on the count of three and climbed into the back. In the corner lay a white middle-aged man. He was wearing once-white clothing, which had become torn and now looked dirty. As the light hit the man's face, he rose to his feet, eyes wide and pale, gaunt face filled with fright.

"No, please no!" the man pleaded, his voice was soft and placid, and his mannerisms timid. Bryan moved over to him and removed the restraints from his arms; his hands were dirty, his nails black and blunt from scratching at the metal doors of the van. As soon as the restraints were off he attempted to dart for the door but was immediately stopped. Grabbing his legs and arms, Bryan and his accomplice began to drag him from the van.

Wriggling like a worm attempting to free itself from the clutches of a bird, the man screamed loudly. The high-pitched shrieks emitting from his saliva-filled mouth got the attention of passers-by; some turned a blind eye while others merely stood and watched as though this was part of some sort of street performance, some strange show for tourists; no one tried to intervene. The pair walked casually through the crowds to the fountain at the centre of the square and without hesitation, they threw the screaming man straight into the water. A larger crowd had now congregated in the already packed space as they seemed to eagerly anticipate the next part of the 'act'.

The frail body hit the water and pockets of steam billowed into the air. A few of the spectators gasped in surprise and wonder. The water bubbled frantically as the man twisted and turned; through his screams he accidently began gulping down mouthfuls of water. His muscles began to enlarge and the already tattered clothes began to tear from his torso and legs; his body tripled in size in a matter of seconds. The skin that encased the muscles hardened to form a thick red jointed shell that encased his entire body. His eyes bulged and stretched so they almost flooded his face and shone a silvery-black colour. As spikes began to protrude from the man's arms and back, the gasps and screams amongst the crowd stopped being those of surprise and became fearful, panicked. Continuing the grotesque metamorphosis further, what had, seconds ago, been hands were now vicious claws with long red nails. The face, too, was turning red; the ears were expanding and the nose shrinking. His mouth became large; his teeth were now individual white blades, resembling those of a shark.

Slowly standing up on its dark red muscular legs the Jakyll rose from the fountain. Water cascaded from the many crevices of its shell and, glaring menacingly at the crowds, it let out an almighty roar that shook those witnessing it to their cores with primordial fear. The crowd began to scream, some tried to flee, others were frozen to the spot, unable to take in what they were seeing. The panic intensified and spread quickly as the Jakyll leapt out of the water and onto dry ground, which sent shudders along the pavement. The air became thick with the sound of fear as people began running away, pushing and pulling each other frantically. The shocked spectators glared with fright and some would have sworn that even Nelson and the great lions in Trafalgar Square also trembled with fear that day.

Salivating, the Jakyll was consumed with the need to feed. Its dark, penetrating eyes scanned the square quickly and located a meal. Its selected prey was a middle-aged Chinese woman frozen in fear. Saliva began to drip from its open mouth as it snarled ferociously. Arms outstretched and legs bent, it was ready to pounce. An instant later it was in the air, sailing through towards her. Legs finally giving way, she fell to the floor in fear; the woman could only stare with abject horror at the creature as its sharp angles and wickedly smiling mouth seemed to float in slow motion towards her. Tears began to fill her eyes as images of her children filled her head. She tried to lift her arms over her head but the weight of the fear had paralysed her body. Just as she was resigning herself to this fate, through the blur of tears she saw a bright jade flash.

Inches away from its prey, the monster was hit with a bolt of blinding light. The impact sent the beast flying off its course and into the corner of one of the fountains. The sheer force of the Jakyll sent shards of stone in all directions. Lifting its head, it turned to look in the direction from which the blast had come. There standing in front of it was a man dressed in a dark black suit, arm outstretched and ready to fight. The man glared at the Jakyll with goading eyes; it was Kristian.

The Jakyll let out another almighty roar as it clambered awkwardly to its feet. Its back was arched and its arms spread as it roared louder still. Kristian removed his sword from its sheath on his back with one swift and graceful move. With a flick of the wrist he arced the blade through the air in a beautifully executed move.

With only a millisecond to react the Jakyll was once again in the air, gliding, but this time towards Kristian. Kristian reacted instinctively, he too leapt into the air, his jump was much smaller and almost before he left the ground, he was landing just over a metre from where he left it. Rolling forward, he moved himself into position. His legs were in a forward splits position, his back arched and his blade close to his chest. With a flick of his neck, he looked up to see the Jakyll soaring overhead. Almost simultaneously and with a single movement, he swept his sword into the air and the blade cut into the hard, deep red shell of the beast's abdomen.

The Jakyll collided with the ground. Kristian stood up effortlessly to face his opponent, who was now again scrambling up to its feet, holding its chest with one long claw. No blood poured from the wound but it was clear to Kristian that he had caused the creature great pain; the large gash was visible along the creature's hardened belly.

Kristian held his sword close to his face so he could see both his blade and the monster before him. Looking into the reflection of his sword, he could make out a pale smoky ring behind him. He understood it was part of Roman and

Kieran's teleportation spell. The ring was currently floating in mid-air, slowly settling down to the ground. Then once it made contact, the spell would be almost complete; all that was needed was for the Jakyll to become trapped in the centre.

The monster charged towards Kristian who leapt in the air, spinning over the charging creature, landing perfectly on his feet. Kristian could now see the smoky magical ring floating behind the Jakyll. As the two opponents were now within easy striking distance of each other, Kristian knew he had to act fast; he stretched out his hand and a stream of bright green energy jetted out. Slamming hard into the Jakyll, it began to force him backwards, but the beast adjusted his footing and countered the blast. Kristian could feel the Jakyll's resistance; it felt like someone had gripped his hand and was trying to push his fingers back. Concentrating harder than he had ever done, he focused more energy into the stream of blinding jade.

The Jakyll's sharp talon-like claws dug into the ground, but did little to oppose Kristian's renewed attack. The Jakyll was being pushed back as its feet were carving up the pavement. It roared with anger and frustration. It was only a metre or so away from the smoky ring that was now just a foot off the ground. The Jakyll glanced behind, the ring of smoke was confusing, it couldn't fathom its purpose, although just its presence gave it the sensation of confinement. It then dived sharply to the left, and the blast of pure green energy caught its legs and sent it spinning hard along the ground.

Kristian not only saw the Jakyll's escape but also felt it, he dropped his palm and terminated its blast. His response was quick, but not quick enough as the bolt of energy collided with one of the fountains; the blast sent rubble flying high. Water began to flow in Kristian's direction. He turned to locate the Jakyll and saw it charging at him again. Acting on instinct alone, he twisted to step away from the rushing water surging towards him. His left foot slid one way as the right one rose in the air; unbalanced and with no power behind it, he barely moved, instead he stumbled. Through all this, the monster had made a giant leap towards him from a few metres away, and before Kristian could react, it had collided with him, banging him hard in his shoulder. Falling awkwardly to the floor, Kristian's sword flew from his hands. He felt immense pain in his shoulder and the coldness of water soaking into his clothes.

He looked up at the Jakyll who unlike him was now already back on his feet, racing towards him. Kristian scrambled to get to his feet but his hands slipped and then, whilst barely at a kneel, the Jakyll pounced on him.

Falling backwards from the impact, Kristian was now lying on his back with the monster on top of him. He let out a blast from his palm, which sent the beast flying upwards a few feet. Kristian quickly turned his body and, using every ounce of strength that he had, he threw himself into the air. Spinning up, he thought that he was clear enough to arch his body and return to his feet.

As Kristian moved through the air the Jakyll was coming down upon him. With a desperate scythe of its talons, the beast clawed Kristian's chest; the stabbing sensation shot through his body but he managed, with a flip, to land himself back on his feet, almost perfectly.

Kristian looked at the Jakyll as it fell to the ground with an almighty thud. The pain in his chest raged and as Kristian looked down he saw rips in his suit. Though he was soaked through with water his chest felt sticky and warm; his hand gently touched his upper body and as it did the pain intensified and sent shocks through his entire being, making his legs twitch. His head began to feel heavy as his eyes lost focus. He found himself fighting to remain alert.

He had been gored by the Jakyll and the pain was almost unbearable, he could think of nothing else. Kieran, watching all this unfold, gasped and moved slightly as though to try and help, but he stopped himself, he couldn't break the spell.

Roman, who was in deep concentration, could feel Kieran's anxiety and followed his eyes towards the injured Kristian.

Both Jonathon and Andrew were standing at the side of the square and when they saw the impact of the beast's claw on Kristian's chest, they both wailed. They knew that if Kristian had been injured, he would be infected. They too were consumed with the desire to help, but Andrew was also in the midst of trying to cast a spell and Jonathon's gift was not of the offensive type. Jonathon instantly left Andrew's side and darted to Kristian.

Kristian felt so heavy, heavier than he ever had felt in his life. His legs were weary under the strain and the pain was all-consuming, he couldn't handle it. He was on the verge of giving up when the Jakyll let out a huge roar, sounding almost victorious.

The sound instantly awoke Kristian from his haze, his eyes locked onto the Jakyll who was staring at him. Kristian began running towards the white ring that now rested on the floor. His pace was slower than he had hoped and the Jakyll soon caught up to him and again leaped upon him and knocked him to the floor. He grabbed the Jakyll's arms and pushed him high into the air, the beast was frantically clawing at Kristian, trying to scratch and maul his face. Saliva from its jaws dropped onto him as he desperately tried to avoid the sharp teeth of the beast. Again, the Jakyll roared and Kristian could feel his arms getting heavier, the teeth were edging ever closer to his face. Bending his knees and bringing his feet up to the Jakyll's chest, he was sure his legs were going to snap at any second. With all his strength, Kristian managed to flick the Jakyll clean over him; the beast did not fly as high as Kristian had expected but luckily the beast continued to tumble along the ground, just rolling over the smoky white line and into the circle. Shaking its head and returning to its feet, the Jakyll looked as astonished as an emotionless face could.

Kieran and Roman could feel that the barrier had been broken. Instantly slamming their hands against one another's, they began an incantation. The white circle elongated quickly into white fog engulfing the monster. Spinning into the air, the smoke twisted like a tornado up into a point high above them where it vanished.

Suddenly the swirling tower of fog and beast were gone, with nothing where they had once been – the Jakyll had vanished. Kristian felt an inkling of satisfaction but this was soon drowned out by a burning sensation that rushed throughout his entire torso. Losing his footing, he stumbled to the ground, but was quickly caught by Jonathon who instantly placed his palm over his wound.

Kristian looked up to see who had caught him but he couldn't make out the face, it was all a blur now and he began to drift out of consciousness. Kieran and Roman were soon on the scene, helping Jonathon to carry Kristian's limp body.

"Can you get him to Andromeda?" Jonathon asked through teary eyes.

"No, it would be quicker to drive," shouted Roman as he pointed to one of the Order's parked cars on the side of the square. Several of the Order security guards were running to their aid.

"Is he going to be okay?" Kieran shouted.

No one responded to the question. No one really knew the answer but it wasn't long before Kristian was being driven off in one of the cars.

The people gathered in the square could not believe what had just happened, they didn't seem so terrified now, just shocked. They began talking loudly to one another about what they had just seen. Some still thought that it had been a street show, others were convinced it was a scene being filmed for a movie or television show. A group of people began to walk towards Roman who was getting into one of the cars. They were shouting at him, demanding answers. He did not give any, but merely looked over to Andrew who was now standing on one of the high walls of the square. The people began to gaze up at him; his old body began to glow and his palms held at his sides began sparkling like stars in the night sky. He was chanting something but no one could hear over the shouts and screams.

As Roman drove off, Andrew looked down upon the people, his eyes a bright white. He scanned the crowed to see if anyone else from the Order remained; they had all left the scene. In then in that instant, Andrew swung his arms out wide and over his head until they collided with a deafening clap. As soon as his hands touched, a bright light shot out in all directions. It spread out fast all over the ground, through the buildings, the cars and the people. It moved so fast it seemed to be more than just light, like a thick bright cloud. It spread as far as anyone could see, the city mile was engulfed by it. After a few seconds, Andrew dropped his hands back to his sides and the light vanished.

The square had changed. No longer was it full of a screaming, panicked mob. The expressions on the faces of the crowd varied from bewildered to lost. Everyone began talking to one another and they all seemed to do a strange little shudder, like a dog shaking itself dry.

Exclamations like "What's just happened?" and "Hey, how did we get here?" began to flow from their mouths. Others began to say things like, "Oh, this is the wrong place, Buckingham Palace is this way, come on," and it wasn't long before normality seemed to return to Trafalgar Square.

Andrew looked around; the spell had worked like the charm it was. The magic had wiped the memories of all those that had witnessed the events and erased any trace of it on recording devices. He contemplated waiting for a car to come back for him, but decided to walk the short distance back to the Order headquarters. As he began to walk away from the scene he looked at the faces of the passers-by. The puzzled looks had disappeared now, and all that were left were the ignorant faces, the blind ones; the happy ones.

...

- Chapter Fifteen -

The Long and not so Lonely Road to Recovery

"Please let me work. Out! Out now!" Susan shouted, ushering Kieran, Jonathon and Roman out of the medical centre. The long room was lit brightly, the staff from the centre were now all working overtime, about twenty people in white coats were rushing up and down the great expanse.

Susan was bent over Kristian examining his injuries. She had never seen a Jakyll wound in practice before, textbooks yes, but the real thing was all new to her. The wound was still open and refusing to heal. Blood had stopped pouring from the gash for some time now but open pink flesh was still visible. She wiped a brown liquid over the wound and began to replace the bandages. Other staff began to connect wires to his chest and prepare an IV drip for the cannula they were inserting into his arm. Susan powered up a variety of machines, which were on a trolley next to the bed.

"Full blood count, U and E and a coagulation screen please, also do whole genome sequencing on the pathogen," she barked her orders at two nurses who were extracting blood via the cannula. The medical team raced around carrying out Susan's orders and as seconds ticked into minutes and then hours the team managed to stabilise Kristian's condition although he still appeared very unwell.

The afternoon soon turned into evening and a member of staff seemed to leave every hour until only Susan and one male nurse were left. Kristian's condition had remained critical throughout the day. His blood pressure and heart rate were abnormally low and every so often Susan would inject a clear liquid into his bloodstream to try and raise them.

"When did you last get something to eat?" Susan asked the last remaining nurse in the centre.

"Hours ago. You?" he replied.

"I'm a light eater. You go if you like. I shall stay here, Kristian appears stable at the moment, I will call if that changes and I need any assistance," Susan said, not looking up from the monitor that was displaying Kristian's observations.

"Are you sure? Do you want me to bring you back anything?" he asked.

"Positive. And no thank you, I shall eat later."

The mood of the room changed on the nurse's exit, no longer bright and busy but sombre and dim. The lights were low and Susan was sitting on a wooden stool next to the bed all alone, staring at her patient. Her glasses hung off the end of her nose as her eyes began to feel heavy and she began the fight to not drift off; it had been a long day. It was not long before she jerked awake, kicking her legs out, clean into the air, throwing off a notepad that was resting on her lap.

Reaching down, she picked up the pad and placed it next to her on the trolley; with her other hand she straightened her glasses. Looking over to Kristian and she wondered how long she might have been asleep; it could not have been more than a few minutes she hoped. She stood up and moved over to his still body. His brow was warm, the sweat was building. She took a handkerchief from her pocket and wiped his forehead.

"How's he doing?" said a man's voice that came from the bed space opposite Kristian's, which was badly lit. Susan turned to look as Jonathon's face became clearer as he moved into the light.

"Jon?" Susan asked, unsure if it was him at first. She paused before continuing, "He's stable for now. It has been a bit touch and go. He's required constant monitoring and intervention to keep him stable."

Jonathon slowly made his way to Kristian's side and gazed down at the young man's pale face. He affectionately stroked his hair to which Susan gave him a sympathetic look.

"It's not your fault you know?" she said reassuringly.

He pulled back his hand and stepped back to sit on the adjacent bed, "Well, it feels like it. I certainly put him in harm's way. Twice now," as Jonathon spoke his eyes remained locked on Kristian's still body.

Susan sat next to Jonathon and put a comforting hand on top of his. "I hate to say this but it's the nature of this business. It is his job to be in 'harm's way', and you know as well as I do, it's yours to put him there," as Susan finished, Jonathon turned to look at her.

"Is it? I keep telling myself that I had no choice, that it's what we do, how we keep the world safe. However, he didn't ask for this, he has never wanted to be part of our world. Was I right in asking him to come back? I don't know. Recently I can't help second-guessing myself all of the time. The job is taking its toll, Susan, I don't know if I'm up to it anymore." He sounded exhausted; his hands clutched hers and she could feel them become clammy.

"Look, it's not supposed to be easy. But you are the best person for the job, you know it, I know it, everyone in this building knows it! You have to make decisions and sometimes it's hard for you, that's because you genuinely care about the people who work for the Order; and I, like many, wouldn't want it any other way. At times like these you should be thinking about all the good things you have achieved, all the important things. Don't for one second think about abandoning us, the Order and this world need you, Jonathon." Her tone was harsh and slightly patronising at times but he responded well to it, it was one of the reasons he came to her for advice.

"Thank you," he said, rubbing his eyes, keeping them dry.

"What else is troubling you?" she asked, sensing there was more troubling his mind than simply Kristian's condition.

"Words help a little, but they don't change anything," he muttered and let out a huff of air, which seemed to release some of the angst he was feeling. "I have a lot on my mind. I'm just stressed and tired that's all. It won't seem so bad after a good night's sleep."

Susan listened and nodded, she knew that he was hiding something. There was something else in this series of recent events that was really troubling him and although she thought that she could essentially extract these secrets from him if she tried hard enough, she decided now was not the time and decided to let it go. Susan knew the only way she could help Jonathon at the moment was to get Kristian better.

"He's going to be okay, you know? So that's one less thing you should worry about," Susan said.

"What is the prognosis then?" Jonathon said as he regained his composure.

Susan returned and sat back on the stool she had dozed off on, placed her glasses firmly on her nose and took out Kristian's notes. "Jakyll venom is a toxin, obviously. Well actually it's remarkable stuff, to call it a toxin would be technically incorrect, it's more like a pathogen, a retrovirus, much like the vampire or werewolf strains. It manipulates a cell's genome; it actually seems to have inserted an RNA sequence into Kristian's cells, which has forced them to replicate until they burst. It's very similar to an HIV virus actually, except that it's targeting a wider range of cells and acting instantaneously. I have gone through the records and all of the cases of infection have involved humans who have died days after the infection and in some cases hours," Susan's voice was typically clinical and Jonathon took in every word she said. He looked panicked, she noticed and so instantly jumped back into her explanation

"Oh don't worry, the infection in Kristian is not as bad as I would have imagined. His body has reacted and produced antibodies already, and some of the cells that would have been hosts to the Jakyll pathogen seem to have formed some kind of resistance to the venom. I have absolutely no idea how or why, but it's good news. My best guess is that his Phoenix is providing a level of immunity. Obviously, there is no direct medical cure, we are just palliating his symptoms but at the rate he's going, I believe he will make a full recovery. A bit of a leap of faith, but I know a lot about these things, so trust me, okay?" she smiled kindly at Jonathon who returned it.

On hearing this Jonathon felt somewhat relieved. *If Kristian pulls through then the day would have been a complete and unforeseen success. The Jakyll captured and no casualties!*

Jonathon stood up and walked back to Kristian's side; he bent down again and whispered in his ear, "Get better soon. Please!" He turned to leave but stopped and looked back at Susan. "Are you sure there is nothing I can do?"

Susan had already contemplated this idea but did not believe it to be necessary or worth the risk. Kristian was recovering and he had his Phoenix to help him.

"I'm sure. I think it's better to let his body clear it out by itself. I don't want to take any risks," Susan said. There were minimal records of people enduring a Jakyll venom encounter and she didn't want to take the risk of introducing the unknown factor that using a gifted power could introduce into the equation.

"I understand. Well, you know where I am, so please keep me informed. And thank you Susan," Jonathon said as he started for the door.

She nodded and watched as he left the room. Standing, she moved over to a chair on the opposite side of Kristian's bed. Her glasses soon fell to the end of her nose as she fought with sleep again; she struggled not to drift off. It wasn't long before she called for the most rested nurse to come and take over the vigil and monitor Kristian so she could go to bed and get some proper sleep.

…

As each day passed, Jonathon felt the job getting immeasurably tougher. His friend and mentor Karl had often told him that it was the hardest job on the planet and that it required the skills of a great juggler. Jonathon often thought fondly of Karl Wolfenstein, the previous Director of the Order.

He wondered how Karl had managed to make it look all so easy. Jonathon was certain that he had more critics than Karl ever did. He knew that he should put such thoughts out of his mind; dwelling on that fact would only prove his doubters right. Jonathon often had these spiralling thought processes when he was alone in his office. Shaking the thoughts clear Jonathon attempted to distract his mind; he reached forward and opened the top folder of a pile on his desk.

It was just another report from the head officer of the Sydney branch of the Order (Amanda Freeman's office) expressing how important it was to renew the alliances with the monks of the Kar'sin, and the knights of the Shing'tao. He threw the folder across the room and watched it flutter into the rubbish bin in the corner. He wondered what the point of that report was, he already knew the importance of the alliance, and that was exactly why he had dispatched Yi-Mao and Brendan to ensure its success and that the continuing alliances prospered.

A slight ringing that had persisted in the deepest region of his head all morning was now manifesting as a full-blown pounding headache. He rubbed his temples and forehead in an effort to ease the pain, then pulled open his top drawer and picked out a box of aspirin. Removing the lid, he emptied three tablets into his palm and threw them to the back of his throat. Swallowing them without water, he didn't wince or gag, clearly used to popping pills in this fashion.

Closing his eyes, he leaned back in his chair. He tried to clear his mind of all thought, to think of nothing, just as Karl had explained once about how he used to function when he was feeling 'the strain.' His headache soon eased off and he arched forwards to pick up another folder. With the folder in his hand, a flash of luminous pink caught his eye. The colour was that of a Post-it note, hidden underneath the many piles of paper on the desk. As he pulled it out from the bottom he accidentally knocked a whole stack of folders onto the floor. He swore as paper and card scattered onto the floor at his feet.

Holding the Post-it note up, he read aloud.

Phone call from Mrs. McKenzie.
She has some questions about Oliver?

Julia

He froze in his chair.

"Oliver," he whispered to himself. With everything that had happened with the Jakyll he had momentarily placed Oliver to the back of his mind. It was very easy in the Order to distance yourself from the families of the workers, even though they were ultimately the people they were working so hard to protect. Although Jonathon was supposed to be somewhat removed from his workforce, he found it incredibly hard to distance himself entirely from them, especially when he was sending them out into the path of danger, potentially, and on occasion, to their deaths. However he found that he rarely thought of the parents, brothers, sisters and children of his people until something like this, this simple note, brought the realities home to him.

He wondered what Oliver's mother would ask him, he was almost afraid to talk to the woman. Would she blame him? Picking up the phone, he called through to Julia. He asked her to put him through to Mrs. McKenzie. As the phone began to ring, he felt a sharp pain in his chest. He grabbed at it and realised that it wasn't a physical pain, it was an emotional one.

Suddenly a voice spoke at the other end of the phone. "Hello?" a strong, harsh female southern American voice spoke. Jonathon took a large gulp before talking, swallowing a metaphorical mouthful of courage.

The call lasted for over an hour, more time than Jonathon could really afford to spend, but he felt he owed her that, and more; he wanted to help ease her grief, she had sounded a broken woman. Although she was grief-stricken she was adamant that Jonathon tell her exactly how her son had died. Jonathon was usually extremely reluctant to discuss and to disclose such information, but on this rare occasion he found himself very forthcoming with her, even though the truth was truly horrific. Oliver's mother knew about the Order, she was aware of her son's work and the risks he faced; she was deeply proud of her son ever since the day he introduced her to his new world.

When Jonathon had hung up at the end of the conversation, he felt compelled to shed a tear but he held it back. A rage of emotions stormed through his heart like a hurricane building up momentum. Guilt, anger and loss were just a few feelings that fuelled the winds of the storm.

"Make amends," he whispered to himself. "Make amends".

...

As Andrew moved gracefully down the corridor he was aware of Kieran racing up behind him and then moving to walk alongside him.

"Sorry, I was asleep," Kieran said, as he caught his breath.

"It's no worry, you made it regardless. We shall make our way together," replied Andrew; this was accompanied by his familiar kind and knowing smile. They continued down the corridor until they reached Jonathon's office.

"So what exactly is the point of this meeting then? I hope it doesn't last too long, I want to go and visit Kristian," Kieran said, more to himself than to his master.

"Susan does not want visitors down there at the moment; he is stable, but remains critical. And this meeting will last as long as it takes," Andrew replied.

Kieran was taken aback by Andrew's stern tone; he had rarely heard him snap like that. They arrived at Jonathon's door and Andrew knocked loudly, it was immediately opened. Jonathon stood, beckoning them in whilst he continued talking on his phone. "Yes, yes I said unlimited, Kara. No, I will get Andrew to sort it out when he gets there. Okay. Okay then, yes. Bye," Jonathon flicked his phone cover shut and placed it on the desk then quickly burst into speech.

"Hello. I'm sorry to arrange this meeting at such short notice but time is not our ally," he raised his eyebrows.

"Is this about Kristian?" Kieran asked.

"No, it's about Oliver's funeral," Jonathon replied.

"Funeral? Surely his family have buried him by now? You released the body weeks ago!" Andrew exclaimed gently.

Sadness filled Jonathon as he leant against his desk and looked at the pair.

"Yes, they did, but his family are poor and the funeral was paid for by the state. He was cremated and the funeral was condensed into a small ceremony at his mother's home. Not fitting, you know. A lot of his family could not make it as they are all spread out over the US and his mother had trouble contacting them," Jonathon's speech was rapid, as though the pace could hide the shame he felt.

"What?" Kieran asked abruptly, he was disgusted at the thought of Oliver being memorialised in such a way.

"I have been very busy, Kieran, the Jakyll and the Dark Phoenix have taxed me to the limit. Once his body was released, it slipped my mind." Jonathon felt ashamed to say it, but it was true, other things had taken precedence and Oliver had sunk to the bottom of his thoughts.

"Slipped your mind?" said Kieran, struggling to conceal his disgust.

Andrew gave Kieran a wary look and in his mind, Kieran heard the words "Know your place."

"I have spoken to his mother today and I promised her a remembrance service, and a plot in their local cemetery, with a headstone, befitting a Phoenix, all paid for by the Order. We shall also pay for all his family and friends to be there."

"Don't the Phoenix have rules about how to commemorate and bury their dead?" Kieran asked.

Jonathon nodded, "Yes they do, but they waive the ritual if the host requests that their family take care of the funeral."

Kieran was amused by Jonathon's response. So do Yi-Mao and Brendan know that he was cremated? Do they know what happened?"

"No, no they don't, but I shall explain when they return," Jonathon said with apprehension, the thought of Yi-Mao's response obviously worrying him.

"Okay, so I assume you want me to go to Alabama and see to the arrangements?" Andrew interjected.

"Yes please, if you would. I think she wants to have it in their local church, she knows what she wants so if you could just help her, look after the financial side. And if you could both be at the service as well, I would like his family to know that we care," Jonathon asked.

"Are we to leave today?" Andrew enquired.

"Both of us?" said Kieran.

"Yes, today and yes, both of you," Jonathon replied. He was starting to get slightly agitated with Kieran's blatant attitude.

Kieran was more than annoyed, he was outraged to hear of the Order's treatment of Oliver and his family following his death but now his concerns were for Kristian, who was still in the Andromeda-Aceso medical centre.

"We shall leave at five o'clock, our time. Oh, what about Adriana? Should we take her?" asked Andrew.

Jonathon's expression changed. He had forgotten about Adriana as well. He had kept her in the dark about Oliver's death thus far, but now it seemed to him that she should be told. His second thought told him that she was on a very important mission in Spain and should not be distracted.

"No, I still do not want to tell her. Not yet anyway," Jonathon said, sounding unsure of his decision.

Kieran could not believe his ears, he knew that she had been kept out of the loop but this all now seemed just heartless; he could not have imagined Jonathon would treat anyone this way.

"Is that all?" Kieran's voice was bitter and sulky.

"Yes," replied Jonathon "Are you sure you will be okay with this, Andrew?"

"Yes. How is this being paid for, may I ask?" Andrew said, his disappointment in the actions of the Order well hidden.

"Credit it all to the New York office and I shall sort it out later," Jonathon replied.

Andrew bowed and made his way out of the door, his hand holding firmly onto Kieran's arm, pulling him along. As the pair exited the room, Jonathon picked up his phone again and sat back in his chair.

Outside in the corridor, Kieran shoved Andrew's hand off his arm and moved to storm away from the old wizard.

"How dare you! Don't you move," Andrew bellowed, his voice filling the corridor. Kieran had never heard him sound so angry. He froze on the spot and twisted back to face him.

"As a member of the Trinity, a certain amount of decorum is expected of you, demanded of you. And your attitude in that office and out here is unacceptable."

Kieran glanced around him; a few people in the corridor had stopped to witness the altercation.

"Look, I'm sorry, okay?" said Kieran, eyeing the onlookers, before continuing in a whisper, "But this is a joke."

"A joke?" Andrew seethed. "You think that remembering a fallen comrade is a joke?"

Kieran moved closer to his mentor, "No, that's not what I mean and you know it. The joke is that this task should never have been set. If he had done his job and paid tribute to a fallen Phoenix befittingly, we could be focusing on more important things right now, like the Jakyll and Kristian. Oh and let's not forget Leceth. Or has everybody forgotten about that little problem as well?" His voice got louder and his face redder with each syllable that passed his lips.

Andrew looked around at the curious onlookers who were gathering in small crowds; he turned to them and spoke calmly and patronisingly, "Don't you people have work to do?" On hearing his words, the crowds all departed and shuffled off back to their posts.

"Follow me," Andrew ordered Kieran, pointing in the direction of his office. They walked down the corridor to the room, which was barely used, and upon entering, Andrew directed Kieran to a chair.

"You agree with me, don't you? How can you not?"

Andrew closed the door and turned to face Kieran. If he did agree with him, it wasn't shown on his face. Kieran now lowered himself into the chair.

"Whether I agree or not, that's not the point. You need to learn your place. Jonathon is the Director of this entire Order, and believe me, he did not gain that position in a lottery, he earned it. So, he deserves our respect, and you will give it to him," Andrew said as he too lowered himself into one of the chairs; he then smirked mischievously at Kieran, "and yes, I do agree with you."

Kieran tried hard but couldn't help but smile back. It was strange for Andrew to get so passionate over anything except magic. It was at this moment that Kieran did not only respect his master as the wisest in the Order, but respected his unfaltering loyalty too.

"I'm sorry. I didn't mean to be disrespectful. It's just that Kristian is lying downstairs and I'd like to be at his side."

"Oh, you will, in time. Don't worry about that. Our little trip won't last more than a few days and believe me when I say that our friend isn't going anywhere."

"It's not that I mind going. I'd like to go really, to the service I mean. It will be nice for members of the Order to be there, but I really think that one of the Phoenixes should go. And in particular, I can't help but think Adriana should be there, or at least told and given the chance to go. This whole thing about not telling her because it would put her in danger on her mission just doesn't sit well with me." Kieran had lowered his voice dramatically and seemed embarrassed, as though he had realised how childish he had been in front of his mentor and the Order's President. "I can't believe that Adriana still doesn't know. Surely her Phoenix must have sensed that something is wrong? I really think we should take her. I don't care what she is doing in Spain. It's just wrong that she doesn't know."

"I agree," nodded Andrew. "If her Phoenix has sensed anything, Adriana might have mistaken it for worry; she knew he was on a mission. We can't know or guess at what she might have sensed. All I know is that she hasn't been in contact with Headquarters, so she can't be too worried. It's very troubling I know." At this Andrew gazed up into the air and was silent for a few moments as though contemplating his next move. "We will take her."

"Huh?" Kieran stuttered.

"Jonathon is our leader and his orders are always very clear. I'm pretty sure he said that *he* didn't want to tell her, so

I will tell her for him!" he smiled from ear to ear at his own audaciousness, to which Kieran beamed back.

Andrew picked up the phone on his desk and gave it a bemused look. "Hmm, modern technology is not my forte!"

"Here let me," Kieran took the phone from him, "it's the new model, isn't it? Who do you want to call?"

"Pauline, I want to ask her if she would be so kind as to pack a few things for me."

Kieran tapped the screen and opened Andrew's phone. It was barely five minutes before the call was over and the two men were discussing the finer details of their task.

...

It was three days ago that the Jakyll had been captured; three days ago that Kristian had been so devastatingly wounded. A lot had happened in the last three days, Kieran told himself. He was now in Alabama, in a car on the way to a cemetery. He sat in the back of a large black limousine with two companions. Andrew, the long-in-years and powerful wizard, sat opposite him; on his lap rested a small, old and fragile spellbook. Sitting next to Kieran was Adriana, a Phoenix Host. A dark dress elegantly hung off her shoulders. Her dark hair complemented her eyes and skin. She was in her early twenties and was naturally beautiful. The only make-up on her face was a little mascara and some light foundation.

Her hair was long and stretched past her shoulders, falling on her chest. She had a single parting, forming a fringe that just covered her left eye. Underneath the shiny locks, her eyes were filled with tears. Gently wiping them every few minutes, she prevented them from running down her face.

Kieran compassionately placed his hand on top of hers, which rested on her folded legs. The soft touch forced her to turn and face him.

"You okay?" Kieran asked, knowing it was a stupid question, but he struggled to think of anything else that he could say.

She smiled half-heartedly and as she spoke, her Spanish accent was evident and strong. "I am okay, thank you. The service was beautiful, wasn't it?" She had liked it; it was fitting, not too eccentric or mundane. It was almost perfect. The almost part being that it was for a man who had died in the prime of his life, a long time before he should have; for a man that Adriana had once loved with all her heart.

The car stopped with a jerk, which caused Andrew's book to close. "Oh, I guess we are here," Andrew said, placing the book down on the empty seat next to him.

Kieran opened the door and was the first to step out; he then helped Adriana who was followed by a slightly unsteady Andrew. The three stood in front of a huge cemetery, with no boundaries for miles. A large red-brick house was the only building to be seen. A long row of cars filled the space outside, most of them hired limousines. Andrew looked at the many vehicles and wondered just how much this was going to cost, then privately chuckled to himself as he realised he didn't care about such trivial things.

Kieran smiled as he saw Andrew secretly smile to himself, he wondered what was funny; his eccentric mentor was always a breath of fresh air, always preferring the happier emotions in life to the sad ones, even in times of sorrow.

The three walked along the long narrow path that stretched around the building; they did not know where they were going, they just followed the crowd ahead of them. Nearly a hundred people were walking in single file along the same tiny path, until after ten minutes of walking, they reached Oliver's final resting place.

The crowd spread out, looking at the empty patch of grass. It seemed so bare. A single red flower stretched out in the sea of green. Andrew whispered into the two ears, "This is his patch. The headstone is arriving on Tuesday, it really is beautiful and befitting of Oliver."

The memorial service had been conducted earlier that day and now everyone stood with his or her own thoughts; their memories of Oliver were no doubt playing in their minds as

Oliver's mother began to scatter his ashes onto the grass. After she had said a few moving words about how Oliver had always looked after his sister and his friends, she knelt down and poured the remainder of the ashes onto the ground.

Adriana could not help but notice how the wind stole more than half of his ashes and took them high up into the sky. She knew that this was Oliver's way of escaping Alabama. He had once told her that his joining with Ethalon allowed him to see the world and get away from the banality of Alabama life, which he hated. Quickly bringing a tissue to her face, she was a little slow as a tear escaped her eyes and trickled down her face, creating a tiny crater in the foundation she was wearing.

As the ceremony finished, the sun was beginning to head towards the horizon. People drifted away until very soon, Adriana found herself almost alone watching the wind take Oliver away forever; she could not bring herself to leave.

Andrew had, some time ago, retired back to the car with his book. Still standing at the grave was the grieving mother, clearing up the overgrowth and shrubs around the outer rim of the patch. Adriana and Kieran stood quietly behind her, watching her with concern.

"Adriana, it's getting late. We should leave soon," Kieran said as he watched Oliver's mother.

"No, I'm fine. You don't have to stay, go back to the car if you like," she replied not looking at the wizard.

"No, I'll stay with you," Kieran automatically replied.

"To be honest, Kieran, I would rather be alone. Sorry, I just want to say a final goodbye," she now looked at him and although he wondered just how alone she would be with Oliver's mother still there, he decided to respect her wishes and he left her side and headed back to the car.

After a minute or so of being alone with her, Oliver's mother looked up and glanced over to Adriana.

"Oh, you still here, my dear?" Her deep southern accent was familiar to Adriana, she could hear Oliver in her words and found it comforting.

"Sorry, did you want to be alone?" Adriana asked.

"Oh no, no, not at all. Did you know my boy well?" she asked, staring unwaveringly at the patch of grass where Oliver's ashes had been scattered.

Adriana had never thought of Oliver as a boy and she had not known him that long, two years, but it had felt much longer.

"Two years," she answered. The way she spoke these words communicated effectively how she felt about Oliver.

"Are you from the Order? Was he... happy there?" said Oliver's mother, moving closer to Adriana.

Adriana considered the question and thought of how to answer before she spoke. "Happy? Well, there was a time when he was. I wouldn't like to presume anything but if he was anything like me, which I think he was, he would have had the best and worst of times at the Order." She was sure she knew Oliver better than anyone but did not want to upset the old lady, or take anything from her, any of the memories she may have had, real or otherwise.

"Do you have one of them creatures in you as well?"

"Yes, I am a Phoenix. I've been in the Order a little longer than Oliver though. I remember the day I met him, even then, he was so brave and somehow he just got braver." She could not help but smile at the memory of him.

"So, you did know him well then?" As Oliver's mum asked the question, her eyes welled up. It hurt her to think that this strange woman who now stood in front of her knew her son in a more intimate way than she ever could, the brave warrior Phoenix part. It hurt her to know it but in a strange way, she was also relieved that her son, her beloved son, had made something of himself. She was so proud of him, but despite the constant pride she felt she couldn't recall an occasion when she had ever told him that.

"There was a time when we were close," Adriana replied almost in a whisper. A large smile crossed the woman's face, as she understood what she had just heard.

"Did you date him?" she looked up as she imagined her son courting such a beautiful woman.

"Yes. Last year," Adriana's tone saddened and she looked down.

"Oh," replied the lady, "I see," she began throwing weeds and mud into a carrier bag.

"Would you like some help?" Adriana asked sincerely.

The woman looked at Adriana thoughtfully. She did not really want any help, she did not need it, but she could see in the girl's eyes that Adriana needed it.

"Yes please, honey. That would be great."

Adriana quickly moved down to her knees and began to pull weeds out of the grass. Oliver's mother pointed towards the deep red flower in the middle of Oliver's patch and spoke. "Lovely colour, isn't it?"

Adriana stared for a few seconds taking in the crimson redness of the flower. It was strangely familiar to her.

"Yes, it is," Adriana said, "it's just right."

...

Kieran swung open the door and hopped into the car. Andrew peered over his book and smiled, "Where's Adriana?" he asked.

"She wanted a moment alone," Kieran's face was sadder than it had been all day.

"Are you okay?" Andrew asked reluctantly; he wanted to read.

Kieran laughed inside, *There's that question again!*

"I'm okay. The day is just getting to me and I'm beginning to think that bringing Adriana wasn't a great idea," Kieran replied.

"She seems to be coping well. She will be fine, Kieran; I will take her home later tonight," the old wizard spoke over his book, not once lowering it.

"I know that she's been strong today," Kieran replied, "but I'm surprised that she wasn't more angry about Jonathon not telling her."

"Well, yes, one would've expected that she could have been angrier, but she and Oliver were only together briefly and whatever feelings there may have been between them, they both believed that the job was more important. Jonathon knew that, as I did, I guess he didn't feel obliged to tell her," Andrew said as he lowered his book.

"Obliged?" Kieran whispered. "They loved each other, Andrew! The only reason they broke up was because they were miles apart and the job, as you know, was getting in the way. It doesn't take away the feelings they had for each other. She feels the same way about him today as she did a year ago, I can tell, I know how that feels."

Andrew tried to lift up his book, he paused, looking over Kieran and out through the window. Something in his words had made him wonder. Kieran examined Andrew's face, he realised the old wizard was contemplating something.

"Aren't you afraid of death, Andrew?" Kieran seemed to randomly enquire of him.

The old man closed his book and placed it back on the seat next to him. "Afraid of death? Hmm, I suppose I am too old now to worry about that. Death comes to us all, well, to the lucky ones anyway!" With this he chuckled to himself.

"Lucky ones?" Kieran asked.

"Death, my young friend, is a gift. Everything ends, and anything that doesn't, never changes, never grows and will never have the chance to meet its God." Andrew continued to look past Kieran and out of the tinted, rain-streaked window.

Kieran had never heard anyone in the Order talk about God; he would not have said Andrew was a believer.

"You believe in God?" Kieran asked hesitantly.

"Of course. Do you not?" Andrew retorted

"Well, no," Kieran answered bluntly. "I've never had a reason to believe. People only pray when they want something. If I ever want something badly enough, I am driven to get it myself. The idea of a god or a creator fits very nicely into our world, but isn't a god just a person with more power than the rest of us? And at what point would you define a powerful person as a god, what power would they have to have?" Kieran spoke honestly.

"They're good questions. However, to me, God isn't anyone. It's more like everyone and everything. His existence allows our and his own miracles to succeed, His through us, for the world, not against it. He is in every void and atom of you. When we die, I believe we meet our maker and they see every piece of us, they see our soul and determine our fate. So, am I worried about death? As a good, true person, I do not fear meeting my maker, I embrace it," as Andrew spoke he looked into Kieran's face, to scrutinise it for his reaction.

"So God cannot walk the earth? That is what you are saying?" Kieran asked.

"If He truly wanted to, I'm sure he could find a way through the world, but I really don't see why He would need to," Andrew answered.

"Well then, how could we determine if any given being was an incarnation of God or not? Would it be the power to destroy and create life? Does that make someone a God? Because, if so, I can do these things," Kieran said with a frown.

Andrew appeared amused, though he grimaced initially in reply before he spoke.

"The power of which you speak certainly does not make you a god, and using that power, merely because you can, would only make you a fool."

Kieran stared, perplexed, at his master.

"I paraphrased from an old saying, from a religion called Oridirin. Not much is known about it, but I think that quote makes it clear. To me anyway. We are not gods, Kieran, and to ever think we are would be a grave mistake. Gods do not need to prove that they can create and destroy; they created those concepts." Andrew reclaimed and opened his book from the seat to signal that he had just said something profound and that to ask any more questions would be ignorant.

Kieran sat and wondered about what his master had just said. What did make someone a god? It was hard to imagine a god in his mind. He had been brought up with the belief in magic and now he had to think about this as well? He continued to analyse what he had heard. Was Oliver lucky then? Was he in the afterlife; with his god? What defines God? He settled his internal debate with the thought that one can only determine what one's true beliefs are when faced with imminent mortality. That would be the point at which truth can be found. To dwell on it whilst alive would detract from the whole point of living. For Kieran, the point of living was to grow one's soul, to better oneself; all other concerns were meaningless.

...

Zhing walked through the large oak doors to a very surprised-looking Stanley. Walking proudly across the lobby, she was in her Phoenix suit and it fitted her to perfection, always enhancing her powerful and regal appearance. She was followed by a red-faced and out-of-breath Rachel who was power-walking to keep up with Zhing's pace.

"Stanley?" Zhing acknowledged, nodding to him as she passed the desk and headed to the elevator. Rachel, too, greeted the guard on passing; as she caught up with Zhing the lift doors opened.

"Tell me again why we just couldn't just teleport inside?" Zhing said as she stepped into the elevator.

"Like I explained, I can't teleport through the mystical barriers that surround the building. I'm not that powerful, and neither is any person, as far as I know," Rachel said breathlessly as she joined Zhing in the lift. "What is that anyway?" she pointed to a silver rifle in Zhing's hand.

"This," Zhing replied proudly "is a gun. It is also my trophy."

Rachel took the rifle from her and examined it. Her fingers stroked the long silver barrel and a strange sensation drifted through her body. The doors opened with a ping to the hustle and bustle of the hub. Zhing strode purposefully through the crowds, down the hallway. As she passed each person, they turned their heads and stared; everyone had been so consumed with the Jakyll dilemma that they had almost forgotten about Zhing's mission to hunt down the Dark Phoenix.

Rachel was three steps behind Zhing, and was even more breathless as they approached Jonathon's office. Zhing tapped on the door and waited for the reply.

"Enter," shouted a different voice to the one they were expecting. It was Peter's voice; the two women gave one another inquisitive looks. The door swung open and they entered. They saw Peter first, sitting on the floor in the middle of the office surrounded by piles and piles of paper. Jonathon sat at his desk, talking loudly on the phone. "Kara, I know you are busy, we all are actually. Please, please can you spare someone?" He waited for the response, "Oh, Zhing?" At this point, he looked up at Zhing standing in front of him and immediately apologised to Kara. "Yes, yes, she is here. Sorry Kara. I will get back to you later about the other thing, bye."

As he placed the phone down, he looked up at the Phoenix and smiled, a wave of relief passing over his face. He rose from his seat and almost knocked Peter over as he enthusiastically embraced Zhing.

"I hear you have been very busy around here?" Zhing said with a kind smile.

Jonathon placed his arm around her shoulder and directed her towards his desk. "Then you have been misled." he smiled back. "We have been *ridiculously* busy around here.

I take it Rachel has updated you on the past month's events?"

"Yes, she has tried," Zhing replied looking over to Rachel who was still engrossed with the rifle.

"Well, I'm sure she has done her best," Jonathon said as he walked over to Rachel and began to study the gun in her hands. "What is that?" Jonathon asked, taking the gun from her hands.

"A trophy!" Rachel said with a hint of sarcasm.

"Interesting," said Jonathon as he twisted it around in his hands. "What do you think, Peter?"

Peter jumped to his feet and stood at Jonathon's side, his hands eager to touch the 'trophy'.

"Well, at a first glance, it looks Vinjian in design. Some kind of non-conventional projectile weapon," he said as he took the gun and held it lovingly, as if it was some priceless artifact he was afraid of breaking.

"Well, Peter, I hate to place more weight on your shoulders but could you take a proper look at it *now*?" Jonathon said, patting him on the back. Peter glanced at him; he was intrigued by the intricate designs of the gun but something about the way Jonathon spoke made him feel like he was being sidelined. "Sure," he replied, "I will start on it right away." A few seconds later, he exited the room with the gun and gritted teeth.

Jonathon was glad that Peter had left so easily, without objection. He wanted a private talk with Zhing. "Rachel, if you don't mind, I would like to speak with Zhing alone for a moment? If you like, you can go and see Kristian; I gather you are eager to see him?" He walked back over to his desk and sat down.

Rachel nodded enthusiastically; she was more than eager to see him, it was the only thing she had been able to think about. She closed the door behind her as she left the room.

"How is Kristian?" asked Zhing with a hint of concern laced in her blunt, professional voice.

"He is okay. Well, when I say okay, I mean that he will be soon. It is good to see you. This thing with the Jakyll and Kristian has changed a lot of things around here."

It was clear from the tone of his voice and the expression on his face that he was deeply worried.

"What is our next move? Have you heard from the Council yet?"

He glanced up and spoke. "No, nothing from them yet. They are probably wondering how we dealt with it so quickly, and without any civilian casualties." He leaned back into his chair and attempted to imagine Leceth and his followers' reactions to the Order's capture of one of their most dangerous weapons. "I doubt that they will let Kristian off regardless, not if they were willing to go this far, but on the bright side, I expect they will not be attempting anything like this again, not for some time anyway. They lost that fight – no casualties and the Jakyll is in our custody." Jonathon let out a victorious chuckle laced with bitterness.

"That's good," Zhing said, pausing for a second. "How did you know where the Jakyll would be?"

Jonathon too drifted off for a few seconds. "You know? I'm still not entirely sure. We knew it was going to be a tourist attraction so obviously, we would have had Trafalgar Square covered anyway, but the fact that Kristian knew, just knew exactly where it was, made it a hundred times easier for us to get all our resources down there. I still don't know how he knew. Could it be a Phoenix thing?"

She looked puzzled and replied, "I'm not sure, I couldn't say, I have never experienced anything like that before. Obviously, I sense things but in Kristian's case, only he knows how he got that information. Perhaps you should ask him when you get the chance. Now, do you want me to get on with writing my report?"

"No, Kristian!" Jonathon blurted out.

"Kristian what?" said Zhing, confused by this sudden outburst.

Jonathon was silent for a moment as he collected his thoughts. "Sorry, your report? Um, no that can wait. There is something I need you to do for me, for Kristian."

She was thrown by this; it was Order procedure to write your mission report straight away. Records are the key to success, she was often reminded by Peter.

"Okay," she said apprehensively. "What is it?"

"I want you to begin investigating Leceth. I want to know his whereabouts over this past month, who he employs, everything," his voice was resolute.

"You want to know more about Leceth?" Her voice was uneasy. She knew the implications of doing this.

"No, not about Leceth. There are dozens of reports *about* him in this building. I want to know what he is doing, where he goes, who he meets with, that kind of thing."

"You want me to spy on him, tail him?" Now she was even more uneasy.

"Look," Jonathon said as he rose to his feet and walked across to her, "I know that this is risky and I'm not even certain that you will find anything. However, I am tired of walking on eggshells around the Council. It is vital we discover what Leceth is up to, for our sake and Kristian's. This is, of course, to be handled with complete discretion."

Zhing, although apprehensive about this mission, understood what was needed from her. She was a true professional and had served the Order for many years. One of her most noble qualities was her unquestionable ability to accept any mission she was given. "Okay. When do I start?" she asked.

"Go and sleep. Start as soon as you wake. Tell no one of this mission. Report only to me or Yi-Mao," as he spoke he placed a hand on her shoulder.

"Okay. I will do, but you should know one thing. Tom is dead, I killed him."

Jonathon felt a little disappointed, but also relieved that Tom's reign as host of the Dark Phoenix, Kronos, was over.

He had guessed as much when he had seen the rifle in Rachel's hands.

"Okay, see Andrew before you leave and make a glimmer stone. I'll get someone to write up a report from the impression left within it. Good work, Zhing, but for now, focus only on this mission. Put Tom to the back of your mind."

She exited the room, not sure how she felt about Jonathon's reaction to her news. She was still pondering on it as she drifted off to sleep that night. She slept for fifteen hours. When she woke the next day she went and saw Andrew first thing; after the glimmer stone had finished absorbing and translating her memories she left it in his care and headed straight to the Great Library, spending three hours there before slipping out of the building unseen, not to be heard from anyone at Headquarters for over a week.

...

- Chapter Sixteen -

Bedside Manner

Slowly opening his eyes, Kristian was surprised by how dark the room appeared. His vision was blurred but he could make out the silhouette of a person. Rubbing his eyes he wondered where he could be; his last memories began to play out in his mind. Thinking strangely hurt, so much so that he had to close his eyes again. His hands were now aggressively rubbing his forehead in a vain effort to relieve the pain. He again slowly opened his eyes. His vision was no longer blurry; the silhouette had been replaced by a clear image. Kristian could not believe what he was seeing. He rubbed his eyes again, this time in an attempt to wipe the image off his retinas, but it was pointless. Shock surged through his entire body and only one thought could explain what he was seeing. "Am I dead?" he asked.

"No, you're not dead. Far from it in fact," Oliver's kind voice filled the room.

Kristian looked around and realised that he was not in the hospital wing where he had imagined himself to be. He was in fact in one of the Order's sparring rooms. He looked around for other people, anyone. His mind was still plagued by the thought that he was dead, despite Oliver's denial.

"Are you sure?" Kristian said as he sat up.

Oliver looked down and smiled at Kristian. He reached out his hand. "Would I lie to you?" he asked.

Kristian thought about it for a second, "Yes, you probably would," he laughed as he grabbed hold of Oliver's hand and pulled himself up.

"Well, not today!" Oliver replied.

Kristian took in Oliver's appearance; he did not look dead. He was the same old Oliver, tall, still handsome and with the same intimidating presence that he always commanded. His sharp jawline and blonde hair was similar in appearance to his own but Oliver was nearly seven years older than he was and therefore had been blessed with growing into his looks. "If I'm not dead, does that mean that you are not dead?" Kristian knew that his question was stupid, but he was hopeful.

"No. Unfortunately, I am very much dead," Oliver's voice was filled with sadness and regret.

"So, is this some kind of dream?" Kristian looked around the sparring room again, "It's a little bit clichéd, isn't it?"

"Well, I suppose." his southern American accent was strong; the roughness of his deep southern drawl suited his appearance, but not his personality.

"So what is this then? Because I am getting tired of this playing in Kristian's head thing. You know, for once I would like to be alone in here," Kristian shouted to empty space.

"Are you talking to me? You want me to leave?" Oliver joked.

Kristian shook his head; despite what he had said, he was pleased to see Oliver. "Are you a memory? You aren't actually Oliver, are you? And we are not really in this sparring room?"

"No, this is the real me. We're not in the sparring room, you're lying in a bed in the medical centre and I am speaking to you from, you know, the other side, so to speak."

Kristian tilted his head to take in what Oliver was saying. It all made sense to him in a very weird way. Talking from beyond the grave did not seem so strange in the world full of vampires and magic. "So why are you talking to me?" Kristian asked.

Oliver began to walk slowly around the room as he spoke. "Well, I can only speak to you now because of your state of mind. You are pretty close to death and therefore more open to communication. Moreover, what can I talk about? Well, I can only talk about the things of which you know," he was reminding himself of the rules he had to abide by, talking to himself more than to Kristian.

"We can only talk about stuff I know? What the hell do you mean?" Kristian asked, confused.

"It's tough. There are these rules. Rules in life that guard the living from the dead. I'm forbidden to tell you about things that are yet to happen," Oliver's voice seemed far away now, distant; Kristian found himself moving closer to understand more clearly what he was saying.

"So you came to me to have a chat about things I already know? All right, it's great to see you and all but I still don't get it. What's the use in that?" Being in Oliver's presence again was comforting, even if Kristian wasn't sure it was real.

"I can only guide you," Oliver whispered. Suddenly it became clear, he had been so overwhelmed by seeing Oliver he wasn't thinking clearly, but now it was obvious why he was here.

"This is about Zelupzs, isn't it? This is about the Sagara prophecy," Kristian had never spoken about Sagara before.

"In a way, yes," replied Oliver, "I know what Zelupzs told you." Oliver stopped walking and gazed at Kristian's face to gauge his response.

"Is it true?" Kristian words slipped out of his mouth before he could think about them.

"What does everything tell you?" Oliver replied.

"Yes, and it's started," Kristian whispered; deep down he knew that things were in motion and the implications scared him to his very core. "It's Leceth isn't it? He's a part of it all."

"He is responsible for my death. It's all connected, don't you think?" said Oliver cautiously.

Kristian fell back to the floor with the weight of what he was being told; he found himself close to tears, but again fought back the urge to let go.

"Hey, don't you cry. Not yet," Oliver said, as he knelt next to his old companion. "It's not your fault. It's just a part of that crazy thing we call destiny. You just have to play the game. Play by the rules," Oliver tried hard to bolster Kristian.

Kristian held back the tears, once again; he had spent so long running but somehow Sagara had finally caught up with him. "You know. I believed that if I distanced myself from our world, then just maybe that would be enough to stop it," said Kristian as Oliver's thumb and first finger gently pushed Kristian's chin and lifted it up so that their eyes connected.

"Listen," Oliver said softly. "What is going to happen cannot be changed. You are a part of it, you have to stop running. What has happened and what will happen is not your fault, you are a cog in a machine."

Kristian did not take any comfort in this; he knew exactly what it meant and what was to come; he pulled away from Oliver.

"There are things you have to do. You must put your emotions aside," Oliver continued.

Kristian shook his head. How could he keep his emotions in check now? The outcome could not be changed.

"It has cost you your life! That is just the beginning!" Kristian shouted angrily, helplessly.

Oliver looked hurt by these words. "Listen, the prophecy is realising itself, you cannot alter the ultimate outcome or its conclusion but you can influence the meandering course it follows to it; there are things you can do to save lives."

"Like what?" Kristian replied defensively.

"You must remain at the Order for starters," he turned away as though looking at a script, but in fact he was contemplating his next sentence. "And there is something else you need to do, something I need you to do for me."

Kristian looked up suddenly, "What?" he asked.

Oliver was once again locked in thought as he contemplated his next words. "It is dangerous. There is something that you've seen before," with these words he pointed towards the corner of the room and suddenly the urn retrieved from the Berlin warehouse appeared. "The urn?" Kristian whispered. "What about it?"

"I need you to destroy one. Not the one you have taken. There are more out there and Leceth has another one." As Oliver spoke now his every word seemed to cause him to become increasingly hazy, as if walking closer and closer to a desert mirage.

Kristian was surprised. Oliver was telling him things that he didn't know, couldn't know. Surely, that was against the 'rules'.

"More? What do they do?" Kristian questioned.

"I cannot tell you what they do. You must find the one Leceth has and destroy it. It has a part of me in it. Not just my heart," as he spoke he winked, which Kristian found hard to discern as Oliver seemed to be struggling to keep his wispy corporeal form intact.

Instantly Kristian knew what the urn's purpose was, or at least what it contained.

"Ethalon? Your Phoenix. He's trapped within the urn?" Kristian jumped back to his feet. "That's what they do, that's it!" At last he felt a little closer to the mystery of Oliver's death.

"I know it's dangerous but can you do this for me?" Oliver asked, his voice fainter than before.

Kristian replied instantly, "Yes". He wanted to get started straight away. "So if I destroy the urn, I free the Phoenix?"

"Yes," Oliver nodded.

Kristian moved quickly towards Oliver and hugged him tightly. "You will be avenged," Kristian said staring at Oliver.

Oliver quickly held him back. "No, this is not about revenge. You cannot kill Leceth. Do you understand? You must destroy the urn, but do not kill him. Promise me that?"

"Why?" Kristian was surprised. "Surely he deserves it after what he did to you?"

"Maybe he does, but you cannot do it. Promise me. Please?" Oliver's voice was full of concern, he looked worried, his voice had returned to a more audible level.

Kristian didn't understand why he couldn't kill Leceth but it would be hard to ignore Oliver's request, and he knew he couldn't go against his friend. However, the thought of not taking care of Leceth was like a knife in his gut.

"Fine. I promise, I will spare his life. Only because you have asked me, but you have to tell me why. Tell me why and I give you my word that I will free Ethalon."

Oliver's face lit up and he re-embraced his old companion. "Thank you. You just can't face him, you can't kill him. Is that clear?" Oliver spoke softly into his ear. "If you face Leceth you will die."

Kristian flinched backwards; his biggest failing was his relentless fear about his own mortality.

"So, you're saying that if I face Leceth I will fail?" Kristian asked, his voice trembling.

"Maybe. I really don't have all the answers. I just know that if you face him, you will change things. You'll die before you should. Trust me, you cannot face him."

Kristian responded by simply bowing his head, he was struggling for words.

"You'll be fine. I have faith in you," Oliver's voice was fading away again, he felt like he was being pulled back; possibly he had revealed too much. The thought of this meeting ending saddened Kristian.

"Will I see you again?" Kristian frantically asked.

"No, not for a while, if you know what I mean? You will be waking up soon. Goodbye." Oliver turned and walked away; he was fading away, faster than before. Kristian's vision became blurry again, he couldn't keep his eyes open. He heard Oliver speak once more, "Tell Adriana… tell her I love her… on second thoughts, never mind… she knows," and with one more smile Oliver was gone and Kristian felt overwhelmed with sadness and the need for revenge before sinking back into a silent darkness.

…

Suddenly aware of something other than blackness he opened his eyes again and wondered if it was another dream, another vision. But, to both his relief and disappointment, it was clear by the pain he felt spearing his side that he must be awake. He slowly became more aware of his surroundings, eyelids were hard to part, sticky and congealed, his body cold against the sweat-damp sheets. Tongue coarse and his skin pale and dry.

He looked about him and quickly recognised the medical centre's starkness, then his eyes fell upon the bed next to him. Turning painfully onto his side, he saw Kieran's face pressed hard against a pillow, his eyes half open.

"You're awake." Susan said, walking towards him.

He attempted to reply but his throat was so dry. Susan sat next to his bed and immediately checked him over. "How are you feeling?" she asked.

"Like I've been hit by a bus… or two," came Kristian's response.

Susan smiled, "You are very lucky to be alive."

Kristian would have laughed at her response if his mouth wasn't hurting so much, not because he found it funny but because of how clinical her tone sounded.

"Well, *lucky* is one word you could use, I guess," Kristian said as he attempted to sit up, letting out a scream as the pain in his side blossomed. Susan placed a hand on his shoulder and gave him a disapproving look.

"I don't think so, mister!" she said as she gently pushed him back down.

Kristian was grateful that she had done so, the pain was unbearable. *I guess the mission will have to wait!*, he thought as he looked over to Kieran.

"How long has he been here?" Kristian said as he directed Susan to look at Kieran with his eyes.

Susan glanced over and gave another disapproving look. "Days," she said. "One wonders if he has any work to do."

Kristian chuckled painfully to himself. "Days? How long have I been here?"

"Six days," she replied to which Kristian let out a long sigh. "You're doing fantastically well though. The viral load is minimal and your body is already working on repairing the damage. You'll soon be in the record books, no one has ever survived a Jakyll envenomation… that we know of anyway." Susan almost gloated as she wrote some notes in the records at the end of his bed.

"How long until you can discharge me?" he asked hopefully.

Susan shook her head. "Several days, maybe a week," to which Kristian closed his eyes tightly in a show of annoyance.

"Can I get a drink or maybe some food? I'm starving," Kristian pleaded, his voice sounding dry and broken.

"Sure, I will fetch you some water. Food, I will have to make a call. We are going to have to structure your diet, I will get you something in a while." As she finished, she walked towards the office and then shortly returned with a large glass of water. "Sip it." she barked as she once again walked away to her office.

Kristian began sipping his drink and as it rushed down his mouth, it relieved the roughness in his throat. He let out a sigh and turned to see Kieran stirring in his sleep.

"Umm, no. Wait! He can't." he uttered from his dreams, then twitched and woke himself up with a start. In a sleepy haze, he looked over at Kristian and it took him about ten seconds to realise that Kristian was awake.

"You're awake." Kieran instantly came to his senses and flung the sheet that covered him to one side. He slid out of the bed and gave Kristian a bear hug.

"Oww," Kristian said, partly sarcastically, mostly painfully.

"Sorry!" Kieran backed off. "I can't believe you're awake. And you're still alive."

"Yes, I'm certainly alive, the pain I'm feeling assures me of that," Kristian replied as he smiled to one side. "How long have you been sleeping here?"

"Oh, um, not long, just a few hours really," muttered Kieran. Kristian knew that this was a lie, not just because Susan had told him but from the look on Kieran's face. "I'm so glad you are awake. I suppose it won't be long before you are back on your feet and leaving us again?" Kieran said sadly.

Kristian almost blurted out that he was planning on staying but he decided to keep that to himself, for now.

"How are you feeling?" Kieran asked.

"Achy. Sore. The usual for someone in a hospital bed, I suspect. But I'm sure it will pass soon. How has it been around here?"

"Good! Well as good as it can be. Just been sorting out the Jakyll. Andrew and Roman have been over at the cells a lot, not really sure what they've been doing. Oh, and Zhing is back, she arrived a couple of days ago but has left already, I don't know where though; no one does," he spoke quickly and didn't stop for breath.

"Cool. Ow!" Kristian gripped his side; the pain seemed to come and go, stabbing him every so often.

"Are you all right?" Kieran asked worriedly.

He nodded and let out a silent yes then sighed heavily after which Kieran stood up. "Do you want me to leave?" he asked. "You need your rest."

Kristian shook his head, "No, it's fine. I'm glad you're here. And I think I have rested enough. You couldn't do me a favour, could you?"

Kieran was happy to oblige Kristian's request of smuggling him in some food. The pair chatted for hours over some fried chicken and hamburgers, which Kieran had smuggled in under a rather neat invisibility spell.

It wasn't long before Rachel appeared and joined in on the smuggling game. The three stayed up late, much to Susan's displeasure. She was constantly ordering them to leave, but after making motions to get up and go the pair would quietly sit back down with Kristian under the cover of a further spell of Kieran's.

It was like being at some old boarding school for the three of them and they enjoyed breaking the rules. This all carried on every day for four days, even getting to the point where Susan complained to Jonathon about their disregard for her. The gang's response to this was simply to get Jean and Sam in on the act. They all stayed up late every night discussing all manner of mystical subjects, ranging from the origins of magic to the mystery that is the Trinity.

"So, you have to have a soul to wield magic?" Kristian asked, confused, during one of the late-night conversations.

"Yes," replied Kieran. "The energy that is used in magic stems from the soul. So, creatures that don't have souls such as vampires and Vinji cannot use magic. And that supports the argument that the Phoenix and the Trinity are alike, that they are living entities, that they are soul-like."

Magic was the most popular topic of discussion for the group and they would often talk about it into the late hours. Soon, a week had passed and each of them began to feel guilty when they thought about how much work they had put off. Kristian had a permanent knot in his stomach that served to reminded him of his promise to Oliver but he was improving almost hour by hour now and the pain had subsided substantially. He soon found himself back on his feet, walking around the ward. Susan found herself longing to discharge him, just to get him and his fellow aggravators out of her ward and her hair.

Eventually, sixteen days after he was first admitted, Susan took his bandages off. The wound had generally healed well, considering its source, but Kristian was left badly scarred, unusual for a Phoenix host, who were renowned for their enhanced capacity for healing. Three large dark grey, angry-looking strokes now lay on his right side. "Wow, that's not going to go is it?" Kristian gasped as Susan inspected the scars.

"I suspect it will fade in time, but looking at it, it might not go completely," said the doctor. "Well, we have your blood results back; it shows an unrecordable viral load and no more evidence of cell damage. You look good. I think you can leave today."

"You seem happier about that than me!" Kristian chuckled as he removed his hospital shirt and reached for the bag of clothes next to his bed. He was changed so quickly that Susan didn't even have time to turn away. Throwing his stuff into the bag, he slung it over his shoulder and kissed Susan on the cheek. "Thank you, Dr. Gambon. You're literally a lifesaver!"

He left the room and took the lift to his living quarters. He threw his bag in and then rushed off to find one of the gang, he didn't care which one.

Susan had watched as the lift doors closed behind him. She fell backwards onto the bed and let out a huge scream. The pure delight that she felt could only be released by such a huge outward expression, what a paper she was going to write!

...

269

- Chapter Seventeen -

The Death and Rebirth of the Old Enemy

'I tracked him to the monastery, taking shelter with the monks there. I thought it risky to try and apprehend him in this place, without a well-thought-out plan, but knowing what I do of his devious nature, I was compelled to make the first move; besides, I could sense him and I could tell he was well aware of my presence too.

Moving deeper into the monastery I spied him in the flesh and immediately launched a barrage of Kar'sin bolts towards him resulting only in plumes of vaporised brick and stone. I waited for the dust to settle to continue the assault. I could see no sign of him amongst the rubble now around me so I made haste down his only possible route of escape. I emerged at the entry to the large ornamental garden; the gates were wide open and in the still of the night I could hear his footfalls moving away, sprinting.

I followed as fast as I could, avoiding the tall trees and overgrown bushes of the gardens; soon I found myself entering a moonlit and deathly silent cemetery. Vaulting a particularly tall wall I landed softly on the grass and spotted Tom only a few metres away. I raised my hands and cast out yet more blasts. One collided with a headstone, the other a tree.

As shards of wood and stone flew past him, he turned and sent tendrils of his own dark black energy at me; the air smelled sulphurous. I had trouble tracking them against the darkness of the night so to protect myself I produced a bold sapphire-blue shield extending out from my palms; the light emitted dimly illuminated Tom's angst-filled face, throwing it into relief. Bolts of his projected shadow slammed into my shield, pockmarking it with spidery impact flecks. Abruptly, he stopped and was off running again. Within seconds I had closed my palms and lowered my shield and was off following, sending as many of my own bolts towards him as I could muster. One caught his legs. He dropped hard to the ground and seizing my opportunity I leapt high into the air, drew my sword and landed within striking distance…'

Jonathon dropped the file he was reading onto his desk as he heard knocking at his door; a stone's impression resulted in a much more poetic report than when it was simply written by an agent: secretly Jonathon enjoyed reading them much more. "Come in!" he shouted.

The door opened slowly and Peter walked in, his suit unusually creased for him; fatigue hung on his face revealing the strain he felt.

"Sorry to interrupt. But I have finished with the gun!" Peter walked in and sat on the chair that Jonathon was pointing to. He handed a report over to Jonathon who gave it a cursory flick through.

"So, what exactly is it?" Jonathon asked.

Peter did not hide the annoyance which now crept across his face. He had worked hard, fitting investigating and writing the report around the vast number of other things he was working on.

"Well, my initial suspicions have been confirmed. It is a specialised projectile weapon. Fortunately, the barrel contained five projectiles inside at the time Zhing came into possession of it. The projectiles are a glass and steel

271

composite with a liquid substance inside," Peter stopped to pull down his glasses. He rubbed his eyes and flicked his fringe to one side.

"So, this is the gun that was used to shoot the vampire that Zhing encountered months ago?" Jonathon asked quickly.

"Yes, without doubt. Well, this one or one of this design. I have identified the liquid as the reactive agent 'Wonto factor three.' It is a well-known toxic agent used to kill vampires," Peter replied.

Jonathon again flicked through Peter's report, reading quickly through the first few pages.

"Thank you, Peter. I will go through this properly later," Jonathon said placing the report on the desk and picking up the one he had been studying previously.

"What's that you're reading?" inquired Peter.

"It is the first-person manuscript from Zhing's glimmer," Jonathon replied.

"Oh, the glimmer that Andrew produced? Who wrote the manuscript?" Peter said, leaning in forward.

"Andrew wrote it up after producing the glimmer. It is very interesting but I've only really just started it. It's quite slow, a lot on her investigation prior to Kristian's intelligence. I am just at the actual confrontation now," Jonathon replied, pulling the file close to his chest.

"Okay. Is she going to write a report when she returns?" Peter was a stickler for paperwork. "Oh, and can I have a look at that when you're finished? Or perhaps you could ask Andrew if he could spare someone to open the glimmer for me?"

"Sure. You can look through it after me. Or you could speak to Andrew if you like, I am sure he would open the glimmer for you. I would have done that myself but I find it much quicker to read than watch it through glimmer and I'm short on time."

Peter stood up and walked towards the door. "Okay, I will speak to Andrew tonight. I need to get some sleep now," and with that Peter exited the room.

Jonathon let out a muffled goodbye as Peter left and then quickly got back to the report and began reading from where he had left off.

'I instantly swung low, aiming for his legs. He drew back quickly as my blade cut only air. I then launched several strokes, aiming left, then right, high. He beautifully avoided every sweep of my blade as it glided unvictoriously past him. He moved back and threw a large bag he was carrying to the floor. He raced away from me, dodging in and out through the many trees that lined the cemetery. I made a long stroke aiming for his lower body; he stepped to one side as the blade locked between two individual trunks. He hit out at my hand and I lost a grip of my sword, he then kicked me in the chest, knocking me back.

He attempted to move closer to me and to strike again but my palms were up and I launched blue energy into his chest, sending him backwards into the trees. I regained my composure, as did he. We stared at each other for nearly twenty seconds, neither of us making a move. He was so close I could hear his heart beating, see the sweat pour from his face. He flinched, reaching for his bag; I sent another blast at him, which he evaded by rolling to one side. When he stopped, he sent a retaliation blast toward me; I managed to produce a small field deflecting the blast to the ground sending mud and grass flying high into the air.

He was at his bag, opening the zip and reaching deep within. I moved quickly, removed my sword from the trunks and, using a headstone, leapt into the air. Landing just a few steps from him, I saw him pull out a large rifle. I spun, kicking the gun out of his hands. I then swung my blade from high, aiming to strike him whilst he was reeling from my kick. The sword hit resistance and as I glanced down I saw Tom blocking my sword with two small blades. Each of his blades resembled the mouth of some monstrous predator insect, two extending blades meeting at the end with smaller sharp razors in the inner space of the blades. The main part of the blade was smooth and long. He pushed up, throwing my sword back and then quickly made a swing at my legs. I jumped back into the air, completing a backwards somersault. Landing on my feet, I looked down in relief. He had missed.

He too was also on his feet and heading towards me. We were both fighting hard. I saw his style was directionless and his technique was clumsy. I felt I was superior, both in swordsmanship and in the use of the weapons we were yielding. After a few more clashes, I brought my blade to my side and took one strong swing to the right. His blades collided with mine and they shattered into useless fragments. After my sword had reached the end of its arc to my left side, I was already sending it back, lower this time. My sword cut deep into his leg and he fell to the ground.

From there he launched a long stream of his blackness at me. I attempted to produce a shield but was too slow. It hit me and lifted me up into the air. As I came back down, I was conscious of the environment around me and hoped I would land on soft ground and not broken-backed over a headstone. Fortunately, I landed on soft grass, rebounding slightly. My chest hurt as I was mildly wounded. I quickly returned to my feet and saw Tom escaping off in the distance, evidently not wanting to remain in combat with me.

He was stumbling, not making too much ground but moving fast for someone with a sizeable leg wound such as the one I had inflicted. I quickly shot some blasts at him. Sapphire flew through the air as he ducked and dived. Each bolt found an alternative target, hitting headstones and trees. Tom looked panicked and I understood in that instant that he was unable to produce a shield from his Kar'sin. His instincts were well honed and he avoided my blasts with some ease. I began to move after him. I paused and aimed my next bolt carefully. A tight, focused beam left my hand; I sensed that it was going to hit him. It collided with his legs; I felt relief as he wobbled. My eyes were locked onto his legs waiting to see them give way but without warning he seemed to have disappeared.

I realised what had actually happened was that his legs had flown up in the air after he had collided with a chest-height headstone. I then made haste to his position. As I got closer, I could see one of his feet poking out from behind the stone. It was still and lifeless. As I got closer still, more of his body came into view and my eyes fell upon his face and neck. His expression was of shock and fear. His head was close to the ground and awkwardly positioned and it was clear to me then that his neck was broken.

I stood there for a few minutes slowing my breathing and taking in the body. I looked for visual signs of life before I moved down and checked his pulse. He was dead.'

Jonathon put down the report with a sigh. It was obvious that Zhing had not meant to kill him with that blow, but he also understood there was little chance of Zhing simply subduing her mark and bringing him back as a captive; she had been in a dual to the death and, fortunately, she had won. He was pleased in many ways but disappointed in others. Tom had had the answers to his questions; answers that could have shed light onto a dark and sinister plan, but now those answers followed him into the afterlife.

...

The wooden post shattered into pieces as a large bolt of raging jade-green energy slammed into its side. Kristian turned and let out a scream of frustration. "Damn it!" He was angry with his self-control. He was honing his non-palm object projection techniques, the goal being to slice the stump cleanly in half. His mind was elsewhere, however, dwelling on Oliver and Leceth.

Moving along, Kristian stepped in front of another wooden post. Closing his eyes, he attempted to focus himself. After emptying his mind he began to imagine a sharp, sword-like mass of energy forming inches in front of the post. He could see in his mind the green bolt slicing through the wood. Suddenly an awful grim image of Oliver's tormented dead face flickered unbidden into his thoughts and, with that, he opened his eyes, startled, losing his concentration. For the second time a post exploded and splintered into tiny pieces, skidding across the floor as his errant projection made contact with the wood.

"Damn it." Kristian fell to his knees and placed his hands over his face.

"Mourning your failures will not solve them, Mr. Wallace," said a familiar and comforting voice from behind him. Turning his head, Kristian was surprised to see the illustrious Yi-Mao standing behind him. Rising to his feet, he was filled with a sense of happiness and comfort. Yi-Mao was his mentor and guide, he brought reassurance and security.

"Master. When did you get back?"

"Just. I had a quick talk with Jonathon and thought I would check in on you next," as he spoke, he walked towards Kristian.

Kristian was pleased that his master's first thoughts had been for him. It had been hard times lately and he was more than pleased to be back in the presence of arguably the greatest leader that the Phoenixes had ever had.

"How was China?" he asked.

"Interesting, to say the least. I spent a lot of time meditating with old friends. I am pleased to be back though and I hear that you've been having your own adventures here?" replied Yi-Mao.

Kristian smiled like a Cheshire cat; that was an understatement, he thought. "Well, first Berlin and then the Jakyll. I suppose you could call that an adventure. I would have described them as nightmares!" Kristian half-joked.

"A nightmare it may have been, but from what I am told, you handled the situations with valour, in true Phoenix tradition despite your time away from us."

Kristian smiled proudly for a second and then his smile faded as he remembered his slaughter of the three men in the warehouse. The events came flooding to the forefront of his mind. "Well, I guess you haven't spoken to too many people then," Kristian said reflectively. "The Jakyll certainly wasn't a resounding success." he lifted his shirt up and showed his master the scars that ran deeply across his belly.

At the sight of the long discoloured scar, Yi-Mao did not flinch. "Well, trophies of our valiant deeds come in many shapes and sizes." As he spoke, he drifted over to the many wooden posts that Kristian had been practising on.

Kristian looked to the floor as he dropped his shirt. He had not thought of his scar as a trophy; the word signified that it was something to treasure, something won, but to him it would be a constant reminder of how slow his technique was.

"In time. In time," Yi-Mao spoke without a catalyst, almost as though he had read Kristian's thoughts. "You have been practising your Kar'sin then?"

Kristian pointed to the floor and gave a disappointed and sarcastic look.

"Not going so well?" Yi-Mao chuckled.

"No, it really isn't. I'm trying to improve my non-palm projection and object projection but it just seems to keep going wrong."

Yi-Mao positioned himself in front of one of the undamaged posts. The room was lit for a second by three bright sharp yellow flashes. Kristian stared in amazement as three intense yellow daggers sliced through the wood leaving a slight smell of scorched pine. The post split into four even pieces and fell to the floor with a soft clatter. Yi-Mao turned and looked at him. "What's so hard?" followed by a friendly wink.

Kristian was impressed. He was also annoyed. He had been practising for most of the day and his technique was still nowhere near his master's. "How?" he cried. "I'm calm, focused and prepared but it just doesn't materialise."

"Show me," requested Yi-Mao, to which the young Phoenix host moved to the next intact post. He attempted what he had practised all day. And like all his other attempts, his outcome was failure. From imagination to realisation, the image of Oliver burst into his mind. The post exploded again in a flash of jade.

"I can see the problem," said Yi-Mao as he turned his back on Kristian and walked a few steps. "You lack determination and you are unfocused as to why the wood needs to be split."

"No, I have focus. I have drive, it's something else," he replied agitated.

"You misunderstand me. You have calm and focus but you are without purpose. You need to understand your goal," Yi-Mao replied calmly.

"The purpose is to slice the wood. My goal is to make two pieces of wood," Kristian replied sarcastically.

"Slicing the wood is a means, not a goal. You need to understand why you want two pieces of wood, and then you will know how to achieve it." As he spoke, he sliced another stump into four parts.

Kristian contemplated what he was being told, beginning to understand. He slowly walked to another post and attempted the projection again. Yi-Mao stood back; Kristian was confident that he had it in him. His mind was closed, his thoughts solely on the task ahead: the goal. He could see the outcome in his mind but immediately and without warning, Oliver's face appeared into his head again and shards of wood were flying in all directions as he opened his eyes. "God damn it!" he cried.

"In time, with practice. Patience is a skill that needs practising too." Yi-Mao walked over and gave him a consoling pat on the shoulder. "Sometimes it helps to sleep on it. Wake up with a new outlook."

Kristian did not see how sleeping would help the problem. The image came without warning and was not under his control. "Sure," he said, sounding defeated.

The pair began to walk to the door together and for an instant he thought about having one more try but as he saw the mess he had made, he gave up on that idea. "I will try again tomorrow, I guess," Kristian said.

The pair stopped in their tracks. Yi-Mao turned to face the young man. "So I assume you haven't told them yet?"

"Told who, what?" Kristian was confused.

"Your companions? And Jonathon; that you are planning on staying for good."

Kristian was almost certain that his master was reading his mind somehow; he wondered for a moment if Phoenixes could do that.

"No, how did you know I was staying? I haven't told anyone," Kristian said.

"Well," chuckled Yi-Mao. "People who are intent on leaving rarely spend hours in the sparring room. And I assumed that you had not told anyone. You seem tense so I took a wild guess!"

Kristian was surprised at how astute his mentor was; he told himself never to be astounded by Yi-Mao ever again, the man was full of surprises.

"So you are staying then? Why haven't you told anyone?" Yi-Mao asked.

It took a few seconds for Kristian to reply; saying the words aloud would make his decision final.

"Yes, I am," Kristian paused again, he knew why he had not told anyone: he was afraid. Telling people would mean he couldn't back out, no more coffee shop, no more Uni – he would be bound to his word. He explained this to Yi-Mao. It made perfect sense to him. It was what he expected from all in the Order. Nobility and pride.

"I am proud of you. You have a bright future here," Yi-Mao said as he patted Kristian on the back.

Kristian again smiled at the wise old master, it was not solely to mask his worries, and in part it was genuine. He was uplifted by the words of encouragement and was filled with the desire to earn that trust, that pride.

- Chapter Eighteen -

Sensitive Truths

The brown leather couch became almost unbearably uncomfortable the more frequently she sat in it. Even the coffee in the café was becoming unsatisfying, almost to the point Zhing thought she might give caffeine up altogether. She had only chosen this spot as it was an ideal vantage point to monitor Passel Tower, a twenty-storey building sat in the business district of Paris. It was the headquarters to Leceth's legitimate businesses; legitimate in the sense that they operated in the mainstream human world.

Leceth often visited the building, usually once a week for a regular meeting with his top staff. It was one of the most advanced vampire-friendly buildings in the world and was the official address for a range of businesses: property management, banks, law firms. The employees of the building's companies were predominantly human; some of them retired from long careers there completely unaware of their proximity to vampires and the sinister reality to their work.

Zhing watched people come in and out of the rotating glass doors and her mind still wondered about how she was going to fulfill her secret mission. Finding evidence of

Leceth's involvement in Kristian's capture or Oliver's murder was always going to be a delicate matter and possibly an impossible one. Breaking into Passel Tower would be too risky, she thought; too dangerous even for her. For days she had watched and logged the comings and goings of noted individuals she had prior intelligence on. The exact course of action to obtain evidence had eluded her and she was beginning to worry she was going to have to give up, or try for permission to break into the ominous building she gazed upon.

Drinking the last of her coffee, Zhing, with a gulp of disgust, considered whether she should stay and have another or head over to one of the two other locations she had been monitoring in the city. Placing the cup down she turned to grab her coat deciding that she would move on, mainly out of boredom than the thought that a change of location might prove more fruitful.

Standing up and sliding her coat on, Zhing was shocked to hear a voice that, although had only been heard once before, was unforgettable; high-pitched and grating, she knew instantly who it belonged to.

"Leaving my dear? Can I not buy you a drink?"

Zhing looked at the short plump man that now stood in front of her. His chubby face rippled as a sly grin stretched his face. His small semicircular glasses rested on the tip of his round, squidgy nose. "Please stay. Let me get you something. You seem somewhat distracted, deep in thought, and I'm sure another drink will help put things into perspective," his voice grated on Zhing and the thought of staying and talking to him repulsed her.

"I'm sorry, I'm on official business and need to get on. Besides you're one of the last people I'd like to spend any time with," as Zhing finished speaking she started for the exit.

The man took a seat; confident and bold, he now spoke with a slightly lower tone. "As you like. Though if you wish to know the answer to your question, Leceth's recent

281

exploits, you might have to forego your disdain of me; please take a seat and accept my most gracious offer of a hot beverage."

Zhing paused in the doorway; her natural instinct compelled her to ignore his taunt but the need to complete her mission overrode the feeling in her gut. Turning on her heels and heading back to the chair she gracefully sat down and without showing any outward sign of conflict or contrition she said, "I'll have a large cappuccino with an extra shot, please."

Admiring her form the man simply acknowledged the request and made his way to the counter. Zhing stared after him taking in his physical appearance; it sickened her as much as the thought of who he was. Anyone who was anyone in the Order had been briefed on his file, how to recognise him in the flesh and of his dangerous nature and opportunistic tendencies which he so often flaunted. 'Mr. Hinkley' was the name he was known by. The Order suspected this wasn't his real name but it was the alias he had been known by for several centuries. Zhing knew he was old, she remembered in a briefing that records on him went as far back as the origins of the Order itself, or that's what Saresh had suggested at that time.

As her eyes fixed on him she could hear the voices of teachers and mentors in her head lecturing her about Mr. Hinkley. The voice of Peter played loudly: 'Mr. Hinkley is of unknown origin. His allegiances are never revealed and his motives for supplying information are often dubious at best. Any dealings with him should be carried out by high-ranking Order officials only. Mr. Hinkley should be treated with extreme caution.' Zhing inwardly smirked at how clear her recollection of Peter's words were, considering she, like most at the London office, tried very hard to ignore everything Peter said.

"The girl will bring our drinks over in a second," Mr. Hinkley said as he wobbled back to his seat. "You look troubled. Don't worry my dear; I'm simply here to help," Mr. Hinkley uttered as he slumped back into the chair.

The words did little to dispel her fears; in fact she found his need to reassure her of his 'good' intentions extremely unnerving.

"I'm not troubled, thank you. So you say you want to help. How?" Zhing's tone was her usual, direct and professional.

The sly grin again stretched across his face and it irked Zhing even more. His hands, which had rested together on his lap, rose to his face with his two index fingers touching his lip. It appeared like he was holding back his words, determining exactly what information he was about to reveal.

"Well, I have some time-sensitive information that may provide you with the answers you seek," his speech seemed even more high-pitched. Zhing winced uncontrollably at his voice and wondered how he knew what she wanted.

"Answers that I seek?" she asked, giving a fake confused expression.

"Yes. Answers to the Order's recent situation. I'm aware of many things. You shouldn't be surprised. You must be aware of who I am and what I do," he replied smugly.

"Of course I know who you are. We have met before, briefly. I am just curious to know what you think it is that I'm after exactly. And how you think you know it?" Zhing's tone was harsh and as she finished speaking a young girl placed two cups of hot coffee in front of the pair.

Mr. Hinkley waited for the server to leave, following her with his eyes, before he responded. "I see you wish me to make the first move. I admire your suspicious nature. I know you are looking into Leceth, I know you are trying to ascertain his recent whereabouts. And I'm also of the belief that you want to find out if he has anything to do with the recent passing of a Mr. Oliver McKenzie. Is that accurate enough?" Again his response appeared smug.

Zhing didn't immediately respond but picked up her cup and took a bitter sip of coffee; with the porcelain still at her lips she gave him a small and subtle nod to indicate that he was, indeed, spot on.

"So now we have the initial mistrust out of the way, we can move on to actual business," as he spoke he grabbed his own coffee and attempted to sit back, but his large chubby body prevented him from looking completely comfortable in the chair.

"So what information do you have? And what do you want in return?" Zhing asked.

"I do like your directness. It is an unusual trait in the individuals I often deal with. You, my lovely, are a breath of fresh air," his compliment felt like anything but to Zhing; she wondered if he could make her feel any more revolted than she felt right now. Before she could say anything he burst back into speech. "Right, answering your questions; I am aware of a situation that, as I said before, is time-sensitive; although this shouldn't be a problem for you. From this most fortunate of circumstances you will find yourself in possession of what I believe to be a set of very illuminating documents. I shall generously give you details so you can take advantage of this opportunity. As for what I want in return for all this, well, I want nothing; I'm giving you this information for free." he winked at Zhing as he finished talking.

Zhing was taken aback by Mr. Hinkley's offer. She had never before heard of him giving anything up for nothing in return. This all seemed out of place and this made her wary of his motives. "For free? Seriously, you want nothing in return? You are willing to give me this information freely to me now?"

"Yes. I can understand your suspicion. You are, no doubt, questioning my motives. I did contemplate asking for something in return, merely to ease your anxieties. But contrary to popular belief, I am not one for playing games. I wish to freely give you this information."

Zhing eyed him up and down. She didn't trust him, everything she had been told about him made her feel uneasy at this offering. "Really!?" she exclaimed. "You expect me to believe that? That I am not about to walk into some kind of trap?"

Mr. Hinkley paused for a brief second; his mind pondered on whether to divulge his underlying motive. He was an extremely secretive individual and being honest about his actions was something he rarely did; it was how he had survived so long. "It is no trap. The information I shall pass to you is genuine," he stopped mid-flow as he composed his sentence. "As you are aware I am a dealer in information, exchanging knowledge and wisdom for more knowledge and wisdom. It's my business to know what is happening in this world. If the truth be known, I believe Leceth is up to something significant, devious. He is an extremely old vampire and his lineage can be traced back to the Old Ones. If he is up to something that would compel him to risk open warfare with the Order, then that is something I need to be aware of and the truth is I am completely unaware of his deeds, which I don't like. Me telling you a snippet of information now will encourage you to, no doubt, investigate further. And investigations lead to more people knowing, which in turn leads to a greater chance of me finding out which, at the end of the day, is my business. The more people know about Leceth and his plans, the more likely I'll hear about it. So you see the information isn't entirely free," as he finished speaking he took a long sip of his coffee nearly drinking it all in one long gulp.

Zhing listened to his words and for an instant she believed what he was saying; in the midst of the secrets and misdirection she knew there was an element of truth to what he was saying. "Okay, say I believe you. There is no guarantee you will hear about what I find out. So why tell me?"

"I will tell you because the information is worthless to anyone but you. There is no guarantee, you're right about that. But it's worth the risk to me," as he finished he polished off the last dregs of his coffee.

"So what do you know?" Zhing asked pushing her doubts to one side.

"Good. What I tell you now is true. Whether you act upon it or not is your own business. You are aware of a man called Reginald Salt?" He stopped, waiting for Zhing to acknowledge that she had heard of Leceth's number-one human accomplice, his most trusted mortal and the director of his day-to-day operations. "Good, well have you heard of a Mr. David Rumble?" Again he paused.

Zhing looked upwards briefly, searching her mind, "No."

"Well I didn't think you would have. Well, David is one of Reginald's personal assistants. And like so many young career-minded men, he has been promoted far beyond his talents should allow. For this we must be grateful. For Mr. Rumble has been struggling for months to carry out his duties and, against protocol, he has been taking some of his work home."

"Work?" she whispered inquisitively.

"Yes. He has taken many documents home from time to time; he currently has quite the substantial load at his home. Coincidently Reginald has requested, in the last few days, that several of these documents, stored away at his residence, be destroyed. Obviously, Reginald is unaware of their whereabouts and David has no doubt informed his manager that he has completed their destruction; but these condemned papers are very much intact and still at his home." Taking a small scrap of paper from his jacket pocket he passed it to Zhing before continuing, "That is his address. I suspect he will destroy them soon, likely tonight when he gets home; hence the time-sensitive warning. You will need to acquire them before he destroys them. It shouldn't be a problem for a Phoenix. He has two vampire guards, but again, no problem for a Phoenix."

Zhing stared at the address; her mind raced with delight and anticipation. She agreed with Mr. Hinkley's assessment that getting these documents should not be too difficult, not for her. Thinking about the potential breakthrough she had been given she wondered whether she should thank him but decided not to. As much as she was delighted at the information she couldn't help the feeling of mistrust and suspicion. If it proved to be accurate and rewarding then she would owe him her thanks, but before this could be determined he was simply a guy with a dubious history who had told her some lies and that was well within his nature.

"Well if it is that time-sensitive, I should be going," she said sipping her half-filled cup and standing to her feet.

"You are an extremely driven young lady. Straight to business. Well I shall wish you good luck. And if you do find out anything please feel free to let me know." He knew she wouldn't but he wanted to say it.

"We shall see," she replied this time sounding smug herself. Zhing left the café before any more communication could possibly take place between the pair of them. Mr. Hinkley watched Zhing through the glass as she made her way down the street. He picked up her coffee and finished it off. Placing it down he felt a sense of achievement and joy. He had passed on everything he had intended to and not a mote more. "Foolish child. Soon, my brothers; soon you will be dead," as he muttered to himself his smile returned, this time taking on a very sinister twist.

...

That night Zhing was upon the large house in the middle of the French capital for which she had been given the address. With bright fierce sapphire blue flashes the two vampires guarding the home had been easily subdued. Moments later Zhing was quickly inside disabling all manner of surveillance systems and overcoming simple magical barriers. The energy produced by a Phoenix was often used to smash through weak protective mystical fields; Zhings powers were well suited for this evening's task.

Her way through the house wasn't silent or stealthy but she had cut the power and fortunately had not bumped into any of the family members that lived there. The house was large but not extravagant; making her way through the hallways she was being guided by the voice of her Phoenix.

Entering a room which the voice inside her seemed to be indicating she should go in to, she found herself in what appeared to be a study. The room was illuminated in blue light as a floating sapphire globe had appeared over Zhing's shoulder as she closed the door behind her. She made her way straight for the desk that had mountains of paper and files upon it. Quickly she began to look through it, collating sheets of paper that looked important. Then her eyes fell upon a red folder marked 'for the shredder' scribbled on the front. Picking it up she flicked it open and began to examine the contents.

Zhing smiled as her eyes widened taking in what she had in her hands. It was her lucky break. It was enough information to draw her investigation to an end. In less than a minute Zhing was outside the house heading for the French offices of the Order of Light with the file and documents in hand.

It had been easy; she thanked Mr. Hinkley in her mind as the details he provided were more than accurate. She wondered how he had come by the information but now it didn't matter. She was thankful that she would soon be leaving France and getting back to London. The last few months had been busy and even Zhing, with her almost fanatical work ethic, wanted a bit of time off.

...

Zhing walked into Jonathon's office without knocking and threw piles of scruffy paper on his desk. Jonathon lurched up from his arms where he was resting. "Zhing?" he said as he blinked his vision clear.

"You might want to have a look at that!" Zhing said as she pointed to the papers she had shoved under his nose. Jonathon picked up the scraps and began to read.

It took him a few minutes to fall upon something that made his entire face light up. "This is good, this is really good!" he said looking up.

Zhing's response was to step forward and to rummage through the file; taking one of the few white sheets out she placed it on top of the pile. "This one is good too," she said through a large smile.

Jonathon's eyes grew bigger and he looked more animated than he had for months. "Well done." He placed the sheets down on the table. "You have done an excellent job, again. You're probably shattered. Go and get some rest."

Zhing stepped back, gave a nod and was gone before he could even say goodbye.

Jonathon picked up his phone. "Can you come to my office, I need you to write something up?" He put the phone down quickly then lifted the receiver again and made another call. "Peter? Meeting in one hour – main conference room. Bring staff. Okay, bye," he dropped the phone back on the hook.

He picked it up again, as Julia walked in, "Type this up for me please," he said as he handed her some papers, "Oh, can you do ten copies of the original as well please?"

He did not wait for her reply; he was soon speaking on the phone again.

"Get me the Council. I want to speak with Leceth!"

...

- Chapter Nineteen -

Friends Forever

It had been nearly four weeks since Kristian had made the decision to ask Jess to leave. He knew at the time that it was the right decision to make but if there was anyone in the world he would have wanted at his bedside over the last couple of weeks, it would have been her.

He was glad that Kieran had agreed to come along with him that day to meet Jess at Waterloo train station. Over the last few weeks, he had felt closer to him, their friendship had grown; regrown to what it once was.

Kieran glanced at his Mickey Mouse watch, "What time is she coming in?" he asked.

Kristian looked at Kieran's watch and smirked. "Ten past. She should be here any minute now," Kristian looked up at the announcement board, scanning for details that he might have overlooked. Her journey had already disappeared which was an indicator that her train had already arrived. "She must be here," Kristian uttered.

The two young men made their way towards the exit turnstiles as hordes of people began making their own way down the platform, heading towards them.

In the midst of them all Kristian spotted the long dark locks of Jess's beautiful hair. He could not make out her face yet, as there were too many people surrounding her, but he just knew that it was her.

"There she is," Kristian said, pointing into the masses.

As Kieran glanced over, she emerged from the crowd and exited the turnstile; she looked over and spotted her friend and her face lit up. Kristian pushed his way towards her and they hugged emphatically, lasting some time Kieran felt awkward as he stood patiently at their side. Jess pulled away from Kristian, looking up at Kieran.

"Oh, you must be Kieran. Pleasure to meet you. Again!" Jess did not wait for a reply and immediately hugged Kieran as well. "I hope you've been taking care of my Kris." she laughed as she rubbed his blonde hair playfully.

"Of course. We all have," came Kieran's response.

At Jess's request, the three of them made their way to one of the station's cafés. Kristian took her heavy bag and slung it over his shoulder. "How are your parents?" Kristian asked. "Is your dad still off from work?"

"No," Jess responded. "He went back last week; his hand is all better now. I'm not even sure there was anything wrong with it to be honest; he's a bit of a hypochondriac really, for an old soldier."

They found a nice round table in a utilitarian station café; the two of them sat themselves down whilst Kieran took their orders and headed for the till.

"So, are things all better now? Does this mean I can come out of hiding?" said a serious Jess. She leaned back in her chair and nodded in Kieran's direction. "He's cute!"

"Hmm, I guess," Kristian said absently, "and, I'm not too sure what you should do really; I'm told things aren't as serious as they were. It feels like things are better now, but I still want you to be extra careful."

Jess raised her left eyebrow as she spoke. "That's not very comforting, you know?"

"Well, if I'm being honest, the repercussions of what I did in Berlin have come and gone, I'm told there's not a lot else the Council can do about it. Jonathon seems optimistic, but there is a meeting this Friday. We shall see about it then," Kristian said, trying to sound a bit more reassuring.

Jess didn't really understand the intricate details of the world Kristian was involved in; how could she when he himself was so uncertain? She gave a smile, which warmed his heart; their hands met over the table.

"I'm sure it will work out. What more can I say on the subject, hey?" said Jess.

"So, is everything okay at home then?" Kristian replied, striving to have a normal conversation.

"Yes, everything is fine, I'm looking forward to getting back to lectures. Have you been in to university at all? I guess not, huh?" Jess said.

"No, I haven't, I think I will have to repeat the whole year. My parents are going to kill me. I can hardly tell them the truth can I? They would never understand," Kristian said mournfully. As he finished, Kieran appeared with a tray of drinks and sandwiches.

"You two caught up then?" Kieran said before taking a sip of his coffee, but it was too hot and it made his lip curl.

"Of course!" they both replied.

"So are you going to show me then?" Jess said to Kristian.

"Show you what?" He knew what she meant but the sheer thought of it pained him. He was not proud of it and did not want to show it off like a trophy, despite what Yi-Mao had told him.

"The scar, of course." Jess laughed. It was obvious that she did not realise how much carrying that scar was affecting him. She just wanted to see proof of her friend's bravery, an extra source of evidence for the mystical world that she struggled to believe in.

Kristian slowly rose to his feet and lifted his shirt. Her eyes did little to conceal the shock she felt at the sight of it. Even Kieran glanced at it in surprise.

"It looks bad!" she said as she ran a finger across one of the grey lines that lay on his abdomen.

"It's okay. It hurts sometimes. It's a trophy I'm told, not sure if I see it like that though," Kristian replied.

"Well, I'm not sure about you, but I would have preferred a medal!" Jess laughed and the two men followed suit.

Kristian dropped his shirt and returned to his seat, desperate to move the conversation on; he picked up his coffee and re-enacted Kieran's failure, taking a sip of the piping hot drink. Jess smirked at Kristian's pained face as she turned her questioning towards Kieran.

The three of them sat and chatted happily like there were no worries in their world for over two hours and four coffees. Kieran and Kristian told Jess all about the Order; they were not even sure if they were allowed but Kristian didn't care, he trusted her. They made plans for the week ahead and, other than going up to the till for drinks and food and the occasional toilet stop, they were content to sit there.

No one interrupted and in the lulls of conversation they people-watched or stared at the large television screen, displaying 24-hour news. They all turned to the TV for one enjoyable report, close to their hearts.

Mass prank or huge cover-up' was the headline and a young hook-nosed northern reporter presented the story.

I stand at the site of what is being called the biggest mystery of the century. Was this damage caused by a ferocious monster that the government is concealing from us or is it the site of the largest organised mass prank?

The report detailed how there was no evidence to the truth about the events of that day in Trafalgar Square, no first-hand witnesses, no CCTV, no recordings of any kind. The only evidence came from the fact that the fountain was damaged and a few people had come forward claiming that loved ones had called them in terror, claiming that a beast was killing people in the square.

Each time the report was repeated, the three of them chuckled. In hindsight, it was not very funny but the thought

293

that they knew the truth was amusing to them. The power of magic was overwhelming to Kristian as he came to realise just how powerful the spell that Andrew had cast had been.

"That was no easy spell. I sure as hell couldn't have pulled it off," Kieran proclaimed.

"Do you have the magic thing inside you as well then?" Jess asked as politely as she could, remembering a brief discussion she had had with Kristian about it.

"The Trinity, yes, but not a Phoenix." Kieran started to wonder if they were telling her too much. He glanced at his watch; as Jess noticed she looked over to Kristian.

"Right, I will have to leave you two. I have a meeting with some of the Order's accountants, as fun as that sounds! Well, it's been a pleasure properly meeting you, Jess, you are exactly how Kristian described you," Kieran stood up and made his exit.

"He's nice." Jess said after Kieran was out of earshot.

"So what do you want to do now? Anything you want, okay? It's on me." said Kristian, delighted that he finally had her back.

"Whatever I want?" she replied unenthusiastically.

"Yeah, we could catch up with some Uni folk, see Jason? Is that still a thing?" Kristian enquired.

"Ha. No, that died a death. You see I had a lot of other things on my mind. Like worrying about you," Jess replied.

"You don't have to worry about me, I am in a good place now," Kristian said, his tone genuine and revealing.

Something was now troubling her. She looked at her friend and realised the truth; she had seen a look in his eyes when he had been talking about the Order and from his last words this had been confirmed.

"You're going to stay, aren't you?" Jess asked.

He was not surprised that she knew, but he still let out a sigh. "God, am I that easy to read? First Yi-Mao, now you!" Kristian uttered.

"Yi who?"

"Ha, that mentor guy in the Order that I mentioned earlier. Well, that doesn't matter. But, yes, yes Jess. I am going to stay. I feel like I have to, it's different this time. It's hard, but I want to as well." Kristian replied. "You all right?" he asked, seeing a worried expression flit across her face.

"Of course," she replied, forcing a smile. "It's your choice isn't it? But I don't want you disappearing from my life, okay?" Jess said as she grabbed his arm tightly.

"Hey! That won't happen, you know that," Kristian grinned reassuringly at her.

"Well, what do you want to do? I have money." he now smirked cheekily as he pushed his chair back and took her hand.

"Well, in that case let's go and get drunk!" she laughed, standing up, "Phoenixes are allowed to drink, right?"

"Abso-bloody-lutely," Kristian roared.

...

The two men sat in almost absolute darkness, the only light source in the room coming from a small desktop lamp. Most of the people that lived in the Order's Headquarters were fast asleep at this late hour but, for Yi-Mao and Jonathon, this was the perfect opportunity to discuss the most secretive of all Order business. The pair had been talking for over an hour in Jonathon's office. The topics of discussion ranged from the events in Berlin and London before it moved on to the mystery of the Quartet.

Jonathon spent a lot of the meeting describing the battle between the Jakyll and Kristian as well as the findings from Zhing and Kristian's investigations. Yi-Mao had been partially briefed on the situations when he was in the Shing'tao temple but hearing it from Jonathon placed it in perspective.

"Well, Kristian has, I think, decided to stay," Yi-Mao said to a bemused-looking Jonathon.

"He's told you this?" Jonathon replied.

"Yes, in confidence. He is a gifted host. More gifted than he realises."

Jonathon pondered on the good news for a second. "That is excellent," he whispered. "I shall obviously keep this to myself, until he decides to tell everyone." Yi-Mao nodded in agreement.

"Brendan and Amar return from Japan tomorrow. I am sure he is eager to get back to investigating the Quartet now that we have discovered the urn," Yi-Mao said.

Jonathon looked a tad worried; he attempted to hide it by covering his face with his hand, as though he was holding his head up.

"You have not told him?" Yi-Mao asked, surprised.

"No, I haven't told him yet. I was trying to keep the knowledge to as few people as possible. I wanted to test my mole theory. I shall tell him tomorrow. I have sent the urn to Kara and her team in New York. Other than her, yourself, me and Kristian, no one else in the Order knows of it," said Jonathon.

Yi-Mao looked at Jonathon disapprovingly. He did not share his belief in his mole theory. The evidence wasn't there to support it, not strong enough to warrant suspicion. "You haven't even told Peter?" Yi-Mao spoke calmly, trying to conceal his disapproval.

Jonathon replied with an ashamed "No."

"You can't be serious, Jonathon?" Yi-Mao said sounding shocked. "Peter is the master of knowledge, Chief Librarian. He will not be pleased to discover that you kept something like this from him," Yi-Mao attempted to regain his vocal composure.

Jonathon looked uneasy. "I'm sure he will be okay, he should understand. I will inform him as soon as Kara has finished her report. I will let him have a look then. It's not that I don't trust him; I would trust him with my life. It's just the more people know, the more it's harder to track if information leaks out."

The pair continued to talk about the Quartet and their theories on possible members. The name at the top of their list was naturally Leceth's.

"Well, it would make sense," said Jonathon. "He's certainly ascended to the head of the Council with apparent ease. He has links to Sauror; the only problem is that we have no evidence apart from the urn, no proof he knows anything about the Quartet."

"He is coming here on Friday. What will you do if he rebuts the evidence that Zhing gathered? Looking through it, it is far from being concrete. He could easily counter it," replied Yi-Mao.

"I know you're right, I've thought that myself. Though, it would be nice for him to explain why his charter jet was on its way to Berlin the night that Kristian was captured. And it will be interesting to hear him explain why he had those assassins on his payroll," said Jonathon. To me, the evidence was all too clear, but then he was biased. The evidence at face value was poor and wouldn't stand up to close scrutiny; everyone knew that, everyone except Kristian.

"So, Kristian believes that this will be enough?" questioned Yi-Mao.

"Well, when I told him what Zhing had found, he made it clear that he thinks we should move against Leceth. I tried to explain the politics of the situation to him, but he is very hot-headed and, understandably, didn't care. To him, Leceth is responsible for the death of his friend," answered Jonathon.

The pair continued to talk about the meeting with Leceth that was planned for two days' time. They talked about the possibility of arresting him but it was clear that unless he confessed, which they both knew was never going to happen, then an arrest was mere fantasy.

...

The music was at a level that was pleasant to their ears, loud enough to hear, but soft enough to speak over, just how Kristian liked it. He and Jess had been drinking for most of the afternoon and evening, going from pub to bar, they were now in a club that had several levels. The level that they were now sitting in was called 'The Lounge.'

They had been joined a few hours ago by the members of the Alpha Team. Jonathon had granted them all a night off, as long as they were fresh-faced at work the following day.

Rachel could not help her drunken desire to drag everyone up onto the dance floor. She was not best pleased that they were now in the quietest part of the club. Jean and Sam were both sitting at one end of a long squishy sofa drinking pints of beer and discussing football.

Kieran, Jess and Kristian were all squeezed onto one couch, talking about the Order and the upcoming meeting with Leceth. The chat was more along the lines of reminding Jess of the details that they had mentioned earlier in the day.

"And so, that is the story of how the Order was formed" finished Kieran, who had rambled on in a drunken state for the last half an hour.

Jess burst out laughing and it was not long before Kristian was laughing too. "What's so funny? Hey, what's funny?" Kieran asked seriously. He looked enraged by their laughing; in his drunken condition, he was sure that they were mocking him.

Before Kieran could say anything else, Rachel came dancing over. "Come and dance with me, please?" she pleaded. She pulled on Kieran's arm and dragged him towards the dance floor leaving Kristian and Jess in floods of laughter.

"I have missed this," laughed Jess as she mockingly punched Kristian in the arm.

He immediately pounced on her and began tickling her to which she screamed loudly. Bringing her to tears, he fell back in his seat. "I'm so glad you're back. So, what do you think of all my new friends?" Kristian shouted.

"I like!" Jess proclaimed.

"Good, 'cause I really like them," Kristian replied, which was overheard by Sam and Jean who simply raised their pints and let out a cheer.

Jess pulled Kristian down close to her. She moved towards his ear and attempted to whisper. "Have you told them yet?"

Kristian loudly shushed her, but it was too late, the two men had heard the her.

"Told us what?" Sam demanded.

Jess started to giggle as she attempted to apologise to Kristian.

"Oh, it's nothing," Kristian mumbled.

"If it is nothing, then you can tell us," Sam replied. Both Jean and Sam had now got up and moved down the sofa. They manoeuvred their way in between Jess and Kristian.

"Come on, tell us," said Jean.

"Guys, seriously, it's nothing," Kristian was blushing and sweating as he tried to sound believable over Jess's hysterical laughing.

"Just tell them!" said Jess. Kristian lowered his face into his hands. Sam pulled them back as Jean probed again. "What is it?"

"Okay, okay. The thing is guys, I've decided that I am going to stay in the Order. It's not a big deal, okay. It just is what it is. I'm gonna stay," Kristian said slowly and soberly.

Sam and Jean instantly leapt into the air in jubilation. It was clear that they considered it a big deal. They started dancing on the spot, and soon Jess was up with them. With excellent timing, Rachel and Kieran reappeared and asked what they had missed.

"Kristian is staying! He told us that he is staying for good," Sam cheered, bouncing around.

Rachel pushed into the middle of the group and joined in with the dancing.

Kieran just stood there in disbelief. "You're really staying?" he mouthed. Kristian nodded, and with that

Kieran's face broke out in a huge smile, which showed how happy he was.

...

- Chapter Twenty -

Hero or Fool

"It was clearly a mistake," said Volvir; pale, wrinkled skin which drooped around his cheeks muffled his voice. "We have now handed the Jakyll over to the Order, who will no doubt subject him to all kinds of tests," Volvir continued as many of the Council members struggled to hear his voice through his sagging lips.

Many people on the Council wondered how Volvir was still a member; he had to be the oldest man alive. He was frail and weak-looking, but looks could be deceiving.

"What else would you have us do, wizard? The Order has for too long treated us with nothing but contempt. They see us as impotent and afraid. We ensured that they rethink that view," came the deep voice of Môn'ark Toral.

"I am sure we've done little to change that view, Môn'ark. Especially as they have now demanded to meet with Leceth. Their success with the Jakyll has emboldened them," Volvir replied.

The Council quickly erupted into a cacophony of shouts with every member striving to put forward his or her views on the matter. The Council's order would often fall apart during meetings such as these; there had been small internal wars fought over such minor trivialities as seating arrangements.

"Silence!" came the cold, slicing voice of Leceth, sitting at the head of the long table. All twelve members of the Council immediately fell to their seats and held their tongues. "I take full responsibility for releasing the Jakyll, and I say it was a failure." As he spoke everybody around the table, except for Isobel, gasped.

"A failure I intended. It was to gauge their reactions, to see how far they would go, to see how they would respond. Many of you have expressed that it would be foolish for me to bow to their wishes, that going to their sanctuary would be a sign of cowardice and stupidity. Do you know what I say to that?" The room remained silent though a few members were itching to speak. "I say to hell with what you think. I was elected as chair of this great Council for a reason. You all know that I can handle the Order! I shall meet with them, listen to them, but if any of you think I shall bow to any demand they make, you are fools. I shall return to this Council, they will not make any move upon me. They will once again respect us, my friends, this I vow, I give you my honour." Leceth rose to some claps while others on the Council looked bemused. The most prominent member who seemed unimpressed with the speech was Volvir, who struggled to conceal his disapproval.

"You wish to add something, Volvir?" Leceth asked as he lowered himself back into his chair.

"Yes, go to the Order if you wish, but don't be assured that they will not try and arrest you. I hear they have evidence linking you to the murder of one of their own," Volvir replied.

Leceth chuckled darkly. "I am well aware of this and in fact, I know the evidence they have. Hear me old friend when I say it is baseless and it is nothing but circumstantial."

"Well, regardless of that fact, you cannot take their word that they will not try to arrest you on your arrival. You cannot trust the word of a human," said Môn'ark in his usual deep, aggressive tone.

Leceth turned his attention to his close ally and smiled intently. "My friend, I do not trust those at the Order at all. However, I have been given assurances from Karnel. He has given me his word that I will be unharmed and free to leave once the meeting is over."

Môn'ark slammed his fist against the table, but it was so grand and thick that it did not move. "You cannot take the word of that traitor. He is worse than a human." His disdain for Karnel covered his face.

"My friend, I do not trust him. But he has given his word on this one thing and I'm sure, like with all Vinji, his word counts for something doesn't it?"

Môn'ark looked like someone had stabbed a long blade through his chest. "Yes, it means something. However, that rat may have the body of a Vinji but he has the soul of a man. His honour is only just above that of a human."

"His word is enough for me, for now," Leceth said as Môn'ark raked his memories for instances where a Vinji had broken their bond.

Leceth waited a few moments before he stood up. "As much as I would love to continue this wonderful discussion, I have a meeting to prepare for. I will be taking Isobel to accompany me, she knows more than anyone about the affairs and workings of the Order." As soon as he had finished talking, he exited the room and the members broke out in conversation again. Isobel was the only one not to enter the debate that followed: Leceth, hero or fool?

...

Kieran paced after Roman whose determined walk was often hard to keep up with. Running late, he was still feeling a little fragile from the excessive drinks from two nights gone. Kieran's mind was pondering on what he was about to witness. The two wizards were nearing the end of a long corridor deep within the bowels of the Cardinal Office. The passage that they had found themselves in was empty of people and access to it could only be obtained via a guarded door off the central level. There were no other doors apart from the one they entered through, now behind them and almost out of sight.

Roman came to a sudden halt as he reached the end of the corridor. Kieran was soon at his side, panting a little from his mini power-walk.

"Well, it's a little narrower than I imagined," Kieran said as he stared at his reflection in the mirror that lay directly in front of him.

Roman turned his head and threw a disapproving expression at his younger companion. The mirror that covered the wall before them was seven foot high and three foot wide, more than large enough, Roman thought, to allow anyone to pass through. Roman as well as Kieran knew exactly where the doorway led and before activating it he quickly gave a flick of his hands and cast a spell. Out of the thin air around them, artic weather clothing materialised on him. His footwear became black winter boots, his jacket changed into a thick brown down-filled jacket. Kieran looked on with mild surprise at the speed; in addition to the outerwear he knew that Roman would have changed his base layers too, it was cold where they were going. Kieran quickly followed suit and cast his own spells, changing his clothing into more appropriate thermal wear although of brighter colours than Roman's.

Next to the mirror there were two podiums, each with a clear football-sized crystal resting on top. Roman waved his hands at the rocks and they instantly began to glow red. At the same time the reflections of the two wizards melted as the mirror itself seemed to turn to water. The puddle on the wall remained vertical, not spilling to the ground; it rippled as Roman turned to Kieran,

"Are you ready?" Roman asked, knowing that Kieran had never visited Carceran before. The portal in front of them was the only way to access the secure, remote prison that had been located in the middle of the Antarctic for nearly three hundred years.

"This part is the easy bit," Kieran replied, knowing full well that the trip there was a lot easier than the trip back. The portal itself was one-way, it only allowed travel to Carceran, those who needed to travel back had to make a very unpleasant trek to get far enough away from the prison's spell boundaries to be able to teleport away. Both Kieran and Roman knew that they could punch through the barriers and teleport themselves back from within the prison, but that would shatter many charms and leave Carceran's location detectable as well as its walls vulnerable; so a hostile trek was unavoidable.

The two men walked through the rippling portal; as soon as they passed the threshold the liquid hardened and the gleaming mirror surface returned; the two crystals' red glow faded. Roman and Kieran appeared in another corridor, the doorway that they had stepped out of was in the centre. There were two further doors at either end of the passageway, one led to the harsh outside, whilst the other opened into the main prison. As the two men approached the great entrance door to Carceran it opened before them; two tall wizards were standing guard, their hands raised with colourful energies flitting about them, spells ready to be discharged if needed.

"Sali Candicus," Roman uttered in greeting; the two guards stood to one side and let the two Trinity wizards enter.

The inside was as cold and harsh as the climate outside; it was all dark grey brick, one long corridor after another. Prison cells came off in every direction and Kieran was surprised to see so many wizards, crystals and symbols adorning the walls throughout the complex. After a few more minutes of Kieran awkwardly power-walking to keep up with Roman, the pair finally reached their destination. Roman traced his hand along some white symbols on the side of a door; they shone as the door's locks clicked into

305

life. As the door slowly began to open Kieran wondered what he was about to see; he hadn't seen the Jakyll since the day it was captured nearly a month ago. Roman, on the other hand, had visited him several times. Ever since joining the Trinity, and therefore being forbidden from participating in the world wizard-duelling championships, Roman focused his time on researching mystical creatures and dark entities; he was first to volunteer to assist with the Jakyll's incarceration.

The door opened and to Kieran's surprise no monster lay within; there, sitting on a bed, was a frail-looking middle-aged man. His skin was gaunt and pale, his eyes were sunken deep into the sockets. Kieran clocked an IV drip that was running into his arm and a plate of jelly-like cubes on a table next to the bed. The man's face lit up as he recognised Roman.

"Roman," the man jubilantly exclaimed.

Roman entered the room and signalled for him not to get off the bed.

"Don't get up, save your strength."

Kieran entered the room and noted, just behind the door, a male nurse sitting on a chair reading notes off a clipboard.

"Sir, I didn't realise you were coming today," the nurse said standing up at Roman's presence.

"Unplanned visit. Just wanted to check in on Mr. Mallory," Roman said as he turned to face the host of the Jakyll.

"Call me Thomas, please. I owe you so much."

"You don't owe me anything, Thomas. I'm just helping you realise your own potential," Roman replied to Mr. Mallory as Kieran cleared the threshold and the door closed behind him.

"Oh, but I do. You have helped so much, more than I ever thought possible. More than I could've dreamed," Thomas said; his face looked joyful, an expression that had for many years never been seen on it.

"Well, you're more than welcome. I'm glad you're making progress. Are you okay for us to talk through how things are going? This is my companion, Kieran, he is like me, a wizard. Would it be okay if we go through your notes together?" Roman signalled to Kieran who smiled towards the stranger at the mention of his name; Thomas acknowledged Kieran's expression with a similar one.

"Of course. Ask me anything. I never imagined I'd feel as good as I do," Thomas replied.

Roman signalled to the nurse for the file who readily handed it over. Roman began to look through it for a minute before passing it over to Kieran who eagerly examined the pages.

"So what rate are we on? And are we using the latest concoction?" Roman asked.

"Yes, it's the concentration I got sent this morning and it's running through at about half a mil a minute," the nurse replied.

"And how's that for you, Thomas?" Roman asked.

"It's good, better than the last. I don't hear the voices anymore with it. I don't feel the change stirring," Thomas said, sounding genuinely surprised.

"That's good to hear. And these gelatin-based supplements; are they working better?" Roman directed his question to the nurse.

"We're getting there, aren't we, Tom? They don't have the same physical effect. There's no hardening of the tongue or any dental change when consumed, though Tom experiences some psychological changes," the nurse replied.

"Yeah, they do work better. My mouth doesn't burn when I eat them. But I hear his voice; I feel his rage, his thirst. It doesn't seem as strong as it used to be, but it's there," Thomas said, his expression now laced with fear.

"Well, I'll revisit the potion we are using to make up the supplement when I get back. There's still room to tweak with mead wort and the solanaceae that we are using to dull the connection between the Jakyll and yourself," Roman explained.

"Thank you again. I still can't believe how much progress I've made these last weeks. Ever since this all started, when the vampires took me, my life's been hell; but in just a few short weeks you here have really helped me. Made me feel like I have a life again, like I don't have to kill myself," Thomas said gratefully.

"So, how much fluid are you able to take?" Kieran asked aloud, not directed at anyone.

"Including supplements and the IV, it's about nine hundred mils a day. That's not including food intake either. So we are nearly where we wanted to be at the start," the nurse answered.

"That's excellent. You're making fantastic progress. Dr. Gambon will be really pleased," Roman exclaimed.

"Yes, thank her as well. She's a little... direct, at times. But she's been great," Thomas said as Kieran stifled a laugh on hearing his words.

The four men chatted for another half-hour, reviewing every aspect of Thomas's intake. They assessed the potions that were used in the IV fluid and the supplements, the strict diet that he was on and even started to examine the accounts of how Thomas felt when he ate. Kieran and Roman didn't have much time, as Jonathon had wanted them back at Headquarters for the afternoon. Soon the two Trinity wizards were trekking through the snow and harsh winds. After nearly fifteen minutes of walking against a blizzard they arrived at a small plateau with glowing crystals in each corner, keeping the area clear of snow and ice. As the two wizards stepped onto the stony surface they both quickly cast their spells and teleported away, both were eager to return to the comforts of the Order.

...

Leceth's car pulled up outside the Order of Light Headquarters and pulled up alongside a tall, stocky but well-built man wearing an expensive-looking suit who was standing outside. Stepping out of the passenger seat, a similarly stocky but slightly shorter man moved to the rear of the car and opened the door for Leceth.

Leceth pompously stepped out of the car and gave a slight tilt of the head to his security guard who had assisted him. He then smiled coldly at the smartly dressed man who was still standing in the same spot. "Karnel," Leceth greeted.

"Leceth" replied Karnel. "I just wanted to be here to reassure you that you have my word that you will not be harmed and will be free to leave following the meeting," Karnel towered over Leceth as he gazed into the vampire's eyes; they glowed, reflecting the street light.

"You're looking very human and I must tell you, friend, it does not suit you." As Leceth was speaking he had turned back to the vehicle and was aiding Isobel out of it.

"Well, I cannot simply stand outside in my usual appearance, can I?" said a defensive Karnel who then changed his tone, turning to Isobel, "Good evening, my lady."

Isobel took a step to Leceth's side and smiled gently at Karnel. The three then walked up the grand steps towards the large oak doors. They were closely followed by four very intimidating security guards. Karnel helped open the doors as the six Council guests entered the building.

In the entrance lobby, Stanley stood at his desk; alongside him were Brendan and Roman. These three, who were among the most experienced Order members, watched as Leceth and his fellow Council companions entered and made their way towards them. Stanley moved and directed the guests towards the large open door that was located just behind and slightly to one side of his desk. As Leceth and Isobel entered the gallery conference room their eyes met with no one: the room was empty. Karnel paused at the entrance and did not follow them in.

"I shall be outside with the security guards if you require anything. Please take a seat, Jonathon will be with you shortly," Karnel said as he closed the doors.

Leceth and Isobel took seats close to where they had entered, which was at the far end of the conference table. Moments later Jonathon confidently entered the room, closely followed by Andrew. The two men acknowledged the two vampires as they made their way down to the opposite side of the large desk. Jonathon took the head seat, which was directly opposite Leceth. As Jonathon stared at Leceth's skeletal face, he was surprised by how classically attractive Leceth appeared, his skin pale but not sallow, his eyes and hair blacker than night. Leceth had an aged face, but somehow retained a handsome appearance. His dark hair was thick and was swept across his forehead, from left to right, almost rakishly.

"Leceth, Isobel," Jonathon acknowledged, a tentative beginning to the meeting. "I have asked Andrew to sit in on our meeting today, I believe it wise, Andrew has had a long career of representing the Order in such matters," Jonathon continued as he fidgeted slightly in his chair, trying to ease his tension.

"Whatever you wish," Leceth said, pausing for a moment before, "To business then!"

"Well, I am pleased that you decided to accept my invitation and to come tonight," said Jonathon. "I did wonder if you would be able to make it, on such short notice," he flipped open his folder as he finished talking.

Leceth let the comments slip. Andrew slid two copies of the report he had typed up regarding Zhing's findings across the table, one to Leceth and the other to Isobel. The two vampires opened the reports and began to read; they sat there for ten minutes digesting the contents. Isobel's expression was changing slightly the further into it she read; it was clear that she was surprised by what she was reading.

Leceth, however, flicked through the papers slowly and nonchalantly, not once did his expression show any hint of

310

emotion. On finishing he simply closed the file and looked up. "So, please tell me why you have called me here today." Leceth's tone showed his revulsion for Jonathon and for the Order.

"What do you mean?" exclaimed Jonathon. "You don't have anything to say about the findings in the report?"

"What in particular should I have a problem with?" Leceth leered. Isobel looked over to Leceth, and gave a curt nod indicating that, having completed the dossier, she was in agreement with his sentiments.

"Well," Jonathon uttered. "Let's start with the two who we known to be on your payroll. Cable, Canola; they both appear in this document," as Jonathon spoke, he lifted up the original and waved it high above his head.

"Again, I don't see why I would have a problem with that. What should I have to say about it? I employed them, yes. As security guards for a warehouse I own... I own many properties that require security." He paused briefly before, "Well, they were employees, before they were brutally killed obviously." Calm tones and a hint of a smile from Leceth.

"So, you admit that you employed two known assassins?" Jonathon's tone showed signs of slight agitation.

"To call them assassins would be, in my book, a form of propaganda. They were in fact some of the finest security guards that I had ever employed, they will be hard to replace," said Leceth, again he remained calm.

"Security guards?" Andrew quizzed.

"Yes. Security guards. They were protecting a family heirloom of mine, which I believe a member of your Order may have stolen," Leceth replied, grinning sinisterly.

Jonathon could not believe what he was hearing, the arrogance of Leceth was sickening.

"Okay, so what about your flight to Berlin the night of the killings, the night that Kristian Wallace was held captive by your so-called security guards?" Jonathon asked.

"Captive?" purred Leceth. "Again, I was merely on my way to collect my family heirloom. It means a lot to me and I personally wanted to bring it to my home in Bath, to Passel Manor. The fact that the boy was in Berlin at the same time is completely coincidental." Leceth had prepared himself well for the inquisition; he had predicted correctly what they would accuse him of having done; of course it helped that he knew exactly what they had on him before he arrived.

"You cannot honestly expect me to believe this?" Jonathon smarted.

"Well, I don't care how you look upon it, your opinion is irrelevant to me. You have brought me here today to show me this meaningless evidence and expecting me to confess to some secret desire to kill this boy, this Kristian. It's absurd! As a matter of undisputed fact, he is the only person who has killed anyone. Recently," Leceth was bold.

Jonathon turned his attention to Isobel, hoping for some backup. "What are your views?" he asked her.

"Mine?" she looked up "Well, I agree with Leceth. I can't see that you have proved anything that would breach any of the clauses of the treaty. And I'm certain the Arbitrators would come to the same conclusion," she folded her arms elegantly and turned her head in Leceth's direction.

Leceth was sitting smugly, tapping a long black fingernail on the wooden table impatiently. Looking down at Leceth's fingers, Andrew noticed three rings. One had a bright blue stone set in it, which was half covered with a silver slot. Another had a strange symbol etched on it, which he could not make out from where he was sitting. The third was large and bulky and looked as though it held something within.

Jonathon stood up, enraged. "I think this meeting is at an end."

"So do I," Leceth said menacingly, rising from his seat. "A word of warning, young man. Don't ever summon me in this fashion again if all your evidence is just a few stolen, meaningless documents," Leceth swiftly turned on his heel and walked away. Isobel remained seated and looked over her shoulder at Leceth.

Before exiting, he made a grand gesture with his hand and said, "Oh, and I would like my 'heirloom' back, Jonathon. As soon as possible," Leceth punctuated the end of his demand by swinging both doors open and storming out of the room.

Isobel rose to her feet. Jonathon glared after her and spoke softly. "How can you pretend to be so blind? What are you playing at?"

Isobel turned to face him and gave him a stern, cold look. "What am I playing at?" she hissed. "You came to Leceth with this?" she threw the report on to the table. "I should ask 'What are you playing at?' You're going to have to do much better than this, Jonathon, for both our sakes. You knew this was weak, hence why you haven't gone straight to the Arbitrators. All you have done right now is tip off Leceth that you're monitoring him."

As she finished she elegantly walked out. Jonathon was frozen in thought.

The doors closed behind her and she could see Leceth nearing the entrance, her unbeating heart skipped an imaginary beat as she could see Kristian moving towards him.

Brendan and Roman were deep in conversation with each other and appeared not to have noticed the unfolding precipitous situation.

"Leceth!" Kristian spat as he made a few strides to position himself directly behind him.

Leceth turned around and as his eyes took in the young man, a large grin appeared on his face.

"Oh, Mr. Wallace? A pleasure to actually meet you in person," Leceth stretched out his hand for Kristian to shake.

Kristian stood unmoving in front of the vampire; a mix of emotions overwhelmed his thoughts as he paused and stared at the outstretched hand.

"Take it," a soft, gentle feminine voice said over Kristian's shoulder.

Isobel took up Kristian's side. "Are you okay?" she directed her question to the young Phoenix Host.

Leceth kept his hand outstretched as his eyes scanned Isobel, she too locked her eyes on Leceth searching his face for intention. Something about her look towards Kristian's enemy revealed something about her. Her tone of voice unnerved Kristian slightly; he quickly hid his thoughts and controlled his expression to as cold and hard a one as he could muster.

Kristian, for a second, glanced at Isobel before his eyes quickly flicked back onto Leceth. Isobel's words and gestures reasserted themselves in Kristian's mind and for an unknown reason he found himself starting to trust them and feel comfort in them. It was then he remembered that he had felt this strangeness from a vampire before.

"Yes, are you okay, boy?" Leceth said.

"I'm good, thank you. Will be better soon," Kristian said as he glared into Leceth's eyes.

"Everything okay here?" a slightly panicked Jonathon asked, as he marched over having exited the room.

"Yes, everything is fine," Isobel said, her eyes connecting again with Leceth's.

"Yes. All is fine," Leceth remarked.

Jonathon moved to Kristian's side and placed his arm over his shoulder. "*Are* you all right, Kristian?"

Kristian looked at Jonathon and could see the concern in his eyes, concern for his safety or worry that Kristian was going to do something very rash.

"Yes. I just wanted to meet Leceth." As Kristian spoke he finally took Leceth's hand. He shook it hard. Pulling his hand back Kristian felt a dig into his hand from the few rings that Leceth was wearing. As Leceth freed his hand and moved it away he noticed Kristian eyeing his rings.

Leceth raised his hand to face level so Kristian could see the rings in their glory. Kristian took in the detail of the three bands, all appearing exquisite in their own right. Two of them seemed very chunky, whilst one was slim.

"Admiring my rings?" Leceth asked over his raised hand. Kristian glared at the rings and then into Leceth's eyes. He had heared the vampire's words but did not respond.

Turning his hand to admire them himself Leceth spoke confidently, breaking the awkward silence. "They are nice, aren't they? They remind me of what I was. I like to have a little something from before I was sired."

Leceth chuckled to himself at some personal joke. "Well I'm busy and have wasted enough time here. Goodnight, gentlemen."

Leceth exited the building, his security scuttling in his wake. Isobel left the building moments later without even a backwards glance.

Kristian and Jonathon watched the Council representatives walk down the steps and into their cars. Kristian wondered how he kept his composure as he remembered staring into Leceth's eyes. He had wanted to hurt him, he had wanted to kill him. A surge of anger welled inside as Kristian felt like he had missed an opportunity to strike his enemy down.

"What the hell are we going to do?" said the young Phoenix, his anger scrawled all over his tone.

"I'm sorry, but there is not much we can do in the immediate. The proof we have is a start, not enough to make any meaningful accusations. We may think we know the truth, but we can't fight him on our whims," Jonathon explained, attempting to ease Kristian's aggression.

His words did nothing to quell Kristian's anger, it seemed to fuel his rage further.

"So that's it? I'm still a wanted man? And the man who tried to kill me, who killed Oliver, just walks free?"

"No, it's not like that. You're not wanted anymore, I doubt that Leceth will follow up the investigation into the deaths at the warehouse. In addition, we will not just let him go! We will keep investigating. Leceth is bold, but he is not stupid. We must tread carefully."

"He needs to pay," Kristian said darkly.

"We will deal with him in time, but not in the ways you are thinking. We will do it my way," Jonathon said sternly.

"Your way isn't working, is it?" Kristian barked back.

"In time, Kristian, these things take time," Jonathon said more calmly now, his hand finding Kristian's shoulder.

Kristian did not care for any more of Jonathon's words. He looked at his boss with contempt, shoved Jonathon's hand off his shoulder and stormed off. Jonathon shouted for him to come back but he was ignored.

As Jonathon looked over towards Brendan, Roman and now Andrew, he spoke to himself. "Okay, round one to you, Leceth. But this is far from over."

...

- Chapter Twenty-One -

The Present, the Past, the Foretold

The last few months had been one long roller coaster ride of emotions for Kristian. For someone who had once been so determined to hide his true thoughts, he was finding it incredibly hard to cope with all his feelings spiralling within. He walked into his allocated living quarters in the Order's Headquarters and slammed the door behind him hard.

"God," he shouted out as he put his fist through the door of the cabinet near his bed. He paced around the room, thoughts overwhelming; a voice deep within was trying to talk him out of what he was planning to do. The promise he had made to Oliver did not seem so unbreakable anymore. He went to give the cabinet door another punch with the same fist when the door he had just slammed suddenly opened and Jonathon walked in.

"Get out!" shouted Kristian.

Jonathon ignored Kristian's outburst, he walked across the room and sat on Kristian's bed. Kristian glared angrily at him. "You need to work on your attitude, young man. You can't keep letting your emotions get the better of you," Jonathon's tone was not that of an angry superior, but his words did feel to Kristian to be a little threatening.

Kristian could not be bothered to listen to anything else that Jonathon had to say. He had heard enough of his excuses. Kristian had convinced himself he knew what needed to be done and was going to do it. He decided that if Jonathon was not going to leave then he would, compelling him to make his way for the door. Jonathon instantly leapt up to prevent him from leaving.

"Come on, now. Why are you so angry? Why are you so stuck on getting revenge? The problem with Leceth affects us all Kristian, not just you," Jonathon said, holding the door and maneuvering himself in the way.

"Does it? Well I think it affects others more than it affects you, doesn't it? Look at Oliver. It affected him, didn't it! Whilst you sat at your desk, bumbling along, calling meetings and making yourself feel important," Kristian knew he was crossing the line, but the anger and the injustice that he felt inside him was so strong it began to spill over. A few days ago he had been having fun with his friends, believing that Leceth would soon be arrested, dealt with. After which Kristian would then be able to stay in the Order, content. But now, after glimpsing into the eyes of evil, he felt so different from what he felt days ago. Leceth had won, again, and easily at that. Kristian had come to his own conclusion that Jonathon's evidence had been laughable in hindsight; Kristian believed Leceth had planned for every outcome. He was obviously involved in a much deeper and darker plan than the Order suspected and Kristian wanted him punished, he wanted to punish him.

"Oliver died to keep the world safe, he wouldn't want the peace destroyed in his name. You are the one who abandoned him to lead your 'normal life.' If you had known him half as well as you think you did then you would know that he would not want revenge for his death," Jonathon pleaded.

"How dare you!" Kristian exclaimed; the words Jonathon had uttered stung, a part of him knew that they were true. "You are the one sending people to their deaths; do you enjoy your job, Jonathon, makes you feel big and special, hey?"

Jonathon's expression changed, Kristian had hit a nerve and he could not help but looked outraged. Kristian had never seen this look on Jonathon's face before. He suddenly seemed taller and bigger than Kristian had ever seen him. Jonathon now towered over him and bellowed in an aggressive voice.

"If you knew anything at all about the Order, you would know that I send brave men and women out to do the job they love and feel is important. You're a selfish and irresponsible child, you left this place because you couldn't handle the responsibility given to you and now you act like its saviour. It is not your job to get justice for Oliver, and how dare you assume it is. Don't think that you are the only person around here who gives a damn. Because you're not. We all have burdens to bear, just that some of us act like adults and professionals." Jonathon turned to face the door and stormed out; he could not endure any more of Kristian's emotional adolescence.

"Well, if you care then do something about it. The peace is just an illusion. When will you wake up? When will you see the battlefront?" Kristian shouted out the door. The words Jonathon had spoken had hit every nerve in his body. Kristian knew Jonathon was speaking truth, deep down Kristian knew it, but right now it did nothing to alleviate his anger, his inescapable desire for vengeance.

...

It had been over an hour since Kristian had had his altercation with Jonathon; he was now lying on his bed. He pondered on the whole situation that he had initially reluctantly stumbled into. He often believed that he was a master at keeping his emotions at bay. *Well, all of them bar anger*, he thought. The constant battle of logic versus his heart had been a laborious and strenuous exercise that had left him tired, his very will fractured.

His head rested against the pillow, his palms covered tightly closed eyes. Images of Oliver, Leceth, Jess, Kieran and the Jakyll stung his retinas. The ache within his mind was only dulled by the wrenching within his heart.

What can I do? How can I stay here? What kind of man am I? How do I avenge Oliver? What about Sagara? Questions came in a constant stream through his mind, at times speaking them aloud, not once giving an answer in words or in his mind. As the questions filled his thoughts he ignored them one by one, thinking that there was no possible answer and therefore putting them away to the back of his mind was his only option.

As Kristian continued in this vein he soon found himself left with two questions which he couldn't quieten; both seemed unrelated but felt connected: 'How do I avenge Oliver?' and 'What about Sagara?'

Their answers brought him to the same violent conclusion: he felt the urge for vengeance and the need to fulfil the promise he had made to Oliver to destroy that urn.

He knew that the plan he was concocting would mean leaving the Order again, but this time for good. He could not comprehend death, especially his own, but knew it was part of his destiny. Facing Leceth and killing him was a choice he was unsure if he had made yet. One thought though plagued his mind above all others: that he had to read it again. Reading it was the driving force that had compelled him to run and hide before; he longed to hide from it again, but he could not escape the Sagara Prophecy.

...

Kristian found himself in the Great Library for the second time since his return. As he sat at one of the oddly placed desks in the Great Hall, a tall middle-aged lady dressed in a tight grey suit strolled up to him and placed a small brown box in front of him. She tilted her head as she put it down and proffered a clipboard with a document attached for him to sign.

After scribbling his name she quickly moved off and left him alone. His hands caressed the box before gently flicking the clip. It opened to reveal several documents bound together; as he lifted them out he could see a glass panel at the bottom underneath which was the original prophecy. The paper was stained yellow with age and the text was in script that Kristian could not read. He stroked the glass as a symbolic gesture to get closer to the prophecy.

From the pile of folders he had placed on the desk he sifted through them looking for the most recent entry; he found and pulled out a thick wedge of A4 paper bound at the side.

The cover of this sheaf had a serial number at the top:

P: AZX32 N:015 T: E

The title of the document was *The Fifteenth Translation of the Sagara Prophecy*. Kristian had read this before, as he held it in his hands that moment felt like yesterday, not well over two years ago. As he read over the summary he was left with nothing but fear; everything he held dear in his life was destined to end; all the things he loved would have to endure a war the likes of which he could scarcely imagine.

He read through the translation of the prophecy, all three chapters, though none of them made sense to him. They appeared to him as riddles, puzzles to be deciphered. He pondered on the usefulness of such a prophecy and why someone would have felt the need to warn of such evils and to do so in such a cryptic way. He wondered if he was dim-witted. *Obviously it made sense to Mr. Eddingtons, the author,* Kristian thought.

The only thing that he felt for sure he understood was that this prophecy predicted a war and the end of the Phoenixes. He had been told when he was young, by Zel, by what Kristian believed to be a higher power, that this prophecy was to come to pass soon, in Kristian's lifetime. Kristian believed it now, he was more sure reading it again of what he now had to do. Oliver was a part of this and had asked him to do something and he was going to do it, he just didn't or couldn't understand why. The prophecy that lay before him brought more questions than it answered, it shed no light on to why he would have to destroy some urn. He had made a promise, he needed to free Ethalon.

"And what is this you are reading?" the voice of Saresh bellowed from afar. "You are just the man I wanted to see. Wait there," Saresh darted off as Kristian began to place the documents back into the box. He didn't want to have another conversation but before he could leave Saresh was already returning.

"I'm sorry but I have a meeting to attend," Kristian lied as he clipped the box shut.

"Oh. No worries, I won't take up too much of your time," Saresh said as he held a book up high and placed it on the desk. "Sit," Saresh directed.

Kristian fell back into the seat as the librarian flicked open the book.

"What's this about?" Kristian asked.

"It's about the name. I have done a little bit of research myself," Saresh said, feeling accomplished with his work.

Kristian felt a little delight at this odd man's unwarranted assistance. Soon Saresh flicked to the page he was looking for.

"There," Saresh pointed to the page. The title made Kristian's eyes widen.

Solasis Krull – it was bold at the top of the right-hand page.

"This book is a consolidation research text," Saresh said looking at Kristian's blank face. "Excuse me. Put simply it's a reference book detailing previous investigations, a good tool to use when you start your own investigations," Saresh spoke joyfully.

The old man began to point out images and ran his finger over certain sentences.

"See, I was right. It suggests that Solasis is either an Ancient or a Traveller. Oh and his name means 'Great Inventor'."

Kristian listened to Saresh's excited voice as he continued to describe the page aloud. Listening as intently as he could, the young Phoenix's eyes fell upon a very familiar image that filled him with glee and fear.

"What is that?" Kristian said pointing to a black and white image of an urn.

"Oh that," Saresh said, "that is one of his inventions. The Urns of Solasis Krull."

Kristian's fingers traced the picture; he had seen the real thing before. The physical urn he had retrieved looked different, but he knew it was the same thing. Everything that had happened to him since he had returned to the Order was connected to this urn; Oliver's death, the vision of Oliver and the memory of Zelupzs, they all led him to this moment.

"What is it for?" Kristian enquired.

"The urn. The urn, as far as I can decipher, is used to… how does it put it, oh yes, 'it is used to contain that which is divine'," Saresh said.

"And what does it mean by that?" Kristian stared into Saresh's eyes quizzically.

"Divine. Well it's subjective. In this context, I believe it refers to the commonly agreed divine lineage laid out in Arnardian law."

Kristian again looked blankly.

"You have never read anything on Arnardian law?" Saresh looked at Kristian's expression - it remained blank. "You black suits! Well you should read up on it, it's fascinating. That's beside the point. So, things it classes as divine, which you would have heard of. The soul, every human has one or at least starts with one. The Phoenix, yes that thing inside you is classed as divine, the Trinity. There are all sorts of classes and types as well; you should definitely read 'Basic Arnardian concepts.'"

"Yeah I will, next opportunity I have. But now, can you tell me more about this urn. It contains the divine. What, like imprisons it? Like it could be used to trap one of these divine things?"

"I guess. I am no expert on this urn, or urns, as it indicates – 'Solasis Krull has made many urns'. I haven't researched them, I'm just going by what it says in this text," Saresh replied.

"So does it say anything on how to destroy them? And what happens to the contents?" Kristian asked, his mind roused by the possibility of completing his promise.

"I think, from the description, it would break like any other urn made of pottery. The markings offer magical protection of the contents, not of the physical object. So, I think it would smash, and the content I assume would be freed. Why do you ask? Have you come across one?" Saresh asked as his eyes widened.

"No," Kristian barked defensively. "I need to go, that meeting. Thanks for looking into that name," Kristian said, not wanting to reveal the truth.

"You're welcome. If you do come across one, you should feel obliged to let me know," Saresh said as he closed the book; Kristian was already on his way out.

"Yes sure. Goodbye and thank you again," Kristian lied, the promise was empty. He had seen one before and he believed he knew where another was, he was going to destroy one, or at least die trying.

. . .

Looking down, Kristian was determined not to talk to anyone; he was going to see Jonathon and didn't want to speak with anyone else. He had made plans to meet up with Jess later but first he needed to be sure of something. He entered the long corridor and was surprised to see how empty it was for a Friday afternoon. As he walked past the various rooms, to his relief, he bumped into no one. He was beginning to regret the things he had said to his boss a few hours ago. He now wanted to apologise; Jonathon was a good man and Kristian believed it.

Stopping in front of the President's office, he could hear voices coming from within. Whoever was in there was shouting. Kristian considered knocking when he heard the distinctive voices of Brendan and Amar. Amar was shouting something. Kristian could not make it out and pushed his ear closer to the door, straining to hear what was going on inside.

"Please," pleaded Brendan. "Promise me, when the time comes."

Amar replied but Kristian could not hear what he said, just muffled mumblings.

The two men became silent and Kristian quickly stepped back and knocked on the door. It opened to the stern face of Brendan who said in his harsh voice, "What?"

"Is Jonathon in Jonathon's office?" Kristian replied sarcastically.

"No, he's in the Great Library," came Brendan's reply.

Kristian turned on the spot and made his way back to the massive doors of the Library. Somehow he must have passed by him, the library was massive and one could have easily not seen someone in there, he thought.

"Hey! You did a good job with the Jakyll, you made us proud." As the words left Brendan's mouth, Kristian stopped in his tracks. Never before had he been given a compliment by Brendan.

Kristian turned to him, "Thanks." He smiled out of respect for his fellow Phoenix before he continued towards the library.

Standing in front of the golden doors he felt the strange tingling sensation he had felt when he had crossed the barrier an hour earlier. It was like walking over a magical threshold but the intensity was stronger. Kristian was about to speak the secret password when the door burst into life. The large cogs that held the doors securely together began to turn, the panels lifted into the air and Kristian stepped back, his eyes reflected the beautifully bright colours that emanated from within the Great Library itself.

Jonathon was walking out and, noticing Kristian, stopped, facing him. He looked forlorn and the pair stood awkwardly together not speaking for a number of seconds.

Kristian was the first to speak. "I was looking for you, I wanted to apologise for earlier."

Jonathon waved a hand in the air. "Ah, not to worry. What is done is done. Thank you for your apology. I too said things I now regret," he walked in the direction of his office and signalled for Kristian to follow.

Entering his office he placed a pile of notes he had made in the library onto his desk. Kristian was a little surprised to see that Amar and Brendan had left already; he wondered if Jonathon had known that they were in his office but did not speak up.

"So, are you feeling calmer about Leceth?" Jonathon asked hopefully.

Kristian was still angry but he had wanted to talk to Jonathon about the Sagara Prophecy; that was what was important to him in this moment. Kristian lied convincingly. "Yes, I have cleared my head. I know that you want what I want. And I know what I said was out of order. I am truly sorry."

"Good," said Jonathon looking incredibly relieved.

Now to the thing that was still plaguing Kristian ever since his discussion with Zelupzs and Oliver. "What do you know about Sagara?" Kristian probed, his voice calm and collected, unlike Jonathon's face which had turned sour, the question taking him by surprise.

Storming over to the door and closing it heavily, Jonathon turned to Kristian. "How do you know about Sagara?" he demanded, quietly but sternly.

"I've read it," Kristian replied.

"But why Sagara? Who told you about it? Who told you to read it?" Jonathon's voice was slightly raised.

"No one told me to read it, I just did. I've never spoken about it before," Kristian again lied.

Jonathon looked him directly in the eyes, ready to read his expression, "Are you sure?"

Kristian could see Jonathon was surprised by the fact he had read it and was asking about it now.

"Of course, I swear," he looked at Jonathon's face and could see a hint of panic in the old man's eyes. "I've read the Eddingtons report on Sagara as well."

Jonathon now looked even more shocked, he moved away to collect his thoughts.

"Do you agree with Eddington's analysis of it? Do you think it prophesies the end of the Phoenix?" Kristian asked.

Jonathon stood stock still, choosing his words before replying.

"I'm afraid I do. I believe that's the correct conclusion from the translation."

Kristian suddenly felt ill, sick to the stomach. Jonathon noticed the worry on his face.

"The Sagara Prophecy is like other guarded prophecies, it's a kind of weapon," Jonathon explained. Kristian gave him a puzzled look. "You see, knowledge is power. I've implemented many things to ensure that it never happens. The prophecy has existed for thousands of years. I wish you had not worried yourself with it. The head of the Order and the leader of the Phoenix order are always entrusted with reading it when they take their posts. It's not the only prophecy out there."

Jonathon could see that the boy was troubled with what he had read of the prophecy and accompanying analysis. In that moment Jonathon was sure that he had been keeping these fears to himself for some time.

"Kristian. It is unlikely that the prophecy will come to pass in our life time, if ever at all."

Kristian looked up at the old man in front of him. "If the prophecy is a great weapon, why isn't it better protected?" Kristian asked, recounting how easy it was for him to find.

"It is in the Great Library so that only the pure of heart can read it. And sometimes the best place to hide something is to hide it in plain sight," as Jonathon finished he walked over to Kristian. "Please don't worry yourself with ancient prophecies or evil leaders. You are young, let the old ones do the worrying."

Kristian did not feel relief, but he had found out what he had wanted to know: Jonathon was aware and he knew about Sagara, that was all Kristian needed to know.

Now Kristian had to go and see Jess, it was the next step of his plan. He stood up and looked Jonathon directly in the eye. "Thank you, Jonathon. I just read it one day, and it sent shivers down my spine. It's frightening, what it says. I guess I have been worried about it. I know I shouldn't and I know you're right. Thank you again. Right, I need to go. I have plans to see some friends tonight." Jonathon listened to Kristian; the young Phoenix's words sounded a little hasty, but to Kristian, his own words felt final.

...

- Chapter Twenty-Two -

Confessions with Friends

The house, though detached, was rather small. It stood on a quiet street on the outskirts of north London. The neighbourhood was filled with these detached nineteenth-century houses, built of brown brick with deep brown wooden window and door fittings. Peter had lived in the house for many years and often spoke of how his parents had once owned it and that he had inherited it after their passing.

The house was filled with many happy memories for him, it was his office away from the Order. His passion for history, both the conventional and the mystical, littered every room except one. In his early years whilst just starting his career with the Order, he had adopted a young orphan boy. Gabriel was the only son of Peter's very close friends, David and Sarah Goldstein; all three had met at Harvard before all ending up in the Order. After Sarah and David's premature deaths, Peter found himself being the closest thing that the young boy had to family. Formally adopting him, he had brought him back to England and raised him in London. Gabriel's room was small and clean. Gabriel, like his adoptive father, owned very little and to him the room had only one purpose: sleeping. It still had the old motorcar wallpaper on the walls that had seen him grow from an inquisitive young boy into a determined young man. Now in his late twenties, like his adoptive father, he worked for the Order, within the Nariasdem.

Peter was wearing the same grey pinstripe suit he wore to work. Grey was the colour for all those who worked in office roles in the Order, the clerks, librarians and anyone who did not work out in the field.

He loved his grey suit. Like the Phoenix attire, he believed it represented something. The grey to him was a sign of brains over brawn. The only thing about Peter's appearance that looked slightly out of place was his gold pocket watch. The golden chain fell down inside his waistcoat and the watch rested in the pocket. He had never been seen without his watch and would often glance at it, up close as though he was keeping time a secret from everyone else.

Peter was sitting in what would have been the dining room if this were an average person's house. In his house though, it was his grand reading room. On a large round table that took up most of the space, books were piled high. He would flick from book to book, looking at different pages, never reading just one book at a time.

Every so often something would grab his attention and he would reach for a pen and write notes in a large open jotter on the table. He would often become so engrossed in his writing he would miss meals, and the old jotter would be filled with essays written over the hours. A ringing sound came from the kitchen, attempting to distract him from his work. He ignored it; his writing got faster and his words became spidery and unreadable. The bell rang again and still Peter ignored it. He knew it was the doorbell but hoped that whoever it was would get tired of ringing and leave soon.

There were then three consecutive rings from someone who was obviously getting impatient on Peter's doorstep. He threw his pen down with a large sigh. He looked down at what he had written. He could understand it, but would Jonathon, he wondered.

Moving into the kitchen and then into the passage, he walked past table after table covered in books. As he reached the front door he began to flick the many locks and bolts. It took him nearly a minute to unlock and upon opening it he was filled with dread.

"Penny!" Peter gasped. It was only in that instant of seeing his colleague that he remembered what he had planned for that evening.

"I'm so sorry, Penny. It is not that I forgot, it is just um… okay, I did forget, but I have a good reason, I have been working on something very important," he stuttered. He felt awful.

Penny looked incredibly disappointed. "Okay," she said meekly, "well if you're busy, we can always make it another night?"

Penny had planned this evening for over a month. After plucking up the courage to ask him out on a date she had planned the evening to the tiniest detail. She had planned a lovely meal at a prestigious restaurant, followed by tickets to the opera. Then a romantic stroll along the river. She had spent hours that evening on her appearance. She was wearing a long green dress that stretched from her ample cleavage down to her delicate ankles, the eye then drawn to a pair of elegant emerald-green high heels. A small silver and green handbag hung from her shoulder.

"No, tonight is fine," said Peter as he saw the hurt on Penny's face.

Stepping into Peter's house for the first time Penny could do nothing but stare. She passed Peter the coat she had in her hand and began to scan the interior. Her eyes were like a camera, taking pictures of everything she saw. After placing Penny's coat on a hook Peter walked her through to the kitchen, navigating around the tables of books as they moved.

"Okay, wait here and I will be down in a jiffy. I shall just go and get changed," Peter darted off down the hall and up the stairs which rose opposite the front door.

Penny looked around the kitchen; it was clean, just cluttered, books littered every surface. Picking up an particularly old-looking one, she began to flick through it whilst glancing around the rest of the downstairs; something piqued her interest in the dining room. She entered it quietly and could not believe her eyes as she recognised a 'Transtext' on the table. It sat askew next to another huge collection of books. The top one was entitled *Myths and Legends of the Great and Gifted*.

Penny began to scan the book's open pages. The more she read the more intrigued she became. "I wonder what he is working on?" she asked aloud.

She flipped over another book from the pile and read its title: *Traveller Codex*.

"Interesting!" she said as her eyes scanned the rest of the table.

Es Ringlet el Curdle read the title of another book which had a picture of a large ring on it. Penny knew what the title meant: *The Ring of Cordell*. She had never heard of the ring of Cordell before but she could read Lower Ancient. She continued reading. She discovered that the ring had the power to allow the wearer invisibility at the flick of its cover. It had been created by a Warlock Cordell over twelve hundred years ago. The picture showed a beautiful silver ring with a blue gemstone in the centre and a half moon-shaped sheath on the right side. As Penny read more she learned how the flick of the sheath over the stone made the wearer invisible. She had heard of invisibility spells, but objects that turned the wearer invisible were extremely rare. Her eyes shot over to the door where a half-dressed Peter stood having announced his presence with a creaking floor board. He was now wearing black trousers, which clearly did not fit, and an untucked light blue shirt. He was in the midst of doing up his tie.

"Oh sorry, I was just…" flustered Penny.

"Not to worry. This is the reason I forgot all about our meal. Jonathon had asked me to look up a few things," he replied as he finally knotted his tie and moved into the room.

"It looks interesting," she said. "What is it?"

"Jonathon asked me to look something up. It's regarding Leceth. Andrew had noticed he was wearing three rather remarkable rings at their meeting. After identifying them on the CCTV taken at the time I was also intrigued," as he finished speaking he placed his hand on the picture of the ring and smoothed it softly as though stroking it in real life.

"It's pretty, isn't it?" Peter said softly.

Penny replied with a simple "Yes".

"I'm almost certain that this is one of the rings that Leceth was wearing. I have also identified another but the third has me a little stumped," Peter said as he opened another book and flicked through the pages.

"*The Myths and Legends of the Great and Gifted*?" recited a bemused Penny.

"Yes, you wouldn't think that this would be very helpful, would you?" Peter chuckled.

He turned the book around and showed her the page he had been reading. It read 'Mark Williams – the unknown gifted.'

Penny knew exactly who Mark Williams was. He had been an ordinary man who, in the sixteenth century, was told by a seer that he possessed an ability like no one ever had had before. However, as he lived his life no extraordinary gift ever presented itself until one day, on his search for answers, he stumbled upon an old woman who could create fire from nothing.

The day he met her they chatted some and then she described how she felt overwhelmed by his presence. In addition, she explained how at that moment she felt that her own power was more prominent, like she almost wouldn't be able to control her flames anymore. Later that day the entire village was wiped off the map by a huge blaze, it killed all the residents. Mark also died in the blaze.

"What has the story of Mark Williams got to do with Leceth's ring?" she asked.

"Well," explained Peter, "there was a story I read a long time ago which described a man who, unknowingly, could increase the powers of other gifted people around him. It said that when he died a dark wizard took his bones and locked his gift within them." Peter quickly scribbled down something on the large open Transtext book.

"And you think it was Mark Williams's bones?" Penny asked.

"To be honest, I was doubtful at first, the story didn't seem factually correct. But now having seen Leceth's ring, or should I say, until Andrew described it to me as the CCTV was too grainy," Peter paused and showed a piece of paper to her. "This is Andrew's description of the ring."

The paper contained a drawing of a symbol, like a fork with seven prongs, each with circles at their ends. "It's Lower Ancient, original form, I translated it as… it says, Mark Williams."

Penny looked more interested as she read the symbol. "Yes, it does say Mark Williams," she was fluent in Lower Ancient original form, as a member of the Nariasdem it was not unusual. "I doubt that that's a coincidence, although maybe Andrew remembered it wrong. It's not as though Leceth gave it to him to examine," she said.

"True but even so it is strange that Andrew just happened to see a ring that fitted with the Mark Williams theory. Also, Andrew described the ring as though it were made of tiny bones. Now that leads me to think I am on the right track," Peter said enthusiastically.

"That's very interesting," Penny said, "what about the CCTV footage?"

"Unfortunately, I cannot make out the symbol from the recording although it looks like there is definitely one there," Peter replied.

Again, something popped into his head and he wrote it down.

"How come you have a Transtext here?" Penny asked, looking down at the book.

"Oh, well, this one is 302. I found it in Camden Market, of all places. I couldn't believe it."

This shocked Penny, a Transtext was one of the most useful and rarest books that the Order used. It was a way of communicating between the offices, much like email, although it predated post. The Transtext was created millennia ago by a group of powerful witches and wizards.

There were three hundred and thirty-three Transtext books and each one had the ability to relay information to the others. Each book contained six hundred and sixty-six pages and to communicate with another one you simply turned to the page number which corresponded to the book you wanted to relay the message to and wrote upon it.

Peter's was open to page sixteen. Penny knew that book sixteen was in Jonathon's office. As Peter wrote on page sixteen on the left hand side, it would appear on Jonathon's page three hundred and two on the right hand side, and if Jonathon was to reply, he would simply write on the left-hand side of page three hundred and two and it would appear on Peter's page sixteen, on the right-hand side.

It was an invaluable tool for the Order. If a book was closed and it received a message from another, it would simply open to the page on which the message sat.

Most of the books were owned by the Order, spread out over the one hundred and fifty offices they had.

"Camden Market? Really? How many does the Order own?" Penny knew a ballpark number but she was sure that Peter would know exactly.

"Oh, um, including this one, two hundred and eighty-one. The twenty-two we do not have could be lost, or even destroyed. We check and look out for them regularly," Peter said continuing to write in his book. "So, do you want to leave now?" he said after resting his pen on the page.

Penny looked at her watch, she knew that they had missed their meal and she could see that Peter was eager to continue with his research.

"Well, I hadn't booked anything really," she lied.

"Really?" Peter replied, not really seeming all that interested.

"If you want, we can just stay here and investigate Leceth's jewellery," she said, though deep down she longed for him to decline the offer and whisk her away.

"Oh, yes, well if you are sure?" he asked in the same tone as before.

"Yes, it's fine," Penny replied as she opened a book and began reading.

Peter smiled. There was silence in the room as the pair flicked through book after book at an incredible pace.

"Okay, a question?" Penny broke the silence. "This ring, Mark Williams's bones? Why would Leceth have it?"

Peter put down the book he was reading.

"Why would Leceth have it? Hmm, well he could wear it for aesthetics. Maybe he owns it so that no one else can, as I imagine he believes if he has it then it cannot fall into the hands of a gifted person, stopping their powers from being enhanced, if the account is true," Peter pondered.

"Maybe," Penny replied before returning to her reading.

"Perhaps we should focus on the third ring," Peter suggested.

"Sure," she replied. "What do you know about it?"

"Andrew described it as being large, bulky and ugly. Try searching this book here," he passed her a tome entitled *The Talismans of the Divine*. She picked it up and flicked through the pages.

Reading the summaries, she was hopeful that she would stumble upon an answer.

Silence returned to the house and they were both absorbed for the next half an hour in their search for the mysterious ring.

"Oh, how's Gabe?" Penny said breaking the silence and looking up from the book.

Peter looked up and smiled at the thought of his adopted son. "He's good. Well, better than good. Did you hear about his recent promotion to head of the Jerusalem office?" He was clearly proud as punch as he grinned from ear to ear.

"Yes, I heard," Penny said quietly. "I heard Ashleen telling people in the canteen last week. All about his promotion and about him taking possession of an omega scroll."

"Ah," he said fondly. "She cannot help boasting. She was the first person he told about it! I didn't hear anything about an omega scroll though, he didn't tell me that. How exciting."

"Oh," Penny replied before continuing to read.

They continued their investigation with little success. The books held no answers.

Hours passed quickly and they soon found themselves in the small hours of the morning, it was 3am.

"Well, I think I should be going," Penny yawned.

"Yes, I think I will retire as well," Peter replied, lowering his book, but not closing it.

Penny had moved into the kitchen before he even stood up. As she walked down the passage she thought about the night she had had. She had enjoyed perusing his vast collection of interesting books, but it was not the romantic evening she imagined, or hoped for. Arriving at the front door, he was at her side.

"How will you get home?" Peter asked.

"The night bus, I guess," Penny replied as she threw on her coat.

"Oh, you mustn't, I shall get you a car," said Peter.

"No, it's fine really. There are still plenty of people out and I don't live far," Penny spoke as she moved to walk over the threshold.

"Well, if you're sure," Peter replied.

As much as she didn't mind taking the bus, a large part of her hoped for Peter to be more forceful, to insist that she take a car. She stepped out of the house and with a simple turn of her head she said goodbye and wrapped her arms around themselves to keep herself warm.

She heard Peter return her goodnight, followed by a clunk of the door closing. She walked to the bus stop passing several drunks and a couple of bad singers. Dissecting the evening she came to the conclusion that, on the whole, it had not been that bad a date, well, not compared to some she had been on in the past. It was just a typical Penny Bright evening, comfortable. Not perfect, not what she wanted, but then, when did anything go the way she hoped?

...

Her embrace was like a tonic, cleansing his soul of almost all his worries and doubts. Kristian knew he loved her more than he thought he could.

"Jess, I'm sorry but I can't stay long, I have a meeting at the Order tonight, it's just been called and I can't get out of it," he was lying and hoped she wouldn't notice.

"Huh? Really? Kieran doesn't have to go in. I called him about twenty minutes ago and asked him to meet us. Thought it would be nice, the three of us again," Jess replied, irking Kristian.

"It's a Phoenix meeting, he isn't invited," Kristian lied again.

Jess took his words at face value but sensed something wasn't right; she hesitated from enquiring further.

The two of them made their way to the pub where they had eaten and laughed many times over the past two years. The Forgotten Onion was a large traditional pub with a traditional menu, conveniently halfway between their university campus and their flat.

It was busy that night but they quickly found a small table in the far corner and four vacant chairs. They sat down, picked up the menus and began browsing through.

Kristian attempted several times to make conversation, he asked after uni, enquired as to what on the menu took Jess's fancy; but the conversations between them were short and dried up quickly. Resisting no longer, Jess demanded, "Tell me what you are really doing tonight?"

"I have a meeting. I told you," Kristian replied bitterly, annoyed at himself that his lies were so transparent.

"Fine," said Jess as she lifted the menu to cover her face.

"Hey, don't be like that, I'm not lying," Kristian said, pulling her menu down.

"You're still lying! I can tell, Kris. Your left eye twitches when you lie," Jess had fabricated this tell but she was a far better liar than Kristian.

Kristian immediately placed his hand to his left eye.

"No it doesn't," he said.

"No, it doesn't, but you've just proven to me that you *are* lying," Jess said angrily. "Tell me what you're doing tonight! I won't drop it until you're honest with me."

Kristian was clearly caught out, he had been determined not to entangle anyone else in his unsanctioned plan to complete his promise to Oliver, no one other than those he absolutely needed.

"I can't tell you," Kristian pleaded.

She slammed her hand down on the table and glared at him; she wanted answers, she wanted truths.

"Fine, okay. I do have something to tell you. I have a mission tonight. That's all. It is important though. I may not get a chance to do it again, it's a big mission," Kristian responded, sounding honest but cryptic.

"Stop talking in riddles!" she cried.

"Okay… But what I'm about to tell you, you must not tell anyone. Promise?"

She nodded her head and extended her hand; Kristian shook it. He moved closer to her ear. "You cannot tell anyone. Remember what I told you about that man on the train, when I was ten. He told me something. Something that only makes sense to me now."

"Yes. You told me what he said," Jess replied, recalling the memory of when Kristian had first told her about Zel.

"Shush! No, I didn't. Not everything. He whispered something in my ear that I'm whispering to you now. He told me Sagara is here, that I'm a part of it and that it would happen in my lifetime."

Jess looked puzzled, she was about to ask what Sagara was when he placed his finger against her lips. "Sagara is a prophecy. You cannot speak of it to anyone. What that man said to me and what I have read is the real reason I ran away from the Order." Kristian was being the most honest he had ever been, not only to her but to himself. "I ran as I stupidly thought that if I got far enough away from that world then what I had read could not possibly come true. I was wrong. I can't escape it; I can't hide from it, there is no running. I need to do something about it. So tonight I am going to free an old friend. It's not going to be easy, I have to face Leceth," as Kristian finished he didn't notice the shocked expression on her face, he only noticed Kieran entering through the pub doors.

"I have to go to the toilet," he said reacting to the wizard's arrival. He quickly leant over and kissed Jess on the cheek, then made his way to the bathroom.

Kieran was soon at her side. "Where is Kristian off to?" he asked.

"Toilet," she replied, deep in thought, almost ignoring him altogether.

"It's not that way," Kieran said, looking around the room.

"Leceth," Jess spoke, ominously to the air.

Dread surged through Kieran. Kristian was heading for the exit, not the toilet. He quickly darted off in the direction Kristian had headed.

Kieran felt the cold biting as he left the building and stood outside; Kristian was nowhere to be seen, gone.

Jess was soon at Kieran's side. "He told me he was going to face Leceth. A 'mission' he said," as Jess spoke she shivered, both due to the icy chill and the spine-tingling reality of what Kristian had finally revealed to her.

"Oh no," Kieran gasped. "I have to go. I have to talk to him," Kieran kissed her on the cheek and flicked his hand in the air and a taxi appeared almost from nowhere. He pointed to it and looked at her. "Get yourself home. I will go speak to Kristian, I promise I'll make all this all right."

Jess walked towards the taxi as thin white flecks of snow began to fall on her face. She was his best friend and never before had she felt so helpless. She turned to look at Kieran before entering the taxi but the young wizard had already left. Jess wondered if she had told Kieran too much or too little.

...

"I know where you are going, I know exactly what you plan to do," Kristian had never heard Kieran so angry or determined.

Closing the door to the weapons storage room, Kristian replied, "So what? Have you come to stop me?" Kristian knew that Kieran would not try to stop him, as much as he could do it, he just would not; Kristian knew Kieran was there to try and talk him out of it.

"I am here hoping that you will listen to reason. You know that you can't kill him. You know that deep down, underneath your anger, your hate, fear and your love, that this is wrong. You will start a war that will take many lives. It's not in you, is it?"

"Not in me?" Kristian replied emotionally. "I will tell you what's not in me. It is not in me to stand aside and let him get away with Oliver's murder. It is not in me to care anymore about the consequences. I have learnt a lot here over the last few weeks. The price of friendship, the price of honour; that it's sometimes worth risking your life for," Kristian said as he scanned the inventory list on a desk.

"Why must you have revenge? Why you? What is your obsession with avenging Oliver?" Kieran yelled at him. "Millions of innocent people could die if there is a war started for your vengeance."

"This is nothing to do with simple vengeance; it is about justice for Oliver." Kristian was blood-red and sweating. His heart was pounding.

"Oh, come on, will you. You never cared for Oliver this much. If you had, you would never have left. This is about feeling guilty and trying to mend your mistakes."

Before Kieran could finish, Kristian had picked him up and held him to the wall, an arm pressed against his neck.

"Don't think that you know me, Kieran, because you don't and you never will. That's the problem, isn't it? That I am risking everything for someone else?"

Kieran looked disturbed, he was seeing a side of Kristian he never thought possible. "Yes you are right; I don't know you at all."

On hearing these words Kristian stepped back and released Kieran from his hold. He was upset by Kieran's sentiments. For him it was not about his self-given mission, it was now about killing Leceth. He had previously given his word that he would not cross that line but things had changed since then. He found himself with an insatiable rage that could only be quenched with death.

As Kieran stood and held his neck they looked at each other. Kristian thought that Kieran looked so weak; for someone so powerful, he appeared vulnerable. He turned on his heel and walked away from him. "Goodbye, Kieran."

"Is that it? You not going to talk about the whys? You're just going to leave and go on your own quest to kill Leceth?" Kieran said.

"It's not a quest to kill him, Kieran. It's a promise I need to fulfill. I knew I shouldn't have told Jess; can't believe she told you," Kristian tried to sound a little conciliatory.

"She didn't really tell me. She let it slip and I could tell from her face that you must've told her something drastic. It wasn't hard to work out what. You really want to do this?" Kieran said, mirroring Kristian's tone.

"I don't want to. I know that this confrontation is something I have to do," Kristian said.

"And you have to do that tonight? Right now?" Kieran asked.

Kristian looked Kieran deep in his eyes, he wanted to quench Kieran's fears so he wouldn't raise the alarm before he had a chance to realise his plans.

Kieran looked back, he was helpless. He was unsure of what the outcome would be, but the impending battle seemed like an avoidable consequence.

"Keeping my promise is something I have to do. Maybe not now, but one day, soon, it is something I have to do," Kristian said as he converted one of the inventory numbers to memory.

"That fight will be meaningless, Kristian. If you're lucky, you will escape with your life, but I'm not sure if you would leave with your soul."

"Maybe not," replied Kristian, "but maybe that price is a fair one."

With that, Kristian left, he was gone. Closing the door behind him he left Kieran alone in the room; he was now left with a dreadful dilemma. Did he go after his friend, try to stop him or even aid him? Alternatively, did he tell Jonathon and get Kristian 'dealt with'. He did not want to betray his friend, but what is the bigger betrayal, he thought; letting him kill, or be killed by an enemy for reasons only he can justify, or stopping him in the name of peace?

...

Kieran sat in the room, thoughts spiralling as he struggled to decide on a course of action. He was consumed with the desire to continue the conversation with Kristian and ensure

Kristian didn't do anything too rash. He bent over the desk in the room looking at the various lists. A few minutes later the door burst open interrupting Kieran's thoughts. A young grey-suited Order member walked in immediately apologising to Kieran for disturbing him, Kieran waved it off and left the room. Standing outside the room he looked at his watch, it had been over half an hour since Kristian had stormed off. Kieran wondered where he might be and he decided, to start with, he would go and search for the rest of his usual group. There was still time to talk to Kristian, to persuade him, Kieran thought as he considered how their conversation had ended. Kieran felt a sense of guilt, a part of him wanted to go straight to Jonathon, the logical part. However, he did not want to betray Kristian. He didn't want Kristian to never want to forgive him. His turmoil was only eased when Rachel appeared in view.

"Rachel!" Kieran shouted down the corridor.

As he got closer to her he noticed she looked very tired and almost upset. Rachel looked at Kieran's neck and saw the red mark. "What happened to your neck?" she asked.

Kieran automatically placed a hand on the mark. "Nothing," he lied as his hand trembled to touch it.

Kieran had to tell her now; he could not lie to her as well, he needed to involve someone he trusted. "It's Kristian," he whispered. "I think he intends on going after Leceth."

Rachel went cold all over. "What do you mean? Are you sure? What makes you say that? Have you told anyone?"

"Yes, he told me. Pretty much. I tried to stop him but he wouldn't listen. He is out for revenge. I've not told anyone, just you. I get the sense that Kristian wasn't going to do anything tonight."

Rachel looked horrified; suddenly becoming tearful, her eyes glistened.

"We can fix this, Rachel, we can!" Kieran consoled. "Even if Kristian wanted to kill Leceth tonight, it would take him over three hours to arrive at Leceth's house form here. We still have time."

"No, you don't understand. I bumped into Kristian about twenty minutes ago and he asked me to teleport him to Bath. He said he has family there. I usually wouldn't but he practically begged me," Rachel spoke with a hand over her mouth, cursing herself that she had inadvertently aided Kristian in his deadly plan.

"His family doesn't live in Bath," Kieran said, as he grabbed her arm and started to pull her along as he paced down the corridor. "We must tell Jonathon. But first, take me to where you dropped him off, we need to try and stop him. If we can't find him we will come back and go to Jonathon together."

"Shouldn't we tell him straight away?" Rachel whispered.

"No, we need to be sure that we can't convince him. His future depends on it," Kieran replied as his pace evolved into a sprint.

…

- Chapter Twenty-Three -

What we Leave Behind

The full moon was fiery red and it lit up the evening beautifully; it was the only source of light illuminating the grounds of the most beautiful house that Kristian had ever laid his eyes upon. He was over the outer wall in moments and soon found himself quickly running in between the trees and bushes within the grounds. It was not long before his back was against the wall of the large stately home. Taking a few steps forward and turning quickly, Kristian scanned the building for a way in; entering the front door was too bold and he wanted something more stealthy.

He noticed an open window on the third floor. The walls to the grand home were too high to climb, but fortunately there was a large oak tree close to the house, and one of the main branches stretched near to the wall. He quickly scaled the tree and was soon crawling across the branch. It was thick and easily took his weight. When he was about halfway along the branch he looked over at the house and realised that he was about as close as he was going to get to the window; he would have to jump the rest.

The window was wide open and the ledge itself protruded far from the wall and looked sturdy. Moving slowly he tried to rise to his feet. His knees trembled slightly, but ignoring the sensation completely, he leapt forward; his body flew considerably far; just making the gap, his chest collided with the ledge. His hands grasped frantically for the wall inside the room, his fingers just finding purchase before he fell.

Kristian pulled himself up and through the window. He was in a large room and the decor reminded him of the main office back at the Order. The room had several cabinets and shelves, which were littered with books. They were similar to the majority of the books in the Great Library, old, thick and treasured. The room was lit by the mottled light of the moon, which passed between the leaves of the large tree.

Walking to the door he stopped to look at several papers laid out on a large desk that consumed one entire wall of the room. The pages were filled with a text that he had never before seen and there was no way of knowing what stories they told. He did not care though, he was there to free Ethalon – Oliver's Phoenix. That was all he cared about; though revenge, taking care of Leceth, was a notion that lingered at the back of his mind.

Slowly and quietly he moved closer to the door until reaching it, and then placing an ear against it, he listened. Not a whisper could be heard from the other side; he gently opened the door. He peered through to see he was halfway along a long corridor, which was about the length of his entire flat; it was unlit and empty.

Kristian exited the room turning right and stealthily made his way down the corridor. At one end, a large window flooded the corridor with red lunar light, the other led to a large spiral staircase. He was headed to the stairs, he knew exactly where he was going; he had studied the plans for Leceth's house at the Order, and he knew that there was only one place in which Leceth would keep the urn.

He walked down the stairs with great care; he had not scouted the place at all well and he had no idea if the house was occupied tonight; he had no knowledge of where Leceth and his bodyguards might be. With that in mind, knowing he would have poor reconnaissance, he had with him a large rifle that Zhing had acquired from the Dark Phoenix. He had stolen it from the Order, the inventory number he was searching for whilst conversing with Kieran. He had also brought his Phoenix blade along with him; he knew he could summon it from anywhere, but having it strapped to his back with its comforting weight seemed to imbue him with an added hunger to complete his mission. The only other thing he took from the Order's armoury was a handgun that was tightly holstered under his jacket. He was not dressed in his Phoenix attire; a new suit was still being made for him after his fight with the Jakyll had all but destroyed his last one.

Instead, he was dressed in a sparring outfit covered by a black jacket. It was simply black, with no symbols. The material was cotton-like, ideal for duelling, ideal for espionage.

He arrived at the bottom of the stairwell; he was now at the mouth of a doorway that he knew led into the main entrance hall. He held his body close to the wall, craning his neck to look into the hall. It was large with grand front doors, several ornate staircases protruding from all sides and paintings covering the walls but it was too dark to make out their subjects.

Opposite the main doors, two smaller double doors were the only other entrance on this level. It was through these doors he knew he had to go, where he believed the urn to be. He stepped back and reminded himself that his actions would be for a just cause, and that he was going to fulfill at least half a promise. He glanced down the hall again and not seeing anyone he made a hasty dash for the small doors.

Within seconds he was against them, clutching frantically at the handle; they were locked. He attempted again, shoving his weight against them. Although small, they were thick and would not budge.

He stopped, realising he was making a lot of noise and that there was no getting in this way. He waited for a long minute to see if anybody would come and investigate, but there was nothing, nobody.

Relieved, he thought that he must be incredibly fortunate in choosing this time to complete his mission.

As time ticked on, he was content that he must be alone in the house. He took another look at the door and knew that although he was alone now it may not be long until he wasn't. He took a single deep breath, held out his hands before him and then suddenly the doors slammed open, hitting the walls, locks broken and metal bent from the force of the solid jade light that ploughed into them.

Jumping through the doorway, he entered another room, resembling the room through which he had entered the house. It had several cabinets filled with books, some were filled with a random assortment of artifacts. Skulls from all manner of creatures filled the largest one and the one next to it contained a variety of weapons. Kristian knew he was in the right place.

He began to carelessly search for the urn, throwing things to the floor and emptying the cabinets, it was satisfying to him. He argued to himself that there was no need to be cautious about accidently breaking the urn during his reckless search, he would have to break it anyway to free the Phoenix.

Ten pleasing minutes of mindless destruction passed and he had made a disaster site out of Leceth's prized possessions. He paused and looked around in the chaos and found himself becoming frustrated; most of the room was destroyed yet he still had not found the urn. "It has to be here!" he told himself.

He kicked a few things in the air and gave another glance around the room, but it was clear that the urn was not there. There was nowhere else in the room it could be hidden. The plans of the building went through his mind as he aimlessly went from room to room in his mind's eye, searching for another hiding place for the urn.

He lowered himself to the floor as he tried hard to search his memories for a clue.

Leceth would keep it close to him, it would definitely be in his home. It was more than a guess; he knew it to be true. It was somewhere in the house, he just had to find it.

He scanned the room again, shelf after shelf filled one entire wall and cabinets lined the opposite, now smashed and broken from his cathartic searching.

A third wall had a few cabinets and then the entrance doors. The last wall had a large glass cabinet on one side that had been filled with gems and jewels minutes ago. Next to that cabinet was an empty space, with a strange symbol on the wall, which he hadn't taken much notice of previously.

An empty space? thought Kristian. He got to his feet and walked over. The symbol was an emblem of some kind, it was made of what looked like shiny silver metal and was protruding slightly. Its design was ugly, the size of an average man's palm. A circular ring filled with twisted metal, it looked like a letter, it resembled an upside-down letter P.

His hand stroked the emblem, images of death rushed into his head. He flinched, pulling his hand away. It was a weird sensation, almost like using a glimmer stone, it felt like it had memories trapped within.

He slowly lifted his hands again and placed them softly onto the emblem. Screams raged in his ears as images of burning villages, of suffering women and children whose eyes were burnt appeared in his mind. Again, he pulled his hand away, nauseated. He swayed on his feet as an overwhelming feeling washed over him; he took in deep breaths and slowed his heart. He shouldn't touch it again, it was surrounded by evil. Then he noticed it, the inner part of the symbol was swaying slightly. "It moves," he uttered.

Reaching out his hand, he attempted to touch the moving symbol. He was instantly whisked away in his mind and found himself in a battlefield, hundreds lying dead around him. People were crawling around him, clutching bleeding limbs. He focused and used all his meditation and concentration training to move the images aside. With his hand against the symbol, he began to turn it. The P within swivelled in its circular holding, as he turned it one hundred and eighty degrees the image broke from his mind and he was back in the room. He shuddered as a large thud rocked the room; the wall in front of him shook as it began to move.

The wall opened onto a secret room; a vault. Lights flickered on revealing a storeroom with treasures that made those in the first room look like cheap knock-offs.

He glared at the wonders that now lay before him; he had only ever seen such striking artifacts before in the Great Library.

A bright ruby-red stone, the size of a fist, rested upon a jacket that was made of scales so thick they must have come from a dragon of sorts.

He glanced around and was suddenly hit by a sense of triumph as he saw the urn resting upon a pillar, illuminated from above, a white light shining directly onto it. It looked exactly like the one he had retrieved from Berlin.

He moved towards it and with his left hand, he reached down and touched the gun that was strapped to his waist.

Before he could take the gun out, his attention was diverted away by another object sitting on the pillar next to the one that held the urn. A dark glass ball rested upon a golden ring; inside the ball, a flame flickered.

All thoughts of the urn left his mind as he was transfixed by the ball. A voice echoed in his mind in a language he had never heard, but the meaning was clear. He found himself moving towards the globe; he did not want to, but he could not stop himself. The flames seemed to grow larger the closer he got.

Inches away from it, his fingers trembled, he wasn't sure why but he felt the urge to touch it. Not more than a second away from touching it, a clatter sounded from behind him and he was immediately brought back to reality. Clenching his fists, he turned around.

"Quite the mess," Leceth's cold voice drenched the room as he clambered over his belongings, which were now lying as debris on the floor. Kristian's hand moved for his gun and he simultaneously turned back to the urn, but could do nothing as he watched it rapidly disappear into a smoky fog. The fog floated through the air and into Leceth's hand, which he held out to his side. The smoke lingered around his palm and then condensed back into the urn.

How? Kristian considered. *A vampire cannot wield magic.*

"I'm sorry boy, but this is worth a lot and they are not easily replaced," Leceth sniggered in his phony arrogant voice.

Kristian took the handgun from the holster on his left side and aimed it at the vampire, so fast he couldn't react. Leceth's face showed a hint of worry as Kristian pulled the trigger. The urn exploded into pieces and a brilliant, bright red flash filled the entire house. The bloody remains of Oliver's heart dropped to the floor mixed with shards of pottery.

Kristian repositioned the gun at Leceth and emptied the barrel into him. Leceth fell to the floor, blood saturated his clothing. Leceth slumped back, lifeless. Kristian walked past him and threw the empty gun down. He knew that Leceth was not dead, but the view was satisfying.

Walking through the front door, three vampires stood in complete shock as their eyes fell upon Leceth's body and then on to Kristian. They suddenly charged at him, he took the rifle from his back and aimed it at them. With a grimace, Kristian fired the rifle's toxic poison into each of them; they fell in turn, each with a cry of pure agony.

As he watched with great pleasure at the vampire's writhing and screaming, he then turned his attention to Leceth's body. His mouth widened as panic stabbed deep in his stomach. Leceth was not there! He turned to look for him, but to his surprise, the vampire was already behind him. Leceth's hand gripped the rifle in Kristian's hand and pushed it up into his face, tore it from his hands and threw it to one side.

Kristian stumbled back, blood filled his mouth.

"I really didn't think you were going to cause me this much trouble, boy!" Leceth shouted.

Kristian was overwhelmed with fear as the thought that he was going to die soon flooded his mind. With that, Kristian leapt to his feet, spat out a mouthful of blood and darted to the front door. Leceth flicked his wrist and the doors slammed shut in Kristian's face, he was trapped. Kristian turned quickly, placing his back against the panels.

Raising his palms, he sent a large bolt of green energy at Leceth. It slammed into a crisp white field, emanating from Leceth's open palm. Kristian was puzzled; *How the hell can a vampire use magic?* he thought.

Leceth sniggered again in his condescending manner as he noticed Kristian's confusion.

"When you are as old as I am, you learn how to bend the rules," Leceth sneered, then closed his palm, pulled back his left hand, placed his right over it and then quietly disappeared into thin air.

Kristian could hear footsteps but they were hard to make out over the sound of his pounding heart; Leceth was still here. Moving evasively from side to side, he tried to avoid the now invisible Leceth. His view of the room lurched as he was thrown into the air. He realised that Leceth had just hit him, his face began to hurt.

Colliding with the floor, Kristian let out a yelp. He pulled himself to his feet as Leceth reappeared in front of the main doors. "I'm going to enjoy killing you," Leceth spoke slowly and with a sinister grin on his face. "How would you like to die, boy?"

Hearing but not answering, Kristian simply took his Phoenix sword from his back and held it out towards Leceth.

"A sword duel! You gravely underestimate me, boy!" with that Leceth vanished again.

Kristian pivoted on his right foot, he held the blade at chest height and swung it to deter Leceth from coming any closer. A cackle from behind him made him turn and look into the room he had ransacked earlier.

Leceth stood there, boldly, with a sword in his hands. It was similar in shape and size to a Phoenix blade. "You are not going to die quickly, I can promise you that," as Leceth spoke he leapt towards Kristian.

Their blades collided, sending sparks into the air. Each attacked and defended, both moving fast on their feet; they were evenly matched.

Leceth was more skilled with his blade, it seemed weightless in his hands, but Kristian was faster, his every move quicker than Leceth's.

The duel carried them around the room as they moved over the remains of the vampires that Kristian had killed moments before. The stench of their foul vampire remains filled the air and made Kristian feel sick, which he tried to ignore as he concentrated on countering Leceth's powerful onslaught.

Kristian caught Leceth's strong upward strike well and pushed him away. They both took a few steps back to steady themselves; Kristian gasped for air. It was almost a weakness to breathe as Leceth stood there waiting, smiling at his far younger, living opponent.

"You know, I have forgotten what it feels like to breathe," Leceth smirked. "I cannot say I miss it though, especially now!"

Kristian heard the taunt and was sickened by the arrogance in his tone. *It will be his undoing*, Kristian told himself. *Use his arrogance.* He launched into an attack, high, low, left, then right. Kristian was using every swordsmanship skill he had been taught, but it seemed like it was in vain. Leceth countered every attack and seemed to predict every move.

Leceth made a sharp swipe at Kristian's face, it was blocked beautifully as Leceth's blade quickly swung out, to which Kristian stretched out his sword and caught Leceth's left arm. Standing back, Leceth looked at his wrist and saw blood seeping out. At this distraction Kristian threw his hand out and launched a bolt of jade with as much force as he could muster. It threw Leceth into the air and across the room with such a force that he smashed through the wall and into another room.

Kristian glanced at the main doors; he could make a run for it now, if he wanted. The thought faded; blinded by vengeance, he ran for the hole in the wall. Diving through into a large open kitchen, he realised how reckless an action it had been. The room was dark and he could hardly see a thing. Whilst taking in his surroundings he saw a flash of silver nearby and aiming a strike in that direction he swung his sword. Again he was in battle with Leceth, this time fighting on instinct alone.

In the darkness he could hear Leceth's menacing laugh; then a sharp pain burst into his right leg then his left arm, he realised he had been cut. The wounds were not severe but he could feel the blood trickling down his body. He needed to get out of this place. He pushed Leceth back and the vampire stumbled, falling over; he looked around for him but could make nothing out in the gloom. He looked about for some way to increase the light in the deathly dark room and contemplated generating some Kar'sin light. Kristian could not concentrate on projection, all his focus was on listening to his Phoenix and letting her guide his blade.

The silence was broken by the menacing laugh again. "You have fought well. You fight like you are going to win, although you know that you will not. What is it you fight for?" There was a silence. "Is it revenge for your dear friend, the other Phoenix? The one who begged me for mercy?" Leceth laughed, more sinister and loud than Kristian had heard before.

"You want revenge for his death? Do you even know why he had to die?"

"I know why you butchered him!" shouted Kristian.

"You think you know, but you do not," Leceth replied.

"You're trying to remove the Phoenix element from the battle; you're deluded if you think that you can contain the Phoenixes in jars," Kristian shouted into the darkness.

Leceth laughed harder than Kristian had heard. "I had not taken you for a fool, boy. However, you are as foolish as your leaders. If you want to know, I shall tell you. Just beg for it." Leceth screamed with laughter as their swords collided again in the darkness. There were brief flashes of light as sparks flew. With each flash, Kristian caught sight of Leceth's threatening and disturbing expression. He moved his blade as fast as he could through the air. Each stroke was coming from Saranthea, he just knew it.

A weird sensation suddenly made his hand shudder, his blade had hit something soft and fleshy. A strange voice in his head said *Shield*, but before he could even register the thought, he was thrown back into the main hall by a bright white flash.

Landing again in the entrance hall, his mouth was filled with blood, which he spat out. His sword was no longer in his hands. He looked over to the hole in the wall and waited for Leceth to emerge. Trying to stand, he felt a punch to the face and then another to his chest. He flew backwards, hit the wall behind him and slid down it.

His body ached so much, he knew he could fight no longer; as that thought passed, Leceth appeared standing over him, holding a hand across his face.

"Oh dear, no gun, no sword. You are all out of tricks, I would say." With that, Leceth bent down and stroked Kristian's face. "Oh you are a handsome boy!" he sneered. Kristian flinched away from his cold touch, "So are you going to beg?"

"Go to hell," Kristian screamed.

"So feisty. Well, I want to correct your misunderstandings. Like it will do you any good, I just want you to die content. The plan is not to contain the Phoenixes by placing them in jars as you mistakenly believe. It is far grander than that. And if you don't believe me, a word of advice: there are currently only seven urns in the world, well, six now, thanks to you," Leceth taunted. He smiled as his finger probed Kristian's wound on his arm, collected blood and licked it off.

Kristian believed Leceth, why would he lie? "So what is the plan then?" Kristian's asked, questioning in his mind what Leceth could be doing other than to trap the Phoenixes within.

"Ha! I've changed my mind; you can die hungry for answers. Just put it this way, the plan is in full swing and when your people realise that the storm is on the horizon it will have already blown their house down," Leceth derided.

As Leceth stepped back, Kristian's eyes fell upon his rings. The three rings on his left hand were impressive to look at. Then something suddenly clicked; Kristian suddenly knew that they must serve a purpose beyond being simple aesthetic trinkets for the vain Laceth. As a sword flew across the air into Leceth's hands Kristian could hear the vampire's voice in his mind, something Leceth had previously said to him.

"Are you ready?" Without waiting for a reply, Leceth drew the sword back and swung it mightily towards Kristian's face.

Kristian closed his eyes, he knew what he had to do and, at that moment, he knew why he had to do it.

The sword came close to Kristian's face, he could feel the faint breeze brush his cheek. Then he opened his eyes, coinciding with a blinding jade-green flash. The sword instantly fell from Leceth's hand point first, stabbing the ground close to Kristian's legs.

With horror twisting his face Leceth raised his left hand to look at it, his fingers fell away with the rings attached to them.

He screamed out in pain as another bedazzling green flash hit him in the chest, sending him across the room.

Kristian looked over at the detached fingers and instantly filled with pride and a sense of accomplishment –

he had thought to use non-palm projection to slice Leceth's hand, he was amazed he had managed to master it.

Pulling himself up, Kristian painfully made his way across the hall. He moved for the rifle; after picking it up he headed towards Leceth. Sitting there on the floor, cradling his hand, Leceth's face was, for the first time, filled with fear. Kristian lifted the gun and aimed it at Leceth.

"How? How did you know?" Leceth shouted.

"Vampires can't wield magic. They don't have a soul. Something you said the first time we met just now came back to me and made me realise that your rings are the source of your power. I take it they all do something?" Kristian smiled in a sinister manner, resembling the one that Leceth had given him earlier.

"You think that killing me ends it? The storm is still coming, killing me, all of this, it will change nothing," Leceth shouted out.

"Is that you begging?" Kristian smiled. "You can do better. And as for changing nothing, I think all this will change something." He pulled the trigger sending a shot deep into Leceth's chest. "It will change someone else's destiny out there. For a new host will be joined."

Leceth started convulsing, his entire body shook and his accompanying screams were so loud that Kristian feared that they could shatter every window in the house. His eyes soon vanished into the sockets as his skin began to melt. He attempted to speak but his voice was garbled. "The defier of death comes. The storm will…"

He stopped trying to speak and in the same instant, he stopped shaking. It was not long before all that remained of the once great Leceth was a pile of moss green sludge.

Kristian dropped the gun to the floor. He could not believe what he had achieved; he was alive and Leceth was dead. He slowly made his way over to Leceth's fingers; gruesomely, he removed the three rings. Inspecting the half-blue gem ring, he could see that it resembled an eye. Accidentally moving the slit across, he vanished instantly;

flicking it back, he reappeared. In amazement, he slipped all the rings into his pocket.

Moving towards the hole in the wall, he glanced back at Leceth's remains. *It was over*, he thought. "But why?" he spoke aloud, his voice confused. He looked at the body, why was he still numb? Questions filled his mind. Why was he still hurting? He had some crazy notion that by killing Leceth he would remove the pain. He was wrong; in fact it hurt more, and the numb feeling was now mixed in with a barrage of emotions.

He tried to shake his mind clear, and moved off to find his sword. Retrieving it from the kitchen, he walked back through the hole.

"Why?" he shouted aloud as he made his way to the main doors. He dropped the sword to the floor just in front of the main doors. Trying the handle, he found the doors still locked. He began to punch it. With each punch his fists bled, the wood splintered and dug deep into his knuckles.

For a minute or more he attacked the doors, with no real purpose other than to hurt himself and inflict more damage

The doors were starting to appear damaged but were still holding firm, he stepped back and glanced down at his blood-soaked hands. He fell to the floor with a loud thud and screamed. Dazzlingly bright blasts of green light flew from all over his body outwards, striking walls, stairs and ceilings; it sent shards of stone, wood and metal everywhere.

As he finished screaming, so too did the jade light. He propped himself up to look at the mess in the room – the death, the destruction. His knuckles sent stabbing pain up through his arms and he could not stop the feelings in his heart. He flicked his legs out and his head fell into his palms. The tears began to pour out. It had been quite some time since he had last cried, he had kept it in for so long, but now had no choice but to open the floodgates.

Kristian sat and cried for over half an hour, for every tear that dropped there was a reason behind it, an emotion or fear that he had kept within for too long. When he could cry no more he simply rose to his feet, his face red and emotionless. He had changed, he had shed much of himself this day, left so much behind here, in Leceth's house.

...

- Chapter Twenty-Four -

The Clean-Up

Bursting into Jonathon's office with concern all over their faces, Rachel and Kieran struggled to catch their breaths.

"What's the problem?" Jonathon asked.

Kieran froze. Rachel spoke and the words left her mouth quickly as if by saying them fast it would make them not true or less real. "It's Kristian. He's gone!"

Jonathon immediately leapt to his feet, knocking papers off his desk as he rose "What do you mean gone? Gone where?" Sweat began to form on his temples as he realised that he knew the answer to his question.

"He's not here, we have searched everywhere. I think he went after Leceth. Jonathon. I'm so sorry," Rachel said emotionally.

"Are you sure? I need to know now," Jonathon bellowed. "Are you sure?"

"I'm certain," Kieran said, not looking directly at Jonathon. He hesitated before he spoke, believing that he was somehow betraying Kristian.

"Damn that boy!" Jonathon's face had turned a deep shade of purple and the veins in his head were throbbing uncontrollably. *How could Kristian be so impulsive? So, stupid?* he thought. Jonathon stormed back to his desk and picked up the phone. "Julia? Wake everyone now. Send them to the meeting room immediately," he slammed the phone down and turned back to Rachel and Kieran "You two, check the building again, check everywhere. Rachel, teleport to his flat if you have to."

"Of course, but I'm sure he's not here. I took him to Bath nearly an hour ago," Rachel admitted. Jonathon's face dropped. He stated that his orders still stood and he waved the two of them off.

The pair rushed off together but they knew as well as their boss that it was pointless to search the building or London for that matter. They knew where Kristian was. "What's going to happen, Kieran?" Rachel asked him, looking up with forlorn eyes. "What will happen to him if he, you know…"

Kieran cut her off and placed his hand on her shoulder, "I don't know, let's hope he's had a change of heart and we find him back in his room or flat. I can't believe he's done this."

With that, they hurried along the corridor towards the elevator, their emotions all over their faces, the panic, the concern, the hope.

Moments later, Jonathon left his office with his secretary, Julia, at his side. She was a large woman and the strain was evident on her face as she struggled to keep up with him pelting down the hallway. The pair entered the main conference room. Yi-Mao and Brendan were already sitting down, looks of bewilderment on their faces, and before Jonathon could take his place at the table, Andrew and Roman entered the room, seconds later followed by Peter. Jonathon took a deep breath and stayed standing to face them all.

"I believe that Kristian has gone after Leceth this evening." The faces in the room all dropped.

"What on earth do you mean 'gone after?' You cannot be serious?" Peter exclaimed, looking extremely worried.

"I am absolutely serious, Peter. I'm not sure exactly when he left or if he has even made it to his destination yet, but we need to get to him now, and stop him from whatever he is planning to do."

"What is wrong with that kid?" Brendan cried. "Why does he think that everything is down to him, like he's so bloody important or something? This is it, Jonathon. Once we find him, that's it, you have to throw him out of the Order. The boy is reckless," Brendan demanded.

"OK, Brendan, I'm sure Jonathon knows how he is going to handle the situation," said Andrew softly. He looked over towards Jonathon. "Don't you, Jonathon?"

"Yi-Mao, Brendan, Andrew and Roman, I want you to get to Leceth's residence, now. Tread carefully though; try to intercept Kristian before he goes any further. Do not let Leceth see him, or you. Moreover, remember, we may be wrong about this, so be wary. We don't want another incident on our hands." As soon as Jonathon had finished speaking he headed towards the door. The four men nodded in agreement as they too made their way to the door. As they exited into the hallway, a flood of people came towards them. Amar, Zhing, Sam and Jean were storming down the corridor followed closely by Kieran and Rachel.

"What's happening?" a voice asked through all the commotion.

"We've looked everywhere and he's definitely not here," said Rachel. "I teleported to his flat and his friend Jess said that she hasn't seen him either."

"Thank you," nodded Jonathon. "The rest of you go into the conference room and Rachel and Kieran will update you. As soon as you have been informed of the situation I want search parties and use all the powers necessary to find him." Jonathon ushered them into the conference room and then turned to Peter who was standing next to him waiting anxiously for orders. "Peter, my office now."

Inside the conference room, Rachel and Kieran informed the rest of the team about what had happened, that they believed Kristian was hunting for Leceth. Kieran did not tell anyone what had happened between him and Kristian though. He knew it was a mistake not to tell them.

...

As the dark figure crossed the threshold into Leceth's house, she noticed how it had been forced from the inside. Her eyes widened as she saw the state of the mansion. *Such destruction,* she thought to herself, *it must have been a fight to witness.* The stench of rot filled the air and blocked her nose.

She closed her eyes. She could feel that Leceth was dead and was somewhere in the house. On opening her eyes, she glanced to the far wall and saw the green sludge on the floor; she knew with certainty that this was all that was left of Leceth. As she walked over to examine the 'corpse', her heels clunked loudly on the marble floor.

Bending down she placed a gloved finger in the moss coloured pulp and swirled it around, "Well Leceth, I suppose immortality is just a word. Although, if you hadn't been so pig-ignorant, maybe you would still be expressing it!" She stood up and flicked the slime off her finger. She moved towards the open doors opposite the entrance. The room was a complete mess. She trampled over the debris and shards of wood and glass towards the vault. She glanced around at the many wonders that lay within. "In here. NOW!" she shouted.

At this command, a horde of people came flooding into the room. "I want everything in here. Forget the things on the floor, just the stuff from the vault. And don't directly touch that globe." As she spoke she took off her robe and threw it over the flame-filled ball flickering in front of her.

She moved back into the hall and suddenly noticed another prized artifact lying on the floor. She glided elegantly, though loudly, towards it. She dipped down, one graceful leg kneeling, as she gripped the hilt. "A Phoenix blade," she whispered. She flipped it around to see the emblem on the handle. "Saranthea," she chuckled to herself.

Her eyes closed and her smile stretched thin; opening them in a flash the look on her face changed, her head turned jerkily to the others. "Hurry up, we're going to have company very soon." She moved to the door as the many helpers followed, carrying the artifacts that had once been in Leceth's secret vault.

On the driveway, a huge van was parked up and her men were filling the back with the prized possessions. She began to walk down the long path, kicking up the gravel with her heels as she did so. The sword, which she now held in her hand, swung back and forth absent-mindedly as she crunched over the stones. In front of the van, a black Jaguar was parked. Similar to the ones driven to the Order some time ago by the members of the Council of Tivernal. The number plate read 'ED4EVA'.

She opened the door and sat in the back, her eyes scanned the blade. She was overjoyed that Leceth was dead. He had been part of the Quartet but she cared less for him than for any of the other members. He was merely an opportunist; he did not care for the group's true goals, whereas she on the other hand was loyal. She cared little for the rewards that would come from future endeavours, but merely for the chaos that they would cause. Whilst she continued caressing the blade on her lap her men finished loading the van and a short five minutes later they were on their way, silently into the night.

. . .

Yi-Mao was the first to step into Leceth's house, closely followed by his three companions.

"Oh dear lord. What has happened here? It looks like hell," Roman said as he looked at the vampire's remains on the floor. He grimaced at the smell of vile rot that filled the room.

Yi-Mao walked over to the green slime. A voice within him was telling him that it was Leceth but he had to be sure for himself. "Andrew, do you have a spell which will determine if this is definitely Leceth?"

"Possibly," Andrew said quietly. He was taking in the mess and destruction and looked sad, not really horrified or repulsed. Just sad and forlorn. He knew that Kristian was reckless but he cared for the boy and now he worried for him, for his state of mind and his well-being.

Yi-Mao bent over and took a piece of fabric from his pocket. He tore a piece off and dipped it into the remains. "We best take a sample of the other three piles as well," he said, looking around the room.

Andrew watched the Phoenix master take a sample with a bit of cloth and as he went to stand up Andrew flicked his wrists and instantly produced a handful of small vials. He moved to Yi-Mao and handed him one.

"If I am to find a spell to determine the owner of these remains I'm going to need a little bit more," Andrew said as Yi-Mao took the vial.

"I've said it before, you're handy to have around!"

Brendan watched the two old friends before making his way over and collecting a couple of vials from the old wizard himself. He turned and went over to another of the piles of rotting slush and took further samples with a look of disgust on his face.

Andrew looked over to the vault and made his way into the room; looking down at the mess he imagined what would have transpired. "It must have been some fight," he said to himself before closing his eyes in concentration. Andrew's body glowed and suddenly turned into a ball of light that whizzed quickly around the room and then zipped off to the rest of the house. Yi-Mao moved to where Andrew had been standing. He stepped over the objects that littered the floor, trying carefully not to stand on anything. He took in the empty vault and its pillars, which had once contained beautiful and priceless antiques.

"We are more than a little late," Yi-Mao sighed with the realisation that someone had already been in this room.

He stepped back out to see Brendan and Roman examining a hole in the wall in the main hall and the room it opened out into. "Anything?" Yi-Mao asked of them.

Both men replied by shaking their heads solemnly. Roman pointed to the opposite side. The others looked over and saw four pale, flesh-coloured sticks. As Yi-Mao walked over to them he realised that they were fingers, Leceth's fingers. The nails were long and dark green. With this, the flash that was Andrew reappeared in the room and rematerialised into the old wizard.

"I have searched the building; there is no one here and no sign of Kristian," said Andrew.

Yi-Mao put one of the severed fingers into his pocket as he listened.

"Time to go I think," Yi-Mao spoke to no one in particular; the men looked at each other, solemn expressions were worn by them all. They were all thinking the same thing. They slowly exited the house in silence and when outside the main door there was a bright flash and they were gone, no longer in the grounds of Leceth's mansion. The four men reappeared a few hundred miles away in central London, just outside the Order's building. They all looked at one another and contemplated the reality of what had just transpired.

"He's killed Leceth, hasn't he?" Brendan whispered to Yi-Mao.

Yi-Mao looked over to his most trusted friend; he wondered how Kristian could have pulled off such a feat. Leceth was no ordinary vampire.

"It appears so. Remarkably, he appears to have killed Leceth and survived," Yi-Mao replied.

"I suspect that we weren't the only ones to visit the crime scene. It appeared as though someone had beaten us to it," Andrew said, speaking over Brendan and Yi-Mao's private whisperings.

"I reached the same conclusion. We need to update Jonathon, it won't be long before the Council is with us," Yi-

Mao said, concerned about what new troubles would come from the Council's indignation.

Andrew and Roman walked off as Brendan held his pace to continue his conversation with Yi-Mao.

"Kristian could have been abducted again? He could already be dead elsewhere," Brendan said, genuine concern about Kristian lacing his words.

"I don't think he's dead. My heart tells me he's alive. If he's been abducted we should soon find out," Yi-Mao replied.

"Find out? How?" Brendan asked.

"Well, if the Council aren't banging on our doors soon, we know they don't have him," Yi-Mao said as he began to make his way through the main doors, Brendan closely following.

...

- Chapter Twenty-Five -

Unbreakable Bonds

"You're late, old man," said a cloaked figure, her voice echoing through the large open space of an old abandoned warehouse. "Could you not find the place?" Again, her voice resonated off the tin walls, the sound shrill and unpleasant as it pained the tall, shrouded man's ears.

"I apologise, my friend. But one could not slip away, I was busy," his voice was soft yet deep and seemed to take longer to traverse the room's entirety; he paced towards her.

The pair now stood directly opposite each other, staring into the darkness of each other's faces, which were both covered by overhanging hoods. The female figure was concealing an object behind her back but her posture was dominant, her head held high. The man's stance was similar but seemed less dominant; his hands were at his side and his head bowed.

"Are you going to tell me what has happened? Where is Leceth?" asked the man, his tone direct.

"Considering you are late, that is hardly the tone you should be taking with me. I did not see you running to Leceth's aid. You didn't even provide the relevant intel, you don't really bring much to the Quartet do you?" her tone was mocking, but generally she viewed him with respect.

"Edith! Enough of this, where is Leceth?"

She stepped back and glanced around at the empty space. "Leceth is dead. We arrived too late. And I thought we weren't to utter names; doesn't that take away the secret part? Shall we take off our robes now?"

"Leceth is dead? Are you sure? What about the Phoenix?" The man spoke quickly, the pitch of his voice getting higher with concern.

"The boy was gone before I got there. Leceth is most certainly dead; I saw the rotting pile of his remains. The place was a mess, let me tell you, that boy put up quite a fight," her voice sounded so cold and malicious, deeply uncaring.

The man raised his hands to his forehead; deep panic rushed through his body and overwhelmed him. "First Sauror, now Leceth. So much for a quartet. We shall have to clean out his place, there is too much there, too much to lose. The Order will no doubt be there to investigate."

"The Order is already there," she interrupted.

"Ah, yes, well of course they are," he said this to himself rather than in agreement with her. "What about the eye?"

Not responding with words, the woman swung around her arms to reveal a large black sack. "Do not worry. I have sanitised the place. Everything of importance has been removed. See whilst you were busy being 'busy', I actually *was* busy."

Looking down at the globe, relief swept over the man and subdued the feelings of worry and fear he had been experiencing moments before.

"Well done. Perhaps the plan isn't completely beyond salvaging. Have you consulted him yet? Have you informed him of Leceth's death?"

"He doesn't require consultation, he is all-knowing." As the woman spoke she held the globe within the cloth so that it was shrouded; holding it up high she allowed the material to fall from around it, revealing the eye. The globe was clear and made of an ancient material, not unlike glass. Within the centre burned a flame. As their eyes gazed into this flame, it grew steadily larger and brighter as though sensing their eyes upon it. It soon became a swirling ball of fire. Bright reds, oranges and yellows flickeringly illuminated a small area around them in the vast dark space.

"Speak." The voice came from within the globe and didn't need the echo of the warehouse to send it around the room.

"Master, Leceth is dead. A rogue Phoenix has slaughtered him," said the male figure.

"Yes, of this I am aware," said the voice. "You have done well to conceal the plan from the Order. They are still blind to my intentions," the voice was dark and fierce, enough to send chills down the spines of any.

"Master?" the man said. "The Order is more than suspicious about Leceth's actions prior to his demise. There will be an investigation, one that we cannot hide from. Perhaps we should abandon the Phoenix plan for now. We can find another way for you to return." As he spoke his voice quavered as though he knew his request would be met with anger.

"NO! My return will herald the destruction of the Phoenix. Why do you fear the Order? The Phoenixes are insects and as such they will be exterminated. Have you located 'The Faithful?'" His voice was darker, angrier and filled with contempt.

"Master, I have found him. But it will, I am told, take some time to release him. And the Juggernaut will soon be with us. Your faithful are returning, but the larger your army grows, the more conspicuous we become to the Order." The woman spoke with glee as though the thought of being caught appealed to her, as though it was part of the thrill.

"You will follow the plan. Soon I shall be among you and you shall receive the rewards. The Phoenix who killed Leceth, I want him found and killed. See to it."

The pair bowed to the globe and Edith spoke. "Consider it done my Lord. What about the Quartet?"

"Môn'ark Toral will make a fine addition, bring him to me. Soon Sauror will rejoin you and the Quartet will be restored. This, my friends, shall mark my return. Now, go and bring 'The Faithful'." The bright light shining from the globe began to fade and soon all that remained was a tiny flickering flame.

Edith dropped the globe back into the cloth and pulled the material around it. She looked at her shrouded companion. She knew who he was, yet she knew the importance of the secrecy.

"What about the informant? Clearly a member of the Order, any ideas?"

"None, but like all 'informants', he or she cannot remain a secret forever. Their identity will soon be revealed to us I'm sure of it," the man replied as he started towards the exit.

...

Jess opened the door awkwardly due to the many bags of shopping she was carrying. Pushing the door with her body, she squeezed in and closed it with a kick. She froze as she approached her door as it was ajar; she was certain she had shut it on the way out. There should be no one home.

She gently placed the bags on the floor as quietly as she could and made her way up the stairs. On arrival at the top step she leaned over and pushed the door open fully; her stomach turned as she felt adrenaline rush through her body. She hoped for a second that it was Kristian, but something inside her told her that it wasn't, something told her to be silent. Tiptoeing in, she looked from side to side, taking soft steps towards the kitchen. Entering it, she saw no one and quickly moved to the drawer on the worktop and pulled out the sharpest knife she could find.

Going slowly from room to room, she searched courageously for a possible intruder; her heart raced. She was more frightened than she had ever been in her life and felt as though she had held her breath since climbing the stairs. She searched for over fifteen minutes, checked in closets and under beds; she finally relaxed and decided that she was just being paranoid. She returned down the stairs, picked up her bags carried them back up and plonked them down on the sofa. She still had the knife dangerously stuffed down her back pocket.

Taking it back to the kitchen and putting it away; she chuckled to herself in relief and embarrassment, although she still felt slightly uneasy. Suddenly a thud came from somewhere in the house and she jumped. She well remembered that Kristian had warned her about people trying to hurt her to get to him and she was suddenly filled with icy fear again.

Composing herself, she tried to convince herself that it was a door slamming, perhaps the downstairs door which she may have accidentally left open. No, she had definitely closed it. She leapt back to the drawer and took the knife back out, and slowly began to make her way out of the kitchen.

She entered the lounge apprehensively and was just about to phone the police when she noticed something different. On the coffee table, which had been empty a few moments ago, bar a few coasters and a newspaper, now lay an envelope. She glanced around nervously and made her way slowly to the table. She was afraid to touch it in case it was booby-trapped, ready to explode once she opened it. After a few moments of staring at the blank white envelope, she put the knife down and reached for the mysterious package.

It was unsealed; she opened it quickly and pulled out the paper within. Unfolding it, she saw her name at the top and recognised the poor handwriting instantly: it was a letter from Kristian. She was suddenly filled with mixed emotions, she was thankful that he was alive but angry with him for scaring her and not showing himself. She sat down and read the letter aloud to herself.

Jessica

Where do I start? How about I'm sorry? That's a pretty good place to start.

I am sorry that I couldn't find the courage to say goodbye to your face. I am sorry that I have to go. I am sorry that you ever got to know me.

I guess I was afraid that you would try and stop me from leaving. I have done something terrible and I have to run. It's the only way to keep the others I care about safe. I know you would understand, that you would hug me, make me a cup of tea, and tell me that you love me no matter what. I know that and that's why it breaks my heart to have to write you this letter. You know me better than anyone else.

I have found out something about me, Jess: I hate revenge. Not because of what it has made me do but because of how it's made me feel. I enjoyed it, Jess, watching that monster die was worth every second of pain I have ever felt. Does that make me the monster? I cannot lie to you. I have lied to myself for too long, but not to you. I'm glad he's dead, I'm glad it was I who did it and given the chance, I would do it again.

Well, I can't stay here all day, watching you walk around the house with a knife like a lunatic!

I want you to know that if I could stay I would. I love you more than I thought I possibly could.

Keep what I have told you to yourself please, don't tell anybody, trust no one.

Burn this after you have read it.

I shall remember you always. Kris x

"I don't, and I will," said Jess as she screwed up the letter and held it close to her chest. Tears began to fall from her face as she knew she was going to have to find him or lose him forever.

. . .

Jonathon walked out through the large oak doors holding a golden parchment in his right hand. He knew as soon as he stepped over the Order's protective threshold he would be gone; he was right. In a blinding flash, he was whisked away, teleporting thousands of miles from London, materialising at the entrance to a remote cavern which the Order assumed was somewhere in northern Iran.

Standing on the rocky ground Jonathon struggled to steady himself. Gazing at where the cavern should be he could see no entrance but he knew it to be there. A solid wall of rock directly in front of him instantaneously burst into life. Changing its shape, it separated allowing a passageway to open. Jonathon cautiously walked down the corridor that now lay ahead of him. The walls of the corridor were smooth and artificial unlike the rock outside concealing the cavern. Ancient flaking scripture lined the walls and Jonathon could not read any of it.

Coming to the end of the corridor he saw an archway adorned with symbols indicating what lay beyond; it was in an Ancient dialect Jonathon couldn't read but he knew exactly what it said, who it announced. Passing under the arch and entering the room he was shocked to see the towering and intimidating frame of Môn'ark Toral. The Vinji's face was filled with aggression and as his eyes fell upon Jonathon he could not help but react.

"You will surrender the boy. There is no other option. The games are over, human." Môn'ark made his way towards Jonathon as he shouted, but Jonathon didn't step back; they both knew that no violent act could take place in the sanctuary that was the 'Hall of Arbitration'.

"I'm here to talk to the Arbitrators, Môn'ark, not you," Jonathon turned away from him and stared at the only thing in the room. Three plinths stood an equal distance from one another at the far end of the hall.

"We shall see what they have to say. This time you have gone too far," Môn'ark responded turning to face the plinths.

Jonathon had never seen the Arbitrators before, but had read every account that previous directors of the Order had written about them. They were known as the guardians of the Treaty; affiliated to neither side, they were the resolvers of disagreements that would otherwise result in war. His eyes examined each of the Arbitrators, they were what were referred to as demigods, half-Ancient, half-mortal, and as far as Jonathon was aware they were the only ones of their kind left on earth. Long ago, Ancients had vanished from the world and shortly after, all their offspring perished. The Arbitrators witnessed the signing of the Treaty between the Order of Light and the Council of Tivernal. The three arbitrators predated the Order, endured the Vinji–human war and were born before the age of man.

Solid as stone, with a bow and arrow strapped to his back, Arcanas stepped down from his plinth and looked at the two mortals he had summoned to his presence. Next to him stood the extremely tall Dardania who was toweringly tall and seemed to have flesh made of vines. Her skin was a thick brown bark. One moment static, the next she burst into life and stepped down off her plinth. The third Arbitrator was Sataki; his flawless skin was like porcelain and appeared similar in build to Arcanas: tall, broad and muscular. He held in his hand a remarkable golden spear.

"We have summoned you both before us as the Council has lodged an official complaint against the Order, raised for the most severe of reasons, and we wish to resolve this matter here and now," Dardania said; all three of the Arbitrators were equal but it was always she who spoke.

"Can I hear the complaint?" Jonathon asked, knowing full well what was about to come.

"The Council has informed us that a member of your kin has, with intention, killed Leceth, the leader of the Council of Tivernal. Do you acknowledge this claim? And if so, what is your response?" Again Dardania spoke.

"I acknowledge that I am aware that Leceth has died. I refute that it was a member of the Order, at this time," Jonathon replied, as honest as he could be.

"What!" exclaimed Môn'ark. "Do not play the duplicity card. You know as I do that it was that Phoenix – Kristian. You will hand him over to the Council or there will be war! He must pay for his actions; the Treaty demands it."

Jonathon took in a deep breath to compose himself. "The Order, like the Council, is investigating what has happened and as of yet, neither has reached a conclusion. So, until we do, I shall not enter into discussion about whom I will or will not hand over to the Council."

"You know as well as I do it was Kristian, investigations are pointless. We demand his presence before the Council!" Môn'ark responded.

"I will not be handing him over to the Council on assumption and accusation alone," Jonathon had turned to speak directly to the Vinji.

Before Môn'ark could reply, Dardania spoke, attempting to bring a sense of calm to the situation. "Jonathon, this allegation is of the most severe kind. And Môn'ark, you must understand the Order's position. This is the first time we have convened in quite a few years and we take these matters seriously. Could we suggest to both parties that we investigate this matter? And whilst we are doing this we suggest that Kristian resides here in the Hall of Arbitration."

"Agreed!" Môn'ark shouted believing that the Arbitrators in time would agree with him.

"I agree that I will adhere to the findings of your investigation. But bringing Kristian here is not possible," Jonathon said hesitating for second, knowing it would invoke a furious response.

"Unacceptable," Môn'ark shouted.

"The Order must understand that our position is not negotiable. We guarantee his safety here until we determine if he is responsible for the death of Leceth. Then if he is guilty the Treaty will demand he is passed to the Council, to face justice. If we conclude that he is innocent then we shall return him to you." Arcanas spoke for the first time.

"I understand and agree with what you are saying. But I can't bring Kristian here," Jonathon said, concealing his anxieties well.

"Why?" asked Dardania.

"I cannot bring him here because the Order is currently uncertain of his whereabouts."

"What? Do not deceive us, human. This is clearly a lie!" Môn'ark bellowed; the Vinji was enraged by the thought that the Order was attempting to mislead the Arbitrators.

"It is no deception. I must confess that Kristian has disappeared and the Order does not know where he is," Jonathon said attempting to reassure those present of his sincerity.

"Well, what more do we need to hear? Running away is a clear sign of his guilt," Môn'ark announced.

"I am unsure why he has disappeared. But I have assigned resources to locate him," Jonathon said.

"We recommend that both sides attempt to locate him and bring him here once he has been found. We shall look for him too. If we complete our investigation before he is found then his outcome will have been determined and he may not be required to stand before us. Do you both agree?" Dardania asked.

Môn'ark agreed but knew full well if he located Kristian first he would not hand him over. Jonathon agreed reluctantly; he felt like he had no other choice. He couldn't risk losing favour with the Arbitrators; if they sided with the Council then the victory of war he was once so assured of, would no longer be a certainty.

"We are glad you both agree. We expect both sides to uphold the Treaty. We shall investigate Leceth's death as a matter of urgency. You shall hear from us in due course. We stress the need for calm during these difficult times and warn you both, we may just be three but our power is absolute," Dardania spoke on behalf of all of them.

Jonathon looked compliant and understood what he had been told but he also knew that their power was not absolute; he also knew that Môn'ark knew that truth as well. That fact troubled him; he needed to find Kristian first but he also needed to find a solution to the problem before he found him. As the meeting drew to a close it wasn't long before Jonathon was leaving the cave and had teleported back to London. He stood exhausted outside the doors to the Order of Light gathering his thoughts before entering; he could only think one thing: *I'll have to break my promise to Kristian. I'm going to have to sacrifice him in the name of peace.* He was sickened to his core, it felt like a betrayal. Then he reminded himself of the only truth that mattered now: Kristian betrayed the Order, risked open warfare that could change the course of history and what was about to happen to him was entirely a destiny of his own making.

For a few minutes he dwelled on the thought; he couldn't help but try and think of a way to avoid surrendering Kristian. He knew that there was no other option but to meet the request of the Arbitrators. It was clear to him now that Kristian was entirely alone; alone and no longer in the Light.

47306266R00233

Printed in Poland
by Amazon Fulfillment
Poland Sp. z o.o., Wrocław